AN
EMPTY
COAST

Tony Park was born in 1964 and grew up in the western suburbs of Sydney. He has worked as a reporter, a press secretary, a PR consultant and a freelance writer. He is also a major in the Australian Army Reserve and served as a public affairs officer in Afghanistan in 2002. He and his wife, Nicola, divide their time between Australia and southern Africa. He is the author of eleven other novels.

Also by Tony Park

Far Horizon

Zambezi

African Sky

Safari

Silent Predator

Ivory

The Delta

African Dawn

Dark Heart

The Prey

The Hunter

Part of the Pride
with Kevin Richardson

War Dogs
with Shane Bryant

The Grey Man
with John Curtis

The Lost Battlefield of Kokoda
with Brian Freeman

Walking Wounded
with Brian Freeman

AN EMPTY COAST

TONY PARK

PAN BOOKS

First published 2015 by Pan Macmillan Australia Pty Ltd

This edition first published 2016 by Pan Books
an imprint of Pan Macmillan
20 New Wharf Road, London N1 9RR
Associated companies throughout the world
www.panmacmillan.com

ISBN 978-1-5098-1541-8

1 3 5 7 9 8 6 4 2

A CIP catalogue record for this book is available from the British Library.

Printed and bound by CPI Group (UK) Ltd, Croydon, CR0 4YY

Visit **www.panmacmillan.com/www.picador.com** to read more about
all our books and to buy them. You will also find features, author interviews
and news of any author events, and you can sign up for e-newsletters
so that you're always first to hear about our new releases.

For Nicola

PART 1
LIFE

Skeleton Coast National Park, South West Africa, 1987

I n all probability, the rest of her kind had been exterminated. Her sisters were all dead and she hadn't seen the father of her offspring for weeks.

Once they had ruled from the icy waters of the Atlantic, so cold she'd hated to touch it when she was young, through the golden dunes as far east as the baking white salt of Etosha Pan, but now she had nowhere safe to raise her youngsters. She trudged along the firm, wet sand, the only living thing visible on a beach littered with bleached bones.

She was hungry, tired and very pregnant, but there was no tree to provide shade, no cool water to slake her thirst, no ready meal to fill her rumbling belly. Gulls squawked at her approach through the golden twilight and somewhere a jackal called, signalling it was readying for its evening patrol.

Darkness would not help her; the sun's pain would be replaced by the cold of the night, which seeped into her old bones.

The setting sun kicked her shadow inland, towards the dunes and the rocky desert beyond. She had hoped to find a dead seal or, even better, a beached whale, but there was nothing. She knew she had to head east, where the sand and rock would eventually give way to golden grass plains, farms with cattle and goats, and dainty springbok. It was risky, because she was an outcast and she would not be welcome, but she had no choice.

Under the bright light of the moon she crested the first dune and trudged into the interior. There was not a sound in her world, not another sign of life. The night, however, held no fear for her, for she was a hunter, a killer, a predator.

Above the wind she heard voices. Men were her enemy. She had learned to fear them. They had probably killed her mate, as they had eradicated almost all of her kind.

Normally she would have run away from the sound of them, but the babies hung heavy in her belly. Soon the cubs would be born and she would need to eat, to produce milk. Without food she would die, her young would die, and the last of the desert lions would die.

She lowered herself and started to slink slowly forward, ears back, tail straight. At the crest of the dune she dropped. Through golden eyes finely tuned to maximise the dullest glimmer of star and moonlight, she saw them. Two men.

The crack of a gunshot echoed across the dunes and made her turn and run, her hunter's heart beating as fast as a fleeing springbok.

She hid in the dunes until just before dawn when a choking, repetitive bark roused her curiosity and her hunger. She crept back to where she had heard the voices and, when she saw the scavenger with his pointed ears and shaggy coat gnawing on something, she charged down the hill. For a moment the brown hyena considered staying its ground, but even in her state she was more than a match for it. Beaten, he scuttled away.

Most of the man's body was intact. She bared her fangs, snarled at the dark in case the hyena was still there, then lowered herself to her belly and started to eat.

Chapter 1

Ho Chi Minh City, Vietnam, 2015

Sonja Kurtz slowed the small Honda motorcycle and stopped outside the ornate French-built Saigon Opera House on the corner of Dong Khoi and Le Loi.

She had grown used to the relentless traffic, the exhaust smoke, the noise and the sheer numbers of people – more like features of another planet than a different continent – which had assaulted her senses when she first arrived in Vietnam. Africa was her natural hunting ground, but predators had to adapt to their environments.

Sonja wore urban camouflage, a cheap open-faced red helmet over piled-up hair; sunglasses; a flower-patterned facemask of the kind locals wore to filter the pollution; gloves and a wrap of cheap fabric around her westerner's legs that a Saigonese woman would have donned to protect herself from sun and grit. From a distance she resembled one of the city's millions of commuters.

Her prey unfurled herself from the green and white Vinasun taxi outside the Union Square shopping centre, as she always did this time on a Tuesday. The woman was tall, blonde, strikingly good looking. She moved with the easy elegance of a giraffe, aloof from the hustle and bustle of the streetscape and the people below her.

The woman was a means to an end, and while Sonja would do her best to protect her, she was also prepared to kill her if she had to. Collateral damage.

The woman, Irina Aleksandrova, lived in a secure complex of villas across the river in Ho Chi Minh's District 7, an expensive new part of the city popular with expats and wealthy Vietnamese, a busy, happening place. Irina was protected in her home, but not on the streets. Sonja had followed the cab on her bike from Irina's home, knowing that on Tuesdays the Russian woman came, religiously, to the old colonial heart of the city, to walk, to shop, to eat and to prepare herself for that evening's work.

As soon as Irina entered the shopping centre Sonja revved the throttle on her bike and drove around behind the Opera House. She parked and handed the attendant a handful of crumpled Vietnamese *dong* notes. '*Cam on ong*,' she said, thanking him.

Sonja took off her helmet, gloves, long-sleeved blouse and wrap and stowed them under the seat. She took her daypack from where it had been nestled between her legs, and pulled out a green peaked cap with a yellow star on the front and put it on. In her faux-military hat, loose-fitting sleeveless top and elephant-printed harem pants she was now a sightseeing backpacker.

Her hair, normally auburn with the occasional mildly annoying strand of silver, matched her target's today, dyed for the purpose and cut in a similar style. Irina never varied her routine or her route.

Sonja unzipped her daypack and double checked the rigid sunglasses case was there, then zipped the bag closed and shrugged it on. She walked past the Continental Hotel, another *grande dame* of the French era, and crossed the road to the shopping centre. The air con was a relief from Saigon's heat and humidity. Sonja picked up Irina in Dior; the only thing that changed in this weekly routine was the brand-name store in which the woman blew her hard-earned fees. Sonja wasn't judgemental about how Irina made her money, but she had never been one to fritter away her own wages on handbags and trinkets.

Motor scooters choked the street and horns beeped as Sonja and her quarry emerged into Dong Khoi again. Sonja settled into position behind her target, close enough to keep visual contact, far enough away not to be noticeable. A party of elderly tourists, cruise ship passengers judging by their shorts, long white socks and clean Nikes, provided her extra cover, and Sonja tagged along at the rear of the group.

She shrugged off the slight feeling of agoraphobia she'd experienced since arriving in Vietnam. She had been born in Namibia, known as South West Africa at the time, a country with the second-lowest population density in the world. Growing up there, and later in Botswana's Okavango Delta, she had only ever known open spaces and isolated pockets of people. Here humans swirled around her, as thick as quelea, the tiny birds of her homeland that flew in dense flocks of hundreds. She forced herself to ignore them.

As Irina passed the imposing People's Committee Building Sonja deliberately looked away from the green-uniformed soldier on duty, his folding-stock AK-47 slung casually across his chest. Pretending to scratch herself, she reached around and touched the familiar hard bulk of the SIG Sauer nine-millimetre pistol sitting snugly in a pancake holster on her jeans belt in the small of her back. She made sure the weapon was covered by her untucked top as she, in turn, passed the guard.

Was she any better than Irina and the other people she was hunting? she asked herself. Not for the first time she answered the question with a mental shrug; good and bad, right and wrong didn't matter any more. Revenge was the only thing that had kept her sane these past twelve months.

After this business was done she could not return to Los Angeles; if she was identified, or the pieces put together, people would come looking for her. LA, in any case, was no longer her home, if it ever had been. No, she would return to Africa. Even if she didn't belong in the country of her birth she would find somewhere to hide there. More importantly, the one person in her life she cared for was there, right now. Emma, her daughter, was on a study field trip, fossicking in the baked dry dirt north of Etosha National Park, for God cared what.

At the cathedral, Irina, true to form, turned left into Hán Thuyên. Pretty girls in traditional *áo dàis*, long silk gowns slit from ankle to waist over matching pants, and with flowers in their hair posed for photographs in a neatly kept park. Irina headed towards the Reunification Palace, but stopped short on the left at Propaganda, a lively restaurant popular with expats.

Sonja carried on to the adjoining eatery, Au Parc, took a table and ordered a cappuccino. Irina, she knew, would be having the *Phở* for lunch. Sonja had become accustomed to the traditional Vietnamese soup of noodles and rare beef; Propaganda served the best she'd tasted. The restaurants were owned by the same people and through an open portal in the adjoining wall she could keep an eye on the target, who sat in front of a wall painted with a colourful faux-political mural.

As she sipped her coffee Sonja wondered what the older Vietnamese, those who had fought in the war, thought of this new wave of consumerism and commercialism, the hallmarks of the enemy they had fought for so long and eventually defeated. Did any war matter, in the long run? Her father had fought in the border war, supposedly against communism, but the party that had won and turned South West Africa into Namibia was still running the country, and it bore no resemblance to North Korea or even communist China. The scattered battles of the Cold War, from the jungles of Vietnam to the thorny bushveld and arid deserts of Namibia, had wrested power from old colonialists and their successors, but had anything really changed? Both here and in her homeland the gap between rich and poor was still great; the urban elite lived the high life on the backs of the rural poor. Communism had not triumphed; the batons of crime, corruption and wealth that power brought had simply changed hands.

But Sonja was not in Vietnam stalking Irina Aleksandrova because of politics or brain-dead ideologies; she was there for a much simpler reason. A man.

Irina was pretty in a sculpted, manicured and made-up way, due in no small part to the time she spent in one of District 9's beauty salons. Sonja normally had no time for such frivolous indulgences, but this morning she had also been coiffed, waxed, spray-tanned, plucked and painted to within an inch of her life.

'Wow,' Ross had said, when she'd walked into the apartment. She had taken his open-mouthed gaping as a compliment, then threatened to shoot him if he said another word.

He'd pantomimed buttoning his lip as she'd unzipped the suit bag bearing the name of the tailor she'd been to. Inside was a cocktail dress, short, backless, with a plunging neckline. Normally the only stiletto she admired came with a point and a blade she could shave her legs with, but she had to admit the pair in the box she'd opened to show Ross were rather fetching. He'd nodded in mute approval. She hadn't dared open the other box, secured with a ribbon that contained the classily provocative lingerie she'd also selected. Sonja liked Ross, a lot, but she did not want to encourage whatever feelings he may have developed for her.

Ross Coonan was a good man, far younger than she, and she had corrupted him enough by enlisting his help, not only with research but to act as her partner today. He was putting himself at risk of arrest and imprisonment, perhaps even death. She had not consciously tried to use her charms to win him over, but she knew from the things he'd said and the invitations to dinner he'd made after they'd finished their planning and briefing sessions that he wanted more than just to help her carry out her mission.

Sonja took a breath and another sip of coffee. She flicked through a gossip magazine, though as it was in Vietnamese all she could do was look at the pictures. There were some American and British actors and singers she vaguely recognised, though she couldn't recall all their names. Her heart lurched when she turned the next page and saw a full-page ad featuring a slaughtered rhinoceros. In a separate picture a Vietnamese man in a suit presented a rhino horn to another man. Sonja bit her lip. She couldn't read the words, but she guessed the intent of the advertisement.

The war against rhino poaching was still being fought in the African bush with guns and bullets, and here, in the number one destination for illegal rhino horn, in what the American military called 'the cognitive space' – the new term for 'hearts and minds'. The fight could not be won by African soldiers and national parks rangers alone; the price of rhino horn was so astronomically high – more than gold, or cocaine – that poachers would keep trying to slaughter the animals despite the risk of being ambushed and shot. Now, various conservation groups were trying to target the customers who bought this worthless substance, prized not for its use as an aphrodisiac, which was a common myth, but more for its purported value as a substance that would prevent hangovers. It had become a status symbol for Vietnam's rich and powerful, who flaunted their wealth by serving drinks in cups made of horn, or ground the horn to serve with alcohol. Cancer sufferers and their families provided a secondary market, clutching at the lies peddled by sellers that rhino horn cured the disease.

Sonja had grown up around rhinos, and while she did not consider herself overly passionate about wildlife, these days the sight of a dead rhino could almost bring her to tears. She had rarely cried throughout her life, and hated public outpourings of emotion; she thought such behaviour weak and stupid. She reached behind her and touched the butt of the pistol. That was her talisman, her strength, the tool of her trade.

While she waited for Irina, Sonja checked her emails on her phone. There was a confirmation message from the airline, a reminder she was booked on a flight to Bangkok the following morning, with a connection to South Africa. This was it; months of planning and weeks of surveillance and reconnaissance had come down to this day, this evening. This was her one shot at righting the wrong that had been done to her and Emma. There was no message from her daughter, and while Sonja knew Emma was out of contact in the wilds of Namibia, and would be for the next few days, she checked each day, just in case.

The phone rang. 'Yes,' she said, recognising the caller as Ross. 'I'm in position.'

Sonja looked through the portal to the neighbouring restaurant. Irina was asking for the bill and opening her handbag. 'Target's moving. Get ready.'

'OK,' Ross replied. 'Sonja, I . . .'

'No names, I told you. Don't get cold feet now. I have to go.' She ended the call, not wanting to give him the chance to air any misgivings he might be having.

Irina walked out of Propaganda. Sonja left a few *dong* notes for her coffee and began to weave her way through the tourists and locals. Irina headed towards the Reunification Palace but turned left into Pasteur. *Like clockwork*, Sonja thought. They passed small eateries, roadside workshops and garages servicing motorcycles. Sonja breathed the familiar scents of spices, food cooking, exhaust smoke, impending rain; it wasn't unpleasant, but every now and then she crossed the perforated cover of a drain and caught a whiff of sewage. She needed the dry air of Africa again, more than she'd realised when she'd been cossetted in America. She tried to push the nagging, offensive thought away, but it had been clawing its way to the surface of her consciousness more and more recently: *Was I really happy in LA?* Sonja hated herself for even considering such a question; she was here because her time in Los Angeles was the only time in her life she had been truly content.

She steadied her breathing. Irina habitually made one more stop before hailing a cab back to her villa. The building was the antithesis of the rest of her whistlestop luxury tour. There was only one reason someone like Irina would enter the dilapidated colonial-relic apartment block. Ross's police sources had told him this place was inhabited by junkies and the dealers who preyed on them. It was a dangerous environment for the take-down, but it was also the only location in this teeming city where Sonja could get to Irina away from prying eyes. If anyone did see her, Sonja had reasoned in her planning, they would be too stoned or too afraid of the law to report her.

Irina looked behind her, but even that move was well known to Sonja, documented in a Post-it note she had placed on the planning board in her apartment. Sonja was ready for it and had ducked into the alcove of a tailor's shop. When Sonja emerged Irina had already entered the apartment block.

Sonja followed her inside and took up a position under the first flight of the concrete staircase, in a foyer that smelled of urine. Irina would be above her, knocking on the door of apartment four. Sonja hadn't got close enough to know what the callgirl was buying, but assumed it would be something high end to match her other tastes. She only bought on the day she was to meet Tran Van Ngo, which she did every week, without fail, on a Tuesday.

Sonja shrugged off her daypack, unzipped it and took out the sunglasses case and a pair of latex surgical gloves. She snapped on the gloves and opened the case. From it she took a syringe. She sent a text message to Ross. *In position.*

Her phone vibrated three seconds later. *Ditto.*

The clack of high heels above confirmed Irina had made her purchase. Sonja removed the plastic cap from the needle on the end of the syringe. As Irina descended the last stair and walked around the bannister Sonja emerged from the shadows. Irina looked surprised but not alarmed to see another western woman.

'I wonder if you could help me,' said Sonja, feigning an American accent. 'I'm lost and I'm looking for the war relics museum.'

'I'm sorry, I'm late,' Irina said, and walked past her.

Sonja had hoped for such a response. She moved behind Irina and, bringing her hand up to cover the other woman's mouth, stuck the needle into her neck and depressed the plunger, shooting the Ketamine into Irina's veins. Sonja dropped the syringe and crushed it with the heel of her hiking boot. Irina stopped her muffled calls for help and frantic clawing when she felt the blunt steel barrel of Sonja's SIG in her rib cage.

'Move,' Sonja hissed, 'or you're dead.' She could feel Irina already becoming unsteady on her feet. By the time they made it to the door of the apartment building Irina couldn't form coherent words and she was becoming heavier in Sonja's arms. Ross was double-parked. A motorcyclist honked his horn and yelled at him to move, but he got out of the little Toyota and opened the back door. An elderly Vietnamese woman was saying something to Sonja while she half carried, half dragged Irina to the car. Ross answered the woman in her language as he grabbed Irina's long legs and slid them into the back of the car.

'I told her that she's just fainted and we're taking her to a doctor.'

'Good.' Sonja smiled and nodded at the woman, then finished folding Irina into the back seat. She closed the door, then she and Ross climbed quickly into the front. 'Now drive. Not too fast.'

In Sonja's rented apartment, an hour later, the Ketamine began to wear off. Irina was tied to a dining chair. Sonja pointed the pistol between the woman's eyes as she hooked a finger in the gag and pulled it from her mouth.

Irina coughed. 'Who are you working for, what do you want? Get me water.'

'You're in no position to make demands,' Sonja said. She faced Irina, while Ross stood behind the woman.

Irina looked around her. 'It's late. What time is it? There are people who will miss me. They don't like to be kept waiting. They'll look for me, kill you.'

Sonja smiled. 'It's not "they", is it, Irina, it's "he". Tran Van Ngo, your regular Tuesday night fuck.'

Irina spat on the floor, then laughed. 'You're going after *him*? That's crazy. Now you will die, for sure.'

Traffic hummed outside and music played in a neighbouring flat. Through the fabric of the blind, the light was fading. 'We're going to call Madam Nhu, and you're going to talk to her,' Sonja said.

'Like hell I will. He'll kill me if he thinks I had anything to do with this. You do know that, don't you?'

Sonja nodded. 'If you don't do what I want, I'll kill you.'

Irina shook her head. 'No way. I'm not going to do it. You can go to hell.'

Sonja picked up Irina's Gucci handbag and opened it. 'I'll meet you there soon for a latte. You know, I thought you were a user, that maybe you were buying cocaine or some designer drug to get you through your weekly appointment with Tran, but I never figured you for a mule.' Sonja pulled out three wads of US dollars and waved them in front of Irina's face.

Irina said nothing.

'How you make your money – screwing people, dealing or couriering drugs – is not my concern. All I want is to get into Tran's villa, past his bodyguards, and have some alone time with him.'

Irina laughed again. 'If you do, you'll never get out alive.'

'That's my problem. Now, we're going to call Madam Nhu and you're going to tell her that you've come down with acute food poisoning and that you can't make it this evening. You're going to add that you've just had a call from an old friend from South Africa, another working girl who came over here to see a client and has a few days spare. You're going to say that your friend – me – would be happy to visit Tran tonight and that you can vouch for her.'

'No.'

'Fine,' said Sonja. She stuffed the SIG into the waistband of her jeans. From behind the white sofa she pulled a plastic tarpaulin and began unfolding it, in front of Irina. She placed it on the parquetry flooring. 'Give me a hand to get it under her,' she said to Ross, who remained out of Irina's field of vision.

'*Really?*' Ross said.

Sonja put her hands on her hips. 'Don't go soft on me. It's simple. I wasn't bluffing when I said I'd kill her. She knows too much.' Sonja hadn't told Ross she was prepared to kill Irina if she didn't cooperate – she'd said they would lock her up somewhere and try another strategy to get to the Vietnamese gangster. The shock in the Australian's voice was helping her convince Irina she was ready to execute her and that this wasn't an orchestrated ruse. 'We dump her body, make sure there's a card from Madam Nhu's in her purse, and I tip off the cops. It shouldn't take them long to call her. In the meantime, I show up at the whorehouse, say I'm a friend of Irina's and looking for her. I also let slip I'm in need of work. I'm tall, now blonde, and I'm a western hooker.

Madam Nhu won't want to offend her number one client so she might just send me to Tran.'

'Sonja . . .' Ross said.

'You can't kill me,' Irina said.

Sonja smiled. 'Don't be silly. Of course I can, Irina. In a heartbeat. If I leave you now and I don't complete my mission, you'll run to Tran, then I'll be compromised. It's a wicked world we live in, isn't it?'

Sonja shoved Irina in the chest, tipping her back on the chair legs, and slid the tarpaulin underneath her feet. 'That should do it.' She moved behind the callgirl, grabbed the back of the chair and pushed it forward. She eased Irina down until her head and knees were on the plastic.

'No.'

'Yes.'

Sonja put the tip of the silencer at the base of Irina's skull.

'All right, I'll make the call!'

*

Sonja was collected from Madam Nhu's in Tran's black Bentley. She had seen the car before and recognised the chauffeur-cum-bodyguard. His suit was a tight fit, from muscle, not fat, and he was slightly bowlegged, as if walking on his toes, expecting a fight. The man said nothing to her as he opened the rear door, reluctantly going through the motions, then slammed it. He checked on her every now and then in the rear view mirror; a bodyguard wouldn't like a change in routine, but a boss would not meet his guests without a woman hanging off him.

She had stood in the tastefully decorated lounge of the well-appointed villa that served as an upmarket brothel. Prostitution, Sonja had learned, was illegal in Vietnam, but it still went on. Karaoke bars and massage parlours served one end of the market, while the upper echelon was catered for in private residences;

it was even illegal for a westerner to have a Vietnamese woman enter his hotel room unless they were married. In Madam Nhu's home the man had frisked her, running his hands up under her skirt and around her breasts and checking her purse as the elegantly turned-out older woman looked on impassively; she had no doubt seen worse humiliations.

They drove through the falling evening. People were still thronging the streets, more of them tourists now, seeking out bars and restaurants. Sonja wondered what the place was like during the war. She'd served with Americans, in Sierra Leone and later in Iraq and Afghanistan. The Vietnam veterans were the oldest of the private military contractors – the media called them mercenaries – but they had the most interesting stories. Some had found it impossible to settle into civilian life after their tour of duty here and had drifted to Africa, rolling from one war and one country to the next. She thought of her homeland, which in reality was a dim memory. She was looking forward to seeing Emma again, but that would have to wait. She forced herself to concentrate on the mission.

The driver pulled up at an ornate wrought-iron security gate. It rolled open without the bodyguard pushing a button; Sonja noticed the security cameras mounted on the gate posts as the Bentley motored through. She waited for the driver to open her door, and when he did, she felt as though she were stepping into an oven after the brief respite of the limousine's air conditioning.

'Miss Schmidt,' a man in a white dinner jacket and black bow tie said as she unfolded herself from the car. It was the name she had given Madam Nhu, and which Irina had confirmed.

'Mr Tran.' She towered above him in her heels, but she and Irina were about the same height, and from her surveillance Sonja had noticed the escort always wore stilettos, open toed. Tran looked her up and down; despite his sartorial cool he appraised her like a criminal judging the value of a piece of stolen merchandise.

His gaze lingered on her pink-painted toenails. 'Delighted to meet you.'

He took her hand and held on to it, looking up into her eyes. 'As am I. But you must call me Ngo.'

She nodded her head. '*Cam on ong.*'

He smiled and led her along a paved walkway to the colon-naded entry of his white stone mansion. 'My humble home.'

'It's beautiful.' She lowered her voice: 'Irina sends her apologies.'

He looked to her again. 'This is most irregular, but I have important guests. I will not say I am happy about this change in plans, about any change of plans, but I thank you for agreeing to, er, fill in for Miss Aleksandrova.'

The thank you sounded anything but sincere, but Sonja was pleased he seemed to have accepted the lie. Her research on Tran Van Ngo, much of it garnered by Ross, told her he preferred the company of western women. Irina was the latest in a string of similar-looking women. She knew from the dossier they had prepared that Ngo was older than his smooth skin and full head of hair would have had her believe; he was sixty-two years of age and had joined the Viet Cong as a boy soldier, just sixteen, and served in the latter stages of the war against the Americans. He had joined the People's Army of Vietnam after the war and had risen to the rank of colonel in the subsequent battles to free Cambodia from the Khmer Rouge, and against the Chinese on Vietnam's northern border.

He had left the army for a career in business and, ostensibly, made his money through import and export. The idealistic teenage communist guerrilla, perhaps disillusioned by wars against other comrades, had eventually realised that power came not from the barrel of a gun but from powders and pieces of green paper: the currency of the foe and the ideology he'd once fought. Ross's sources said Tran had made his fortune in heroin, women – he supplied young Vietnamese girls, some underage, to gangster contacts in Cambodia – and, lately, rhino horn. His legitimate front and the washing machine for his cash was a property development business.

'I have many business contacts here tonight. My company is developing luxury apartments and a new hotel on the coast at Da Nang.'

Sonja nodded. 'Irina told me.'

He stopped as they entered the foyer. 'What else did she tell you?' His tone was low and annoyed.

'Nothing. She likes you, you know?'

He frowned, but Sonja sensed him relax, or try to relax. No boy could resist having a note passed about him between two girls in school.

'Irina and I have a business relationship, just as you and I will have a business exchange this evening. Nothing more. Do you understand?'

'Yes.'

'Good.' He held out his arm, bent at the elbow, and she took it. 'When you've finished charming my guests and I've done my business with them I'm going to take you upstairs and make love to you.'

Sonja nodded. 'I understand.'

'I don't have a wife, in case you're wondering,' he said.

'It's none of my business.'

'And I don't care if Irina "likes" me or not. I pay for what I want, what I need. I have no need for sentimental attachments. I just want you to be clear about this.'

'I'm clear.' In fact, she felt the same way.

Chapter 2

Namibia

Emma Kurtz hurt all over. The sunburnt skin on her shoulders stung where her sweat-soaked safari shirt rubbed against it. Her knees were throbbing, her back was aching, her lips were split and chapped and her right hand was cramping from holding the trowel for hours on end.

A shadow passed over her, blessed relief for an instant, until it moved. 'Not quite as glamorous as you first thought, eh, Miss Kurtz?'

Emma blinked and saw the sun backlighting the wild mass of curly white hair that flanked Professor Dorset Sutton's bushy-bearded face. She tried to speak, but her throat was so dry she had to swallow first. 'No, Prof,' she croaked.

'Lara Croft swanned around in her black tank top and short shorts and Indiana Jones spent more time machine-gunning Nazis than digging, but it's nothing like the movies, is it?'

She was annoyed at him, but bit back a reply. She knew where the Lara jibe had come from. She'd dressed pretty much as he'd described, right down to the ponytail, on the first day of the dig, yesterday, and she'd paid the price of not covering up under the unforgiving African sun.

Natangwe, kneeling a few metres to her right, gave a soft laugh.

'Got something to add, have we, Mr Heita?' Sutton strode over to him. 'You're searching for your country's history, young man, not digging a shit pit. Go easy with that trowel.'

Natangwe was swaddled in a jumper and jeans and woollen balaclava, like it was the middle of winter rather than forty degrees Celsius. Emma had thought him the silly one, but he'd been protected from the sun's rays. Emma was still coming to terms with Namibia and the people who lived here. She'd marvelled at the sight of female road workers, toiling over boiling tar in the ferocious heat but, like Natangwe, cocooned in winter woollies at the time. The whites swaggered about in short denim shorts that looked like Daisy Duke's cast-offs, and the Herero women wore voluminous approximations of Victorian hooped skirts.

Although Emma had been born in the UK she felt a kinship to this quietly baking landscape. Her mother and the grandfather she'd never known had been born here, and Grandpa Hans's grandfather had come here from Germany at the turn of the twentieth century as a soldier. Her grandmother, however, was English, and she had hated Africa. She'd left Grandpa Hans in Botswana and Emma's mother, Sonja, had also eventually run away from the old man. Emma had never known her biological father; he'd been killed in the troubles in Northern Ireland, where Sonja had served as a soldier in the British Army before Emma was born.

Lately, Emma had felt a sense of dislocation, not as acute as her mother's but confusing nonetheless. When Sonja had taken her from the UK to live in Los Angeles, at first Emma had revelled in the novelty of seeing so many places and stores she'd only ever seen on TV. But it wasn't home. She had no friends of her own

age there and, given that she wanted to be a battlefield archaeologist, she and her mother had jointly decided that the best
place to study was Glasgow University, a world leader in the field.

'I can't believe you want to study old battlefields,' her mother
had said to her as they'd waited at LAX to board the flight to
Scotland.

'Mum, it's hardly surprising when you think about it.'

Sonja had agreed with a sad frown. Emma had not been a
perfect teenager; in fact for a few years while she'd lived with
her gran she'd hated her mother. Sonja was no ordinary single
mother; she provided for her only child by working overseas in
the world's conflict zones, as a bodyguard and private military
contractor – a modern-day euphemism for a mercenary. Emma's
circle of friends were left leaning, opposed to the wars in Iraq and
Afghanistan, and Emma had been too ashamed to tell them what
her mother did.

Emma had learned, though, that things were not black and
white, and that her mother was not some mindless killing
machine. Sonja had told her of progress made by the coalition forces in Afghanistan, and of the horrors the Taliban and
Al Qaeda had perpetrated against their own people, particularly
women and girls. Even in the safety of Los Angeles, living in a
mansion with staff to cook and clean for them and nothing to
worry about, Emma had awoken more than once to the sound
of her mother screaming herself through to the tortured end of
another nightmare.

Her bloody mother. She was gone, again, and Emma had been
angry when she'd received a short message with a satellite phone
number, in case of emergency, and no answer to her emailed
questions about where her mother was going or what she was
doing.

'It's called conflict archaeology, Mum,' Emma had said at the
airport. 'It's more than just digging up old battlefields; there's

also an anthropological dimension, finding out how and why people became involved in conflict and how they acted.'

'*Ag*, rubbish, man,' her mother had replied, waving a hand in front of her face. 'People have always killed each other, always will. That stuff is better left buried in the ground, but I'm happy you're just studying war, and not doing something stupid like I did and joining the army.'

Professor Sutton shuffled off. The dig site was an old cattle farm that had been acquired by the government and now leased to a mining corporation. Although the company had the land, it couldn't commence mining until an archaeological survey had been done on several locations that had been judged most likely to contain evidence of early settlement. They were digging on a low rise, near a seasonal stream that ran through the plain. They had removed the topsoil of the area pegged out by Dorset Sutton and were doing the backbreaking work of searching for finds.

Dorset had published an article in the *Journal of Conflict Archaeology* at Glasgow University about his discovery of an old German *Schutztruppe* camp in the south of Namibia, on the edge of the Namib-Naukluft National Park, and Emma had summoned the courage to write to him, explaining her family's connection to the country. He'd been affable, charming and welcoming in his reply, and told her he'd be happy to have her on a dig in the future.

True to his word, Sutton had agreed to her request to join him on this dig, and here they were. She would gain credits towards her degree at Glasgow and, just as importantly for Emma, she would have the chance to connect with the land that had been part of her family's troubled life for more than a century. But things were not turning out as she had expected.

'I think the *baas* gets off on making life hell for his underlings,' Natangwe said out of the side of his mouth.

Still kneeling, Emma straightened her back, took off her hat and wiped her grimy brow. 'At least he's an equal opportunity abuser.'

Natangwe snorted. He was handsome but also opinionated, and he walked with the swagger of a young man who had a sense of entitlement. His father was a veteran of the liberation war and a staunch SWAPO party supporter, Emma had learned on the drive to the dig from the capital. She wasn't shy, but her mother had told her that in the army, or in any group of strangers, it was sometimes best to keep a low profile, to go about one's work quietly and professionally, so she hadn't been as forthcoming about her own background. Her grandfather had served in the old South West African police special unit, *Koevoet*, which meant 'crowbar', a force infamous for its ruthless efficiency in the war, and this would not have endeared her to the likes of Natangwe.

'You don't sound German, Emma Kurtz,' Natangwe had said as he laboured beside her. 'Where are you from originally? Your accent isn't Scottish either.'

Emma put her hat back on. 'All over, really. I went to school in England, lived in the States for a while, and now I'm at Glasgow for the next couple of years.'

'But your father, was he German?'

'Kurtz is my mum's name. She was a single mother; I never knew my father. But she was born here, in Namibia.'

Natangwe nodded and that seemed to be the end of the conversation. He went back to his digging. She wondered if he thought less of her because of the little she'd revealed about her heritage. Emma herself didn't really know how she felt about her family's connection with this starkly beautiful country, but she was here to confront the Kurtz family's history, even if it might be painful or, like now, awkward. It was hard to imagine Namibia at war, but it had been from the mid-1960s to the late 1980s as SWAPO fought for independence from South Africa, which regarded the old South West Africa as one of its provinces.

Emma scratched at the dry, sandy earth. She had thought she would be ready for her first dig; her lecturers had all taken great pains, often, to remind the students that archaeology, working on a real dig, was backbreaking work. She couldn't have imagined, though, that she would be as close to tears as she had been last night when she'd lain her weary body into the squeaky camp stretcher. Emma paused to swig lukewarm water from her bottle.

'Come on, Miss Kurtz,' Professor Sutton called from the other end of the trench, 'history's not going to reveal itself, you know.'

'Bastard,' she whispered.

'How will you feel,' Natangwe said, not looking over at her, 'if we do find a mass grave?'

Excited, Emma wanted to say, but she held her tongue. She knew what Natangwe was getting at. One of the reasons for the dig was that the local people's oral traditions held that dozens, perhaps a hundred or more, people had been massacred in this area, captured rebels who had been summarily executed by a detachment of *Schutztruppen* in 1904. Conflict archaeology, by its nature, revealed the worst of human nature as well as the best. Acts of bravery and barbarity featured in all wars, but Emma knew from her reading that the German colonialists and their army had brutally suppressed several rebellions in South West Africa. That was all in the history books, but if they were lucky – such an odd word to contemplate in this instance – they might find forensic evidence of a war crime.

'How long had your mother's family been in Namibia?' Natangwe pressed her as she kept on scraping. 'What don't you want to tell me?'

Emma sighed. His arrogance annoyed her, but on reflection she told herself she had nothing to hide. 'All right. My great-great-grandfather served in the *Schutztruppe*.'

'I wonder if he executed prisoners, or poisoned wells, or raped women, or imprisoned and worked them to death in concentration camps like Shark Island,' Natangwe hissed.

Emma looked over at him, but Natangwe kept his eyes on the ground, meticulously brushing away the sand, though he now worked with an urgency that Emma hadn't seen in him before. Emma had been honest with him, and this was what she got: a lecture and suppositions. 'He was a soldier, that's all I know for sure.' She was doubly glad now, though, that she hadn't mentioned her grandfather's role in the more recent war, and nor would she.

He looked up at her, his eyes boring into hers. 'So, what, it's OK to commit war crimes if you were only following orders?'

Emma sighed. She had feared that this type of exchange would come up at some time. Her mother was right; it was better to stay in the background, to be the grey person who didn't attract too much attention. What little she knew about her grandfather, Hans, came from his embittered ex-wife, her grandmother, and it did not give her grounds for much hope that her forebear had been a noble soldier with a conscience who would refuse an immoral order. Hans, Gran had let slip once after too many gins, was a murderer; he'd beaten a captive SWAPO guerrilla to death during an interrogation.

She took a breath. 'Natangwe, I don't think I'd be here if I thought for one moment that everything about the colonial era in this country was good or morally correct. I think what we're doing here is confronting the past, not leaving it buried, where some people want it to stay. The Germans only ruled Namibia as a colony from 1884 to 1915, but they left a lasting legacy here. It's in their architecture, their roads, their language and their food, but even their own government admits their wrongdoings. Don't hate me because I'm trying to find out more about where I come from.'

Natangwe stopped his brushing and scraping. 'An apology won't bring back the sixty thousand Herero killed by the Germans, most of them worked to death in concentration camps, let alone the tens of thousands of my people killed in the liberation struggle.'

Emma felt dejected, but went back to work with the trowel, scraping at the dirt without much enthusiasm. She heard a vehicle engine in the distance and when she looked up and saw it was Alex's Land Rover, she smiled.

They had all been introduced to Alex Bahler yesterday, when they'd arrived at the dig site. He was a wildlife researcher, involved with a carnivore research program to help conserve and protect the cheetah and the endangered desert lion.

Desert lions had once roamed up and down the Atlantic coast from the water's edge to far inland, Bahler had told them, but they had almost been wiped out by humans – farmers who viewed them as a threat to their livestock, and trophy hunters. By the 1990s, when intensive research began, there were thought to be just twenty left, but their numbers were slowly coming back. Alex's role was to monitor the movements of collared lions at the far eastern extreme of their home range, where they occasionally came close to Etosha National Park. Cheetahs, Alex had explained, lived a similarly perilous existence; those outside of protected areas were frequently shot and poisoned by sheep and cattle farmers.

Alex was working with a number of farmers in the area on a project to trap and relocate cheetahs and lions. He was Namibian German, aged in his mid-twenties, just a few years older than Emma, and he was, she thought, quite gorgeous. Dorset Sutton shot Emma a stern look as Alex pulled up near the dig, clearly telling her to get back to work.

Despite it going against her training Emma stabbed the sand, hard, with her trowel. She wanted to pierce the heart of this barren, inhospitable place. She scraped the dirt away but then something unusual happened; the trowel snagged.

At first Emma thought she'd caught the blade on a root, but looking around she realised that wasn't possible on this open plain.

Gently, she extracted the point of the trowel, placed it down, and picked up a paintbrush. She carefully brushed the grit from around the object, then lowered her face and blew at the sand covering whatever it was underneath. It was fabric.

She glanced to the side; Natangwe was ignoring her. Professor Sutton was deep in conversation with Alex Bahler, the pair of them poring over a map spread across the bonnet of Alex's Land Rover.

Emma took off her leather gardening gloves and used her finger-tips and the brush to uncover more. It was fabric, all right. Her heart started beating faster. Was this a rebel prisoner, shot in the head by someone her great-great-grandfather may have known? Her fingers touched something hard. She blew and brushed.

It was metal, and as the dust parted under her breath she saw, surprisingly, a rusting zip.

A zip? Such a thing wouldn't have been around in the early twentieth century. She knew she should call Professor Sutton over, but she wanted this find for herself. Screw her mother, she did not want to be the grey man or grey woman or whatever the military called the quiet achiever. She wanted her professor's praise, and she wanted to show Natangwe that it *was* worth her being here, and that she would uncover whatever secrets this grave had to offer. She picked up the trowel again, now carefully using it to scrape away more sand. The pointed tip hit something hard.

Emma gasped. It was a bone.

Chapter 3

There were a dozen people in Tran Van Ngo's large formal lounge room already. The men were middle-aged and up, the women looked in their twenties, mostly. The dress was elegant. It was clear to Sonja that this was a gathering at which to flaunt trophies and chattels, not wives.

Sonja took a glass of champagne and passed on the food. She was the only westerner in the room, but she didn't feel as though she was attracting any more stares from the younger girls than might be expected. Her face might have been new, but Tran's predilections were clearly not.

Tran introduced her to a couple standing near them by her assumed name of Ursula Schmidt – it was actually her aunt's – but then began to speak to the man in Vietnamese. The man's partner, a pretty girl who was introduced to her as Cherry, stepped aside from the men. 'You're new,' she said.

'I actually feel very old compared to you and the other women here,' Sonja replied.

Cherry tittered and put a hand in front of her mouth. 'Ngo likes his women . . . sorry.'

'Old?'

'I was going to say, white,' Cherry said. 'Where is Irina?'

'She's not well. I'm a friend.'

Cherry lowered her voice. 'I hope she warned you about Tran. Be careful. Irina told me Tran can be violent, especially if business is not going his way.'

'Why are you telling me this?'

'I think maybe this is why Irina decided to be sick tonight. Maybe she thinks he will be kinder to a stranger, not take it out on her. If you are lucky, all he will want is sex, and not to hurt you.'

Sonja sipped her champagne. 'Thanks for the warning.' With this new information her revenge would be even more satisfying. Sonja had hit her own father, just before she'd left home, after seeing him beat her mother. Much later she'd reconciled with the old man, who had done his utmost to atone for his earlier sins, but the day she had knocked him to the floor and walked out on him had been one of the best of her life until they'd made amends.

Tran and the other man came over to them. 'Forgive me,' Tran said in English, 'some boring business to attend to. I hope you ladies are enjoying yourselves.'

'Of course,' Sonja said.

A young man threaded his way through the small party of guests and stood beside Tran, who eventually acknowledged his presence. Tran said something to the man, who nodded.

'My personal secretary,' Tran said to Sonja. 'I have a small presentation to make to our esteemed guests. Afterwards, we celebrate.'

Tran called for everyone's attention and Sonja and Cherry drifted to the fringe of the group. The young Vietnamese girl translated, quietly, as Tran held court.

'He's thanking all the men here for their support during this challenging time for him, developing his new hotel and apartment complex.'

Tran concluded his speech then nodded to the young man Sonja had seen him speaking to before. The young man went to a table at the edge of the lounge room and began ferrying gift-wrapped packages to each of the men in the room.

Sonja finished her champagne and set her glass down on a side table as the first of the gifts was unwrapped. There were soft murmurs of surprise as each of the elongated boxes was opened. From the first box, and then the others, the owners each held aloft a pointed horn.

'Rhino,' Sonja said softly.

'It's the only income stream he's got these days,' Cherry whispered. 'The Americans are shutting down his drug shipments and his property development is failing due to oversupply. These gifts are worth a fortune; they say he's been stockpiling rhino horn.'

Sonja had to put a hand on a wing-backed armchair to steady herself. It was not like her to let emotions affect the execution of a mission. She had prepared for this moment, mentally and physically. Hours and hours spent in the gym had helped her to shed the few extra kilos an easy life in LA had brought on, and she'd closely examined the chain of events that had led her here as well as researching the trade in rhino horn. In between she had fired hundreds of rounds at the pistol range to blow off steam. She was ready, completely, for what had to be done.

'Are you OK?' Cherry asked.

'Fine. I don't usually drink champagne.'

The six horns being fondled, passed from businessman to concubine and back again, had a combined value of close to a million dollars. It was just a commodity to them.

Sonja gravitated to the edge of the room. She thought of the blood spilled in Africa to make this moment happen, animals and humans slaughtered in a war over something with no medicinal properties at all. Just as it sickened her, it steeled her.

She needed fresh air. Sonja walked briskly to the front door and down the stairs. She rested her hand on the balustrade and willed herself to stay calm. She was in *control* of her feelings. It was what made her good at her job. Sonja despised weakness – in others, yes, but most of all in herself.

'Miss Kurtz?'

Sonja forced herself to stay still, to not turn.

'That is your name, isn't it? Or do you prefer Ursula when you're working undercover?'

She looked around then and Tran's chauffeur was there, an iPhone in his left hand, held up. He snapped a picture of her. 'What are you doing? My name is Ursula Schmidt, not Kurtz.'

The man's other hand moved inside the left lapel of his suit jacket and drew out a small-calibre semi-automatic pistol, a .32 by the look of it, with a silencer attached to the end.

The man's face was impassive, his tone deadly. 'I don't like a change in the routine. I went to Irina's villa complex. She's not there, not home ill as she told Madam Nhu. I spoke to the security man on the gate; Irina went out for her normal Tuesday appointments this morning and never returned. He was concerned.'

Sonja held her hands up, palms out. 'All right, the truth. She's sick of Tran, tired of the way he beats her. He's not worth the money but she was too scared to confront him. She has another lover. I am Ursula Schmidt.'

'Your name is Sonja Kurtz. You are here in Vietnam to assassinate Mr Tran.'

'Rubbish. Where would you get such a ridiculous story?'

The man used his thumb to select the gallery icon on his phone's camera. He tossed the iPhone to her and Sonja caught it. 'Have a look.'

Sonja had taken her mother's nationality when she left Africa and joined the British Army. She had seen dead bodies in Northern Ireland, where she had served in a special intelligence surveillance unit, and she had witnessed mayhem and massacre from Sierra Leone to Afghanistan as a mercenary. She was, some of her male counterparts would have grudgingly admitted, hardcore, unshockable. Now, though, the air was stolen from her lungs and she felt as though she was sinking, sucking in water as she gazed at the naked, tortured and lifeless body of Ross Coonan.

She swallowed back bile. Ross was a good man who had risked – and now lost – his life to save the rhino. She would not give this pig the satisfaction of seeing her puke. 'Irina?'

'I took her to Madam Nhu. We'll finish her, slowly, later. The boss owes a favour to one of the triads.'

'How did you find them?' She was in shock, still trying to digest the news that Ross was dead.

'The journalist has been sniffing around the boss for a long time. We are not stupid. We have informers who have been monitoring his movements. I asked around my network after I dropped you here. A street-side noodle vendor said Coonan had been seen with a woman who fitted your description. You think you're smarter than us, but you are not. You are a stranger in this land and we Vietnamese have been killing foreign invaders for centuries.'

'You've told Tran Van Ngo all of this?' Sonja asked.

The chauffeur shook his head. 'I called his assistant.'

The young man who distributed the rhino horns, Sonja thought.

As if on cue the immaculately groomed man appeared on the doorstep. He conversed rapidly in Vietnamese with the chauffeur.

The driver turned to Sonja. 'I will take you somewhere secure. He will tell the boss you were unwell, having caught whatever Irina had. The boss will be displeased, but there will be no messy scene in front of his guests and he will be happy when he learns we have disrupted your mission.'

'I'm going to kill you,' Sonja said evenly.

The man chuckled. 'Going to scratch me to death with those fake nails? I frisked you, remember?'

'Get her out of here,' the secretary said.

'No.' Sonja put her hands on her hips. 'You're right, my mission's over. In fact, my life's pretty much over. Shoot me here. Hopefully the sight of a dead body will cramp Ngo's business deal.'

'Come with me, you stupid, insolent woman.'

'I'm going to scream. Ngo's going to lose so much face he'll be the invisible man.' Sonja took a breath and opened her mouth. The chauffeur aimed between her eyes.

'Shut her *up*,' he said.

The young secretary moved behind her and clamped his hand over her mouth. Sonja was ready for him. She raked her shoe down his shin and drove her stiletto heel into his foot. At the same time she grabbed his arm, dropped and rolled him over her shoulder. The chauffeur fired a double tap, and the secretary's body took one of the rounds as she flipped him into the bodyguard. Sonja had figured she could take one of the bullets and carry on, as long as it didn't sever an artery or take out a major organ.

The three of them fell to the ground. Sonja smashed her fist into the gunman's face and knelt on the wrist of his gun hand. She reached to the back of her head. The long, pointed hatpin she'd used to pin her hair up came free. She put one hand over the man's mouth and drove the pin into the side of his neck. In and out, half a dozen times, she gouged around under the skin, shredding the carotid artery. The secretary didn't move; the other man's bullet had been a lucky shot, for Sonja.

'You're not going to call a woman stupid again, ever.' Sonja held her hand over the chauffeur's mouth until he died. When he was still she grabbed him under the armpits and dragged his body into a thicket of bougainvillea by the entrance of the mansion. She did the same with the secretary.

Satisfied the men were hidden she washed the blood from her hands at a garden tap against an exterior wall of the villa. She walked back into the house, pausing at the mirror in the foyer to put her hair up again and check her makeup. She'd worn red for a reason; the few dark spots hardly showed. Killing the two men had settled her; she no longer felt incapable of dealing with the sight of the rich businessmen fondling the rhino horns like phallic compensators.

Inside, the horns had been cast aside in favour of Johnnie Walker Blue Label and Courvoisier cognac. She still felt sickened but her pulse was slow, her vision clear. The red mist had come and gone. She vectored towards Ngo.

He stopped a waitress and took two glasses of champagne from her. 'I was told you were ill.' He handed Sonja one of the glasses.

'Some fresh air helped. I'm still getting used to your climate.'

He looked at her and reached out his free hand. It took all her courage not to flinch. He tucked a stray strand of hair behind her ear. None of his guests were nearby. 'You're beautiful, Ursula.'

She sipped her drink. 'You told me you didn't do sentimental.'

He smiled. 'I lie for a living. This is all a charade, and to tell you the truth, I am tired of it.'

'The property development?'

'That, and the expensive gifts. I am throwing good money after bad, as the English say. You think me foolish, I'm sure.'

She regarded him dispassionately and spoke the truth: 'I think you're a man.'

'You should have been a diplomat, but I suppose a woman in your line of work is just that.'

His eyes were not those of a predator; they were tired. He looked small, as if his tailored suit would have to be taken in because he was shrinking. She forced a smile at his joke, in reply, but he saw through it.

'You look sad,' Ngo said.

'I am *not*.' The image of Ross's body haunted her.

'I didn't mean to offend.'

She took a breath. 'Sorry. No, look, I've had a very good time so far. Very rewarding.'

Ngo raised his eyebrows. 'Really? How so?'

She caressed the side of the glass, collecting the condensation brought on by the warmth of the night, then licked the cool wetness from her fingers. 'I've met a man of power, of intelligence, and humility.' She glanced around. 'How long will this go on?'

He looked over his shoulder. 'I must work the room some more. This is my last chance to save the development, Ursula. I won't lie to you; I was hoping Irina would be here as she is very important to me, but in the same vein I will tell you, honestly, that I am also glad you are here instead of her. I am thinking that I very much want to be alone with you, sooner rather than later.' He stared into her eyes.

Sonja ran her tongue quickly over her glossy lips. 'Me too.'

'Give me thirty minutes. Circulate, look pretty.'

She winked at him. 'I'll try.'

Cherry found Sonja again and, despite Sonja's reluctance, took two cold rice paper rolls from a waiter's platter. 'You should eat something. Are you OK now?'

'I'm fine,' Sonja said. 'Never better.' Her gaze drifted to the gifts of rhino horn scattered about the room.

Handing out the rhino horns had been an ostentatious gesture, Sonja thought. It told the other men that Ngo was not on the ropes, financially, which he apparently was. Horn was only worth what someone had paid for it. The Mozambican poachers who had risked their lives to shoot the animals from which the matted lumps of keratin came had been paid a pittance compared to what the substance would fetch once ground and sold on. Ngo could have made serious money out of trading the horns, but he'd used them as currency, instead, to curry favour. It was a ballsy move, and one that would cost him dearly if these other men did not bankroll him.

Sonja wondered what else the gifts signified. Was there something bigger going on here than a last-ditch attempt to shore up an overdue hotel and apartment complex? Was there something Cherry didn't know and that she and Ross had missed in their research?

She had been trying not to think of him, at least not until after the mission, but visions of Ross's tortured body scrolled yet again across the inside of her momentarily closed eyes. Ross had told the chauffeur everything. She was not surprised – in real life most people told everything they knew under torture, believing the lie that they would be spared if they revealed the truth. Ross was one more casualty in this war, one more reason for her to do what she had to. She spared a thought for Irina, more collateral damage.

'Looks like we're leaving,' Cherry said, breaking into Sonja's thoughts.

'Oh, yes.'

'It was nice to meet you, Ursula. Perhaps we can have coffee some time.'

'Yes, perhaps.'

Cherry took her hand and looked into her eyes. 'Good luck, whatever it is you're here to do.'

'What do you mean?'

Cherry glanced behind her, nervously checking for her partner. She lowered her voice. 'I hate this life, these men. The things they are involved in, that Irina is involved in, are terrible. There are drugs, guns, even children being traded by these men in their smart suits. They kill, Ursula, often for fun. Be careful.'

'Of course, but you've nothing to worry about.'

Cherry opened her Gucci clutch bag and took out a tissue. She reached up to Sonja's face and dabbed at her left temple. 'You missed a spot of blood.'

Cherry snapped her purse closed and rushed to answer the beckoning wave of her man. A chill ran down Sonja's back. Evil was good; the worse this man was then the more satisfaction she would have in bringing him down. Sonja went to Ngo's side, near the entrance to the mansion. He was farewelling another man and a woman. The man, much older than Ngo, took Sonja's hand. 'Hello,' the man said.

'Ursula, allow me to introduce General Nguyen. The general was a great hero of our liberation war against the Americans.'

'You're still in the army?' Sonja asked.

'Formerly. Ngo indulges me with an honorary title. You're German?'

'Yes, though I've lived overseas for many years.'

'I've only been to East Berlin, and that was in the bad old days, before the wall came down,' Nguyen said.

'I would have thought for Vietnam that the old days were good, with East Germany as an ally against the capitalist west,' Sonja said.

General Nguyen smiled. 'I'm something of a progressive socialist. East Germany was a failed state, but in Vietnam we value free trade and entrepreneurial spirit. That's something some of our Russian friends have also embraced, eh, Ngo?'

'Yes, quite,' Ngo replied.

'I haven't seen you here before,' the general said to Sonja.

'No, I'm new to Vietnam, I was invited here by a friend.'

'Irina.'

Sonja nodded. 'She's unwell.' She glanced at Ngo, who looked distinctly uncomfortable.

'Ah,' Nguyen said, 'so you're both in the same business?'

Sonja was surprised by the elderly man's directness, but the woman on his arm, whom he had not bothered to introduce, could have passed for his granddaughter. This was a party where women, escorts, had the status of pretty baubles. 'Yes, you could say that.'

'Ah . . . so perhaps, Ngo, you were holding out on us, eh?' The general laughed and clapped Ngo on the arm. 'We must go. We have a long night ahead of us, yes?' He looked to the young girl for the first time and she lowered her eyes.

Sonja was pleased when the general and the last of the guests finally left. Her whole operation had been compromised and Ross was dead. Other people, notably Madam Nhu, would be aware of what was going on and it wouldn't be long before someone called Ngo to check on her whereabouts.

Ngo glanced at his watch. 'Right, I just need to discuss some follow-up matters with my secretary, then we can spend some time together.'

'I think you'll find he's gone,' Sonja said. 'When I went outside earlier, for some fresh air, I saw him walk out the gate with your driver.'

Ngo frowned. 'Really? That is annoying. He was not dismissed.'

Sonja reached out and put a finger on Ngo's chest and looked into his eyes. 'I'm pleased you're not putting me off any longer while you do business. I have work of my own to attend to.'

He smiled. 'Oh, do you, and what do you want to do?'

'You.'

'I know that it is rude to keep a lady waiting. Perhaps we should conclude our business upstairs, in private.'

Sonja laid a hand on Ngo's shoulder. 'You can seal this deal wherever you want, at your desk if you wish.' She leaned forward and kissed him. His lips were soft, like a woman's, and he made no attempt to invade her mouth with his tongue. Their meeting was sensual rather than urgent.

He broke from her and took her hand. 'There is champagne in my bedroom, come with me.'

'Yes, sir.' She lowered her eyes.

Ngo opened the door to a large, tastefully decorated master bedroom. The style was modern, minimalistic, the colours cool.

An air conditioner hummed. Ngo went to a silver ice bucket by the side of the bed and took out a bottle of Dom Pérignon. 'I've been looking forward to this.'

She smiled.

Sonja was pleased she wouldn't need to bother with the messy work of using the hatpin again. She opened her clutch bag, took out the chauffeur's pistol and shot Ngo between the eyes.

He fell backwards, dead before he hit the floor, but to make sure, she put two more shots through his heart. 'Me too.'

Chapter 4

Sonja sat in the business class seat of the Thai Airways Boeing 777 and took out her iPhone. She plugged in the earbuds and fitted them then switched on the phone, which she'd set to flight mode.

She had promised herself that after the business was done in Vietnam she would not watch the video again. She had seen it so many times, on the television news, on Facebook, on Twitter, on the documentary they had made about rhinos and at the Emmy Awards where they had presented him an honorary award. Sonja hated maudlin shows of emotion, but it seemed no one else in America did. Strangers had stopped her in the street after the news had aired worldwide, recognising her from some paparazzi snaps that the networks were re-running as stills.

She had been careful, after it happened, moving out of the big house and changing location twice to escape the vultures of the media. A few photographers had tried to get pictures of her at the funeral, but she'd worn a headscarf as well as dark glasses. After the wake they'd tailed her and Emma. Sonja had opened the door of the Hummer, climbed out and stood there, still in her disguise, and waited while they had taken their pictures. After they were sated she had called each of them over, one by one, and whispered into their ears, in case they were carrying digital audio recorders, that if they continued to hound her and Emma she would find out where each of them lived and hurt them, in some small but unforgettable way.

There had been stories about her, the television star's girlfriend, that pieced together some of her life in the British Army, and as a mercenary. There was vision of the conflict in Namibia's Caprivi Strip from several years earlier, and allegations of Sonja's involvement in fomenting a brief and ultimately unsuccessful revolution by ethnic Caprivians against the legitimate government. It had all died down, eventually. The press had a short attention span.

She opened the video she had saved to the phone. It was a montage made by some stalker or other, cheesy with its gospel music background. His face appeared.

Sonja reached out with her trigger finger and caressed the strong jaw, the thick dark hair.

Sam Chapman, wildlife documentary maker and conservation hero. RIP, read the crawler line under his picture.

Sonja caught her breath. It was always the same. She felt her throat tighten and the tears begin to form. The video began, showing him riding in the back of an open Land Rover in South Africa's Kruger Park. He jumped down from it and swaggered through the bush behind a Shangaan tracker. The macho act was just that, a performance for the cameras. The rangers accompanying him carried guns, but Sonja knew how much Sam had hated firearms. He'd made her sell all of hers, which she'd resented at first. In time, though, she had come to believe that she could live in a world without guns, bullets, knives and bloodshed.

She had been wrong.

Damn it, *damn him*, she had been *wrong*. She cuffed her eyes before the tears began. Again she watched the scenes of a rhino being darted, its horn drilled and then infused with a poisonous dye. Tran Van Ngo had not cared about poisoned rhino horns; no doubt he sourced horn that was yet to be contaminated. Sam was talking, caressing the massive head of the drugged rhino. He'd loved animals.

'*I've never loved a human being as much as I love you,*' he had said to her, his last words before he'd boarded the flight from the States to Africa.

And her reply? She shuddered as she remembered, reliving the pain, hurting herself all over again. '*Get on the plane, you* fokken *sissy.*'

Sam had laughed, as he always did, at her mock disdain for public affection and endless protestations of devotion. She loathed Valentine's Day, barely acknowledged anyone's birthday except Emma's, and had pretended to vomit when Sam had bought her a locket to celebrate the one-year anniversary of their meeting.

She felt for it now, under her bush shirt. In it was a picture of him. She'd never told him she had cut one out of a celebrity magazine and put it in there, the night after he'd given it to her. Sonja had put it in the drawer of her bedside table, pretending that she never wore it.

They had Skyped, the day before it happened. He had been in a luxury safari camp in a private game reserve on the edge of the Kruger National Park. She had kidded him about how this was Hollywood's idea of roughing it in the bush.

He laughed and she thought her heart would turn to molten honey when he smiled and winked at her.

'*Hey, you're wearing the locket,*' he said, and reached out to the screen of his iPad to try and touch her.

With one hand she'd met his fingertips, with the other she had clasped the locket. '*I'm embarrassed now,*' she had said.

'*Don't be, it's OK to love.*'

And there was the problem. The Thai flight attendant stopped beside her. Sonja paused the video and removed a bud. 'Vodka and tonic, double.' It was her third. *Fuck it*, Sonja thought. Drink wasn't the answer, but it was a good short-term alternative.

Sonja closed her eyes and rested her head back against the seat. She needed to sleep. She had gone from Tran's in a cab direct to Ho Chi Minh City's Tan Son Nhat Airport, arriving in time, as planned, to catch a flight to Bangkok. Still pumped when she got off the plane, she had tried to level out with a couple of drinks in the lounge while she killed the more than two hours before the flight to Johannesburg, which left at a quarter past one in the morning. The flight was ten-and-a-half hours, plenty of time to sleep if she could stop the thoughts that were whirling through her mind on an endless loop.

Killing Tran was never supposed to bring closure, a stupid word invented by soft people who couldn't face reality. The only thing she had closed was the door on one gangster's life. Her mission had been payback, nothing more, but it had gone horribly wrong with the death of Ross. Sonja knew that if Sam had been alive he would not have approved of her taking out a kingpin in the wild-life trade, no matter how passionate he was about saving rhinos. But she didn't come from the same world as Sam.

They had met in Botswana. He had been hopelessly lost in the Okavango Delta, stuck on the real-life set of an absurd reality TV show that had gone wrong. He had been dropped in the bush like some survival expert, but in reality Sam was a scientist, not an SAS operative. She had saved his life and then had become embroiled in a plan to blow up a dam. They had made an unlikely pair, the mercenary and the television pretty boy, but she had loved him.

Emma, unlike Sonja, had actually heard of Sam Chapman and she had been over the moon when Sonja had announced that she would be going to Los Angeles to live with Sam.

Emma had been on the cusp of finishing her schooling and Sonja had given her the option of staying at boarding school in England or coming to America with them. Emma had finished high school in California.

Sam had doted on Emma and her daughter had adored him. For a time Sonja had recognised her own pangs of jealousy. She and her mother had raised Emma, but the truth was that Emma's grandmother had done most of the work while Sonja was away earning money in the worst places on earth. Sonja had been through a trying time with Emma and had only just reconnected with her when Sam had come into their life. But Sonja had got over her need to be over-protective and revelled, if only for a short time, in being able to share the trials and tribulations of a teenage girl's transition to adulthood with someone else.

The flight attendant returned with the drink. As she leaned across Sonja to place the drink on the small table between Sonja and the next empty seat, she saw Sam's face, frozen on the small screen.

'Oh, I loved him so much.'

Sonja nodded, tipped a splash of tonic into the vodka, and took a deep sip. 'So did I.'

'He made advertisements, in Thailand and other countries in Asia, telling people not to buy products from elephants or rhinos that had been killed. He was a very good man.'

The woman left and Sonja touched the screen again, remembering how soft his skin had been. She closed her eyes and fancied she could almost smell him, almost feel his touch. When she opened her eyes the screen had gone to sleep. She switched the phone off. A flush of anger replaced her indulgent reminiscing. Her mission had cost the life of a good man, tortured to death, and God alone knew what horrors Irina would be subjected to as payback for her complicity in getting Sonja across Tran Van Ngo's threshold.

Sonja's anger, in turn, morphed into self-loathing. It was the same as it had been in the aftermath of Sam's death. She *knew* he had signed on to make *Wildlife Frontline*, a series of documentaries about national parks rangers around the world who were involved in the deadly business of counter-poaching operations, because of her. He had denied it, but she'd known he was trying to impress her, trying to prove he could be as brave as she had been.

In fact, as she'd tried to tell him, she didn't consider herself brave. She was no more than a tradesperson, doing the only job she had been trained for. She did not put herself in harm's way in war zones because she was brave or noble, or fighting for some cause or other. '*It's just bloody money, Sam,*' she had tried to tell him.

'*And it's money for me, for us, if I make* Wildlife Frontline,' he'd countered. A second later, though, he'd recanted. '*No, I'll tell you the truth, it's more than money; you and I both know that the men and women who are trying to stop rhino poaching in Africa, trying to stop people killing tigers in Asia and orangutans in Borneo and Sumatra are good people doing a valuable job. I want to tell their story.*'

She had envied him his idealism, but when he had told her he planned on going on patrol with rangers in the Kruger Park as part of a filming trip to South Africa she had said she would come with him, to provide security.

He'd been mad, telling her that he could look after himself.

Sonja drained her drink and pushed the call button for the flight attendant. *No, Sam, you couldn't look after yourself, and I should have been there to protect you.*

She'd been with Sam long enough to know that shooting a documentary involved long days of work for Sam and that she wouldn't have had much time with him even if she had tagged along, so she had decided to stay in the States – a decision she knew she would regret forever. She had imagined, hoped, the night-time anti-poaching patrol would be set up and filmed in some safe area of the reserve; so much of reality television was anything but. However, as bad luck would have it the real patrol Sam and his crew were filming had heard shots in the night, near the Stolsnek rangers' post in the south of the park, and they had been first on the scene. Rangers had opened fire on the poachers and the Mozambican criminals had returned fire with an AK-47. Sam had been hit in the chest.

A helicopter had been called and Sam had died in the air over White River on the way to the Nelspruit Mediclinic.

Death followed her, always. She knew that depression would come hard on its heels and that she would keep it at bay, through alcohol, until she ended up as she had last time, after the funeral, with the barrel of her Glock in her mouth in the middle of the night. Perhaps, this time, she would have the guts to go through with it. If she believed in the hereafter, or in any form of religion, she might take solace in the thought that she might be reunited with her beautiful Sam, floating with him on a fucking cloud or, better yet, roaming some dry golden savannah with him for eternity, arm in arm, kissing as they wandered amid the animals he had given his life for.

But that was just bullshit. Even if it were true – and she had no problem with people believing in God – she, Sonja Kurtz, had led a life that would end in only one place.

Hell.

*

As Alex and Emma approached Namutoni Camp, the white tower of the fort now visible, Emma checked her phone and saw she finally had a signal. She tapped out a message: '*Hi Mum, where are you? I need your help*', but before she could finish the sentence with '*identifying a military uniform*', her finger slipped and hit send.

'Damn,' she said.

'What is it?' Alex asked.

'Just tried to send my mum a message and I've lost the signal again.' It was more than an inconvenience; Emma re-read the fragment she had been able to send and realised her mother would probably freak out. She hoped the signal returned soon.

Alex had driven her into Etosha National Park and they were approaching the northernmost rest camp, Namutoni, the closest place to the dig site that had mobile phone coverage. They had entered the park through the King Nehale Gate, crossing open grasslands where cattle ranged, before coming to the fence that stretched to the left and right as far as she could see, and marked the border of the game reserve.

'This is the Andoni Plain,' Alex had told her on the drive in, 'part of the same ecosystem as your dig site, but this area is protected.'

'It's beautiful.' The vast expanse of pale green grass waved in the light breeze under a cloudless sky tinged blue-grey by a layer of dust that hung permanently just above the horizon. This was wild, empty Africa, just as Emma had imagined it.

'It's fantastic cheetah country; despite the fence they still get through, into the cattle lands. Also, there are populations of cheetah living in the communal lands, where the local people graze their cows and goats.'

Alex slowed as they passed a waterhole on their left. It was full from the recent rains and Emma was surprised to see a flock of a hundred or more pink flamingos wading in the shallows, searching with their beaks for food. 'Gosh, they're beautiful, I wouldn't have expected to see them here now. Isn't this the beginning of your winter?'

He nodded. 'The summer rains lasted a long time this year, so Etosha is still very green, but by the end of our winter many of these pans dry out and the ground is just white limestone rock and dirt.' They left the flamingos and drove the rest of the way to the camp.

Emma had seen this part of Etosha before, but only briefly. She, Natangwe and Professor Sutton had driven to the dig site via the park, but it had been a quick one-day transit. Professor Sutton had taken the time, though, to give them a lecture at Namutoni, in the whitewashed fort, about the battle that had been fought here in 1904, as it was central to the theory that they could possibly find human remains at their dig site. Fort Namutoni, along with another garrison at Sesfontein to the west, in Damaraland, marked the northernmost extent of German military occupation of the colony at the time, Sutton had explained by way of introduction.

'I know there was a battle here during the Herero War,' Alex said as they drove through the gates of the camp, 'but not many details. But from what I learned at school, I believe most of the fighting was further south of here.'

'You're right,' Emma said, secretly pleased that she knew more about this part of his country's history than Alex did. It would be a chance to dazzle him with what she had read, and learned from Professor Sutton. 'Samuel Maherero, leader of the Herero, rebelled against the Germans in central Namibia and tried to get your other peoples, the Owambo, the Damara and the Nama to join him.'

'The Nama and the Witbooi did, eventually,' Alex said.

'Yes,' Emma replied. She had been intrigued by the politics of the time; the Witbooi, under Hendrik Witbooi, had originally fought *with* the Germans, but he and his men were shocked into changing sides after the Germans ordered them to shoot Herero prisoners of war. 'But initially only the Ndonga, part of the Owambo, joined Maherero.'

Alex nodded. 'They're from near here; the gate we entered through is named after their King Nehale.'

'Exactly,' Emma said, enjoying playing teacher. 'King Nehale attacked the fort here, but seven *Schutztruppen* fought off hundreds of the king's warriors then slipped away to safety. King Nehale took the fort and destroyed it, but it was eventually rebuilt.'

'I'm impressed,' Alex said. 'I wish I'd known you in high school; I might have got a better mark in history with you as a tutor.' Alex parked his truck near reception and they got out and wandered towards the imposing building that dominated the flat landscape around it. 'So this fort isn't the original?'

Emma shook her head. 'No, it's a rebuild. The Germans apparently planned a punitive mission against King Nehale, but according to the history books the German military decided against this as they were tied up further south, fighting the Herero and the Nama, who'd joined the fight by then.'

'But isn't your dig trying to find evidence of some mass grave of victims from the war? They couldn't be the men killed here at the fort as you're more than seventy kilometres away.'

'You're right. There's a strong tradition in local oral history that Ndonga women and children were killed and their village destroyed some time during the war. Professor Sutton thinks it might have been an unauthorised revenge raid by a rogue element of German soldiers when they went back to start rebuilding the fort. It's something we just don't know much about, but if it's on the site of the proposed new mine it's worth investigating.'

Emma checked her phone as they walked through an archway into the courtyard inside the fort. 'Still no signal. This is so frustrating.'

Alex smiled at her. 'No, this is Africa. You can't expect things to work out here like they do in LA or Glasgow,' he said.

He was right. 'Believe me, things don't always work in Glasgow, and if you think African bureaucracy is bad you should try applying for a Green Card.'

'Did your message get through to your mom?'

She nodded. 'I think so, but I've lost signal again so I can't get a reply. My mum is going to freak. She'll think I'm in some kind of trouble based on what I was able to send her.'

He pulled the brim of his bush hat down lower over his eyes. 'There's not much trouble you can get into out here; believe me, I know. I've tried.'

Emma laughed. She decided she loved her chosen field of study, even if the work on the dig site was punishing. It had all been madly exciting since she'd found the body, but it was also nice to get away from the dirt and the dust for a couple of hours, and even better to be able to do so with Alex.

Emma felt a thrill course through her body every time she remembered that it was she who had found the mysterious dead man. They were now trying to work out who he was and what he was doing north of Etosha. Professor Sutton had, reluctantly, agreed to her suggestion that she try and contact her mother. Sutton had asked, full of arrogance, how Emma's mother could possibly help identify a man in what appeared to be a military uniform, and then had raised his bushy grey eyebrows in surprise when she had whispered to him that her mother was a mercenary who had served in various African countries with military types of all nationalities.

'So, how come your mother is an expert on military uniforms?' Alex asked. She had told him she needed to talk to her mother to help identify the body's clothing and Alex had offered to drive her to Namutoni as the camp usually had a good phone signal and was the nearest supply of fuel; he also needed diesel for his truck.

'She joined the British Army when she was very young, then worked as a military contractor and sometimes as a bodyguard around the world. She has contacts all over.'

'Cool,' Alex said. They wandered slowly around the interior of the fort. Instead of soldiers' quarters it now housed a bar, two curio shops, a small store selling drinks and basic foodstuffs for tourists staying in the camp, and a restaurant.

Emma frowned. 'Not really. She was away more than she was home and, honestly, I think the whole bitch of war thing screwed with her head a bit. She gets bad nightmares and sometimes goes on benders. It's been worse since her boyfriend was killed.'

'*Bitch of war?*'

Emma felt bad having used the nickname; she didn't hate her mother any more. Their relatively brief time together in LA, with Sam as part of their little family, had been great, but she'd seen her mother unravel and withdraw into herself. 'Like "dog of war" – mercenary – except she's a woman.'

They walked into one of the curio shops and Emma idly inspected some carved wooden bowls.

'My father served in the north during the bush war,' Alex said. 'Like most of the whites he was in the SWATF – the South West Africa Territorial Force. He was a part-time soldier, but he saw plenty of action. He has nightmares as well.'

Emma checked her phone again; still no reply from her mother. She didn't even know what country Sonja was in, though she carried a satellite phone for her work so she should be able to pick up Emma's message anywhere. 'War sucks.'

'I don't know,' Alex said.

'What do you mean? Nothing good ever comes out of it.'

Alex shrugged. 'I just know that despite all the bad stuff he must have seen, when my father gets together with his *boets* – his old army friends, who are like brothers to him – they only talk about the good stuff. Everyone was conscripted and they all, like, have this shared experience.'

Boys, was all Emma could think. She shook her head.

'Are you all right?' Alex asked.

'I'm fine.' She wanted to change the subject. 'The dog tag on the body said "*Brand, H*". That's not a common name, is it?'

'*Brand* means fire in Afrikaans. I don't know. We could google it, except we have no phone signal, no computer, and I haven't got a data bundle on my phone.'

'Me neither,' Emma said. 'I'm still on roaming and I need to get a Namibian SIM card and load some data. Do you think they'll sell them here?'

Alex just laughed. 'Come on, I think I should get you back to the dig after I refuel the truck.'

Emma didn't want to go back just yet. Not only did she want to wait, no matter how forlornly, to see if she could regain signal so that her mother could call her back, but she also wanted to spend more time with Alex.

They walked out of the curio shop into the courtyard. Tourists milled about taking photos. 'Hey,' she said, nodding to the bar in the corner, 'we've come all this way, why don't we have a beer?'

He pushed back his hat. 'Sure, why not?'

It was cool and dark and the long narrow room inside the fort's walls was divided by a bar faced with rough-sawn half-round slabs of tree trunk. The barman said hello and asked what they would like.

'The locals all drink Tafel,' Alex said.

'Well, when in Rome,' she said.

The barman served them cold Tafel lagers in brown bottles and Alex led Emma outside to an unmarked doorway next to the gents' toilets.

'Where on earth are you taking me?' she asked in mock horror.

'I spent plenty of holidays here so there's one thing I know about this fort that you don't.'

She followed him up several flights of a long, narrow concrete staircase until they emerged at the top of the fort's high tower.

'Wow.' She looked around at the 360-degree panorama of the wide, flat expanses of Etosha National Park. Beyond the waterhole on the camp's perimeter a line of zebra snaked its way towards the life-giving source.

'I wonder if they were scared,' Alex said, after they'd admired the view. 'Those seven guys, fighting off hundreds of men who wanted to kill them.'

'My mother said once that she never had time to be scared when people were shooting at her. It was only later she was scared, when thinking how close she'd come to being killed.'

Alex leaned against the parapet and took a sip of beer. 'We were taught as kids that the *Schutztruppen* were heroes, and that the Germans brought civilisation to primitive people. Nowadays we're all seen as war criminals, no better than the Nazis.'

She leaned next to him. 'I'm guessing that like all men, like all soldiers through history, there were good guys and bad guys.' Her mind went back to their own missing soldier, or whatever he was. 'I wonder who he is.'

'Your dead guy?'

She nodded and took a sip of beer. 'Yes, my *dead guy*,' she said. 'Professor Sutton thinks the body could be twenty or thirty years old.'

'That surprises me,' Alex said. 'There's so much skin on him, and he still has his hair. I thought he must have only been dead a couple of years or so.'

'No, we learned at university that different climates and soil types play as much of a part in decomposition as time. It's so dry out here, with so little rainfall and moisture in the ground that he's been sort of mummified. Also that accounts for how his uniform, if that's what it is, is in such good condition. Professor Sutton wants to take him to the university in Windhoek and do an autopsy on him, but we'll have to call in the local police as well and that might complicate things.'

'The guy could have been murdered, no matter how long ago it was. Unlike the war during the colonial times most of the action in the seventies and eighties *was* up here in Owamboland. That was where SWAPO had their support and the South African Army and the local security forces were here in force.'

'But how did he end up here alone in an unmarked grave?' Emma asked rhetorically. She looked at the screen of her phone and selected the picture gallery. She flicked through the pictures she'd taken of the body, and the close-ups of his clothing and the faded patches on his outfit.

'Well, he can't have just fallen out of the sky.'

Emma looked up from her phone. 'Wait a minute . . .'

'What?' Alex sipped some more beer and gave a look like he'd just swallowed a mouthful of lemon juice.

'I think you might have solved part of our puzzle.'

'How do you mean?'

'He was wearing a one-piece outfit, like a flying suit, maybe?'

Alex mulled over his inadvertent discovery. '*Ja*, but if he fell out of an aeroplane his body would have been pulverised.'

'Maybe he crashed his plane,' Emma said, 'and walked till he starved to death or died of thirst.'

'Well, there was a big air force base not far from here, at Ondangwa.' Alex rubbed his chin. 'Where you found him is not that far away from civilisation, but I suppose if you were injured or disoriented you could wander around the plains until you passed out or died of thirst. So do you think we should look for a crashed plane now as well?'

'I don't know,' Emma said. 'Hey, you know a lot of the local farmers in the area, don't you?'

'Yes. I visit them all regularly to ask them about cheetah sightings.'

'Maybe some of their elders would remember a plane crash in the area, from the old days.'

Alex nodded. 'I'll ask at the *kraals* next time I'm doing my rounds,' he said.

Emma finished her beer, and thought more about the dead man, trying to piece together the clues in some way that made sense. 'But if the man was a pilot who had crashed his plane, then surely the locals would have reported finding it to the police.'

'I'm not so sure about that,' Alex said. 'If your professor's right and the man died between twenty and thirty years ago, then you have to remember this country was at war. He could have been killed by SWAPO guerrillas or sympathisers.'

'I'm going to try and email the pictures to my mother. She'll know what some of his badges mean. I'm supposed to be meeting her in a few days in any case. She's flying to South Africa and we're going to spend some time together.'

'Where?'

'We hadn't decided. My mother likes to be mysterious about when and where she'll appear,' Emma replied with a distinct roll of her eyes. She glanced at her watch. 'Hey, I should be getting back to the dig site.'

Alex took her empty bottle from her and led her back down the staircase. 'There are a couple of villages on the way back, not far off the main road,' he said over his shoulder. 'Why don't we call in and ask if any of the old folks remember a plane crash?'

Professor Sutton would be annoyed if she returned later than she'd told him, but Emma didn't care. They walked back to Alex's truck and he took it to the camp filling station to top up with diesel. As she sat in the cab Emma looked up at the fort and, as Alex had, tried to imagine what it would have been like being stationed in such a remote and hostile outpost. She also wondered how it was that her victim of a more recent war could have ended up separated from his comrades and buried in an unmarked grave.

She was confident that someone, somewhere in this sparsely populated country would remember the missing flyer – if that was what he was – and, besides, Alex wanted to spend more time with her, and that was just fine by Emma.

Chapter 5

Hudson Brand felt like he was going to throw up. It was intensely unfair, he mused as he lay in bed, to have drunk as much as he had the night before, then slept several hours, and still be on the verge of nausea. He opened his eyes, but the act of blinking just made his head hurt more.

A spurfowl was screeching its demented rooster-like wake-up call from the bush outside the house in the Hippo Rock wildlife estate on the banks of the Sabie River. Across the river was the Kruger National Park, and Brand and the Australians he'd been drinking with the night before had been treated to a close chorus of lions calling from the reserve as they'd worked their way through a cooler box of Windhoek Lager and several bottles of Zandvliet Shiraz.

Brand sat up in bed and his head started to spin. He swung his legs over the edge, stood shakily, took a deep breath and for a second thought he was going to be OK. Instead, though, the bile rose up, almost gagging him. He strode to the en suite and got to the toilet just in time.

When he was finished, his head still pounding, he found that the house owner, his friend Cameron, had two Panado in the cupboard under the sink. Brand couldn't thank his absentee landlord enough. Cameron and his Australian wife, Kylie, were living in Sydney, and Brand was housesitting Cameron's place at Hippo Rock. The Australians he'd been drinking with were miners who were in South Africa attending a conference, and Brand had hosted them in Cameron's house for the night. They'd left already, in God knew what sort of state, for an early morning game drive in the park. Brand took the pills, wiped his mouth and brushed his teeth.

He used the outside shower, the piping-hot water from the large head warding off the morning chill, and was treated to the sight of a lone bull elephant munching his way through the reeds in the bed of the Sabie as he washed.

Brand lived a bachelor's life, and the two slices of bread and half a carton of milk past its use-by date that he found in the fridge would not come close to aiding his recovery. Grease was needed, and lots of it.

He dressed in his khaki bush shirt and shorts, pulled on his Rocky sandals and put on his Texas Longhorns cap. There was little of him that was rooted in the country of his birth, but the Longhorns would always be his team, and the hat had survived several near-death experiences and had become a talisman for him.

As he drove his old Land Rover along the winding dirt road to the estate gate he tried to recall which nightmare he'd had the previous evening. Sometimes the drink warded off the memories, but the cognac he'd taken with a cigar at about two in the morning had brought the horrors back into sharp focus.

Brand signed out of the estate, handing the clipboard back to the security guard, Lawrence, who smiled, perhaps at the bloodshot eyes or the alcohol fumes on Brand's breath. It was a bright sunny morning. Brand turned right onto the R536 and drove past the old Lisbon citrus estate and Sabiepark, another housing estate, and crossed the bridge over the Sabie to the Paul Kruger Gate entrance of the national park.

'*Avuxeni*, Abbey,' he said, bidding the national park security guard on duty good morning in Xitsonga.

'*Ayeh imjani*,' Abbey replied.

'*Kona*,' Brand said, completing the ritual by lying that he was fine. He went into the gate office and filled out the form to gain entry to Kruger, once more exchanging pleasantries, this time with Precious, the woman on duty. Finally, with his park permit in hand he went back to his truck and Abbey let him through the boom. A pair of frisky impala rams chased each other across the road in front of him.

A few kilometres into the park he turned left towards his destination, the Skukuza Golf Club. The club was set on a nine-hole course adjoining the staff village that serviced Skukuza, the park's headquarters and largest tourist rest camp. In the bad old days of apartheid the golf course had been restricted to white national parks staff members only, but in the Mandela era it, like so many of the country's assets, had been opened to all comers. It was still a bit of a secret and the course and its bar and restaurant – the best in the park – was mostly the hangout of locals and seasoned Kruger visitors.

Brand liked the idea of golf, but not enough to actually pick up a club. There was a competition of some sort on today and the car park was full. Brand walked to the serving counter and ordered his breakfast by ticking the relevant boxes on a form; it was one of the clubhouse's little idiosyncrasies, but it ensured you got what you asked for, mostly. Inside the clubhouse, which was open-sided where it looked onto the ninth green, an official was wrapping up a briefing on the day's tournament and Brand was able to grab a table on the lawn in the sun as a trio of golfers headed for their buggy.

'Hudson, howzit? Man, you look like *kak*.'

Brand turned and squinted. He looked up and saw the imposing bulk of Captain Fanie Theron. Theron was a detective who specialised in wildlife crimes – poaching, smuggling and the sale of living and dead animals, birds and reptiles. He'd been seconded to the operations centre that had been set up at the Skukuza Airport to coordinate the fight against rhino poaching – though it was more like a war than a fight given the current body count.

'I feel how I look, Fanie. How are you?'

'Fine, fine, fine. You should give up the drink, like I did.' Theron was dressed in shorts and a pink polo shirt.

Brand resented the man's jollity; 'I liked you more when you were a hungover drunk. At least you dressed better.'

Theron laughed and sat down.

'What's the news from the front line?' Brand asked. Just talking was an effort, but Theron was a good guy, and a good contact. He was the intelligence officer for the operations centre and had an overview of everything happening in the field. Brand had tipped him off a couple of times about suspicious characters in the nearby town of Hazyview, and his information had led to the break-up of a poaching gang.

Hudson Brand's day job and passion in life was working as a safari guide. His trips into the Kruger National Park and his occasional work as a walking trails guide in the adjoining Timbavati Private Game Reserve were all that kept him sane and alive these days, but he moonlighted as a private investigator, specialising in suspect life insurance claims for a law firm in England. He kept a close ear to the ground in the Lowveld, and had a few paid informers who kept him up to date on the local crime scene and in particular which policemen, doctors, undertakers and churchmen were desperate enough for cash to falsify police reports, death certificates and burial certificates for people who wanted to fake their own deaths and have a relative claim on their policy.

'Tran Van Ngo was assassinated, gangland style, in his home in Ho Chi Minh City yesterday,' Theron said.

A waiter brought a plunger pot of coffee. 'Can we have another cup, please,' Brand said. Theron nodded his thanks. Brand recalled the name: 'The Vietnamese kingpin named in the media a couple of months ago?'

'That's the one. And here's the other news; Ross Coonan – the journalist who made the allegations against Tran, the one who wrote that book you were in – was found dead in an alleyway nearby around the same time Tran was killed. Coonan had been tortured.'

'Shit,' Brand said. He remembered Coonan well. The young Australian had written an in-depth exposé on the rhino horn trade and had not pulled any punches. He'd interviewed Brand about his experiences in Angola. A retired South African Defence Force general had tipped off Coonan that Brand had some infor- mation about the smuggling of elephant ivory and rhino horn out of Angola near the end of South Africa's border war in the country. Brand's story had rated a few paragraphs in Coonan's book.

The waiter returned with a cup for Theron and Brand poured for both of them. A pair of warthogs snuffled in the grass on their knees a few metres away, near the green. 'What's the theory on Tran?'

Theron stirred in milk and sugar. 'Tran was a major player in the rhino horn market, of that Coonan was one hundred per cent correct. He was up to his neck in a failing property development in his home country, but he was still bankrolling several poaching gangs working out of Massingir in Mozambique. The word is that he was stockpiling horn; as we get better at catching and killing poachers the street price is going up. Tran is – or was – a gangster, so he had his enemies, but he was in the business of being nice to his business partners, not pissing them off. The hit was professional – there were two other KIAs found in the garden, Tran's bodyguard and his personal secretary.'

'Well, whoever he was,' Brand sipped his coffee, revelling in it, 'he gets a high five from me.'

'You need to move with the times, Hudson.'

'What do you mean?' Brand asked.

'Our liaison man in Vietnam says the local police there are looking for a woman, blonde hair, possible German or South African accent. She went to Tran's purporting to be a hooker, but she nailed the John.'

'Any thoughts on who it might be?' Brand asked. The waiter brought his bacon, eggs, beans and cheese griller sausages, and he could already feel the cholesterol going to work on his hangover as he breathed it in.

'Nothing so far,' Theron said. 'What do you think? Know any *boere meisies* looking for some payback?'

Brand tucked into his breakfast. As a matter of fact, he did have an idea who might have had the motivation, the skillset and the guts to carry out a hit half a world away. 'Only person I can think of was last seen in America, so it's probably not her.' Brand set his cup down. 'Probably not. At least, I wouldn't want to try and arrest her.'

*

Sonja's flight from Bangkok arrived on time at 7.30 am and she cleared immigration and customs at Johannesburg's OR Tambo International Airport without a problem. While she waited for her rucksack to emerge on the carousel she took out her phone and turned it on. A few seconds later it beeped, first with the message welcoming her to the phone provider in South Africa, and then with an SMS from Emma.

'Hi Mum, where are you? I need your help.'

'*Fok*,' she said aloud in Afrikaans, startling the elderly woman next to her, who moved her trolley further along the carousel. Sonja tried her daughter's number, but it went straight through to voicemail. 'Howzit, it's me, I'm in South Africa,' she said. 'Call me or SMS me. And next time, don't just send a message that says "*I need your help*". Bye.'

She had not wanted to sound angry or panicked, but knew she had failed. Sonja told herself Emma was fine. The girl was in Namibia, not Afghanistan. The country of her birth had been through several periods of terrible violence, but these days it was quiet, peaceful and stable. The crime rate was low and the people friendly, and Emma was in the middle of nowhere.

Was that part of the problem? Sonja wondered. Had Emma or someone on her team suffered some terrible accident, or been bitten by a snake? Did they need Sonja's bush knowledge? For once she regretted not giving Emma a specific date and place to meet up. Years of subterfuge and not knowing how long missions would take had led to her always keeping arrangements on a need-to-know basis.

Her bag popped out and she hoisted it onto her shoulder, not bothering with a trolley. Sonja was supposed to be catching up with some friends in Johannesburg, but she quickly sent them a message saying she would have to take a raincheck as something had come up. She decided to head straight for Namibia. Sonja went out into the arrivals hall and walked to the Parkade complex where the rental car offices were located.

Sonja had drunk herself to sleep on the flight and managed to catch a few hours of rest. She did the car rental paperwork, found her Nissan X-Trail in the garage and tossed her bag on the back seat. She headed out onto the R24; her planned route would take her around Johannesburg's northern and western suburbs, then onto the N14.

Once clear of the western outskirts of the city Sonja felt she could breathe more freely. She was heading for the Kgalagadi Transfrontier Park, on the border between South Africa and Namibia. If she couldn't make it today, she would reach it the day after. All she could think to do in the absence of speaking to Emma was to drive towards her dig site. She turned off the air conditioner and wound down the window. The morning air was still crisp and the African sun streamed in through the windscreen. The cloudless blue sky and the grassy farmlands, already turning golden under the endless winter sun, stretched to eternity.

It was good to be back in Africa. This was South Africa, not Namibia, but the landscape reminded her of her youth. She cruised through tiny towns with little other than wheat silos, a pub and a butchery selling biltong. Burly farmers in Toyota *bakkies* lifted a finger off the steering wheel to wave good morning to her; African farm workers trudged slowly to another day's work.

Sonja spied a cafe and bar, co-located, pulled over and parked in front, got out of the Nissan and stretched. She walked into the cafe, which was empty and called, 'Hello?'

A girl in her late teens, blonde, in jeans and a thick pullover, came out from the kitchen. '*Goeie more, Tannie.*'

'*More,*' Sonja replied, biting back a retort that she was not the girl's aunty. Sonja had grown up speaking German and English in her home, but there were many Afrikaner families in the farming district of Okahandja so she learned to speak her third language fluently. *Tannie* was a term of respect for an elder and, Sonja reflected, she was certainly old enough to have earned the name. She didn't like to think of herself as 'old', but while she kept herself in peak physical shape – a prerequisite for her job – no amount of working out or running could remove the wrinkles at the corners of her eyes and mouth.

Sonja ordered coffee and eggs and *boerewors*. The girl apologised that she spoke little English and Sonja told her it was fine.

It was, in fact, nice to be speaking the old language again. It made her feel like she was closer to where she belonged, wherever that might be. Perhaps, she thought as she moved out onto the *stoep* of the cafe to catch some morning sun, she could move to a *dorpie* like this, a small town where she could reinvent herself and live in peace.

She dialled Emma's number and the phone went through to voicemail again. 'Dammit.' Sonja felt her anxiety level ratchet up a notch. She'd be angry with Emma if her call for help turned out to be something minor.

A Toyota Land Cruiser *bakkie* pulled up. Two fat men in shorts and camouflage jackets got out of the cab and a third, who had been sitting in the open on a canvas-covered seat in the back, climbed down. He swayed as his feet hit the ground. His friends laughed at him and the pair joked in Afrikaans that the man in the back couldn't handle his liquor. They looked like hunters, Sonja thought. They nodded to her as they walked through to the adjoining bar and, once out of her sight, started to laugh.

The waitress brought out Sonja's breakfast, then rolled her eyes as one of the men yelled out for service from the bar.

Sonja cocked an ear when she heard raised voices inside. In Afrikaans, the men were asking why the young woman couldn't serve them alcohol at this time of day.

The girl screamed.

Sonja set down her knife and fork and slid off the picnic table bench. She walked inside and saw the man who had been in the back of the *bakkie* lying across the bar, his feet kicking in the air as he swung himself over. His friends were laughing as the man removed a bottle of brandy from its holder. The waitress tried to grab it and he reached around and slapped her on the bottom. This provoked more guffaws from the men.

The waitress retreated and reached under the bar for a wooden club. She brandished it at the man, who swatted the baton away with a meaty hand.

'Put the bottle down. I'm calling the cops,' the girl said.

Sonja stood in the doorway of the bar, as yet unseen by any of them. If the men were smart, they would leave now. The waitress put down the club and picked up the handset of a phone on the bar. She was tough, Sonja thought; she probably had to be to work in a place like this.

'*Poepol*,' the girl said to the man with the brandy, who was struggling to get his fat belly back on the bar. He stopped when he heard the insult and reached for the phone.

The waitress turned her back to him and the man grabbed the phone with his free hand and wrenched the cord from the wall socket. The waitress responded by slapping him in the face.

Sonja clenched and unclenched her fists. The incident was escalating. She prepared herself, mind and body, for what was to come. She felt a sense of calm wash over her. Her pulse rate slowed and she breathed deeply and evenly as she strode across the otherwise empty barroom floor.

The man with the brandy tossed the phone away and grabbed the waitress's arm. She screamed again and one of the other two men reached across the bar and yanked her by her ponytail. The third man backed away, his face going pale.

'Enough, guys,' he said to his friends, but they were beyond listening.

'Bitch hit me,' said the fat one with the brandy. He pushed her against the bar.

Sonja went to the man holding the waitress's ponytail, coming up fast and silent behind him. She grabbed a fistful of his mullet haircut under his baseball cap and slammed his face down hard and fast into the wooden bar top, shattering his nose. The third man started to close on her. 'Back off,' Sonja hissed.

'Get her, man.' The fat man kept his hold on the struggling girl and smashed the neck of the bottle of brandy against the bar, shattering it. He held the jagged edge against the waitress's neck.

The man who had urged moderation kept coming towards Sonja. She put her hands up, palms out, as if submitting, but when he was close enough she delivered a vicious kick to his scrotum. As the man bent double Sonja grabbed a fistful of hair and rammed her right knee up into his nose. Blood spattered her skin below her shorts and she let him fall to the ground. The man whose face she had driven into the bar staggered towards her and swung a wide punch at her. Sonja dodged to one side and jabbed two fingers, hard and fast, into his already broken nose. The man howled like a jackal and sank to his knees.

'Get out or I'll cut this one's pretty face,' the man behind the bar screamed. He had the barmaid in a headlock now, his free hand around her neck and the broken bottle close to her skin.

'Ja, right.'

Sonja turned and walked outside. She knew the idiot with the broken bottle would not hurt the barmaid, but that didn't let him off the hook. She peered into the cab of the Land Cruiser. As she expected there were three rifles inside and the men had, sensibly, locked the vehicle. She picked up a brick lining a flower bed outside the bar, smashed the driver's side window and the truck's alarm started screaming. A grey-haired man in a butcher's apron came out of the biltong shop next door.

Sonja reached into the cab through the shattered glass, unlocked the driver's side door and opened it. 'Nothing to see here, Uncle,' she said to the butcher. The man took a step towards her, but backtracked into his shop as Sonja slid one of the rifles from its padded canvas bag and chambered a round.

She walked back to the bar, the butt of the rifle snug and comfy against her shoulder as she raised the telescopic sight to her eye.

The man who had threatened the barmaid was leaning against the bar now and the girl had backed away from him. When he saw Sonja he swayed upright and raised the broken bottle and moved towards the barmaid again. 'I'll kill her!' the man with the bottle screamed.

A bottle of Jägermeister schnapps exploded behind and to one side of the man's head, showering him with spirit and shattered glass. The barmaid laughed as the man cowered. Sonja worked the bolt and took aim. Her second shot took out a bottle of scotch.

'*Sheesh*, man, not the Klipdrift Premium!' the barmaid cried. Sonja liked her style.

'Next shot's for you, *outjie*,' she said to the fat man.

The man dropped the bottle and backed away from the girl half a pace, giving the barmaid the chance to vault across the bar. The man who had grabbed her hair was trying to get up again and the girl kicked him in the stomach and spat on him as he doubled up again.

'Say sorry. Apologise to her,' Sonja said to the man still behind the bar. She chambered another round, revelling in the smooth, slick action of the rifle.

He bared his teeth and she shifted the end of the barrel until the crosshairs of the sights were between his eyes. Her finger curled around the trigger and everything slowed around her. She could snuff this fucker out in a heartbeat.

The girl laid a hand gently on Sonja's shoulder. 'No, hey. He's not worth it. The cops will have heard the shooting; they're just up the road and they'll be here in a minute.'

'Say it,' Sonja said again. She lowered the rifle, tracking down over his nose and chin, along his sternum until she was aiming at his balls. 'Last chance.'

The man licked his lips and looked down at where Sonja was aiming. 'Sorry,' he croaked.

'That's better. Are you OK?' Sonja asked the girl.

'*Ja*, I'm fine, but you'd better get moving. The owner will be here soon and he won't be too happy about you shooting up his bar.'

Sonja turned, walked outside and shot out the first tyre of the Land Cruiser. She chambered a round and shot out another tyre. She removed the bolt from the rifle and dropped it through the metal grille of a stormwater drain. She went to the truck and did the same with the other two hunting rifles.

The incident had pumped her full of adrenaline and it felt good. It had also felt satisfying to feel the rifle bucking under her control. It was the same when she'd killed Tran Van Ngo. There was no remorse, no fear, no nerves, just the calm satisfaction of a job well done. She had felt incomplete in America, living the life of a glorified housewife or Sam's red carpet plus one. Sonja leaned into the cab of the Land Cruiser and opened the glove compartment. As she'd hoped, there was a pistol there, probably the owner's. It was a nine-millimetre Glock. She slid the pistol into the waistband of her shorts, pocketed a spare magazine and walked back to her rented Nissan.

Blue lights were flashing in her rear view mirror, but the police *bakkie* pulled off the road and parked in front of the bar as Sonja accelerated up the road, a smile on her face for the first time in quite a while.

Chapter 6

It was mid-afternoon when Sonja entered the town of Kuruman. She was tired from the flight and she knew it would be unwise to drive through the night. There was no chance of her reaching the Kgalagadi Transfrontier Park before nightfall and she knew accommodation options would become fewer and further between if she kept travelling.

Kuruman was a popular stopover place and there were dozens of signs for bed and breakfasts. The main street was choked with minibus taxis and honking cars; she had hit the town in its mini evening rush hour. She decided that tomorrow she would take the shorter, gravelled road to the Kgalagadi park, via Hotazel and Van Zylsrus, so she took the turnoff to Hotazel and began to look for a place on the outskirts of town.

A sign for a bottle store tempted her and she pulled over, walked in, and bought a bottle of Klipdrift, two litres of Coke Light and a bag of ice. She carried on and randomly decided she liked the sound of the Azalea B&B. It turned out to be a good choice, a nice place off to the right of the main road on a suburban back street. The owner was friendly without prying, and showed her to a comfortable room with en suite, a television, and a fridge. He said he could organise dinner for her, but she'd snacked in the car through the afternoon to keep herself awake, so she passed on the offer.

In her room she poured herself a brandy and Coke, added ice, kicked off her hiking boots and lay down on the bed. Sonja tried Emma's number again, but there was no answer.

Don't worry, she told herself. Sonja finished her drink and nodded off. She awoke two hours later, the sun low outside and slanting in through the room's window. The news in Afrikaans had just begun on the television. Video of a rhino flashed up on the screen and she turned up the volume.

Another three rhinos had been killed in the Kruger Park overnight, and in a separate incident another poaching gang had been ambushed by rangers and South African National Defence Force personnel in the reserve; one poacher had been killed and another wounded.

'Should have shot the wounded guy,' Sonja said out loud. She drained her Klippies and Coke and made another.

'*Coming up, later tonight*,' said the news anchor, '*50–50 has a special report on rhinos in Namibia and how that country is managing to protect its population of wild animals*.'

It was masochistic, Sonja realised, for her to want to watch another program about rhinos. Too often, these shows mentioned Sam, as he was without doubt the highest profile casualty of the war against poaching. But Sonja was interested in the upcoming segment on *50–50*, the popular South African nature-based current affairs program. She had wondered, when considering the rhino problem in the wake of Sam's death, why the country of her birth had been relatively free of poaching.

There had been the odd incident, but the number of animals killed, however, was a tiny fraction of the losses in South Africa.

Part of the reason, she was sure, was logistical. Namibia's

rhinos tended to be in remote, sparsely populated parts of the country, with limited road access in and out. By contrast, there were hundreds of thousands of people living along the borders of the Kruger National Park and there was no fence between much of South Africa and neighbouring Mozambique, where many poaching gangs were based. They had a relatively short walk, through thickly vegetated country that allowed concealment from aerial patrols, to get to Kruger's rhinos. Namibia's desert-dwelling black rhino, however, traversed wide ranges of open territory.

Sonja would be interested in what other theories the program's journalists came up with. She poured herself another brandy and Coke and checked her emails on her phone while she waited. There were a few messages, one from a friend serving in Somalia who had been out of contact with the big wide world and had only just heard about Sam. She hated receiving condolence emails and had long since given up replying to them.

There was a statement from her bank, but she didn't need or want to open it. Sam had been an only child and his mother, his sole parent, had passed away, so Sonja was the sole beneficiary of his will. She had been financially secure on her own – she'd made sure she had put aside a portion from her contract fees for Emma's schooling and future as well – but now she wanted for nothing. Nevertheless, she had put herself back out into the market for some military contracting work. There was the offer of a personal protection gig from an old friend now working in Dubai – he was looking for a woman who could be the body-guard for a sheik's wife. Sonja screwed her nose up; she didn't want to come out of retirement to spend her time following a rich woman through handbag stores.

Slightly more interesting was a message from a South African ex-recce-commando. Before she'd met Sam she'd had a fling with Piet in Iraq; despite his reputation for toughness he was a big softy with lovely blue eyes, but she could conjure no memories of happiness or ecstasy these days. Piet was in the Central African Republic. The South African National Defence Force had been involved in a full-on shooting war there trying to protect the government from an uprising by Muslim extremist rebels. Piet and some other private contractors were running private security there.

It's hectic here, Sonja. Maybe you should stay in California, his email read. She smiled; Piet would know such a comment would be like a red rag to a bull. Emma would be furious once she found out Sonja was getting back into the fray, but as much as Sonja had loved being able to reconnect with her daughter and spend time with her she would go crazy sitting around in a mansion in LA.

Sonja wallowed in her self-pity and encroaching drunkenness. She got up to go to the toilet and tripped over her backpack. As she reached out to steady herself she knocked a lamp off the bedside table. The lampshade came off and the globe popped, covering the carpet in broken glass.

'*Scheisse.*' She'd spoken German, for the first time in a long time, she realised as she sat back down on the bed and stared at the glittering fragments on the floor. She remembered her father, Hans, belting her across the back of her skinny legs the first time he'd heard her say that word, 'shit'. She also remembered Hans slapping her mother in the face.

Sonja looked to the wall facing the bed, and saw her face in the mirror. She saw the first tear rolling down her cheek. She picked up the lampstand, stared at it for a few seconds then tugged it, ripping its cord from the power point, and hurled it at the mirror. The glass shattered and cascaded down onto the writing bureau and the carpet. She was a one-woman wrecking ball who destroyed everything and everyone who got close to her. It was probably too late to really save her relationship with Emma in any case.

'*Mein Gott, reiss dich zusammen!*' she said out loud after splashing water on her face in the bathroom, but try as she might she didn't seem to be able to pull herself together. It seemed being so close to home meant her German was coming back to her thoughts and words.

Although she knew she shouldn't, Sonja made herself another drink and flopped back down on the bed. The program she had been waiting for, *50–50*, had begun. She sat through a story about lions being reintroduced into a national park where the species had been shot out decades ago and then, after the commercial break, the story about rhinos came on.

The small screen of the television didn't do justice to the majestic landscapes of Namibia, but all the same it moved something inside her to see the endless skies and red, flat-topped mountains. There was vision of a black rhino, lying at first then standing and trotting towards the camera; the rhino had his head up and sniffed the air as he paused.

'*And one of the men in the front line of rhino conservation,*' the announcer broke in, '*leading a team of local people backed by international NGOs in this fight to save a piece of prehistory, is Stirling Smith.*'

Sonja nearly spilled her drink as she clumsily set it down on the bedside table. She scrabbled for the remote and turned up the volume.

'Stirling?' she said. *Her* Stirling. It was him, framed close-up on the screen now, and that was his voice speaking. He was heading up the rhino research and conservation project in the Palmwag Conservancy in Damaraland.

Sonja slid herself along the bed until she was sitting at the foot. She reached out and touched the screen as he talked about rhinos. Sam had been the true love of her life, but once upon a time she'd thought that the only man for her was Stirling Smith.

Chapter 7

A t the dig site they had a couple of free-standing camping gazebos that could be shared among the students to keep the worst of the sun's fury off a couple of diggers at a time, but one of them was now covering the remains of Harry Brand.

They had dubbed him 'Harry' by consensus. Emma took off her hat and wiped her brow and looked across to where Dorset Sutton knelt, meticulously brushing away the sand and grit from Harry's boots.

That morning, just after dawn, he'd asked them to assemble around the body, before Natangwe left to do the shopping for the next few days' provisions.

'We must not forget,' he had said, standing at the body's head, 'that here lie the remains of a human being, just like us. Whatever his nationality, whatever his race, whatever his religion and whatever his politics, he was flesh and blood, with a beating heart, a soul, and a life. You may call him "Harry" if you wish, at least until we know his correct name, but we must not make light of him or treat him as an object of fun or ridicule, any more than we would if one of our own family members was lying here.'

Emma had noticed Natangwe fidgeting and shifting his weight from one foot to the other. 'But Prof,' he'd chimed in, 'this man was probably part of the security forces, the men who brutalised my people. He might have dropped bombs on women and children.'

'Natangwe,' Emma had hissed.

'No, no, Emma, don't be so quick to criticise,' Dorset said, not unkindly. 'Natangwe, I know your father was a member of the liberation army, your family's role in the struggle is well documented. Inevitably, the work we do, uncovering the past, scratches at the scabs of barely healed wounds. We must – you and I both must – try to view the events of the past as historians, as archaeologists, as investigators, not as participants, or the family of participants. We must confront the sins of the past, and try to understand them through our work, just as we must celebrate bravery and heroism and other noble deeds. If you don't think you can treat this body with respect because he may have fought against your father, then I think you must either resign from this program or ask for me to be dismissed from the university.'

'You, Prof?' Natangwe asked. 'I didn't mean any offence to you; I just don't know if I can salute the remains of a man who may have killed innocents.'

'I'm not asking you to *salute* Harry here any more than I'm asking you to forgive me. It may be, though, that you can't see past your family's own history.'

'I still don't understand what this has to do with you, though, Prof,' Natangwe said.

'I served here as well, Natangwe. Before studying history and archaeology at Wits I, like every other able-bodied white man living in the old South Africa, had to undertake national service. I served as a gunner in an Eland armoured car, with the Umvoti Mounted Rifles. I did two tours in the old South West

Africa, today's Namibia. I didn't kill anyone, civilian or soldier, but I was trained and ready to. If you can't abide respecting Harry's dignity as a human being then perhaps you can no longer respect me.'

Natangwe said nothing for a couple of minutes, and Emma's heart had pounded. Their exchange was simply bringing into the open the sorts of questions that she had been grappling with. She was worried Natangwe wouldn't like her if he knew more about her family's history in the war, but now Professor Sutton had brought the simmering tension to a head.

'I'm sorry, Professor Sutton. I do respect you and I do want to be here.'

Dorset walked around Harry to Natangwe and taken his hand in his. He looked into Natangwe's eyes. 'You don't need to be sorry, Natangwe. When I was your age, serving here in the heat and the dust, thousands of kilometres from home and worrying that some other poor bugger might kill me with an AK-47 or an RPG round, I hope I would have been as respectful of a dead enemy as you have been. I learned through the course of the war that we were all victims in some way or another and, in the end, the ideologies we were fighting for all counted for nothing. Namibia has emerged as a beautiful, peaceful country and I'm proud to be here and proud to play a small part in unearthing its history.'

'I understand, Prof,' Natangwe said.

'Thank you. Then let us continue,' the professor said to them.

*

Natangwe Heita thought about Emma Kurtz as he waited for the Chinese man in the general trader's store to fill the requirements on the shopping list.

She was of German Namibian descent and her family had left the country at the end of the war. Emma hadn't said why, exactly, but Natangwe assumed that her white supremacist parents couldn't have countenanced the idea of living in an independent country, ruled by the majority, or that her father had done such shameful things during the war that he was too scared to face his victims.

In fact, Namibians had proved extremely tolerant of their former oppressors. Sure, the issue of the genocide came up often for discussion, as did the question of land ownership – much of the country's most productive land was still in the hands of a white minority, many of them living abroad – but all in all he felt he lived in a progressive, peaceful society. Still, if he ever brought home a German girl he knew his father, who had served as a freedom fighter in SWAPO's military arm, the People's Liberation Army of Namibia, would hit the roof.

His attention was distracted, at least temporarily, by the girl who strode into the store.

'Give me a Coke,' she said to the shopkeeper.

Despite the girl's curvaceous beauty, she needed to be taught a lesson in manners. 'I was here first, sister,' Natangwe said.

'I'm not your sister, and I'm in a hurry. I have a deadline.'

'Well, I've got a bunch of starving archaeologists waiting back at camp. A deadline? Are you a journalist?'

She tossed her head, flicking an errant dark curl from her face. 'Yes, I'm a journalist, for *New Era*. You might have heard of it.'

Straight out of university, Natangwe guessed, which would account for her age and the fact she was here, in the middle of nowhere. 'Of course I know it. The government-owned newspaper; which minister is telling you what to write today?'

She frowned. He had clearly scored a point. 'It's *not* like that. We are encouraged to be independent, and to voice the people's problems. We don't just toe the party line, you know. Anyway, why am I bothering to justify myself to you? What did you say about archaeology?'

81

He decided not to goad her any further. 'I'm studying archae-ology. A few of us are on a dig not far from here. We're looking for a mass grave from the Herero War.'

Her plucked eyebrows formed double arches. 'The genocide? Serious?'

'Very serious,' he said, savouring the reaction his revelation had provoked. 'How much is that?' he asked the shopkeeper.

The man evidently couldn't speak English as he simply pointed to the figures on an old-fashioned desk-top calculator he'd been entering the prices into. Natangwe knew only too well from his history studies the dangers of racial stereotyping, just as he knew the debt his country owed to the People's Republic of China for its support during the liberation war, however the presence of so many Chinese trading stores throughout Namibia concerned him. This was, he thought, a type of neo-colonialism where traders had been dispatched to the remotest corners of Africa to peddle Chinese-made goods. As well as limited range and stock of basic food supplies – bags of maize meal, cooking oils, canned goods and long-life milk – this little shop was overflowing with mass-produced, cheap consumer goods. There were radios and clocks, blankets and clothing, rubber sandals, lanterns, chil-dren's toys, a couple of bicycles and just about everything else in between.

'Tell me more,' said the woman. 'I'm Aggie, by the way.'

He felt like he was getting somewhere. 'Natangwe. Nice to meet you, Aggie.'

'Have you found any heroes from the war against the Germans?'

Natangwe hesitated. She was back to business and he didn't know how much he should tell her. The find was interesting, though not in the way they had all been expecting. It was a mystery, and he wondered what ramifications the finding of a dead white man in the desert might have. At the very least the man's family would want to know his fate. It might make an interesting story, he thought. He corrected himself; it *would* make a good story for a young journalist consigned to a beat far from Windhoek.

She changed tack. 'OK, if you're not going to tell me anything I can't waste my time talking to you here in the middle of nowhere. Coca-Cola Light,' Aggie said slowly and loudly for the benefit of the shopkeeper. She tossed some coins on the glass-topped counter, above a selection of flashlights and pocket knives. 'Goodbye, Natangwe,' she said, and turned on her heel.

'We found a body,' he said, the words tumbling out.

Aggie stopped and looked back over her shoulder. 'Man or woman?'

'Man.' He felt safe giving away that small amount of information, and she wasn't leaving.

'Executed? Killed in battle?' she pressed.

'We don't know,' he said, rationalising it was best to stick to the truth.

'Hmmm.' She frowned. 'That's not very interesting. And I *do* have a deadline.' She reached into her purse. 'Here's my card. You can call me on the cell number if you have something really interesting to tell me. Maybe I'll come out and do a story on your dig?'

He liked her. She was confident and beautiful. 'I could show you around, give you a briefing on the battle that took place in the area.'

Aggie faked a yawn. Natangwe felt a little hurt and annoyed, but she laughed. 'I was just kidding. It *could* be interesting, but I can't just go wandering off into the wilderness without a story to follow. My editor puts enough pressure on me to come up with news every day, so I can't waste hours listening to a history lesson, no matter how important you and your fellow archaeologists think it is. Tell me more about this body, something I can use. Where's your dig?'

Dammit, she was sucking him into revealing more information than he'd intended to give her.

'Go on, tell me where you're scratching around. I'll be able to find out from the local authorities in any case.'

'On the site of the new mine, about forty kilometres east of here.'

'Ah, yes, I know it. There's some local opposition to the mine. If your find is controversial it might stop the project from going ahead. This could be *big*.'

Natangwe groaned inwardly. He really hadn't thought through the potential consequences of what he was doing. The reporter, Agnes Aikanga, her card informed him, was right, though. The point of the dig, from the mining company's view, was to find nothing of interest. The government outwardly supported the dig, which the mining company was paying for, but Dorset Sutton had hinted that there would be people high up in the administration who wanted the mine to go ahead as badly as the company did. It would bring employment to impoverished local communities, resources income for the country through taxes and who knew, perhaps even some cash to some politician or bureaucrat's back pocket. Dorset, however, said that they needed to stay true to their calling, to seek out the truth through their digging. They were there to reveal history, he had said, not provide the answers other people wanted.

Natangwe realised Aggie's newspaper could actually help ensure that what they had found was never covered up. The discovery of the body – whoever he was – warranted a full investigation. For all they knew he could have been the victim of a murder rather than a casualty of war.

'We found the body of a white man, from the liberation war, we think. He seems to be wearing the uniform of a pilot, so we think maybe his plane crashed or was shot down somewhere. His surname is Brand, first name begins with an "H". That's all we know. Maybe your newspaper could even help us identify him.'

'Wow,' Aggie said. 'I've got to call my editor.'

*

Emma noticed that Professor Sutton had been quiet since the exchange with Natangwe that morning. She welcomed the absence of his brusque instructions and frequent criticisms, but as she watched him Emma also wondered if his revelation about his war service had brought back some painful memories. She set down her trowel, stood, straightened her aching back and took her water bottle over to where Sutton was working. He didn't bother looking up as she stood next to him, casting her shadow over him.

Emma cleared her throat. 'I'm just on my break, but thought I'd see how you were doing.'

He brushed away some more dirt from Harry's boot. Emma looked into the dead man's empty eye sockets. At first she had been so excited to discover him she hadn't been concerned by the physical sight of a dead person, but since this morning she'd been feeling mildly freaked out about being around Harry. It was, she realised, Sutton's simple but poignant reminder to them all about what, or rather who, they were dealing with that had brought about the change in her attitude. Seeing the skull, with its layer of stretched, mummified skin drawn across the cheeks, made her feel incredibly sad all of a sudden. Harry must have had a family, perhaps a wife or a girlfriend, maybe children, and they would have had no idea what had happened to him, only knowing that he'd never come home.

'Like I said, I didn't kill anyone during the war, but I did lose a couple of friends. You never really get used to it, you know,' Sutton said, without looking up. 'And the memories, they stay with you.'

'I understand.'

He looked up at her, pausing in his work. 'Do you, Emma?'

'My mother gets nightmares.'

'You couldn't get through to her, when you and Alex went to Namutoni?'

'No, there was no phone signal,' she said. He had changed the subject, just like her mother did when she tried to ask her about her sleepless nights, or about the places she had served and worked.

'Do you think Natangwe was all right, when he left to do the shopping?' Dorset asked her.

Emma was surprised. She didn't think the professor would care what one of his students thought of him, but Natangwe's comments had obviously unsettled the old man more than she had guessed. 'He seemed fine. Before he left he told me he was sorry he'd interrupted your speech. He's a hothead, that's all. He's in the SWAPO Party Youth League and you know what student politics is like.'

Dorset nodded and went back to brushing away the dirt. 'There has been so much blood spilled on this continent,' he said without looking up, 'that I wonder if we'll ever be able to dig anywhere and not unearth more sorrow.'

'But you were right,' she said, 'this is our job, to bring history to light and not shy away from it. It's good to remember the past, and to understand and learn from it, so that the terrible things that happened won't ever occur again.'

Sutton sighed. 'Yes. The only problem is that mankind's been saying that since the dawn of time, and we never learn.'

*

Sonja cleaned up the mess in her room as best she could, filling the tiny waste paper bin with broken glass from the mirror. She left an extra five hundred rand on the writing bureau and a note that said, '*Sorry*'.

She made herself a cup of coffee in the room, but skipped breakfast. It was good to be moving again and she wound down the window of the X-Trail rather than using the air conditioning and let the hot wind blast away some of her hangover as she drove out of Kuruman.

The road soon turned to gravel and she had some fun driving too fast and deliberately drifting through some of the bends. At tiny Van Zylsrus she filled up the car's tank and then went to the hotel across the road, where she had a cold Windhoek Lager and a cheeseburger at the bar to take care of the remnants of her post-binge illness. Sonja knew she couldn't go on like this. She needed to get her mind back into shape. She'd worked out and stayed away from liquor for a month prior to the Vietnam mission and had felt the better for it. She needed to keep up that regime, but it was hard.

As she hit the road again she thought about Stirling. It had been a surprise seeing him on the television last night and, in her drunken stupor, she had googled the lodge where he was based, Desert Rhino Camp, and found a phone number. She had almost called, but by morning had thought better of it.

Things had not ended well for them the last time she'd seen Stirling, in Botswana. She'd been on another mission then, to blow up a dam that the Namibian and Angolan governments were building on the Okavango River, where it passed through the narrow corridor of Namibian land known as the Caprivi Strip. The dam was a threat to the wildlife-rich wetlands of the Okavango Delta and the Moremi Game Reserve; downstream in neighbouring Botswana a group of lodge owners had banded together to oppose the dam. When their lobbying efforts failed they employed Corporate Solutions, the mercenary outfit Sonja had worked for back then, to destroy the dam.

Stirling, who had been managing a lodge in the delta, was a good man, too good for her, and in the end he couldn't support the plan to destroy the dam as it also involved fomenting an insurrection by separatist rebels in the Caprivi Strip. He'd tried to foil the plan and Sonja, who had despised Stirling's betrayal at the time, had questioned why she had ever found him attractive. She had ended up with Sam, who'd been caught up in the insurrection while making a wildlife television documentary, and had not given Stirling a second thought.

Until now.

Stirling had been right, she had to concede, to oppose the plan Corporate Solutions had hatched. The rebellion against the government of Namibia had failed. She could have blown up a dam without starting a war. Perhaps she was getting maudlin in her advancing years, but she regretted adding to Africa's long tradition of bloodshed.

She had actually met Stirling years before the dam episode. They had been teenage sweethearts and he'd wanted her to stay in the bush with him, in Botswana, but Sonja had run off to England and joined the British Army. She wasn't like Stirling; she couldn't manage a safari camp because she couldn't be bothered pandering to the needs of overfed, overpaid guests, and while she loved the outdoors and appreciated the continent's wildlife, she wasn't a bunny hugger like Stirling. Her father had taught her to shoot and she'd hunted for the pot when they had lived on the farm in Namibia. Stirling had never killed anything larger than a mosquito, and she knew he abhorred the work she did.

Sonja made Twee Rivieren, the main camp of the Kgalagadi Transfrontier Park, just after lunch time. She had been here on a family holiday in the old days, when it was still known as the Kalahari Gemsbok National Park. The newly named park was the first of a series of 'peace parks' to be opened in Africa. These transfrontier parks, which were springing up all over southern Africa, dropped fences and streamlined crossings and management where two wildlife reserves adjoined each other, but were in different countries. Here at Twee Rivieren in the east of the Kgalagadi park, one could cross from South Africa to the neighbouring national park in Botswana to the north, while Namibia was just across the western border of the reserve.

Sonja walked into the impressive new thatch-roofed reception and administration area and presented herself to a woman in a South African National Parks uniform. She had decided to stop here for the night. After exchanging pleasantries the woman consulted her computer and made a clicking noise with her tongue. 'We've nothing here in Twee Rivieren, ma'am, but I can book you into a chalet in Mata Mata for tonight.'

Sonja cursed silently. It wasn't the woman's fault. While the woman processed her booking Sonja read an information sheet on the park and noted it would take her about three hours to get to Mata Mata, and she needed to reach the camp before its gates closed at dusk. 'Thanks,' Sonja said when the woman handed her a printout of her booking.

Mata Mata was on the border between South Africa and Namibia. Sonja was persona non grata in Namibia; the same events that had put a wedge between her and Stirling were also the reason she couldn't legally go back to her birthplace, but if her daughter was in trouble she would find a way into the country. Nothing would stop her.

Chapter 8

Matthew Allchurch had teed off at the eighth hole on the course at the Steenberg Golf Estate when his phone beeped. He usually switched the damn thing off when he played, but he'd forgotten.

He'd sworn after selling his profitable law practice in Cape Town six months earlier that he would consign the device to the dustbin, but it seemed impossible for anyone, even a retired advocate, to live without a phone.

He checked the message and felt the beat of his heart quicken. *Thought you should know, the body of a flier has been found in northern Namibia. Call me when you can. Andre.*

Matthew immediately abandoned the game, giving brief apologies to the three friends he normally played with, and drove his buggy back to the car park. In the car he took a deep breath and called Andre Horsman, but he was told by the receptionist that Andre was on the other line and would call him back.

Matthew started the engine of his Range Rover, his retirement present to himself, and drove, too fast, out of the estate and up the hill towards his home on the slopes of Table Mountain, over-looking Tokai. Andre's office was in Constantia, not far away, and Matthew resolved that if Andre hadn't called him back within an hour he would drive there.

He pressed the remote to open the swinging security gates and drove down the driveway, not bothering to open the garage in case he did have to leave again soon.

The dogs, Fabian and Soda, started barking, and they galloped up the steep lawn from the koi pond at the sight of Matthew walking out onto the balcony. His wife, Helen, was in her broad-brimmed khaki bush hat. She looked up and waved to him, then followed the dogs.

Matthew was in the study turning the computer on when Helen walked in. 'Well, this is a surprise. You couldn't have finished your game already.'

'No, something's come up, love.'

She peeled off her gardening gloves. 'Just as well you weren't half an hour earlier or you would have caught me with Charles the gardener making passionate love in that illegal marijuana patch he's growing down past the pool house.'

Matthew only half heard her joke. He typed '*flyer found Namibia*' into the search engine.

'What is it, Matthew?' his wife asked him.

The search just yielded useless results, so he tried '*body of pilot found Namibia*'.

'Andre sent me an SMS while I was on the golf course.' He looked up at her. 'The body of an airman or a pilot has been found in Namibia.'

Helen put a hand over her mouth and sat down in the chair on the other side of his desk. 'No. Is it –?'

Matthew scanned the results on the screen. 'I don't know, love, Andre didn't say anything in his message. Hang on, here's something.'

He clicked on a news item dated that morning. It was from a Namibian newspaper called *New Era*. The headline on a story by Aggie Aikanga said: *Mystery body found in desert archaeological dig may be a wartime pilot*. As Matthew read the story Helen got up and moved behind him. She scanned the item over his shoulder.

'It's not him,' she said, with what sounded to Matthew like a mixture of relief and sadness. 'It says the man had dog tags identifying him as "H. Brand".'

Matthew nodded, then felt himself slump a little in his seat. 'No, it's not him. But Andre thought it worth mentioning the article to me. Perhaps there's some connection to Gareth.'

Helen straightened and put a hand on his shoulder. She gave him a little squeeze. 'You know the names of all the crewmen who went missing on that aircraft. "Brand" isn't one of them.'

She was right. Matthew knew that also missing on Gareth's flight were the senior pilot, Captain Danie Bester, and a load-master, Jacobus Venter. But all the same there was some reason why Andre had messaged him. Perhaps Andre had seen a different version of the article, one that didn't carry the name found on the body's identification disks, but when Matthew tried a variety of combinations of words in the search engine he kept coming back to the same story. He felt as his wife had sounded: a mixture of relief and the annoyance that came when one reopened a healing wound.

'I'll get Sophia to make us a cup of tea,' Helen said as she walked out of the office.

When the air force officer and the padre had come to their home, in the more modest area of Fish Hoek at the time, the news they'd brought had nearly destroyed Helen. She hadn't wanted to let them into the house, rationalising that if she didn't hear the words then it wouldn't be true. They had, both of them, clung to the one word, 'missing', for a long time, years, in fact.

After a while, especially once South Africa's war in Angola was over and South West Africa had become peaceful Namibia, the fact that their only son, Gareth, was still listed as 'missing' proved more of a cruel taunt than a glimmer of hope. Helen had been an emotional wreck for years, crying every day, but Matthew had turned his attention and his energies to finding out what he could about his son's disappearance near the end of the war.

Matthew looked at the framed photo on his desk, the one he said 'Good morning, my boy,' and 'Goodnight' to every day. Gareth had just earned his wings as a pilot in the South African Air Force when his parents had cajoled him into getting the studio portrait done. He'd been excited, he'd told his father, at being deployed to South West Africa so soon after graduation. He had wanted to fly jet fighter aircraft but had to do his time flying a maritime patrol aircraft, an old Second World War vintage Douglas DC-3 Dakota as it turned out, but Gareth was simply happy to be flying operationally, putting his training into practice.

The war in Angola had become one of full pitched battles on air and land, with tank battles and aerial dogfights between South Africa on one side and the Angolan military backed by the Cubans on the other. Still, father and son had assured Helen repeatedly that Gareth would be flying patrols over the Atlantic Ocean, not dodging Russian-made surface to air missiles or Cuban-piloted MiG interceptors.

Again, though, the seemingly random way in which Gareth's aircraft had simply disappeared made the loss of their son even harder to bear than the ordeal faced by other parents and loved ones whose sons had been killed in action in the border war.

Andre Horsman had been Gareth's temporary squadron commander and it had been he who had penned a letter to Matthew and Helen, praising their son's commitment to the unit and the war effort, and stressing that in the short time Gareth had been with the squadron he had left his mark in a positive manner.

The National Party government in apartheid South Africa kept as tight a muzzle on the press as it could and released rosy pictures about the war in Angola and the fight against communism. Even though he considered himself politically liberal, Matthew realised that censorship was part of the war effort. However, he had quizzed Andre in a subsequent letter about why there had been no reporting in the South African newspapers, radio or television about the loss of a transport aircraft; surely, Matthew theorised, this would be too big a story to keep quiet.

Andre had telephoned him from South West Africa and used veiled speech to ask a favour of him.

'Please, Matthew,' Andre had urged him, 'don't talk about the matter we have been discussing in our letters in public. Gareth was doing something of utmost importance for the war effort, and if our enemies knew even vaguely about where he was flying to or from, then it would put many South Africans and many more of our allies at risk.'

Matthew had toed the party line for a long time after that, but with the change in government in 1994, when Nelson Mandela came to power, Matthew could see no reason why he should not be given access to information about the mission Gareth had been flying. Terrible things had emerged from the Truth and Reconciliation Commission about the crimes and human rights abuses perpetuated in the name of apartheid – and on the ANC side – and Matthew could not imagine his son had been involved in anything as bad as all that. He had discussed the matter with Andre, who had by then left the air force and set up an import-export business, specialising in electronic goods, remote control model aircraft, drones and other gadgets made in China. With sanctions lifted South Africa was now back in the international business community.

'Matthew, not even I know everything that went on with some of the missions we flew,' Andre had told him, several years earlier. 'I later found out that sometimes our security forces used our aircraft to commit war crimes; we would be tasked to fly some prisoners back from Angola or Owamboland to another base in South West and the aircraft would be diverted over the Skeleton Coast to the Atlantic Ocean. Sometimes,' and Andre had pinched the bridge of his nose at this point, 'sometimes those prisoners were tossed out of our aircraft alive into the ocean, far from shore.'

'My God,' Matthew had said. A chill of dread and shame had run through his body; had his own son been involved in such missions? If Gareth's plane had crashed while taking a cargo of men to their deaths then it was no wonder the authorities would want it covered up. Even if the Truth and Reconciliation Commission could help him uncover more information about Gareth's mission, did he want his son's name dragged through the press as being complicit in mass murder? Gareth's death had left Helen desolate and empty for years; news like that might kill her.

Instead, Matthew had gone through the snail-paced, resistant, frustrating channels of bureaucracy to trace air force records from the new regime. No one seemed particularly interested in helping him, but the replies he did receive were adamant that there were no records of a South African Air Force Dakota being reported as missing in action, crashed or downed by enemy fire on the date of Gareth's disappearance or for a period of a month on either side of that day.

Andre had stayed in contact with him. He didn't discourage Matthew's attempts to find out more through official channels, but always he would remind Matthew that there were some mysteries that were better left unsolved.

'The government is very clear on this, Andre. There are no records of an SAAF DC-3 Dakota going missing at the time of Gareth's disappearance. What aren't you telling me?' Matthew had demanded one day in the golf club bar, raising his voice.

'Shush, man, shush.' Andre had run a hand through his thinning hair. 'Look, they are right and they are wrong. An aircraft did disappear that night, but it wasn't an air force Dakota. It was a civilian registered Angolan version of the same type.'

'Andre, for God's sake, what was Gareth doing flying an airliner?'

Another piece of the puzzle had been revealed but it hadn't helped much. South Africa, with financial backing from the Reagan administration in the United States, was supplying arms and ammunition to Jonas Savimbi's UNITA guerrillas. Much of it went by road, via Rundu, but sometimes special consignments of cargo and people went into and out of Angola by air.

'Gareth was working for our State Security people on his final mission, Matthew. I couldn't have told you this at the time. They were dealing with the CIA – it was all on a need-to-know basis, and even as Gareth's squadron commander I didn't need to know. All I knew was when he was going, and when he was due back, and the night he was supposed to return to us he never did.'

'If you didn't know where he was going, or what he was doing, how did you mount a search for him? *Did* you search for him, or was that a lie, too?' Matthew had fumed.

Andre had told him that he had pieced together the known movements of Gareth's last flight and he and Gareth's squadron mates had mounted their own search. Gareth had flown from Ondangwa air force base in South West Africa north, presumably to Angola. He had delivered cargo, or possibly flown there to pick something – or someone – up, and then returned to Ondangwa. His take-offs and landings had been recorded by air traffic controllers at the air force base – there was no hiding that, Andre had said.

'Yes, but where did he go after that?'

Andre had looked around the bar, as if he still feared someone from the old regime was eavesdropping on him. 'I spoke to a ground crewman at Ondangwa who had refuelled Gareth's aircraft. He said Gareth's last words to him, when the man had remarked how warm the evening was, was that it would be cooler over the Skeleton Coast and the Atlantic.'

Matthew had been shocked by Andre's revelation, and the unnamed crewman's words. The clear implication, based on his earlier conversations with Andre, was that Gareth had been flying a load of live cargo, prisoners of war, who would be dropped to their deaths over the cold grey waters of the Atlantic Ocean.

Matthew had hidden all this from Helen, and had told himself the best thing he could do was stop searching for answers about Gareth; he didn't want to find them any more. However, a couple of years earlier Matthew had created a Facebook account and against his better judgement had joined a number of groups online dedicated to veterans of the fighting in Namibia and Angola. On a site for SAAF veterans he posted a simple message asking to connect with anyone who had served with Gareth Allchurch.

To his surprise, a man had contacted him a month later. His name was Roland Pretorius and he had been a pilot in Gareth's squadron. Pretorius lived in Darling, a quaint town in the wine lands north of Cape Town, and he'd agreed to meet with Matthew next time he came to the city. They scheduled a time and place, but Roland hadn't shown up. Matthew found out through posts from relatives on Roland's Facebook page a few days later that he had been killed in a car accident.

In a way, as terrible as the news was, Matthew had felt relieved. If Roland Pretorius had been coming to tell him his son had been involved in murder, Matthew didn't want to hear it. Now he felt the same mix of anticipation and dread as he waited for Andre to call back.

'The hell with it,' Matthew said out loud. He phoned Andre's office again.

'Matthew, howzit,' Andre said.

'Fine, but cut to the chase, Andre, what's all this about, and who's this guy "Brand" who they've found in the desert?'

'There was something else I didn't tell you about the night Gareth went missing, Matthew, but I didn't know until now that this other thing was connected to the missing aircraft.'

'Really?' Matthew scoffed. 'I'm hardly surprised you've left something out.'

Andre ignored the barb. 'Matthew, the night Gareth and the others went missing another *oke* who used to work out of Ondangwa sometimes also went missing. His name was Hudson Brand.'

'Another of your flight crew?' Matthew said.

'No. He was a foreigner, a half-Portuguese–Angolan, half-American guy. He was one of the CIA liaison officers to UNITA and he used to organise the supply flights from Ondangwa into Angola. I knew of him, but never met him personally, because I never needed to.'

'So you think he was on Gareth's aircraft?'

Helen walked into the office carrying a tray with two cups and a teapot on it.

'Matthew, I'm sure he was on that flight, but there's something else.'

'What?'

'I was just making some calls before you rang. I did a search online this morning and found out that unless there are two half-American, half-Portuguese guys called Hudson Brand, then this guy is not dead – he's very much alive.'

*

Hudson Brand ended the call and looked out over the waters of the Sabie River, which swirled around the bulbous, smooth, pink granite rock that gave Hippo Rock wildlife estate its name.

Across the river was the Kruger Park, the happy place he could go to, mentally and physically, when the past reared up to try and devour him, as it was doing right now. He hadn't known the name of either of the pilots on that aircraft, and had made it his business, when he'd made it out safely, never to ask.

Now he knew a little about the younger man, the co-pilot. Gareth Allchurch, aged twenty-one, son of Matthew and Helen. Matthew had spoken with the familiar grasping, heart-wrenching tones of the bereaved who will never understand why their son had to be taken from them at such an age. That was war for you.

No.

He corrected himself: Gareth was not killed in a war, he was killed in the commission of a crime. So, too, did the others die not for a country or an ideology, but for cold, hard, dirty cash. Brand felt sick to his stomach, and for a change it was not the drink.

He had turned his back on that business decades ago, but he knew, always, somewhere in the deep recesses of his mind, that he would have to confront the deaths of those pilots one day, and that he would be found accountable. Brand had been brash, cocky, a young field officer on his first posting in the actual field. He had returned to the country of his mother's birth and he had thought he was there to do good, to fight communism, and to support gallant freedom fighters.

It was almost inconceivable to him now, all these years later, how foolishly naïve he had been, how ready to swallow his own government's propaganda. Angola had not been a noble crusade; there was nothing good about the country, the politics or the war on either side of the political divide.

Allchurch had told him about the discovery of the body in Namibia and Brand had googled the article on his phone. 'Are they your dog tags on that body, and if so, whose body is it?' the man had asked him.

'I don't have to answer any of your questions,' Brand had replied, tempted to end the call there and then.

'Please,' Allchurch had begged, and the guilt rose up in Brand, not over the body he had left in the middle of Namibia somewhere – that was Jacobus Venter and he'd been a prick of note – but over the fate of the two pilots. Brand didn't know how complicit they'd been in that mission, whether they were just blindly following orders, or whether they were crooked as well and stood to make a cut from the flight.

'Are you still there?' Allchurch had said.

'Yes.' Barely, he thought to himself.

'Look, I don't care about the body they found in Namibia – unless it's my son with your dog tags on him, of course.'

'It's not,' Brand had assured him.

Brand had heard the man exhale loudly – a mix of relief and despair, probably. 'This is the closest anyone has come to locating any trace of my son's flight. Even if I can't find him I do want to know what my son was doing and what happened to his aircraft. I want to meet you, as soon as possible.'

Brand, to add to the shame he already felt, tried, in a cowardly manner, to talk him out of it. 'You don't want to know what happened to that flight,' he had told Allchurch.

'You don't understand, Mr Brand,' Allchurch had said. It had been easy for the man to track Brand down – his cell phone number was on his personal website which advertised his services as a safari guide. 'I *need* to know everything about my son's last flight. I want to find out what happened to him and his aircraft – I know it was a civilian registered DC-3 Dakota and that it was some sort of hush-hush mission – but there's no excuse after all these years for the truth not to be known. I read online you're also a private investigator, and you were on my son's last flight. Please, Mr Brand, I need to know what he was up to.'

'Up to?' Brand said. 'He was just the co-pilot.' At least Brand hoped that Allchurch Junior hadn't been involved in what was going on that night.

'I need to know, though, if he was a party to the cold-blooded murder of prisoners of war.'

Brand was momentarily confused, but he knew enough of the dark deeds of those days to put two and two together. 'No, Mr Allchurch, Gareth didn't kill any innocent men. If you're talking about people being dumped at sea then that's not the sort of mission your son was flying. He didn't kill anyone.'

'Really?'

'No, he didn't kill any innocent people,' Brand said.

'That's something of a relief, but I still want to meet you. You're in the Lowveld, yes? Where exactly?'

Brand had not been eager to give out his address, but if Allchurch had found him via the web it wouldn't take him long to track him down.

'On the edge of the Kruger Park, near Kruger Gate.'

'I can be on a flight to Skukuza tomorrow,' Allchurch said.

Brand had reluctantly agreed to meet him. He tried to remember what the two pilots looked like, but it had been dark and his only memory of them was of ghostly faces illuminated at first by the muted glow of their cockpit instruments and, later, by the fire.

Gareth Allchurch hadn't killed any innocents, but Hudson Brand had, including Matthew Allchurch's son.

Chapter 9

Sonja was pissed off and not even the lions could lift her mood.

She motored slowly along the dirt road that followed the course of the Auob River as the two magnificent black-maned Kalahari lions ambled their way towards the Montrose waterhole.

Normally the sight of their rippling muscles, their luxuriant manes and their chilling golden eyes would have pleased her. As a child, visiting Etosha National Park with her parents, lions had always been her favourite animal. Here in the Kgalagadi Transfrontier Park she was as close as she would get to wildlife on this trip, but even having one of the big boys just a couple of metres from her car, close enough to smell his musky scent through the open window, was not enough to distract her from her thoughts about her daughter.

The lion on the other side of the road stopped, lifted his tail and aimed a high-pressure jet of urine at a small thornbush as he marked his turf. He moved on a few paces and curled his lips back from his teeth, inhaling the scent of another cat. Sonja had no territory any more, no mate either; all she had was Emma.

When she reached Mata Mata, she checked in then drove to a row of connected chalets. The front of each room looked depressingly narrow, but once inside she found the rooms were quite long. Her room was also enticingly cool; she dropped her rucksack on one of the single beds and flopped down on the other on her back and checked her phone. There was still no message from Emma and the worry nibbled away at her common sense.

It was part of coming down, as well. She was still wired from the mission in Vietnam, and from taking on the morons in the bar. She couldn't sit still in a rest camp in the desert.

Sonja got up off the bed and went to the small kitchen at the front of the chalet. Her bottle of brandy was nearly empty and she was almost out of Coke Light. At least drinking gave her something to do. It was a short walk to the camp's small shop, which sold basic provisions for campers and self-catering visitors.

Sonja walked past the reception building, which doubled as the border post with Namibia. The new flag of the country of her birth – red, white, blue and green with a yellow sun in the upper left corner – snapped in the breeze across a token expanse of no man's land between two gates. She was a little surprised to see two white women on the far side nod their thanks to a Namibian policeman in a mottled brown camouflage uniform then walk through to the South African side of the border. They each carried a pair of white plastic shopping bags.

The women chatted to themselves and, noticing Sonja said, 'Hi, howzit?'

'Fine. And you?' Sonja replied.

'Fine. You're not on your way to the camp shop, are you?' one asked. They looked like Johannesburg housewives on holiday – blow-dried hair, painted nails and jewellery, bling in the bush.

'*Ja.*'

'Oh, no, no, no,' said the other. 'You really *must* visit the little *padstal* just across the border on the Namibian side. It is simply *divine.* We just took the last of the springbok *wors*, but their biltong is to die for and there's the loveliest selection of home-made jams and preserves.'

Padstal was Afrikaans for a roadside stall or farm store. Sonja had imagined there was nothing but desert on the other side of the border. 'How did you go about crossing the border? Did you need a passport?'

'No,' said the first woman. 'We're from Joburg, we're not crossing into Namibia with our vehicles so we didn't even *bring* our passports. Just say hi to the policeman on the gate and tell him you're going to the little shop and he'll let you through.'

'Thanks,' Sonja said, experiencing a jolt of adrenaline. 'I might just do that.'

The women walked down the hill to the camping ground and Sonja turned and went back to her chalet. As well as her large military-style rucksack she had a small daypack that she used as carry-on luggage. Into the smaller bag she stuffed her wallet, lightweight US Army quilted nylon sleeping bag liner, a pair of compact binoculars, a spare pair of cargo pants and a T-shirt, some underpants and a second sports bra. Her Leatherman multi-tool had been in her check-in bag for the flight, so she took it out and threaded its pouch onto her belt. From her wash bag she took soap, toothpaste and toothbrush. She took off her sandals and put on socks and her hiking boots. She was wearing short khaki shorts and a tank top, so she liberally smeared her arms and legs with sunblock and tossed the bottle in her daypack.

She unwrapped the Glock pistol she'd taken from the hunters from the towel in the bottom of her rucksack. She put the spare magazine in her pocket and stuffed the pistol in the waistband of her shorts, nestled in the small of her back.

Sonja quickly packed the rest of her things in her rucksack and put it in the boot of her rented car. She drove the X-Trail the short distance to the Mata Mata camp store and parked it under the shady tree out the front. It would be a few days, she reckoned, before anyone thought to check why the car was still there, and where she had gone. Sonja locked the car and put the keys in the exhaust pipe, then walked to the border of South Africa and Namibia.

As she approached the first gate she waved to a South African policeman sitting on a chair in the shade of the overhanging roof of the reception and border control office. 'Howzit,' she chirped brightly to the man. 'I'm just going across the border to the shop, is that fine?'

The man gave her a thumbs-up and waved her on.

Sonja felt a buzz as she walked through the no man's land area. The policeman in camouflage touched the brim of his cap as she approached. 'I'm sorry, I don't have a passport, but is it all right if I just pop across to the shop?'

The policeman smiled. 'Welcome to Namibia.'

*

Alex Bahler thought about Emma Kurtz as he drove the white dusty road through Etosha National Park. He was driving from Halali Camp, where he'd spent the night, his sleep disturbed by honey badgers raiding the dust bins in the camping ground.

He believed strongly in his work; in fact it was more of a calling than merely the subject of his postgraduate thesis. He received a basic allowance from the overseas charity that raised money in Europe and America, but he did not feel like this was his job. It was a way of life, and he wondered if he would ever find a woman who would share not only his passion for wildlife, but the privations that came as part of a life lived in the bush on a shoestring budget.

Emma clearly had at least a superficial love of the wild, judging by her reaction to their brief drive through Etosha from the King

Nehale Gate to Namutoni, but what foreigner didn't think they'd fallen in love with Africa after their first visit to a national park or a game reserve? He'd seen girls, foreign students and volunteers, who'd visited his camp and accompanied him on drives, burst into tears at the sight of their first elephant. In the end, though, they all went back to Munich or Melbourne or Milwaukee or wherever they came from.

As he drove, instinctively scanning the grasslands for the silhouette of a cheetah sitting upright, surveying its surrounds, his mind turned over their conversations about recent military history and the army.

He didn't take war lightly, but he did know that when his father and his uncles, and just about every man over the age of fifty in Namibia or neighbouring South Africa got together over a beer, they started talking about their army days and the war in South West Africa and Angola. They were never stories of death or sorrow or trauma, they were tales of mischief and drinking and flouting the regulations.

He was smart enough to know that Namibia's war of independence had caused nothing but grief and hardship for most of the people caught up in it. There had been no crushing victory by SWAPO, and while the white population and their African conscripts had held the line against Sam Nujoma's People's Liberation Army of Namibia, when South Africa finally agreed to pull out of Angola and South West, then free and democratic elections were always going to deliver the country to the black majority. Emma knew the history of his country, better than he did, and she didn't seem hung up on politics, even though her family had lived through the war. She intrigued him.

Perhaps his one hope of impressing Emma would be to help her find the identity of the man they had discovered, the one they had taken to calling Harry. Their visits to local villages had so far turned up nothing.

If there was one person who knew everything that had ever happened in and around Etosha and the surrounding area, it was Oom Otto Stapf. *Oom*, the Afrikaans word for uncle, was not just a customary term of respect for an elder but also Otto's enduring nickname. He had been a head warden of the park back in the 1980s and he and his wife, Ria, now owned a small private lodge and campsite just outside Andersson Gate, near Okaukuejo.

Alex checked his phone as he drove and saw that he had signal. He pulled over, selected Oom Otto's number and dialled.

'Alex, how are you, my boy?' Oom Otto said as soon as he answered.

'Fine, *dankie*, Oom, and you?'

'*Ja*, fine thanks, but busy. I've got a party of German guests I'm taking for a drive in the park today.'

'Sorry, Oom, I can call back later if that's better.'

'No, no. It's fine. I've just sent them into the restaurant at Okaukuejo for lunch. I'm heading to the waterhole now, so I can talk.'

'I'm going to be in the camp in about ten minutes, can I meet you there by the waterhole, Oom?'

'Sure, man.'

Alex ended the call and drove the rest of the way to Okaukuejo, Etosha's largest rest camp and its administrative hub. The reception and restaurant area was dominated by a tall round watchtower that was visible for miles around. Tourists were browsing in the curio shop and the camp store and filing into the restaurant for lunch. It was busy, as always. Alex preferred to stay in the quieter camps, especially Halali, but Okaukuejo and this part of the park were justifiably popular with tourists and tour guides because of the densities of game. Each camp in Etosha had a floodlit waterhole on its perimeter, and while all of them attracted game, Okaukuejo's was literally teeming with animals twenty-four hours a day.

As he navigated his way between the bungalows that over-looked the waterhole Alex caught sight of half a dozen elephants plodding in single file across the white stony ground on the far side of the oval-shaped waterhole. An electric fence set in front of a stone wall, both about waist height, were all that separated the awe-struck tourists sitting on park benches from the giant pachyderms. To make the encounter even more memorable the elephants, all bulls, walked around to the camp side of the waterhole and pointed their ample behinds at the tourists as they lowered their trunks into the water and greedily started to drink, just thirty metres from the nearest onlookers.

Alex raised a hand to shield his eyes from the midday glare that bounced off the limestone rocks and dusty lands beyond, where thousands of hooves and pads had worn down the remnants of dry, golden grass. He scanned the people sitting around the wall until he saw the distinctive, unkempt silver mane and long bushy beard he was looking for. 'Howzit, Oom?'

Otto looked up, put down a sandwich he'd been eating, stood and clasped Alex's hand in a meaty paw, squeezing so hard that Alex could barely reciprocate the handshake. 'Fine, fine. How are you, my boy?'

'*Lekker, dankie*, Oom. Thanks for your time.'

'For you, always. You know how interested I am in your predator research.'

Alex explained about the archaeological team finding the body outside the northern boundary of the park.

'Yes, I'd heard about that.'

'You had?' Alex was surprised.

'Yes, it's been in the news. I knew the dig was going on, a friend of mine in the local community told me about it. There were a lot of rumours about the siege of Namutoni and what did and didn't happen there during and after the battle. Not all of it went into the official history.'

'I didn't know it had already been in the media, Oom.'

'There's a thing called the internet, Alex.' He laughed. 'Like I say, I envy you being stuck in the bush out of contact with the world.'

'OK, well, Oom, I've been trying to help the archaeologist. I asked around a couple of the local villages outside the park to see if anyone remembered an aircraft crash during the war, or a plane going missing, northeast of Namutoni, but no one remembers anything.'

Otto picked up his sandwich and took a bite. 'I was going to call the police later today, after I saw the article online this morning. Back in '87, at least I think that was the year, I was head warden and I got a call from the air force base at Ondangwa. A South African named Horsman told me that a DC-3 Dakota had gone missing and that the air force would be flying search missions over the park. I asked him why the aircraft had been flying over Etosha and where it was heading, and he told me it was none of my business.' Otto took a pipe out of the pocket of his sleeveless photographer's vest and began filling it.

'Would it have been unusual for the aircraft to be flying over the park?'

Otto shrugged, put a lighter to the bowl of the pipe and puffed on it. 'Nothing was "usual" in those days, boy. The South Africans did what they liked here. The word was that they were killing buffalo, elephant and rhino up in the Caprivi Strip and in Angola, and I was very particular about keeping the military out of the park as much as I could.'

'Did you check with the villagers outside the park?'

Otto exhaled and nodded. 'This Horsman asked me to check with what he called the *natives* around the park to find out if they had seen anything. I found a headman, dead now, who did see a burning light in the sky on the night in question, and I reported this back to the air force straight away, naturally. From what Matthias, the headman, said, it seemed the aircraft was heading west, but when I told Horsman this he still refused to say what the Dakota's destination was and whether this was on course or off course. I also got the feeling he didn't know for sure. I was told not to say anything to anyone, especially the newspapers, about this missing aircraft. I found it all very strange, but as I say, my boy, they were unusual times. It was a war, after all.'

'What do you think happened, Oom? Did some SWAPO guys shoot down the plane?'

Otto seemed to mull over the question as he drew on his pipe. 'I suppose it's possible, but we never had them operating with surface to air missiles in our area. It could be that it just developed engine troubles or something of that nature. We had a couple of days of air force helicopters and fixed wing aircraft flying over the park, concentrating on the western section, but they never found anything – at least not in Etosha or the immediate surrounds or I would have heard about it.'

'It could even have crashed further to the west of the park,' Alex said, thinking out loud.

'It could have gone anywhere, my boy. And if the pilot kept flying west there's nothing but a hell of a lot of nowhere out there, through Kaokoveld, the Palmwag Conservancy, all the way through to the Skeleton Coast National Park and the Atlantic beyond. If their Dakota had crashed anywhere along that route they might never find it, and no human being might ever pass within sight of it.'

'What if the plane crashed near where the body was found – maybe he was the only survivor and he walked off to look for help and somehow died of thirst or his injuries?'

Oom Otto seemed to consider the proposition, but in the end shook his head. 'If the aircraft crashed within a hundred kilometres of where those people are digging I would have known about it. We patrolled the park constantly and there were plenty of people living outside Etosha, farming, even during the war. We communicated with them all the time.'

'Maybe he parachuted out as a way of escaping the fire that Matthias says he saw?' Alex said.

'Or maybe he just fell out?'

'I don't think so,' Alex said. 'I had a look at him and he looked intact. He must have had a parachute. Also he'd been laid out on his back, with his hands across his chest, like in a Christian burial, so it wasn't as if the dirt and dust just covered him where he'd died.'

'Hyena or jackal would have finished him well before the earth swallowed him,' Otto said. 'Something, or someone, killed him, and someone buried him.'

A herd of zebra was cautiously approaching the waterhole, the stallion way out in front of the mares and two foals. The nervy animals would pause every few steps to listen, look and sniff the wind. It was hard, Alex thought, to imagine his homeland at war, with burning aircraft lighting up the night sky and men being left in unmarked graves. It had happened, although he'd been too young to remember anything more than the presence of uniformed soldiers and armoured vehicles on the roads on his way to and from school.

Otto stood, tapped out the remnants of his pipe tobacco on the stone wall and put a hand on the small of his back. 'But now I must go and find some lions for my tourists.'

Alex stood and shook his hand. '*Baie dankie*, Oom.'

'Pleasure. I hope I can be of some help. But may I ask why you're so keen to help these researchers?'

Alex waved his hand. 'It is nothing. Just helping out some fellow students.'

Otto winked. 'You sure it's nothing to do with that pretty girl you were seen with at Namutoni yesterday?'

Alex laughed. 'You really do know everything, don't you?'

111

Otto's reference to Emma jogged his memory. After the older man had gone, Alex took his field notebook out of his top pocket and opened it to the page where Emma had written her mother's satellite phone number. Emma had asked Alex to send a message to her mother and had written it down for him. He took out his phone and typed the message: *Hello, this is from Emma via a friend's phone. Emma says she is fine and needs some help with identifying the uniform found on a dead man she has discovered on her archaeological dig. She is sorry for not getting in touch sooner, but phone signal here is bad. She sends her love and will text a picture of the man's uniform when she can.* Alex pressed send.

*

Emma was sheltering in the shade of one of the gazebos as they recorded and tagged the artefacts they had found on and with Harry's body. They had placed each of the articles in a tray as they had recovered them from the body, and Emma and Natangwe were now recording them and securing them in plastic snap-lock bags.

Professor Sutton watched over them with arms folded and a serious look on his face. 'Be careful, Emma, some of these finds can literally fall apart in your hands.'

'Yes, Prof,' she said, trying not to sound resentful. She couldn't have handled them more gently or with more reverence if she'd tried. 'One man's Seiko diving watch. Time, 11.20. Do you think that's when he died, maybe when he hit the ground if his parachute didn't open properly?'

Natangwe wrote the site location, date, Emma's initials, and an item number on a bag, then slipped the watch into it and sealed it.

They had all been madly theorising about how Harry might have come to be here and how he died. Sutton stroked his beard.

'Hard to say. More likely that the watch just ran out of battery life. Also, what happened to his parachute?'

'The material might have come in handy for poor people in the area,' Natangwe said. 'If it was silk or nylon it could have been used as blankets or to waterproof a shack or a mud and cow dung hut.'

'Maybe, Natangwe,' Professor Sutton said.

'One man's wallet, empty,' Emma said, delicately slipping the wallet into a bag. 'I can't believe that it's survived so well.'

'Leather sandals from ancient Rome have been found at Hadrian's Wall, Kurtz, so it's not surprising his wallet has survived nearly thirty years.'

Emma bit back a retort. Older people all thought her generation believed they were entitled to instant respect and that they couldn't be taught anything – she'd heard such ranting before. Sutton was probably deliberately goading her, but she would not rise to it. 'Yes, Professor. I should have thought of that.'

'Hmph,' was all he uttered.

'One photo, found in Harry's left breast pocket. This is so sad.' Emma looked at the girl in the bikini. The photo was cracked with age, but not faded at all. She was blonde, a little on the chubby side, but she had a beautiful smile. There was nothing written on the back, but Emma supposed it was Harry's sweetheart.

Professor Sutton blinked and looked away, but made no comment on her observation. Perhaps there was a heart in there somewhere, she thought. He had removed the finds from the body and left it to the students to catalogue them. He'd told them not to go near Harry since he had finished excavating around him. The other gazebo was over the body now, and Sutton had cable-tied green shade cloth to the poles to form a screen around Harry. Emma guessed it was out of respect, but she desperately wanted to have another look at him, as heart-wrenching as that experience could be.

Emma held up another item found next to the body.

'One, what is this, a vest of some sort?'

'It's a webbing vest,' Natangwe said confidently, 'the kind soldiers carry their ammunition in.'

'More likely, Natangwe, it's an aircrew survival vest, given that we now believe Harry came to us from the sky,' Sutton said. 'Contents?' he asked Emma.

Emma looked at the items that had been removed from the nylon webbing vest. 'One first-aid bandage, called a field dressing according to the lettering on it.' She placed the wrapped package in a plastic bag. 'One length of nylon cord; one mirror.'

'That would have been used for signalling,' Sutton said.

Emma nodded. 'And that's about it. If it's a survival vest there's not much in there that you could survive with. Why wouldn't they have something like, I don't know, maybe a compass or a map or some high-protein food, something like that? What's missing is more interesting than what's here.'

'Indeed,' Sutton said. He pointed over to the enclosed gazebo. 'I would have expected to find a map, water, a compass, perhaps a signal flare or a hand-held radio, but there is none of that. It seemed Harry was robbed not only of what cash he had in his wallet, but of things that someone else might need to survive out here in the wilds.'

'But who would have taken those things, and left the other bits and pieces?'

'In case you're wondering why I cordoned off Harry's body, it's because this morning I found two stab wounds in his torso, under his sternum. I'm going to contact the police.'

'Wow,' Emma said.

'I have to contact the police anyway because of the estimated age of the body. If Harry was a wartime flier he should have had all the things Emma mentioned, and probably a sidearm – a pistol,' Sutton said. 'I believe that whoever took all that paraphernalia from Harry could very well have been the man who killed him. What we have here, now, is no longer a dig, it's a crime scene.'

Chapter 10

Sonja heard the far-off growl of a vehicle engine. She stopped, shrugged off her daypack and took out her binoculars. She had been following the course of the Auob River since illegally crossing the border the day before, staying off the road to avoid leaving tracks, sticking to the high ground on the southern side of the dry riverbed. She focused the binoculars and made out a white Land Rover Defender, not the type of vehicle that the Namibian police or immigration officers would have been driving – they used Toyotas.

Dodging tufts of hardy desert grass, Sonja jogged down the red sandy hill and waited by the side of the road. She stuck out her hand and waved it up and down, hitching for a lift, African style. The cloud of dust behind her was preceded by the Defender; her sort of vehicle, she mused with a smile, tough, no-nonsense, and prone to the occasional breakdown.

The driver showed no indication of slowing until he came close to her, then he put on his brakes and came to a halt fifty metres past her. Sonja waved away the cloud of red dust that enveloped her and saw the driver's reverse light come on.

The electric passenger side window was wound down and Sonja saw a man with spiky grey hair and flabby jowls behind the wheel. He greeted her in Afrikaans, then switched to English. 'Can I help?'

Sonja beefed up her German accent and pointed in the direction she had come from with her thumb. 'Hello. I am hitchhiking across Africa. Can you take me to Windhoek, perhaps?'

The man laughed. 'You'll die of thirst out here in the desert, and while Namibia is a safe country I wouldn't recommend hitchhiking anywhere these days.' He ran a hand through his hair. 'Well, I'm not going as far as Windhoek, but I'm going as far as Mariental. I was just visiting a parishioner on a farm here, her husband passed away recently.'

'You are a minister?'

'A pastor. Lutheran.'

'Then I think this is my lucky day, to be picked up by a church man and not a murderer.'

He laughed again and reached over and opened the passenger door for her. 'I'm Herman Lotz.'

'Ursula,' she lied, once again.

Lotz had a cooler box on the back seat of the Land Rover and he invited her to take a drink, either a bottle of water or a beer. 'I'll have a Tafel. Can I get you one?'

'I'll have the same.'

Sonja opened the beers for both of them and handed one to the pastor. The air conditioning was a welcome relief from the dry heat outside. Sonja could have survived in the desert for days on end, but she was in a hurry to get to Etosha and find Emma. She had slept in the desert the night before, covering herself first in her nylon sleeping bag liner and then with a layer of sand to further insulate her from the bitter cold of the evening.

Sonja had eaten some of the biltong she'd bought at the farm shop on the Namibian side of the border and drained one of her water bottles, which she'd replenished by digging a hole in the sand at a bend in the dry riverbed. When the subterranean water had started welling up to the surface she'd waited for it to clear then patiently filled her empty bottle.

Pastor Lotz asked her about her travels so far, and she made up a route from Maputo on Mozambique's Indian Ocean coast, across South Africa and into Namibia.

'An attractive woman like you must be careful, though, about accepting lifts from strangers.'

Sonja noticed the way his eyes kept travelling via her breasts and legs after each exchange in their conversation. A thought crossed her mind; she would have to find another lift in Mariental, and that could take time. 'Sometimes strangers can be fun, intriguing.'

She saw his Adam's apple bob. He licked his lips with a darting tongue like a snake's, and then looked across at her. 'You like strangers, eh?'

'Some. Big, strong ones.'

They approached a bend in the gravel road and when the pastor changed gears he let his hand slip off the stick and onto her knee. She made no attempt to move it, instead she shifted her knee closer to him. He licked his lips again.

'I've never done it with a church man.'

He swallowed and looked straight ahead. His face was beginning to colour. 'You like the thought of that?'

She finished her beer and dropped the bottle in the footwell, then covered his hand with hers. 'Very much. Inside every saint there's a sinner.'

He glanced at her. 'I shouldn't. I am married.' Yet he kept his hand where it was.

Pastor Lotz slid his hand from her knee back along her thigh, towards the hem of her shorts. Sonja sighed, in reality out of perverse disappointment that he had succumbed so easily. So predictable.

Before he got too carried away she called: 'Stop.'

He looked at her, eyes wide. 'What do you mean?'

'No, silly. I don't want you to *stop*, I just don't want you to crash the truck and kill us both. Pull over.'

'OK.' He took his hand off her and slowed the vehicle, bringing it to a halt under the shade of a tree.

'Get out, get ready for me. I want you in my mouth, then you can do me from behind over the engine.'

Lotz nearly fell out of the truck in his eagerness. Sonja shook her head and quickly checked the centre console box between the seats. In it she found some of his business cards. She got out her side of the Land Rover and as she walked around the front of the truck she took out the nine-millimetre pistol from her waistband with her right hand and her iPhone from her pocket with her left.

The pastor had his pants down and his semi-erect skinny white penis in one hand, furiously tugging himself to full arousal. Sonja kept the pistol behind her back but raised the phone and took his picture.

'Hey, what are you doing? I don't care what kind of kinks you're into, but you can't take my picture. I'm a public figure.' He shuffled towards her, his feet hobbled by his shorts around his ankles, but stopped reaching for the phone when she levelled the pistol at him.

'My God!'

'You should have thought about Him before you started groping me. I took one of your cards; it seems your church has a Facebook page. How very modern of you.'

'Please, please don't put my picture on there. My wife, my congregation . . .'

'Move away from the truck.'

He shook his head. 'No! You can't leave me here in the middle of nowhere.'

She raised her aim to between his eyes and he backed away from the edge of the road, into the sand. 'I'm borrowing your Land Rover for a while. You'll get it back, or I'll send you a message on Facebook telling you where to collect it. Now pull your pants up; you'll get sunburn otherwise.'

Red-faced he raised his shorts and buckled his belt. 'What will I tell my wife?' he whined.

She was tempted to insult him some more, or maybe shoot him in the genitals. 'Tell her you love her, every day, if you mean it.'

'I do, I do. I'm so sorry. Please don't leave me here.'

Sonja got in the truck, reached into the cooler box the pastor had on the back seat and tossed him a couple of bottles of water. 'Tell your wife your Landy broke down and you hitched a lift home. Tell her the truck's in the garage for repairs, and tell your God you're sorry.'

*

Hudson Brand met Matthew Allchurch at the small but tastefully decorated dark grey terminal building at Skukuza Airport, in the Kruger National Park. Allchurch had taken the direct Airlink flight from Cape Town.

'We could have talked some more on the phone,' Brand said as he shook the older man's hand. Allchurch's clothes were casual but tailored, chinos and a blue cotton shirt. The rest of the Embraer aircraft's passengers, a tour group, wore matching green and khaki safari wear.

'You can't hang up on me this way,' Matthew said. He carried a leather cabin bag, which he hoisted over his shoulder.

Allchurch completed the formalities of paying for a national park permit at the window next to the small gift shop, and Brand then led him out of the terminal, past a life-sized sculpture of a rhino, to the car park. 'So, where are you staying, Matthew? I can drop you somewhere if you need, after we've talked. Do you have luggage?'

'No luggage, and I'm not staying.' Allchurch said. 'I'm catching the afternoon flight to Johannesburg and then connecting to Windhoek.'

They got into Brand's battered Land Rover and he started the engine. 'That's a roundabout way to get to Namibia from Cape Town.'

'If my information is right, Mr Brand, you were the last person to see my son alive. I would have flown to Ulan Bator to see you.'

'Call me Hudson, or Brand, folks use either. Well, have it your way, but we can drive to Skukuza camp at least and get a coffee or a drink there.'

'Fine.'

Brand drove out of the car park, past the Joint Operations Command anti-poaching headquarters located next to the airport, and turned right at the end of the access road. He slowed to cross the single-lane low-level bridge over the Sabie River. Brand pulled into one of the parking bays on the bridge, designed so that people who wanted to watch animals or birds could stop and let other vehicles pass.

'Some hippo over there,' Brand said, pointing to a pod that occupied a pool.

'I'm not here to go on a game drive, Brand. What was my son doing on his last flight?'

Brand sighed. 'Flying the aircraft.'

'I'm not in the mood for jokes.'

'I'm not making light of it. As far as I could tell, your son and the other pilot were simply there to fly the Dakota. They didn't seem to be involved in the business at hand. In fact, they were a fill-in crew. The regular pilots had both come down with food poisoning in Angola. The replacements were flown up to us.

Somebody pulled some strings to make sure our flight left on schedule.'

Brand waited for a game viewer to pass and then crossed the remainder of the river and turned left at the four-way stop. They followed the river for a few hundred metres and he glanced at Allchurch who was silent, digesting what must have been new information.

'Who were the other pilots, were they South African air force?'

'No, not air force, they were civilians,' Brand said, 'one was South African and the other was Portuguese.'

'Do you remember their names?'

Brand searched his memory. Most of his contact had been with Venter, the loadmaster, though he'd seen the pilots around the forward operating base in Angola a few times. 'No. But if I heard them I'd probably recognise them.'

'Was Roland Pretorius one of the civilians?'

Brand turned right at the next intersection and accelerated up the hill. He thought a while, remembered a tall man with dark hair, sideburns and a moustache. 'Yes, that's one of them, the South African. How did you know that?'

'He contacted me out of the blue a couple of years ago. He told me he had some information about Gareth's last flight. I checked the squadron history book and the list of members' names I had also obtained – I probably know more about that squadron than some of the men who served in it – and Pretorius's name wasn't on either. I wondered if the man was a con artist who had heard about my searching and was going to string me along with false information. In any case, he never made the meeting; he died in a car accident.'

Now it was Brand's turn to be silent. Pretorius and the Portuguese guy had been company employees, CIA contractors. They were ex-military mercenary pilots who were paid to fly where they were told and not ask questions. Venter had hinted that they, like him, were on the take as well. It would have been convenient for a lot of people for Pretorius to die in a road accident before spilling the beans on those flights out of Angola.

'What was the mission?' Allchurch asked, filling the void of silence. He paid no attention to the journey of seven giraffes browsing the trees at the side of the road.

'That depended on who you were talking to.' Brand turned right at the big four-way stop just outside Skukuza and drove through the gate into the camp and down the road past the clock tower and conference centre to the Cattle Baron restaurant on the river.

'Please don't talk in riddles, Mr Brand – Hudson. This is very important to me.'

It was important to me, too, Brand thought. It had nearly cost him his life, and it had ended his career with the CIA. Still, at least he hadn't lost a child. He felt sorry for Allchurch, but his intelligence background made him wary of sharing secrets with a stranger. 'Officially, which was still unofficial as far as anyone who asked at the time was concerned, we were supposed to be dropping arms and ammunition to a UNITA unit that had got itself cut off and surrounded.'

'UNITA, the anti-communist guerrillas,' Allchurch said.

Brand got out and Allchurch followed him to the riverfront, where they took a table on the deck. 'Yep. The CIA was bank-rolling UNITA, importing weapons and supplying cash to their leader, Jonas Savimbi, to continue the fight against President Dos Santos and FAPLA, the Angolan Army.'

'And we South Africans were at war with Angola because they were supplying bases and aid to SWAPO, the people trying to overthrow South West Africa.'

'Correct,' Brand said.

'You were there with the CIA?'

Again, Brand's initial instinct was to reveal as little as possible. 'I was a captain in the US Army Rangers,' he said truthfully, though leaving out the next step in his career path, his secondment to the CIA. 'I was like the bag man, making sure the money from the Reagan administration bought the right stuff and that it and the cash got to the right people and wasn't siphoned off along the way.'

'Not easy, I imagine,' Allchurch observed as Hudson beckoned a waiter. 'I've done pro bono legal work for some NGOs and I know how international aid can be siphoned off by corrupt parties; I assume it was even harder to keep track of money and weapons.'

Brand ordered a coffee, as did Allchurch. 'You're right,' Brand said, 'but I became more interested in what was coming out of Angola rather than what was going into it.'

'Such as?'

Brand watched some tourists wandering along the pathway and fence that separated the camp from the Sabie River. The house where he lived was on the other side, just a few kilometres up river. The tourists had only just spotted the old bull elephant that was browsing in the reed bed. Brand had seen him as soon as they had approached the cafe, but he hadn't bothered to point out the animal to Allchurch. That was what had nearly got him killed. 'Ivory.'

'Yes, I've heard those stories, that UNITA and even the SADF were poaching wild animals in Angola.'

'The Angolan bigwigs wanted to line their own pockets as well as fund the war effort, and there were some senior South African military people, too, who realised there was a buck – quite a few bucks, in fact – to be made in smuggling stuff out of Angola. Elephant herds were decimated, ditto the rhinos. Tusks and horns were shipped out and sold on the black market, and plenty of diamonds left the country too.'

'Was my son killed flying diamonds out of Angola?'

Brand heard the sense of distress and futility in Allchurch's question. 'Could be.' Venter had bragged about making a fortune from diamond smuggling and Brand had encouraged his boasts, hinting that he was looking for a way to make money on the side as well. Unbeknown to Brand, Venter had taped him using a Walkman, and so had evidence that seemed to prove that Brand was interested in getting in on the racket. The tape later came to light, part of Venter's personal insurance policy. 'But there was more than diamonds on the Dakota your son was flying. There were half a dozen bundles on board, each made up of four wooden crates made for carrying artillery rounds; hundreds of kilograms of stuff. They had parachutes fixed to them, so they were going to be dropped somewhere.'

'But not in Angola?'

Brand waited before answering as the waiter set their coffees down in front of them. 'No, not in Angola. We started across the border from the Caprivi Strip, in Angola, and flew south-west, into what's now Namibia; it was clear from the start that we weren't going to resupply a besieged UNITA outpost with ammo. We landed at Ondangwa air force base in South West – Namibia – and refuelled.'

Allchurch ignored his coffee. 'That's a long way south of the border. Where were you headed after that?'

Brand shrugged. 'That's what I was trying to find out, where all this stuff was destined for. The fact that UNITA and the South African military were smuggling ivory and rhino horn out of Angola was pretty much an open secret, but the vast majority of it went by road, through Rundu, into South West Africa, then South Africa and somewhere beyond. The trade in wildlife products made me sick, but I was more interested in what was on these covert flights flown by freelance pilots, and where they were headed.'

'So you got yourself on one of the flights?' Allchurch asked.

Brand nodded. 'I didn't know it when I boarded the flight in Angola, but I'd been set up from the start. The man whose body was found at that archaeological dig is Jacobus Venter. He was a crewman on the DC-3 Dakota that regularly flew stuff out of Angola. I'd been buddying up to him, trying to find out who was running the smuggling outfit, and he asked me if I wanted to go on a joy ride and help him push some cargo out of the back of the airplane.'

'But why bother investigating in the first place?' Allchurch interrupted. 'You were an American adviser – of some sort – not some international policeman.'

It was a good question, and, in hindsight, Brand wished he'd never begun his unofficial investigation. 'You're right, but I was concerned that there were Americans involved in shipping shit *out* of Angola, not just guns and money into it. These flights flew under the radar, literally. I was curious about where they were headed, as well as what was on board. I was also naïve, a boy scout, and I'd become fascinated by Africa's wildlife. So much of what I found in Angola wasn't right. It was supposed to be one of Reagan's noble crusades against communism. I bought the propaganda bullshit and when I got to Africa I found we were propping up an illegitimate force whose leaders were more intent on making money than winning a war.'

'So your superiors didn't know you were investigating those flights out of Angola?'

Brand gave a little laugh, although it had been anything but funny at the time. 'I believe my *superiors* and some of their counterparts, South African spies, were running the smuggling operation, outside of the regular cross-border smuggling route.'

'So what happened after you landed?'

Brand sipped his coffee. 'We took on fuel at Ondangwa, and another passenger.'

'Who?'

Allchurch was impatient, like a dog going after a bone. 'I don't know. I'd never seen him before; a white guy, South African, in uniform, but no rank or other insignia. Maybe late twenties, early thirties. It was night; I was taking a piss when he boarded the aircraft, at the last minute, and he sat up front with the pilots. I was down the back with Venter so I never really got a good look at the guy's face.'

'And Gareth?'

'One of the pilots, the younger one, I guess it was your son, checked that the cargo was secured OK, but didn't say too much. It was like he was just following orders, not asking too many questions. If he was surprised that we were inside South West Africa and not flying over some drop zone in Angola, then he didn't show it. When I'd first shown up at the strip Venter had a map out and was briefing your son and the other pilot, so *they* knew where we were headed, even if I didn't.'

'What about the other man who boarded the flight in Namibia, what was his role?'

'He was there to kill me.'

Chapter 11

The pilot and co-pilot flew by the light of the moon, their faces illuminated by the dull glow from the plane's instruments. Other than that, no lights showed from the inside or outside of the Dakota.

The man who had boarded the Dakota at Ondangwa stood behind the pilot, one hand resting on the back of the seat. In his other hand he held a nine-millimetre pistol. He was talking to them.

Brand struggled to hear the conversation as he lay on the cold metal deck of the cargo hold, which vibrated beneath him. His head throbbed and he tasted the blood that had run down from the wound in his hair, where he'd been clubbed by the butt of the man's pistol soon after they'd taken off from the air force base in South West Africa.

Through slitted eyes – he was still pretending to be unconscious – Brand saw the man with the pistol turn and wave to attract the attention of the loadmaster. 'Get ready to jettison the baggage,' the man called from the front of the aircraft. Above him, Brand's peripheral vision registered the loadmaster, Jacobus

Venter, giving a thumbs-up to the new guy, who was obviously the most senior man on board.

One of the pilots, the younger one, was glaring back over his shoulder at the newcomer. He'd been shouting at the man before, though Brand had been coming out of his unconsciousness at the time and the pilot's words hadn't registered. The boss man, as Brand had come to think of him, waved his pistol in the young pilot's direction and the man returned his attention to flying the aircraft.

The space between Brand and the cockpit was stuffed with cargo. The six bundles were each surmounted by a cargo parachute and the static lines of the parachutes atop them were drawn and attached to an anchor cable that ran the length of the Dakota's fuselage. It would be hard to navigate a way to the front of the aircraft, and vice versa.

Brand sensed Jacobus Venter looking down at him, and closed his eyes. He lay motionless. He felt a brush as Venter stepped over him, the toecap of his flying boot dragging across Brand's chest. The crewman had moved further aft. Brand risked a glance. Venter was donning a slim-back free-fall parachute, the kind where the wearer had to pull a ripcord to open the canopy, as opposed to the static line parachutes used on the cargo and by paratroopers, which relied on the line fixed to the cable inside the aircraft to deploy the parachute. As a US Army Ranger, Brand was also a qualified paratrooper.

The collapsible troop seats that ran down the interior of either side of the fuselage had been folded and stowed. Stuffed into one of the sections of seating was the khaki-coloured military chest webbing that Venter had been wearing over his aircrew survival vest when he was on the ground in Angola, before they'd taken off. The man wore his personal weapon, a pistol, in a shoulder holster, but Brand could see a wicked-looking hunting knife taped to one shoulder strap of the webbing.

Brand's hands were tied behind his back and his ankles had been bound once he'd been knocked out; he needed to get to that knife.

Venter was moving to the cargo door. It would take him less than a minute to open and secure it, Brand knew. He wouldn't have enough time to get to the chest rig and pull out the knife, so when Venter's back was to him he rolled, instead, until his bound hands could reach a ratchet tie-down device at the base of the rearmost crate. Working by feel, Brand thumbed the release and pulled down on the handle of the tie-down. The aircraft lurched as it hit a pocket of turbulence and the nylon strap that ran through the device instantly became slack.

Freezing air blasted the inside of the Dakota and Brand glimpsed stars in the night sky as the loadmaster secured the door open. Brand rolled, fast, back to the approximate position where he'd been lying. He knew that the door had been opened for one reason: to get rid of him.

As Brand had hoped, when Venter turned back to him the man's eye had immediately been drawn to the loose cargo. The line of crates sat on tracks of roller conveyor, which allowed them to be rolled into and, eventually, out of, the aircraft, when they were dropped to whomever they were intended. Brand still hadn't figured out where or when the cargo would be dropped, but he knew that as he had been left at the aft of the aircraft, the last thing to be loaded, he would be dispatched through the open door first, with no parachute. He had no idea how long he'd been unconscious, so he had no idea where they were.

Venter keyed the switch clipped to the front of his flight suit, no doubt informing the pilot of what had gone wrong. The man with the gun had his back to them; he was still leaning against the pilots' seats, looking out through the cockpit windshield into the night sky. The loadmaster dropped to one knee and heaved on the rear crate, manhandling it back into place on the roller conveyor and pulling on the nylon strap to tighten it once more.

'Hey!' said Brand, loud enough for Venter alone to hear.

Venter's head snapped around. Fortuitously, the aircraft bucked at that precise moment as it hit another pocket of turbulence and the line of crates, still not secured, rolled back against the loadmaster. He couldn't reach his intercom without letting go of the cargo, which lurched and heaved forward again, almost pushing him over. Brand finished the job by rolling onto his back and kicking out with his tied feet, smashing the soles of his army boots into the crewman's face. Blood spurted from Venter's nose as his head snapped back.

It was an all or nothing move and Brand had put every ounce of strength and every scintilla of anger he felt at Venter's betrayal into the force of that kick. He looked down over his feet, waiting to see if the loadmaster moved. If the blow had only stunned the man temporarily then Brand would be finished. He watched and waited two more seconds. Venter was sprawled on the floor of the aircraft. He felt nothing for his victim; Brand had been abandoned by everyone – the South Africans, the Angolans, and his own people, the CIA.

Awkwardly, he rolled onto his belly and then got to his feet by sliding up the inside of the fuselage next to where the loadmaster's gear was stowed. Working by touch in the gloom he managed to unhook a strap that stowed the seating. The crewman's webbing dropped and Brand reached for the knife. He sat down on the canvas sling seat, reversed the knife and began to rub at the rope binding his wrists. He felt pain and wetness as the blade sliced the inside of his forearm; at least the blade was sharp. The man at the front of the aircraft, between the pilots, looked back. Brand lowered his head as he continued to saw his bonds against the knife.

Pain surged into his fingertips as the tight rope finally parted and circulation returned.

Brand then checked the pouches of Venter's chest webbing and found an emergency signal flare. Next he needed to get to Venter and take the loadmaster's pistol. He would retake this aircraft, killing the man up the front and holding the two pilots at gunpoint. As Brand reached for Venter's weapon the explosion of a gunshot filled the cabin with light. A bullet tore at the sleeve of his bush shirt.

'Shit!'

Brand dropped to his belly and as he grabbed Venter's gun, the loadmaster started to come to. Brand punched him in his shattered face. With the man down again Brand raised his hand above the nearest crates and fired back, two shots. He angled his aim high, to miss the pilots. The blind shots didn't work, though, and another bullet zinged dangerously close to him and drilled through the Dakota's thin metal skin. Brand heard angry shouting from the pilots.

'You're dead, Brand. You've got nowhere to go!' the boss man called from the front of the darkened fuselage.

Brand had been suckered. He'd thought he'd won Venter's trust, after nights of drinking with the man, listening to him brag about the money he made on trading diamonds and how many hookers he'd screwed in Joburg, but all the time Venter and the other man they had taken on board, presumably Venter's superior, had been setting him up. He didn't know the identity of the man who was shooting at him, or what the man had told the pilots or how much they knew about this dirty business – they, after all, were late replacements direct from the air force. One thing was for sure: Venter and his boss intended to kill him and dump his body out of the Dakota all along. Brand didn't want to charge the man with the blazing gun for two reasons; one, he didn't want to get shot, and two, he didn't want to kill one or both of the pilots as he would have no chance if the aircraft went into an uncontrolled dive. He'd lost his one advantage, surprise.

Venter came to again and grabbed Brand's gun hand, around the wrist. Brand knew Venter had been ready to push his unconscious body out of the aircraft without a second thought. Likewise, it was pure instinct that now enabled Brand to plunge Venter's own knife up and under the other man's rib cage. Brand twisted, rupturing the lungs and pushing for the heart. Venter's eyes went wide as he tried to speak. The grip on Brand's wrist eased and he felt Venter's blood rush out of him, down over the knife. He pulled the blade out and stabbed Venter again, then rummaged through his vest.

'Now!' the man from the front yelled.

Three more shots tore through the metal around him and, from the noise and the impacts, Brand worked out that they were coming from more than one person. One of the pilots, the elder of the pair, had climbed out of his seat and was also shooting at him. Brand's hand closed around a metal tube, the signal flare. He pulled the cap off one end, reversed it, and slid it onto the other end of the tube.

Brand changed his mind about hurting the pilots. He raised the pistol over a crate and fired a couple more shots, then stuffed the gun down the front of his bush shirt. A bullet splintered the crate he was sheltering behind as he raised his hands again. He slapped the cap at the base of the flare with the palm of his left hand, causing the striker pin inside it to hit the igniter at the base of the tube. Men screamed as the interior of the transport aircraft was filled with smoke and the brilliant red incandescence of the flare. The Dakota lurched. Brand coughed.

Still, though, bullets clanged around him. At least no one forward could see him, thanks to the flare's choking smoke. However, his cover was being rapidly sucked out the open cargo door. Brand grabbed Venter by the shoulders and dragged the loadmaster to the hatch.

The other man's body jerked in his arms and Brand felt a hammer blow on his right thigh. He slumped to the floor of the cabin, unable to stand. His brain dimly registered that he'd been shot, but when he looked down he saw the bullet had gone through the crewman's heart before it had entered his own leg. Clipped to the rear of Brand's safety harness was a tail-like strap about two metres long, with a snap hook at the end of it. Had he been doing the job he'd been co-opted for he would have secured himself to a point in the aircraft so he could stand in the door and safely help the loadmaster dispatch the crates.

Brand unfastened the snap hook and attached it to a buckle on the harness of the parachute Venter wore, another safety precaution for the man's job of seeing paratroopers and cargo out of the hatch and on their way.

Acrid black smoke had replaced the red of the flare. Brand looked up and saw the man from the front bathed in the glow of flames. One of the pilots was doing his best to douse the fire the flare had started with an extinguisher, but he seemed to be losing the battle. The mystery man with the gun seemed to care nothing about the fire or his own safety. He was climbing over the crates, heading to the rear of the aircraft. He raised the pistol in his hand and took aim.

Brand wrapped his arms around the dead loadmaster and, holding him in a bear hug, toppled out the open door of the Dakota.

As they plummeted through the freezing night sky Brand clawed at the blood-covered body, frantically trying to find the parachute's ripcord. He had no idea how high they'd been flying, but he knew he had precious seconds to deploy the parachute. The two of them tumbled, end over end. It had been the desperate move of a man with no options, but he knew he would have died if he'd stayed in the aircraft.

Brand felt metal, then made out the D-shape of the cord's handle. He slipped his fingers, already numb, through the ring and pulled with all his might. For a second he thought it was too late, or the parachute had malfunctioned, but in an instant the loadmaster's body was wrenched from his arms as the canopy deployed, separating them in mid-air.

Brand dropped, and only the buckle he'd attached to the loadmaster's harness stopped him from falling to the ground. He swayed sickeningly, suspended beneath the dead man as the desert below seemed to rush towards him. He'd be lucky if he survived the landing, he thought, especially as there was a good chance the body above him might crush him when they both hit the ground.

He craned his neck and saw a glow in the sky; it was the Dakota, still flying, but it was burning.

*

'I landed hard, knocked myself out again, and Venter's body damn nearly killed me when it landed on me,' Brand said to Allchurch, who sat over his cold cup of coffee on the deck overlooking the river at the Cattle Baron restaurant at Skukuza, his mouth half open.

Allchurch licked his lips and, after a few seconds, seemed to return to the present. 'My son, Gareth, didn't shoot at you?'

It had been dark, a mid-air gunfight had been going on, but Brand was sure he'd remembered the facts correctly. There had been a distinct age difference between the pilots and Allchurch had said his son had only just been commissioned. 'That's right. He stayed at the controls. The senior pilot had drawn his weapon and was shooting at me while your son flew the Dakota. Hell, I didn't blame the guy; I was busting caps and trying to set fire to his aircraft. I knew the only way out for me was out the rear hatch.'

'And Gareth had argued with the man who boarded the plane at Ondangwa?'

Brand nodded. 'Guess he wasn't expecting the mystery man to start beating on one of his crewmen – that is, me.' He saw the conflict crease Allchurch's face. On the one hand, his son may have been a stand-up guy, but on the other the man who was telling him all this, Hudson Brand, had most likely caused the deaths of Gareth and the other two men. 'I'm sorry.'

Allchurch let out a long sigh. 'I don't know what to make of all this. The more I learn, the more questions there are, it seems. How badly damaged was the Dakota?'

Brand shrugged. 'There was a fire on board, but the pilot was going at it with the fire extinguisher after he finished shooting at me. Those DC-3s were tough old birds.'

'How did you make it back to civilisation?' Allchurch asked.

'I'd been shot in the leg, but it was a through-and-through, a flesh wound they call it in the movies. I took my dog tags off and put them around Venter's neck; I figured that if the plane made it back to base they'd cast me as the villain of the piece. I took what I could find from his pockets and survival vest and set off. I walked a few hours through the night using the stars to guide me, but I guess I was still suffering concussion or blood loss because I passed out when I reached a road. I woke up in a military hospital. The last thing I remember was hearing lions calling; guess I was lucky I didn't get eaten.'

'The authorities thought you were Venter?'

Brand nodded. 'Anyhow, I checked myself out before people could start questioning me, and hitchhiked back up north, to the Caprivi Strip. I had friends there I could trust, in 32 Battalion. They were tough dudes, but they were honest, no-nonsense, and I'd shared my suspicions about ivory and rhino horn being smuggled out of Angola with their CO, who was as pissed off about the situation as I was. When I got to their headquarters, Buffalo

Base, they put me up, no questions asked. I contacted the CIA field station in South Africa and they told me I was suspended, pending an investigation into improper conduct. I tried to tell them my side of the story, but they said my superior in Angola had a tape, made by Jacobus Venter, in which I said I wanted in on the diamond smuggling business.'

'You were set up,' Allchurch said.

'Royally. I tried to find out what happened to the Dakota, but the word came back that it had disappeared. An aerial search was mounted from Ondangwa, but turned up nothing. Part of the problem was that no one knew or no one was saying where the aircraft was headed. All they had was its last known refuelling spot. I'm guessing one of my bullets or the flare I fired off took out the radio, otherwise there might have been a mayday call.'

'What happened to you after that?'

'I threatened to go to the press about the CIA's involvement in smuggling diamonds, ivory and rhino horns out of Angola, and the agency threatened to terminate me – kill me – if I did. I backed down and 32 Battalion offered me a slot, on account of me speaking Portuguese.'

Allchurch pushed aside his cold coffee. 'I want you to help me find my son's aircraft, Brand, and to find him.'

Brand sighed. 'Namibia's a big empty country, Mr Allchurch, full of desert. Besides, the Dakota could have crashed into the Atlantic.'

'The Atlantic? What makes you think they were headed to the coast? They weren't going to push prisoners of war out to feed the sharks; you said yourself they had cargo on board.'

Brand had made a slip-up; his mind had been wavering between past and present. Maybe he'd done it intentionally, subconsciously; maybe he, too, wanted to put the flight and the fate of the pilots to rest. 'All of the bundles of boxes that were going to be dropped that night were wrapped in heavy-duty black plastic sheeting, and under that was another layer of waterproof tarpaulin. I had to cut through the two layers with my pocket knife before I got to the boxes. I'd seen cargo dropped out of airplanes in the past, but never wrapped like that. There was no point.'

'Unless someone wanted those bundles to float.'

Brand nodded. 'My theory was that whatever was in those boxes was going to be dropped at sea, or maybe on a beach, and the wrapping was designed to keep them afloat.' He'd given the mission much thought over the years, trying to work out a plausible scenario. 'Also, there were half a dozen self-inflating containerised life rafts on board that Dakota. That's way too much capacity for that type of aircraft, even if it was full of passengers, which it wasn't. I figured that maybe after he'd kicked me out of the airplane, Venter was going to attach those life rafts to each of the loads so that when they hit the water the rafts deployed, helped keep them afloat and made them easier to spot.'

Allchurch took a sip of cold coffee. 'But who would be operating a ship out there to pick up the cargo?'

'I don't know,' Brand said. 'But I've thought about it. Wouldn't have been a South African or a Namibian vessel – if the receiver had been from either of those countries, it would have been far easier to land the aircraft at a remote strip or even on a stretch of road in South West Africa. Whatever was in those bundles was destined for somewhere overseas, out of Africa.'

'Someone who couldn't land a ship in a South West African or South African port?'

Exactly, Brand thought; with his analytical legal mind, Allchurch was coming to the same conclusion he had reached. 'It could have been any nationality, but the Russians were operating off the Angolan coast at the time, bringing in supplies for the Angolans and the Cubans, and operating fishing trawlers and fish factory ships.'

Allchurch pieced together more of the puzzle. 'If the cargo on board the Dakota was destined for a ship, it couldn't have gone through Luanda Harbour as that was controlled by Angolan government forces, and it probably couldn't have flown over the coast of Angola.'

Brand nodded. 'The Cubans had the capital ringed by anti-aircraft missiles and radar sites. A Russian ship, however, could stay in international waters and move to a location south of the Angolan–South West African border, and wait there.'

Allchurch raised his eyebrows. 'An international smuggling conspiracy?'

'Could be. Not all the Russians were dedicated servants of the state and the party. In Afghanistan their military set up a sophisticated operation smuggling heroin out of the country to the west. It's quite possible a Russian sea captain and his crew wanted a slice of what was going on in Angola on dry land.'

'Come with me to Namibia. Help me find my son's aircraft, find my son.'

Whether he subconsciously wanted to or not, Brand knew such a quest would uncover nothing but trouble. 'Namibia's Atlantic coastline is thousands of kilometres long and there are tens of thousands of square kilometres of desert and nothingness between where I fell out of that bird and the ocean. You wouldn't even know where to start looking.'

'No,' Allchurch agreed, 'but you would.'

'What makes you say that?' Brand knew he was not dealing with a dummy. Allchurch had run a successful legal practice; his mind was sharp and he was driven by a force far stronger than anything else known to man: the love of a parent for a child, and the anguish at losing that child.

'Because you have a map.'

'Who says I do?'

'You did. You told me Venter briefed my son and the other

139

pilot from a map, and, later, that you stripped Venter's body of useful equipment. You took the map from the loadmaster's body and you knew that you were going to be set up as the fall guy by the people who were behind the smuggling operation. That map, and whatever Venter had written on it, would corroborate your story that the crew – at least Venter and the usual pilots – were setting off not to supply some Angolan freedom fighters but to deliver a load of valuable cargo to a Russian ship off the coast of Africa.'

Brand was right, Allchurch was smart. 'Say you're right, why would I still have it?'

'You've got that map stored somewhere with anything else that's of great value to you, either in a safe deposit box or at your home, right now. There's a flight leaving for Johannesburg in two hours and a connection to Windhoek an hour after we land at OR Tambo airport. I've booked your tickets, but first we're going to get that map.'

Brand mulled over the facts of the case as he knew them. That aircraft had disappeared, and so, too, had the pilots and the man who had boarded in Ondangwa, who was in on the dirty operation. The other fact was that the tape Venter had left behind had killed Brand's career with the CIA and resulted in his never returning to the country of his birth.

He didn't regret his life, as it had turned out. He no longer thought, as he had briefly back then, that there was any glory or worth in the war he had fought, but he had served alongside some of the best men, black and white, that he had ever met in his life, and he had made life-long friends with many of them. He loved the new South Africa, his adopted homeland, and seeing the continent's wildlife up close every day had restored his faith in God, if not in humanity.

If Allchurch could, however remote the odds, find that aircraft, it would bring, Brand firmly believed, nothing but trouble.

But that trouble would have a name, a shape and a form. The people behind the mass slaughter of wildlife, and the exploitation of dirt-poor Angolans slaving in illegal diamond mines, might just surface again, after nearly thirty years, to claim their loot. And if they did, Hudson Brand would be there. If he could not bring them to lawful justice, he would kill them.

'The map's at the house I'm staying at, about twelve klicks from here. It's in a metal .50-calibre ammunition box, waterproof and fireproof, with my birth certificate and a picture of my mom and my first girlfriend.'

Allchurch smiled. 'You're not just a safari guide, I've learned. You're a tracker, a hunter of people. We're going to find that aircraft, and we're going to find my son.'

The odds were still crazy, but Brand thought that even the act of searching might still flush out his real prey, the man or men who had set him up, and the customers they'd been dealing with out in the icy nothingness of the Atlantic.

'I have to warn you, Mr Allchurch, that if the people who were behind that mission are still alive and they get wind of what we're up to they'll be coming after us. They'll want to find that aircraft just as much as you do, and they'll be prepared to kill to get their hands on it.'

The smile left Allchurch's face. 'Please, call me Matthew. A part of me, most of me, died the day the air force came to tell me my son was missing. I love my wife, more than anything on earth, but until we can finally lay Gareth to rest once and for all or find out what happened to him we're just two people marking time until we die and join him. I don't care if that happens sooner rather than later, and if it happens looking for my boy, then so be it.'

Brand wasn't as ready to die as Allchurch was, but he did feel bad about what had happened to the man's son.

'Hudson, I know my son wasn't killed in action, and that he may very well have died because of what you did up there.

But I want you to know that your story, while upsetting, has been something of a relief for me. You were acting in self-defence and, if you're right, my son behaved in an honourable way. I still need to find the wreckage of the Dakota and, hopefully, Gareth's body, so I can bring him home and give him a Christian burial.'

'Let's go,' Brand said.

Chapter 12

Windhoek was different in many ways from the city she remembered from her youth, but familiar in others.

Sonja realised that part of what she was experiencing was to do with returning to a country that had been conquered – no, liberated was the word, she mentally corrected herself – by the people she had been taught to hate.

She did not, in fact, hate the Herero or the Owambo or the Damara or any of the other peoples of Namibia. As a child she had feared the dire threat of armed SWAPO guerrillas attacking her in her bed but, ironically, when that nightmare became a reality she'd fought back and set in motion a life that would be defined by guns, wars and killing. She didn't hate the pastor from whom she had stolen the Land Rover and, in fact, was feeling a little bad about the way she had treated him. He was a dirty old man, but Sonja realised her concern for Emma had brought out the lioness in her, when she probably could have hitched a lift with the man, easily fending off his advances, and hired a car in Mariental.

Her journey from the red sands of the Kalahari had taken her through the grasslands and rocky kopjes that sprang up north of Rehoboth, then finally through the pass between the Khomas Hochland and the Auas mountains. After several hours of driving she had finally seen the city – not really more than a large town by world standards – sitting familiarly in a natural bowl of hills. A sign to 'Heroes Acre' pointed to the right. The monument was a daily reminder that Namibia had won her freedom through blood. There were no monuments for the losers, and Sonja had read online a few months ago that even the old statue of The Rider, a mounted member of the colonial *Schutztruppe* cast to commemorate those German soldiers who had fallen in battle against the Herero and Nama at the beginning of the twentieth century, had been unceremoniously relocated from outside the front of the *Alte Feste*, Windhoek's Old Fort.

New housing developments cascaded down the hills and there were more tall buildings but, again, even these were modest by the standards of other world capitals. The main road into town, which had been called Kaiserstrasse in her day, had been renamed Independence Avenue. She followed it until she came to the street formerly known as Harold Pupkewitz, and turned into what was now known as Nelson Mandela Avenue.

There were plenty of bed and breakfast places to choose from in the suburb of Klein Windhoek, which had once been a whites-only neighbourhood and even now seemed reserved for those with money and status, regardless of colour. Sonja buzzed the intercom at the security gate of a place on the corner of Barella and Nelson Mandela streets and the gates opened. A woman told her there was a room free and Sonja checked in. The place was tranquil, with nice gardens and a pool. Half a dozen vehicles spoke of travelling salespeople and overland tourists. She parked the Land Rover next to her room, took her pack and Lotz's cooler box inside and flopped down on the bed.

Sonja was filthy and needed a shower, but she grabbed the remote for the TV and turned it on. Then she took out her satellite phone, opened the balcony door and placed the phone on the outside table. She went back inside, but as soon as the phone acquired enough satellites for a connection it beeped, signalling a message. Sonja went straight out and checked the phone.

'Hell,' she said. There was a message from a friend of Emma's. Her daughter was fine and wanted nothing more than some information on a military uniform found on a body she had dug up on her archaeological dig. Sonja didn't know whether to laugh or to scream. She had broken several laws to get into the country and to travel this far, and now it seemed she could have stayed in South Africa.

She felt foolish. She couldn't tell Emma she had been worried sick about her. Instead, she sent a short return message. *Tell Emma I love her and have crossed into Namibia. Will travel to her dig site and see her in three days. Please ask her to contact me.*

Inside the room, she saw that the local Namibian Broadcasting Corporation news had started. She sat down on the bed and unlaced her boots, wrinkling her nose at the smell of her socks. She stopped peeling them off, however, when the announcer mentioned something about two Chinese nationals being arrested at Windhoek's airport for attempting to smuggle fourteen rhino horns out of the country.

Sonja turned up the volume.

'*The men, who appeared in court today, were denied bail. They were charged with possession of fourteen rhino horns,*' said the announcer. '*Save the Rhino Trust manager, Stirling Smith, in Windhoek today for an international conference on rhino conservation, told NBC the seizure, while welcome, raised some serious questions.*'

Stirling's face appeared on the screen. '*The interesting thing about this arrest is that there haven't been fourteen rhinos poached in Namibia in the last couple of years,*' Stirling said. '*It's possible this haul came from a stockpile somewhere, perhaps of privately owned rhinos that had died or been dehorned in the past. It's a real mystery.'*

The announcer wrapped up the story, giving the police's estimate of the street value of the seized horns in Vietnam, where the Chinese men had been destined for; Sonja whistled through her teeth when she converted the Namibian dollar value to one and a half million US dollars.

She needed a drink, but first she needed to shower. When she was finished in the bathroom she put on clean underwear and her shorts, brushing the worst of the dust from them, and her spare shirt and sandals. She took the Glock with her, left her room and used the remote control to open the security gate.

Joe's Beerhouse always came up in conversation when people talked about nightlife in Namibia, and Sonja had passed the place on Nelson Mandela earlier when she'd been looking for somewhere to stay. Due to Windhoek's elevation it was chilly outside, but Sonja had long ago learned to ignore the elements unless she was at risk of exposure or dehydration. Joe's didn't look like much from the street, just a cement slab wall topped with razor wire in a semi-industrial neighbourhood, but as she walked through the car park and inside, a tourist's oasis revealed itself.

Eclectic didn't do justice to the selection of antiques, bric-a-brac, street signs, colonial memorabilia, African objets d'art and plain old junk that cluttered just about every free inch of wall and ceiling space and much of the floor of Joe's. Not so much a bar as a collection of bars all rambling off a central pebbled walkway, the place was already filling fast even though it had only just gone six o'clock.

The maître d' stopped Sonja and asked if she could help.

'Table for one.'

'Do you have a booking, ma'am?' the woman asked.

'No, sorry.'

The woman sucked air in through her teeth. 'We're very full. I can see if I can find you a seat at a long table, will that be fine?'

Sonja shrugged. She didn't want to converse with strangers, but she had to eat something. 'Sure, I'll wait at that bar over there.'

The clientele spoke a variety of European languages and some American English. Apart from a few local businessmen in short-sleeved shirts and chinos the dress of the day seemed to be safari chic; Sonja eased her way through a sea of khaki. She took a seat at a polished wooden bar, only noticing as she lowered herself that she was actually sitting on a toilet seat stuck to the top of a stool. She shook her head and ordered a half-litre of draught beer.

Sonja swivelled on her toilet seat, looked behind her and saw the face of the man she had been watching on television not half an hour ago, the man she had once thought she would spend the rest of her life with.

He had seen her; he stood up and walked towards her.

'Sonja? It is you. Sonn. My God.' He lowered his voice. 'What are you doing here? I can't believe they let you into the country.'

Sonja took a long sip of the beer the barman handed her. She wasn't feeling up to facing her past just yet. She was saved by the return of the woman who was going to show her to her table.

'I'm going to eat. Alone.' Sonja hopped off her stool and followed the waitress to an area cordoned off with clear plastic sheeting from the outdoor bar area. A fire blazed and Sonja took her seat at the end of a long wooden table set for about twenty. The group hadn't arrived yet. She picked up the menu, doing her best to ignore Stirling, but he had followed her.

He pulled out the chair in front of Sonja and sat down. 'Aren't you at least going to say hello?'

Sonja pretended to study the menu, and eventually looked over the top of it. 'The last time we saw each other you left me high and dry in the Caprivi. Good people were killed.'

Stirling looked around, as though, Sonja thought, he expected her to be under surveillance. 'You started a *war* in a peaceful country for nothing.'

'Well, that depends on who you talk to.'

Stirling sagged back in his chair. A waitress came and asked them if they wanted more drinks; Sonja ordered a brandy and Coke and Stirling asked for the same. Funny, she thought, he'd never drunk spirits when they were teenagers, only the occasional beer. He ran a hand through his hair, still thick, she noticed. 'I was sorry to hear about Sam, really.'

Sonja gritted her teeth. He didn't have the right to even mention Sam's name and her anger was only tempered by the wave of sadness that rose up again. All she could do was nod.

'He was a good man.'

'You don't have to tell me that,' she hissed.

Stirling, wisely, did not reply, but she was still in no mood to talk to him, no matter how many memories came flooding back of their childhood and youth. They had played together as children, his family managing a lodge and her father working there as the maintenance man. All he'd wanted to be when they were small was a safari guide and all she'd wanted at one point, until she reached the age of nineteen and realised she needed to get out of Botswana and see more of the world, was to be Mrs Stirling Smith. He was now living his dream and her life had been a series of bloody nightmares in the world's great shitholes. She had, Sonja conceded, found the excitement she had been looking for, but it had come at a cost.

'What are you doing here?' he said, trying to change the subject. 'Planning a coup?'

She almost laughed. He could still disarm her, and she didn't like that. She worked hard to stay annoyed at him. 'If you must know, I've come to visit my daughter.'

'Emma?'

'I haven't had another.'

'What's she doing here, training the Namibian Defence Force how to water-board people?'

'You're very funny, you know that, Stirling? No,' she added with a touch of parental pride, 'she's at university, studying archaeology, high distinctions every year.'

The waitress came with their drinks, and the tour group noisily speaking French started taking their seats. Sonja polished off the last of her existing beer and handed the glass to the waitress. The booze was helping her keep her emotions in check around Stirling.

'You must be proud of her.'

'I am,' Sonja said, 'proud she didn't end up like me.'

'I think that hurt me most, you know,' Stirling said, 'when we met up last time and I found out you'd had a child. It was what I wanted most for us, when we were younger – for you to stay in Botswana and for us to make a family.'

'For God's sake, Stirling, man-up, you sound like a girl.'

He smiled sadly. 'You're still in touch with your emotions, I see.'

She did not need her old boyfriend psychoanalysing her, so she decided to change the conversation again. 'I saw you on television, just now.'

'I did a couple of interviews today,' he said. 'Rhino poaching's getting out of hand in South Africa and it looks like it's spreading to Namibia, although they've had a pretty good record so far.'

Sonja remembered seeing rhinos in the delta when they were growing up, but more and more often Stirling's father, and sometimes Hans, her father, were called out by rangers to inspect the carcasses of slain animals. All the rhino in the Okavango Delta had eventually been wiped out, and those few that were there today, she knew, had been imported from South Africa.

'We've had another day today of lecturing each other and sitting around tables trying to work out a solution to the problem, but we just keep moving in circles. It's hard to work out the best course of action.'

Sonja knew the best course of action, and she had planned it and executed it. Tran Van Ngo was dead and buried, one less cashed-up kingpin to finance the poachers in Mozambique who were slaughtering rhinos in the Kruger and other national parks and private reserves. Sonja wasn't under any illusion that her actions would stop the rhino trade, but they might slow it a little. It was a war, and like any other war the way to win was to take the fight to the enemy, ruthlessly, and to cut the head off the snake, as the Americans used to say in Iraq.

'What are you thinking?' he pressed her.

She realised she'd been lost in her thoughts. Sonja couldn't tell Stirling about what she'd done in Vietnam – he might sell her out to Interpol, she mused, half seriously. Stirling liked picking good causes, but he lacked the guts or the balls to do the dirty work.

'I was thinking that I don't ever want to think about rhinos or rhino poachers again.'

Stirling took a breath, then a sip of his drink. He grimaced, and she could tell he had only ordered the drink to try and impress her, or to find some common ground with her. 'I really am sorry about Sam. I know I didn't like him when I met him in Botswana, but he genuinely cared for wildlife and, in an odd way, his death did a lot of good. It focused attention in the US, if only for a short time, on the challenges we're facing in Africa to protect the rhino, and it resulted in a huge increase in funding for a number of anti-poaching projects.'

Sonja felt like stabbing him in the heart for the remarks he'd just made. 'There was no sense in his death, and nothing good came of it. There's no cause worth dying for, believe me.'

Stirling had always backed down on the few occasions they had argued when they were young lovers in Botswana. He hadn't fought for her when she'd left Botswana for England. As a result, his response surprised her.

'That's bullshit, Sonja, and you know it. Are you playing the hardcore mercenary now? Are you going to tell me money is the only thing worth taking up arms for?'

She was tired of this argument; it was one she'd fought back and forth on both sides in her own mind over the past twenty years. The wars she had been embroiled in had been over things that meant nothing to her – religion, oil, diamonds, more religion. 'I don't even think the money's worth it any more.'

Stirling leaned back in his seat and raised his eyebrows. 'Too much competition these days, eh? Too many ex-GIs and SAS guys going down the private military company route? You being undercut, Sonn?'

'Don't mock me. But, for what it's worth, you're right. Besides, I've realised there are some things more important than money.'

'Hallelujah.' Stirling threw his hands up in the air. 'Sonja Kurtz joins the human race, at last.'

She felt like a cornered animal. Her instinct was to lash out, to attack, to go on the offensive. 'Get fucked, Stirling.'

The French woman seated next to her muttered something in disgust. Sonja couldn't have cared less. Stirling reached out across the table now, for her hands, but she withdrew them. After a second she realised she had picked up the knife from the table, a reflex action. Embarrassed, she replaced it, worried Stirling might think she was a nut case. *You are a nut case*, she reminded herself. Still, she didn't want him touching her, for a number of reasons.

'Sorry,' he said, and placed his hands palms down on the table. 'All I meant was that Sam's death did bring the rhino problem into sharper focus and sparked a huge outpouring of support, financial as well as moral, for people putting their lives on the line to save the rhino.'

'It still wasn't worth it,' she said.

'You'd die for Emma, right?'

Sonja exhaled. 'Of course.'

'There you go, some things are worth fighting for.'

It was still a stupid argument, she thought. An increase in donations from well-meaning animal lovers in America and other countries where Sam's documentaries were shown on TV was not worth the loss of his life and the knife that had been stuck in her heart. Stirling was probably right, though: if Sam had truly known the risks associated with filming a night anti-poaching patrol, instead of blithely ignoring them as he had, he still would have gone.

But that was not reality. In the real world, in Sonja's world, people went to war for stupid reasons and they got shot and killed and at the end of the day it made no difference at all. Yes, she would put herself in front of a bullet or a speeding car or a charging lion to save her daughter, but beyond that there was nothing on this earth 'worth' dying for.

'What are your plans while you're in Namibia?'

She tried to focus on the question instead of on Sam's smile and the smell of that cologne with the gay-sounding name he'd insisted on wearing. 'Plans? I don't have any plans, Stirling. I'm not a tourist. I'm going to see my daughter sometime in the next few days.'

He reached into his pocket and pulled out a business card which he slid across the table to her side. 'I'm sure she'll be happy to see you. Here, take this, call me if you're heading to the Palmwag area. It's spectacularly beautiful country and I'd love to show you some of it.'

Sonja was almost going to throw the card back at him. She decided she'd been churlish enough, but she still didn't want to play nice.

'Maybe. I'm leaving. See you round.' Sonja got up.

'Sonja?'

She didn't turn; she walked into the courtyard of Joe's and then out of the crowded bar full of happy, laughing people.

PART 2
DEATH

Huis kind had survived war and drought, and miraculously they still roamed the desert.

He had been kicked out of his small family as soon as he reached maturity, when his golden hair had bristled into a mohawk, but now he carried a full mane, a luscious deep russet with black hair lining his chest. He was a male in his prime.

He had mated, and now he was hungry. The prides were small here, just two females, sisters. If they had cubs already, they had hidden them somewhere so that he wouldn't kill any young ones he hadn't sired. It was brutal, but it was their way of keeping their blood lines pure, of surviving.

Ahead, on the wind, he heard the clanking of goat bells, smelled the little creatures.

The last thing he should do was risk his life for the tiny meal of a goat. Nonetheless his hunter's instinct carried him on, listening for the bell and the bleating.

He came to them on dusk and watched the goats and the small boys who tended them. It was dangerous, but to not eat out here was to die. He was in luck. Beyond the goats, he made out the braying bulk of a donkey.

Around his neck was an orange collar. He shook his head and felt its ever-present, slightly annoying weight. At least it gave him a neck rub.

He eyed the fence and picked the best place to jump it. He crouched, then darted to the fence and cleared it in one bound. The goats scattered in panicked terror as he cornered the donkey. He went for its throat and clamped his jaws. Blood spurted.

Before he could feast, though, he heard the roar of an engine and the night was suddenly lit up. A vehicle arrived and caught him in its headlights.

Too late, he realised, the *kraal* and the boys were a trap. A man in the back of the vehicle pulled the trigger. Darkness descended.

Chapter 13

Emma scratched at the dry earth with a trowel while Alex, who had just arrived back at the dig site, stood watching her. 'Who is this guy your professor has gone to collect, anyway?' Alex asked.

Emma straightened her back, took off her hat and wiped the sweat from her brow. 'I don't know. His name is Andre Horsman or something, but all the prof would say beyond that was that he's a retired South African Air Force guy who contacted Sutton saying he knew who Harry was.'

'Interesting,' Alex conceded. 'But how did he get in touch with your professor out here in the middle of nowhere?'

Emma had asked the same question of Professor Sutton. 'Turns out he's a major shareholder in the mining company that we're all contracted to, for the archaeological survey. He pulled some strings and the mining company sent someone out to the dig site to tell Sutton he'd better talk to this guy.'

Alex nodded to the portable gazebo, under which Natangwe sat, reading a book. 'How come you're the only one working?'

Emma shrugged. 'Crazy, I guess. Sutton said that as long

as I didn't disturb the crime scene, where Harry was found, I could poke around a bit more if I wanted to. Natangwe's sulking.'

'Is he still in trouble for letting out the news about Harry?'

'Yes,' Emma said. 'Sutton was furious with him. He even confiscated Natangwe's phone so he couldn't tell anyone else. Not that there's even a signal here. Natangwe called Sutton a racist, and Sutton threatened to have him expelled from university. Natangwe's always spoiling for an argument and Sutton's a stubborn old man.'

Alex plucked a stray spear of yellow grass and chewed on the end of it. Emma went back to digging. It was pointless, she thought, but as tortuous as the work was she had found she had become addicted to it. The excitement of discovering Harry did not make her want to rest on her laurels, it made her want to keep scraping and sifting at the dirt to see what other treasures or sorrows the African earth might reveal.

'I can't stay, Emma. I have to head west, towards the Skeleton Coast. Something has come up. When I sent your message to your mother from Okaukuejo, I received some bad news.'

Emma stood and saw the concern creasing his face. 'How bad?'

'XLR 501 has stopped moving.'

'That sounds like a car or a spaceship or something,' she said. Her lame attempt at lightening his mood failed. 'XLR 501 is one of our collared desert lions. He's the dominant male of a couple of small prides. When his GPS collar does not record a change of position after twenty-four hours I get an SMS. It usually means an animal is dead. There are no other males in his area, so I'm worried he's been shot by a farmer. This could be a disaster for the desert lions.'

'Oh my God, Alex, I'm so sorry. I didn't mean to joke about it.'

He ran a hand through his thick blond hair. 'It's not your fault, Emma. I'm sorry, but I must go.'

She'd heard it said, on campus, that the zoology students who went into the field to research wildlife often looked like the animals they were studying. Alex was leonine, in a way, with his wavy hair, but his body was lithe and wiry, like a cheetah's. Alex got into his truck, started the engine and roared off, leaving a cloud of dust in his wake. Emma walked over to where Natangwe was sitting. She had left her water bottle next to Alex's in the shade to stop it heating up, and took a long swig.

'We're not going to find the remains of any Ndonga here,' Natangwe said, putting his book down on his knees.

'How do you know, if we don't look?'

He shrugged. 'It just doesn't make sense that there would have been a village here, even back in the 1900s.'

'The professor thought it was worth looking,' Emma said. She thought it odd to be fighting the irascible academic's corner, but she liked a good debate and was happy that Natangwe was at least talking.

'The Owambo, of which the Ndonga are part of, aren't nomadic people. They settle where there's water and pasture. There's no evidence of a permanent river for miles around here. Sutton was relying on some half-remembered oral histories, or maybe he decided to do the dig here precisely so we *wouldn't* find anything.'

Emma thought Sutton was many things, but corruptible wasn't one of them. 'Seriously, you think he'd take money to turn up a nil result?'

Natangwe shrugged. 'I don't know. Maybe I'm being too hard on him. All I know is that the sooner I can get off this dig and onto something of real significance, the better. So where did your boyfriend go in such a big hurry?'

'He's not my boyfriend. It's terrible; he just heard that one of the desert lions he's been researching has possibly been shot by a farmer. How could someone do something so thoughtless?'

Natangwe closed his book. 'That's a typical western response to human–wildlife conflict. You're automatically assuming the farmer has done something wrong.'

'Well, if he's killed an endangered lion then that's wrong.'

'What about the farmer's cattle, or sheep or goats? They're worth money.'

'You can't compare the worth of a goat to a lion,' Emma said. 'And by the way, Alex isn't my boyfriend.'

'Your people, the Germans, cleared the lions and other big game from the fertile plains of Herero land, yet you cry foul when an African farmer tries to protect his flocks, or even his family, by killing a predator.'

'Do you believe all the lions should be shot at then?'

'No, that's not what I'm saying,' Natangwe said, 'just that you have to see both sides of the story. It's cool that the desert lions are coming back from the brink of extinction, but the very thing that nearly caused them to be wiped out in the first place is happening again; the reason they were all shot in the past was that they were raiding cattle – white people's cattle in most cases. Now when an African farmer kills a lion you western liberals think he's evil or backward or uneducated.'

Emma sat down in an empty camping chair in the shade. She was hot and tired and wondered whether it had been a good idea to strike up a conversation with Natangwe after all.

'Anyway,' he said, 'isn't that why we're here, to try and shed light on conflicts of the past and hopefully learn from them?'

'I guess,' said Emma.

They both heard a far-off engine at the same time and looked up to find an approaching cloud of dust. It was Professor Sutton's Land Cruiser. They got up to meet him when the vehicle pulled up. There was another man with him of about the same age, perhaps late fifties or early sixties, and a much younger guy, who smiled at her as soon as he climbed out of the vehicle.

Emma felt suddenly self-conscious, all sweaty and covered in dust. The man who had caught her eye had dark hair, thick but cut short, finely chiselled features and she could see from the way his T-shirt clung to his body that he was ripped to shreds. He wore an elephant-hair bracelet and what looked like a very expensive diving watch.

'Emma, Natangwe, this is Mr Andre Horsman, from Cape Town, and his nephew . . . sorry . . .'

'No problem, Professor,' said the man, looking straight at Emma, 'Sebastian Lord.'

'Sorry, yes, Sebastian,' Dorset said. 'He and Andre just flew into Ondangwa today on Andre's private plane.'

'Howzit,' Horsman said to both of them, and shook their hands.

'Andre's got some information about our mystery man and how he got to be here. I'll put the kettle on while he explains.' Sutton opened the back of his vehicle and took out a gas bottle and cooker and a battered black kettle.

Horsman cleared his throat. 'I served in the air force, near here at Ondangwa, during the war. The man you found was on board a transport aircraft, a DC-3 Dakota, that went missing on a resupply mission in 1987. We don't know exactly what happened on the flight but finding the body here gives us another piece of the puzzle. From what Professor Sutton's told me about the state of the body you found we've surmised that the man was able to parachute out, which would seem to indicate some sort of problem on board – either that, or he accidentally fell out, which seems less likely. While he probably survived the jump, given what the professor told me about the state of the body, we think he was then killed – stabbed, according to Professor Sutton – by insurgents.'

'Freedom fighters, you mean,' Natangwe said.

'Have you told the police all this?' Emma asked.

TONY PARK

Dorset poured boiling water into three mugs. 'We went to see the police at Ondangwa. They're going to get their own forensic people to examine Harry, but they seem to think Mr Horsman's theory is sound.'

'Please, call me Andre,' Horsman said, and thanked Sutton for his coffee. 'I was in charge of the search and rescue operation that looked for our missing aircraft and it's pained me ever since that we didn't find any trace of the Dakota or the men on board her. You finding this body, and now learning what happened to him, makes my sense of failure even more acute. If we'd tried harder or, more importantly, if we'd been looking in the right place, we might have found him in time to save him, and found the aircraft, even if it was wreckage.'

'What do you mean "if you'd been looking in the right place"?' Natangwe asked.

Horsman nodded. 'The flight plan for the Dakota's last mission would have seen it heading northwest of Ondangwa, towards Angola, yet here we are south of the airbase, on the edge of Etosha National Park, which is very strange.'

'We've found out that some local people reported seeing what looked like an aircraft on fire, heading west from here, back in 1987,' Emma said.

'Yes, your professor told me,' Horsman said, 'which is precisely why I'm here. I want to start the search for the missing aircraft again, now that we have a starting point – here where Hudson Brand met his fate.'

'You'd need an aeroplane to do that,' Emma said.

'Well, as Dorset pointed out, I've got one,' Horsman replied. 'I flew to Ondangwa myself, in my twin-engine Beechcraft. I'm ready to start looking now, as soon as my aircraft's refuelled.'

'Would there be anything left of an aircraft after thirty years?' Natangwe asked.

Emma interjected. 'Yes, quite possibly. We studied the discovery and recovery of the *Lady Be Good* at university.'

'What's that?' said Natangwe.

'An American B-24 Liberator bomber,' Dorset said. 'It got lost in a sandstorm over Libya during the Second World War. The crew bailed out when it ran out of fuel and the bomber flew on for a little further and crash-landed. It was remarkably well preserved by the desert conditions, not dissimilar to those in Namibia, if Andre's Dakota crashed between here and the Skeleton Coast. The machine guns on the *Lady Be Good* were still serviceable and when the wreckage was inspected, decades after the crash, a thermos was found on board and the tea inside it was still drinkable.'

'Surely it would be like looking for a needle in a haystack,' Emma said. 'You've only got a vague report that it flew west of here.'

'You're right, of course,' Horsman conceded.

'But that's where you – we – come in,' Professor Sutton said. 'Mr Horsman – Andre – needs some extra eyes to help with his search. He wants us to fly with him and Sebastian, to help scan the desert for the missing aircraft.'

'Wow.' Emma turned to Natangwe. 'Isn't that awesome?'

Natangwe frowned. 'Professor, are we not supposed to be looking for victims of the genocide?'

Dorset folded his arms and regarded Natangwe. 'It looked to me, Mr Heita, as though you were sitting in the shade reading, rather than looking for heroes past.'

'I was waiting for some direction from you,' Natangwe said defiantly.

'Well, now that we have found a body from recent times we should stop digging and wait for the police to investigate. In any case, our time here was only ever going to be brief, as our budget was limited. You look surprised, Natangwe. Are you?'

'So this was just about window dressing for a mining company,' Natangwe said.

Emma felt a little cheated, although she countered her lesson in real-world cynicism with the knowledge that they – she, in fact – had unearthed a modern-day archaeological mystery and what seemed like a valuable clue in the puzzle that might just locate a missing aircraft. She couldn't understand why Natangwe wasn't as excited as she.

'I think it might be better if we went back to the university,' Natangwe said.

'Speak for yourself,' Emma countered. 'Sure, I'm disappointed we didn't find what we came for, but isn't unearthing the remains of a man missing for decades and giving his family some closure just as important?'

'Natangwe,' Professor Sutton said, 'I intend on taking Andre up on this new project. If we find this missing aircraft it will be worldwide news – well, at least Africa-wide – and it could very well turn out to be one of the most important archaeological finds in Namibia. If you'd rather go back to varsity then I'm sure we can drop you somewhere on the main road and you can hitch-hike or get a bus back to Windhoek. Emma, are you coming with us?'

'Absolutely! One thing, though, Prof, I'll need to call my mother as soon as we get signal to let her know where we're going. She's on her way here.'

'Who knows where our search might take us?' Horsman said. 'However, why don't you just tell your mother to meet you at, say, Namutoni Camp in Etosha in a few days? I can drop you there at the appointed time. If we haven't found the aircraft then you can decide at that point whether to leave with your mother, or stay with the search. She might even want to join us.'

'Cool,' Emma said, then looked at Natangwe again. '*Please*, Natangwe, stay with us. It'll be awesome.'

'So you said. I'm still not sure.'

Sebastian, who had remained quiet so far, took a step closer to Emma, but directed his words to Natangwe. 'There are families in South Africa who have no idea what happened to their loved ones on that flight. My uncle's been talking about finding this Dakota ever since I was a kid. Please, it would mean a great deal if you could help us.'

Natangwe frowned.

Emma detected a slight scent of cologne on Sebastian. She had never dated a guy who wore a scent, but she loved the smell of this man. 'So, where do you fit in with the mining company?' she asked him.

He looked at her and smiled, his teeth even and white. 'Nowhere. I'm in my uncle's business, import–export. I look after a lot of his overseas work, travelling to factories in Asia, checking on our Australian operations, going to design fairs and trade shows in Europe and America, that sort of thing. He's a big shareholder in the mining company and I'm just kind of tagging along.'

'Nice work,' Emma said.

Sebastian laughed. 'It's a living. I studied law at university but I've found business far more interesting. Andre's company is rapidly growing. I give him some limited legal advice, but I love the travel. I think what you're doing, though, is fascinating.'

Emma heard a far-off drone and turned around to the north, shielding her eyes as she peered through the heat haze. 'Dust trail from a vehicle. All of a sudden it's like Grand Central Station here.'

Dorset frowned. 'Well, whoever it is they shouldn't be here.'

Natangwe looked at the approaching speck. 'It's Alex.'

'He left not long before you arrived,' Emma said to Dorset. 'One of his lions has probably been killed by a farmer.'

'They're not *his* lions,' Natangwe said. 'They belong to the people of Namibia.'

'Quite,' said Dorset.

'Time is wasting,' Horsman said. 'Shall we get moving?'

'Wait,' Emma countered. 'I have to see what Alex wants, it must be important for him to come back.'

Horsman checked his watch and looked at Sutton, who shrugged his shoulders. Alex's truck took shape and Emma broke away from the men to greet him. 'What's up?' she asked as he opened the door.

Alex got down from the driver's seat and looked past her to the men. 'That's Sutton's mystery man – or men?'

She nodded. 'They want to take us flying, over the desert, to look for Harry's aeroplane.'

'I've just come back to pack up.' He walked back to his truck and opened the door.

She went to him and put her hand on his arm. 'I've got an idea. The collar on your lion, it's a GPS collar, right, not a radio collar?'

'Yes.'

'So you know, more or less, where the lion is, right?'

'Yes, I know where he is, or to be more precise, where his collar is. Sometimes a farmer will kill a lion then take the collar somewhere else and burn it, or try to make it look like the collar fell off. I'm actually more worried about the females in his area. There is a small pride of two lionesses with two cubs. XLR 501 was near them. I need to know if those females are all right, but they are not collared. The collar that stopped moving is several hundred kilometres away. I want to get there before nightfall.'

'All right, wait here. Don't leave just yet.' Emma walked over to the two older men. 'Professor, Andre, Alex has a problem. He needs to get to the last known location of the lion as soon as possible, and to check on another pride.'

'Andre is looking for an aeroplane, Emma, not lions.'

Horsman raised his eyebrows. 'Emma, does Alex know that you're leaving with us now and what we're looking for?'

Emma nodded. 'I just told him. He could help us look for the Dakota, as well. He spends all his time in the bush and his eyesight is amazing.'

Horsman rubbed his chin and looked to Sutton. 'What do you think?'

'I think it's a great idea,' Sebastian said.

Dorset looked back towards Alex. 'I suppose it's the right thing to do.'

Emma returned to Alex and recounted her conversation with the men. He wasn't as excited as she'd hoped. 'Emma, all my equipment is in my truck. If I fly over the pride and they're out in the desert we most likely will not be able to land and there will be nothing I can do for them.'

'No,' she agreed, 'but at least you'll know where they are and if they are OK?'

Alex shrugged his shoulders, but agreed to come. Emma found herself hoping it was partly because he wanted to stay in her company.

*

Sonja woke, hungover again, and ate a full cooked breakfast at the B&B in Klein Windhoek where she had spent the night. She settled her bill and loaded her meagre belongings into the pastor's Land Rover.

'Where to next?' she asked herself out loud as she started the engine. Her question was as pertinent to her life at the moment as it was to the journey ahead. She had no idea what she would do with herself. She didn't have to go back to work as a military contractor, but nor could she see herself whiling away her days and years as a Beverly Hills widow. The thought of moving to Scotland didn't appeal to her either. She would have loved to be near her daughter and spend more time with her, but even though their relationship was stronger than it ever had been, she knew enough about young women to realise that the last thing a university student needed was her mother hanging around. Also, she'd had enough of windswept, rainy moors and freezing weather in her brief time with the British Army; the rest of her career had been spent fighting wars in warmer climes.

Sonja had toyed with the idea of setting up her own contracting business, but with the coalition forces pulling the plug on Afghanistan there was a reduced demand and an over-supply of ex-soldiers. Iraq was looking promising again with the rise of Islamic State, but the redeployment of troops from the west had been minimal so far. She quite liked the idea of Kenya – Al-Shabaab was a threat and the beaches were nice. However, she simply couldn't muster much enthusiasm for any of them. But her current concern was more immediate. Emma was fine, and now Sonja had a few days to kill.

Sonja turned on the heater in the truck – it was chilly here in the capital – and switched on the radio. A Hitradio Namibia announcer was giving the national weather forecast, in German. The seaside town of Swakopmund was going to reach an unseasonal twenty-nine today.

She put the car in gear and waited as the B&B's manager opened the security gates with a remote control. 'Swakopmund it is,' Sonja said to herself as she rolled out onto Barella Street then turned right into Nelson Mandela Avenue.

Sonja drove through Katutura, which had been the official location for the black people of Windhoek, segregated from the whites who lived in more upmarket suburbs such as Klein Windhoek. Katutura itself had been divided into different areas for different tribes; Herero on one side of the road, Owambo on the other, and Nama in another location. The mechanics of the apartheid system, which had filtered across into South West Africa, seemed absurd when viewed through the prism of time, but as a child she had thought it all perfectly normal.

Clear of the city the smooth tar road took her north towards the town of her birth, Okahandja. An uneasiness, like indigestion, grew in her with each passing kilometre. On the one hand she wanted to see how the town had changed – what was the same, and if any of the precious few pleasant memories of her childhood could be rekindled – and on the other, she dreaded it.

If Sonja had one guiding motivator or a creed in her life it was her desire – her need – to move forward. It was like the first time she'd been in an ambush, in Sierra Leone: her army training had overcome the instinctive need to run away; instead she had charged into the barrage of rebel fire and broken through their lines. To dither or to turn one's back was to present more of a target; to push on, to drive through the fire was to get past it, and either move on, literally, or turn and fight on one's own terms. As she left the hills of the city for the open, grassy plains and farms of her childhood she realised that was why she was finding it so incredibly hard to get over Sam – for the first time in her life she seemed incapable of fighting through the sorrow and the pain and moving on. She was stuck in the purgatory of here and now. Her drinking was what they called in the army a 'combat indicator' of a problem – that, and all the other fucked-up shit she'd been doing lately.

But how to move on? She had been alone before Sam, and content to find sex when and if she needed it on a casual basis, or to take matters into her own hands, so why should it be so impossible for her to move on from Sam, to lay him to rest, and to return to that same state?

Why? She knew the answer; it was because she was not the person she had been before she met Sam Chapman – she was half that woman. She was like any of the many soldiers she'd known in Afghanistan who had lost a limb, or two, to an IED. They spoke of the pain of a phantom limb, still feeling the missing arm or leg when they closed their eyes, but the illusion of the physical presence was compounded and tortured by a feeling of agonising, twisted pain. That's how her heart felt.

A road sign said Okahandja was ten kilometres further down the road. Her family's farm was on the other side of the town, heading north, and her route would take her to the west. She didn't mind that she wouldn't be passing the farm and even if she had, she would not have turned off on the gravel road that led to the house where she had grown up.

The place held few fond memories for her. There were some, of course – riding her horse with her father alongside her, camping in the bush with him and him teaching her about tracking. The war had put an end to those good times. Hans taught her to shoot, not only for the pot but also to defend herself. Her little fingers had bled and been covered in blood blisters as she learned to load a twenty-round R1 magazine with 7.62-millimetre bullets in under seven seconds. Her father had inherited the farm, but he was not interested in cattle; he preferred to go off hunting with his friends, and when the war intensified he'd been more than happy to leave the territorial forces for a fulltime posting to *Koevoet*.

Her mother had been left to run the farm and she had hated it. She was British and loathed the hot summers and the endless dry winters. When the terrorists mortared the farm and a group of them tried to get into the farmhouse, Sonja had killed her first man; she was aged ten.

The tall communication tower in Okahandja came into view and she remembered it from Sunday trips to town for church. There were no happy Sunday school memories, just those of her father coming back from the bush, dirty and sweaty in his camouflage uniform and green canvas boots, and wanting nothing more from his wife and family than a safe place to drink himself into oblivion.

Sonja knew, now, what he had been through. She had been there herself – was there now – and the rational part of her mind kept reminding her that she could seek help if she wanted. Sonja had made her peace with Hans, before he died. He had sobered up, found God, and remarried.

Mercifully, a new bypass had been built around Okahandja so she was spared any further pain that the town's old buildings and streets might have dredged up, and instead hit the road, which turned southwest, towards the coast. The country here was thorny bushveld, game farms and some cattle. On the side of the road warthogs fossicked with their snouts in the dirt, and through the trees she caught glimpses of the occasional farmhouse or hunting lodge, some with Bavarian-style high-pitched roofs. There was little to distract her from her thoughts, which was a pity.

Sonja remembered the morning Sam had left for Africa. She had tried hard not to recall those last precious hours, but now, lulled by the monotony of the countryside and the long straight road that she navigated on autopilot, his voice came back to her.

'I'm sorry,' was the first thing he had said to her when she'd opened her eyes.

They had fought, late into the night, as he packed. One of his faults was that he was disorganised and always left his packing until the last minute. She, on the other hand, always had a bag ready to go, a legacy from her time as a military contractor when she could be called away at a moment's notice. He'd once accused her of being ready to walk out on him, if the going got too tough. That barb had hurt her more than anything else he'd ever said to her.

He gave in too easily, another of his faults. She was still angry, when she'd woken, and ready to go a few more verbal rounds with him, but he'd kissed her, on the forehead then on the lips. She had sighed.

'I still think you should let me go with you, and . . .'

He'd kissed her protest away, gently. 'I told you last night, I *need* to do this shoot, and I don't need you to be my bodyguard.'

Sonja had frowned. She had known, and still understood, even after what had happened to him, that he was right. Perhaps she could have shot the poacher who killed him, or given him better first aid, or taken a bullet for him, but that was all academic. Sam was right: he had needed to go to South Africa by himself, as much as it wounded her.

'I don't want to go away with you being mad at me,' he'd whispered, and moved his hand between her breasts, tracing a line down her sternum, over the flatness of her belly.

She was still mad at him, but when she looked up into his eyes as he lay there propped on one elbow, she felt her anger cool. He was just too goddamned sexy. Sonja had drawn his face to hers and kissed him deeply.

He had teased her, as he always had, until she was close to orgasm and she'd climbed on top of him, the way they both liked it. She had climaxed almost immediately, and rolled off him, but he'd then moved between her legs and entered her again, looking down at her. Her body was still quivering, still acutely sensitive from the first time, and each long thrust of him was like a mini jolt of electricity; it set her on edge with desire and she locked herself around him, drawing him deeper into her.

When he was finished he stayed there, melded to her. She hadn't wanted to let him go, and when she'd closed her eyes she'd been annoyed when she'd felt a tear squeeze through her tightly shut lids.

'Hey, hey, my big tough girl, what's this?' He'd kissed the tear away.

'I'm just tired, that's all,' she'd replied. She hated showing weakness, and hated women who cried over nothing. 'My eyes are sore.'

He had smiled down at her and kissed her again. 'Are you going to miss me?'

'No.'

He'd laughed, and she'd felt it through her body. Even so, she couldn't stop another couple of tears welling.

'Oh, baby, it's all right. I'll be home before you know it.'

Sonja had felt the anger return then. She hated it when he was condescending to her, treating her like a child. 'Don't call me baby! I'm fine.'

'I love you, you know?'

'Yes.'

He'd chuckled again, then withdrawn from her. He got up and stepped into the shower. She'd thought of joining him, but decided against it. It was bad enough he'd seen her cry; she didn't want him to think she couldn't live without him. She had to let him go.

In the Land Rover, driving through the heat haze, she screamed at the top of her voice, until her vocal chords ached.

Chapter 14

Windhoek's Hosea Kutako International, Hudson Brand mused, would have to be one of the few capital city airports in the world with not a building visible beyond the terminal complex. As far as he could see was flat, dry landscape studded with hardy blackthorn acacias.

He and Matthew Allchurch disembarked from the South African Airways flight and walked across the baking black runway to the terminal building. They cleared immigration without delay or issue, along with the other tourists who had been on the flight.

'I did my military service in Pretoria, as an army lawyer, before things got busy in South West Africa,' Allchurch said as they walked through the arrivals hall to the car rental desks. 'I've never been to Namibia. I always thought – hoped, in an odd way – Helen and I might come here to lay Gareth to rest or to bring his body home.'

'Try not to get your hopes up, this is still a long shot,' Brand cautioned him.

'I gave up getting my hopes up decades ago, Hudson.'

They picked up a Jeep from Avis and Brand said he was happy to drive. 'It'll take us about five hours to get to Etosha,' he added.

They skirted downtown Windhoek and Brand was relieved when Allchurch said he wasn't hungry after eating on the aircraft and was OK to keep going. Brand always felt most relaxed when on the move; he found if he stayed in any one place for too long the demons from his past started catching up.

Brand mulled over the case, for that was how he viewed this arrangement, as he drove. Once clear of the city, the countryside was empty of people and distractions. Matthew Allchurch would be happy if he found his dead son's body, but Brand had a nasty feeling in his gut that the publicity of the discovery of Venter's body – still listed in the media as himself – would flush out some ghosts from his past who were very much alive. That wasn't necessarily a bad thing. Even after all this time, and despite being disillusioned with America at the time, the way he had been summarily dismissed from the CIA still rankled.

It wasn't that he regretted having to turn his back on the States – he had carved out a better life for himself in Africa than he probably would have in the US – but his name had been tainted, and in some records deep in a vault in Langley, Hudson Brand was still branded a criminal. The war in Angola had left him feeling bitter and cynical, and even if he'd wanted to challenge the way he'd been dismissed or appeal the ruling, by the end of the conflict he couldn't be bothered. He'd seen enough of the way foreign powers – be they the Americans, Cubans or Russians – meddled in the affairs of other countries to know he didn't want to re-join the company. But even if he was willing to put the past behind him he knew there would be others from that time who could not afford to forget him, or the fact he was still alive.

'What are you thinking?' Allchurch asked from the passenger seat.

Brand looked straight ahead. 'I'm wondering why I'm still alive, specifically why the people who planned that mission your son was on let me live.'

'Maybe they didn't know you were alive,' Allchurch replied. 'You said yourself you put your dog tags on Venter's body and then disappeared from your old job and joined 32 Battalion.'

'That's true, but I contacted my superiors in Langley, over the head of the local station chief, a guy called Brett Martin, as soon as I could after surviving the jump from the Dakota. They told me Martin had filed a report on me and I'd been terminated from the agency, and that they were sending people to get me. They never did. I fought in 32 under my own name, and I haven't tried to hide my identity since then. Hell, I'm easy to find – you contacted me through the website for my safari business and a couple of my cases have made the press here in Africa.'

Allchurch exhaled. 'So you think your immediate supervisor, this Martin fellow, was guilty, involved in the illegal smuggling of valuable goods out of Angola?'

Brand shrugged. 'Could be. I never really got on with Martin, and he pronounced me guilty without even hearing my side of the story. As it was, he died a few weeks later in a grenade attack on his office in Namibia. Maybe he fell foul of his business partner. I've thought that could have been the mystery guy on board the Dakota.'

'Perhaps the trail to you ended when the Dakota crashed.'

'Maybe.' Brand instinctively patted his top left breast pocket for the pack of cigarettes that wasn't there.

They were quiet for a while as the rented Jeep ate up the kilometres. They passed through the regional towns of Okahandja and Otjiwarongo. Brand kept a close eye on his rear view mirror.

Allchurch looked out to his left, over the bush-covered plains. Occasionally they passed a camelthorn tree, nurtured to maturity by water trapped in the drainage line on the side of the road.

Tall barbed-wire fences marked the boundaries of game farms. 'This country is beautiful. Wild. Do you think if there's anyone left alive who knew what was on board the Dakota that they'll come looking for it, now that the discovery of the body has been in the news?'

'I'd bet my shirt on it, and that's about all I've got at the moment.' Brand glanced in the mirror yet again.

Allchurch leaned over to Brand's side of the car and looked at the dashboard. 'Hey, I don't want to sound like an old woman, but aren't you travelling a bit too fast?'

Brand glanced down and saw the speedometer needle creep above the one hundred and forty kilometre per hour mark. 'Not a bit.' He pushed his foot down a little harder and checked the mirror again.

'What are you up to, Hudson?' Allchurch asked, his voice raising an octave.

'Sorry, don't mean to alarm you.' Brand moved his toe to the brake and the Jeep bled off speed until the needle was hovering around eighty. He looked in the mirror again. 'There's a town coming up, Outjo; nice little place. We're going to stop there.'

'All right,' Matthew said, 'and then you can tell me what's going on.'

'Probably nothing.'

Outjo had the feeling of a town trapped in time, somewhere around the mid-eighties, Hudson thought. There were a couple of cafes and curio shops to serve the tourist traffic on its way to and from Etosha, and delis, bakeries and supermarkets for the locals and surrounding farmers. It had a feeling of general orderliness. He'd passed through similar towns in the old days, but this part of the country had been spared the worst of the war, which was mostly fought in Owamboland, or further north in Angola. After being kicked out of his CIA liaison role in Angola he'd spent most of his time based in the far north of Namibia, in the

Caprivi Strip area at Buffalo Base, 32 Battalion's headquarters on the banks of the Okavango River. From there he and the Angolan soldiers under his command crossed the border into Angola on lightning-fast, hard-hitting raids. He was there for the last big battle of the war, at Cuito Cuanavale, where the South Africans, including his battalion, went head to head with the Cubans and their allies in a battle the likes of which the continent of Africa hadn't seen since the Second World War. Brand still shuddered when he remembered the smell of blood, the rumble of tanks, the screech of artillery shells overhead and the terror of Cuban MiGs raining ordnance from above.

Brand slowed, casting an eye over the shop fronts, then pulled into a service station. An attendant came over and Brand got out of the vehicle and opened the fuel cap.

'Say, do you know where the Portuguese bakery is around here?' he asked the attendant.

'Yes, just down the road, take the first left and it is on your right.'

'Much obliged.' Brand paid the man, got back in and drove out of the service station.

'We're going the way we came,' Allchurch said.

'I need to visit a bakery.'

'You're hungry?'

'I know the baker, an old friend.'

Brand took the turn and saw the O Portuga Bakery on the right. He made a U-turn and pulled up outside it. Brand turned to Allchurch. 'Wait in the car. I won't be long. I'll bring you a custard tart – this guy makes the best ones this side of Lisbon.'

Inside there was an African woman serving and in the rear of the shop, seated at a wooden desk staring at a computer was an enormous, swarthy man. Brand thought the kitchen chair he was sitting on was in danger of collapsing at any minute.

'*Ola*, Joao.'

The man raised bushy grey eyebrows and looked over the top of the screen.

'You never could keep your eyes off porn for long, could you, you disgusting bastard. Only difference now is you get it online instead of in those Scandinavian volleyball magazines.'

The man made two fat fists and pushed them down on the desktop as he struggled to get up. His fierce scowl suddenly softened, though, and his mouth split into a beaming grin under his ashen Viva Zapata moustache.

'Hudson Brand?'

'The very same. How you been, Joao?'

The man came around the counter and engulfed Brand in a bear hug. Brand felt his ribs giving way from his sternum. 'My God, I can't believe it's you, after all this time, you useless Yankee prick.'

'Let me go, you stink of garlic.'

Joao dropped Brand then nearly winded him with a slap on the back. 'Come out the back. We must drink brandy.'

'No beer?'

'Breakfast is over.' Joao led Brand through the bakery, past hot ovens and a young man kneading dough. They emerged into a small courtyard with a home bar in one corner under a thatched roof. There was a bottle already on the table and Joao took a glass from behind the bar and half-filled it. 'It's good to see you again.'

Brand clinked glasses with him. 'How's the bakery business?'

Joao shrugged. 'It's OK. People need bread. It's better than the old days.'

'I'll drink to that.' Brand took a sip.

Joao drank half his glass then narrowed his eyes. 'What do you want, Hudson?'

'I can't just look up an old war buddy?'

'I don't see you for thirty years and you walk into my bakery. Shit always followed you, Hudson.'

Brand didn't have time for chit chat. 'I need a piece.'

'What makes you think I deal in guns?'

'You always loved guns. Even if you're not dealing, you'll still have a collection stashed away somewhere.'

The baker raised his bushy eyebrows again. 'You going to kill someone?'

'I hope it won't come to that, but I'm going to be doing some digging into the old days. Some people aren't going to like what I might find.'

'CIA shit?'

'Something like that.'

'I like it here, Hudson. It's a nice country – overly bureaucratic – but the SWAPO guys leave us in peace. I employ Angolans, illegals mostly, but the government turns a blind eye. I don't want trouble.'

Brand nodded. 'I understand. Sell me something untraceable. No one will know it came from you.'

Joao stared at him across the table for a few seconds and Hudson almost believed the old Portuguese army officer who he'd fought alongside in 32 Battalion really had gone completely legit. Joao had been ruthless in battle, but he was devoted to his Angolan foot-soldiers and Brand wouldn't have been surprised if some of them had worked for him in the bakery. 'Wait here.'

Joao disappeared out the back gate of the courtyard, and after a few minutes returned and set a long green canvas safari bag down on the table with a loud clunk. He unzipped it.

Brand whistled through his teeth. 'Where the hell did you get an Uzi?'

'You want paperwork and service history you've come to the wrong baker.'

'Understood.' Brand picked up the stubby Israeli submachine gun and pulled back the slide. It was clean and lightly oiled, in good condition. Also in the bag were a couple of nine-millimetre Glocks and a Russian-made Tokarev.

Brand placed the Uzi to one side and checked out a Glock. 'I'll take this one, plus a couple of spare mags for each of them.'

'Five hundred,' Joao said.

'Namibian dollars?'

The other man laughed. 'Funny guy. US dollars.'

'For crying in a bucket, Joao, I'm probably not going to make that much money on this case.'

Joao reached for the pistol. 'Then give it back. I heard you were a private investigator. I thought you'd be licensed to carry your own gun.'

'I didn't think I'd need it in Namibia, I heard it was a peaceable country, and I had to leave South Africa in a hurry.'

'What made you change your mind?'

Brand looked over his shoulder, through the bakery. He could just make out Allchurch, leaning against the Jeep and talking on his phone. 'You remember how sometimes we'd be in the bush, in Angola, and everything would go quiet; the birds would stop singing and even the damn flies would quit buzzing?'

Joao nodded.

'I got it now.'

The Portuguese ran a hand over his moustache. 'OK, four hundred for the Glock and the Uzi, and I'll toss in the ammo and some spare mags for free.'

Brand pulled out his wallet and counted the cash. It almost tapped him out, but Allchurch seemed to have plenty of money. The two men shook hands and Joao wrapped a meaty arm around Hudson. 'Stay safe, brother.' He put the Uzi in an over-sized shopping bag.

Brand tucked the Glock into the waistband of his cargo pants and covered it with his shirt. He went out through the bakery and got into the Jeep.

Allchurch closed his door. 'What's in the bag?'

'Not bread.'

They drove through Outjo and the C38 opened up ahead of them, long and straight. Four kilometres out of town Brand caught the glint of sunlight on a windscreen, off to his left down a gravelled farm road. As he flashed past the turnoff he saw a black BMW X5. He reached around to the small of his back and pulled out the Glock. Steering with his knees, he racked the pistol then placed it on the seat between his thighs.

'What the hell is that for? Is that what you were buying in the bakery?'

Brand focused on the rear view mirror. Allchurch looked over his shoulder. 'Are we being followed? Is that what this is all about?'

Brand floored the accelerator, pushing the speedometer up to one hundred and fifty. He glanced at Allchurch, whose face was looking pale. 'He's catching up to us,' Brand said. 'Open the bag.'

'Shit. Who could it be?' Allchurch pulled out the submachine gun. His eyes widened.

Brand grimaced. 'Could just be some local thug who tailed us out of the airport car park, maybe waiting for a good place to take us down.'

'This is Namibia, not Johannesburg. These are the people from your past, aren't they?' Allchurch asked.

Brand felt bad that the lawyer might become a target on account of his own past, but Allchurch was the one who'd dragged him to Namibia. 'You knew this could get messy after your air force friend told you about what was going on with Gareth's flight, and after you heard my story. You want out? I'll turn around and outrun these guys and take you back to Joao, the baker. He'll look after you until you can get a lift to Windhoek and fly back to Cape Town.'

Allchurch looked over his shoulder again, then back at Hudson. 'No. I've come here to find out what happened to Gareth.

If whoever's following us sees you as a threat then they know something. I'm in if you are.'

'All right, then load a mag in the Uzi and cock it.' The BMW was looming close in the mirror. 'OK. We can't outrun him, but we can out-drive him. Hold on.'

'What?'

Allchurch let out an involuntary scream as Hudson swerved off the tarred road onto the gravel verge. As the Jeep bled off speed the BMW shot past them. Hudson swung the wheel hard to the left and headed away from the highway and into the grassy veld studded with bushy blackthorn acacias. The two of them bucked in their seats as the Jeep bounced over the uneven terrain. The vehicle was all-wheel drive, but it wasn't designed for serious off-roading, and hummocks and rocks scraped noisily on the undercarriage as Brand weaved between the stunted thorny trees.

Hudson looked around and saw that the BMW had stopped and made a U-turn. The driver hurtled back to where they had left the road and pulled off onto the verge.

'This is far enough. If we go further we might do some serious damage to this thing. Lie low and let me do the talking.' Brand stopped the car in the shade of a tree and got out, the Glock in his hand. He took up position on the far side of the Jeep from where the BMW had stopped, about a hundred metres away.

Allchurch ignored him and got out. He crouched beside Brand, cradling the Uzi. 'Are you sure this is a good idea?'

Brand watched the other vehicle intently as he spoke. 'This is a long shot for a pistol, but we've got some cover and they're in the open.'

The two front doors of the BMW opened simultaneously and two white men got out. The car was pointed towards Brand and the men were obscured from view behind the opened doors. 'Stay right where you are and raise your hands where I can see them,' Brand yelled.

'You want to see our hands?' the driver yelled.

'You heard me, smart man.' Brand had his pistol trained on the driver's side door.

'No problem.'

Both men raised their arms at the same time, lightning fast. 'Get down,' Brand said to Allchurch as he squeezed off two quick shots then pushed the other man to the ground with a hand on his shoulder. A dozen bullets raked the Jeep, punching a line of holes in its silver bodywork.

'What the hell was that?'

Brand moved to the rear of the SUV and popped off another two shots. He was answered with two fierce bursts of fire. 'They've both got AK-47s.'

'I thought you said we'd be out of their range,' Allchurch said.

'Of a pistol, yes, but not Russian assault rifles.'

'What do you want?' Brand yelled at the top of his voice.

He was answered with two more bursts.

Brand scooped up a handful of dirt, held it up and let it trickle through his palm.

'What are you doing?' Allchurch said.

Brand nodded. 'Checking the wind. It's in our favour.' He motioned with his left hand for Allchurch to lean back, then raised his right and shot a hole in the lower left-hand-side rear panel of the Jeep. Petrol jetted from the ruptured fuel tank in a fast, steady stream. Brand reached into his shirt pocket and pulled out the Zippo lighter he always carried with him, even since he'd given up smoking. He ripped up a handful of dry grass, flicked the Zippo and held the flame to the kindling. 'When this goes off, run for it. Head away from the road for a hundred metres or so then cut north, parallel to the road. I'll be close behind you.'

Brand risked a look around the edge of the Jeep and saw one

of the men moving while his buddy covered him. The stationary gunman fired a burst which stitched the Jeep.

'Ready?' Brand said.

Allchurch paused, looked into Brand's eyes, then nodded. They both rose to a sprinter's crouch and when Hudson tossed the burning grass into the pool of gasoline they both took off. As fast as they were, Brand felt the heat from the *whoosh* scorch the skin on his back through his safari shirt. 'Run, Matthew!'

Satisfied his client was not holding back, Brand peeled off to his right, sooner than Matthew, and cut a wide circle through the scrubby thorn trees back towards the road. When he glanced over his shoulder he saw heat haze rippling up through the air from the burning Jeep and fire sweeping through the grass and undergrowth at a rapid pace, towards the road.

The gunmen were shouting to each other and had both now left their car. Brand saw one of them, through the rising curtain of smoke, sprinting back towards the parked BMW. It was exactly what Brand had been hoping for; the grass fire might not have been an inferno, but if it reached the car it would destroy it, leaving the hit men without wheels.

Brand reached a cluster of head-height trees at the edge of the cleared grassy verge on the side of the highway. When the man who had gone to save the BMW broke from the bushveld Brand was ready for him, kneeling in an ambush position with his Glock extended, his left hand cupping his right. As soon as the man got to the driver's door and stopped moving Brand fired. The Jeep, now engulfed by fire, exploded behind him, covering the noise of gunfire. His first shot punched a hole in the man's chest, the second went through his throat. Brand was on his feet, running, before the gunman had hit the ground.

His heart was pounding and his breath was coming in great lungfuls, expelling through his nose like a blowing racehorse when he crouched beside the man. Brand shoved him, but there was no movement. 'Damn.' He'd hoped to question him.

Brand climbed into the BMW, relieved to find the electronic key still in place. He punched the ignition button, put the vehicle in gear, and stood on the accelerator. Dirt and rocks fanned out behind him as he tore up the grass verge alongside the main road. As he steered he looked left, hoping for a sign of Matthew. When he had gone two hundred metres he pulled over, left the engine running and got out.

'Matthew! Where are you?' There was no answer. Brand pressed the button on the side of the Glock and let the magazine slide out into his left hand. He still had rounds left. He started to walk into the bush again, the pistol up and leading the way. 'Matthew!'

Adrenaline coursed through him and the heat of the day and the smell of the bush took him back to Angola, where this mess had all begun. There was a purity to combat, man against man, that had been missing from his time in the CIA and his life as an investigator.

'Hudson, run! Get away from . . .'

Allchurch's warning cry was snuffed out with a dull thud and a scream. 'Shit,' Brand whispered to himself.

'I'm going to kill him, Brand,' a voice called out from the bush ahead of him.

Brand looked behind him. The BMW was waiting, its engine purring. Fire crackled and roared in the wind, the flames and smoke licking across the road. This guy was going to kill Allchurch in any case – he wouldn't be the kind to leave witnesses.

A gunshot rang out and Brand heard Allchurch scream. 'My bloody hand!'

'I just shot off his little finger, Brand. I'm going to kill him slowly while you run away and save your own worthless skin. Don't worry, I'll come find you later.'

'I've got your car, you *poes*. I'm going to get the police. They'll find you.'

The other man laughed. 'This is Namibia, it's an easy country to get lost in. Say goodbye to your friend. I'm going to shoot his cock off next.'

The noise of an engine made Brand turn around. A battered Isuzu *bakkie*, a pickup with 'OJ' Outjo licence plates, emerged from the roiling smoke. The vehicle stopped, the driver's side door opened and a man got out.

Brand smiled and started walking into the scrub. 'I'm coming for Allchurch, whoever you are. I'm holding my pistol up.'

'Come in slowly and your friend gets to leave, almost in one piece.' The man laughed at his own joke.

Asshole, Brand thought. He pushed a thorny branch aside and was confronted by the barrel of an AK-47. The man holding the weapon was about fifty, hard-faced, the nose red from drinking but the eyes clear. He'd spoken with an Afrikaans accent. 'Who do you work for?'

The man chuckled again. 'Drop the gun. Get down on your knees.'

Brand tossed the Glock into the grass between them. 'We can make a deal.' He lowered himself down slowly. 'I know where the Dakota is.'

'I'm not here to make deals.' The man raised the butt of the AK to his shoulder and sighted down the barrel. 'I'm here to kill you, Hudson Brand.'

'Then why haven't you pulled the trigger? You think I came all this way to *look* for a plane that's been missing in the desert for thirty years? I'm not that stupid. I've known where it is for a long time.'

The man licked his thin lips with serpent-like speed. 'Then why haven't you found it sooner?'

'You know what's in it?'

'I don't care what the fuck's in it, I'm going to kill you now.' The man curled his finger through the trigger and started to squeeze.

Matthew Allchurch screamed for mercy as the single shot split the burning afternoon air.

Chapter 15

Joao the baker emerged from the thornbushes, a .375 hunting rifle with telescopic sights gripped in his meaty hands.

'Good shot,' Brand said.

'You know me, I never miss. How is your friend?'

Brand had taken off his bush shirt and wrapped it tightly around Matthew Allchurch's hand. 'He's probably in shock. Bastard shot off his little finger, but he'll live.'

'Don't talk about me like I'm not conscious,' Allchurch said. He tried to stand, using his good hand to lever himself up, but when he made it to his feet he started to sway.

'Take it easy, Matt,' Brand said, hooking an arm around him. 'You've lost blood.'

Joao nudged the body of the gunman with the toe of his desert boot. The heavy-calibre bullet from the hunting rifle had taken off the top of his head. Matthew Allchurch glanced briefly at the dead man and started to heave. 'Easy,' Brand said. 'Joao, check that one for ID.'

The Portuguese knelt and rifled through the dead man's pockets. 'Nothing. No wallet, no driver's licence, not even a receipt for petrol. Also, nothing on the one you capped by the BMW.'

'Professionals. Let's get to the car – can we go in your *bakkie*? Matthew here needs a doctor.'

'I know one, back in Outjo. We can go to my place; he'll make a house call. You want to tell the cops what happened here?'

Brand imagined the investigation, the delays, perhaps some time in a police lockup. 'What do you think?'

Joao stroked his long grey moustache. 'I'm doing OK with the bakery, but I've got some history. I don't want to get dragged into this.' Joao led the way back to the road, with Hudson shouldering Matthew. When they reached Joao's truck they lifted Matthew into the back and used a rolled tarpaulin as a cushion for him to lie against. Brand then went to the assassins' BMW and torched it, the same way he had destroyed the Jeep. He didn't want the local police to find any evidence of him in the car. They drove back to Outjo, leaving the twin pyres of the burning vehicles and the smoking remains of the grass fire which, fortunately, had not jumped the main road.

*

Sand blew across the road in front of Sonja but through the gritty curtain she began to make out the distant blue line of the Atlantic Ocean.

The backside of Swakopmund revealed itself first, an industrial estate, filling stations and vehicle workshops. Somewhere out here in the desert, she knew, were mass graves of Herero and Nama people who had died in the Swakopmund concentration camp during the independence war against the Germans. Emma was trying to uncover more grisly evidence of that time. Sonja knew that the desert winds often exposed bones and the ragged remains of clothing.

As Sonja drove closer to the coast, passing first through a

new extension of housing along the Swakop River that hadn't existed when she was last there, the trappings of the modern world gave way to the Germanic orderliness of the seaside resort town. Swakopmund was a perfectly preserved little piece of Bavaria perched incongruously on a desolate coast of Africa. In a colonial anomaly the British had taken possession of Walvis Bay thirty kilometres to the south, the best deep-water port on the Atlantic coast and a chunk of land around it, leaving the German administration to develop Swakopmund, a poor second choice, as its prime sea port. Swakopmund almost became redundant, however, when the British took over South West Africa during the First World War, but reinvented itself as a seaside holiday resort after the second.

The town centre and the waterfront had retained its original German colonial feel, unchanged since the brief period when Kaiser Wilhelm owned this little piece of Africa. Its street layout and earliest buildings had been designed in Germany and all of the materials shipped across the ocean and the town assembled, almost in kit form. Sonja's aunt, Ursula Schmidt, had a place on the beach where Sonja and her family used to visit once a year.

Sonja remembered swimming in the Atlantic, still cold even in summer, while her mother lay on the sand under an umbrella reading a book. Her father would drive north along the coast on day-long fishing trips and arrive home as red as a boiled lobster, reeking of beer and schnapps, but proudly holding aloft a dead fish, dripping blood.

Sonja took a slow drive around town, and found it little changed from her childhood memories. The stately old hotels with their steep-pitched roofs, the Lutheran church, and the railway station – now also a hotel – were preserved and freshly painted, and the odd German street name had even survived. Some of the merchandise in the storefronts had moved with the times; there were African curio shops that would never have been seen when she was a child, and boutiques full of designer safari gear, but there were still the familiar cafes and pubs.

Sonja pulled up outside a bottle store, went in and selected a sixpack of Windhoek Lager dumpies. She put the green bottles on the counter and greeted the woman at the cash register in German. She replied in the same language. German-style beer, and still the language of a colonial power vanquished more than a century earlier. Her country was bizarre, yet beautiful.

She walked down the street, carrying the beers in a plastic bag and pausing now and then to look in the tourist shops. In a small arcade she came across a bookshop. She browsed for a while and picked up a copy of a book about the war against the Herero and the Nama. When she was a child her teachers had taught her that the Germans had brought civilisation, education and health care to South West Africa, not concentration camps, forced labour and summary executions. She placed the book back on the shelf, then picked it up again and paid for it.

Sonja walked out into the sunshine. The wind was brisk and chilly, but the sky was endless African blue. It could change in minutes, she knew; and every evening a cold, wet blanket of fog rolled in off the Atlantic and sometimes hung around for days. If she was welcomed in Namibia, which she was sure she would not be, would she come back? It was a question to ponder over a few chilled beers, but first she would see if Tante Ursula was still in her house on the beach.

*

'You should rest,' said the doctor, a Herero man with a shaved head and a beer belly that almost rivalled Joao's.

Matthew Allchurch looked from the doctor, who was now washing his hands in the sink of the kitchen in Joao's house, not the most hygienic of surgeries, to Hudson Brand. 'We need to keep moving.'

Brand knew the physician was right, but Allchurch also had a point; lingering in one place would not help them find the missing aircraft and would also make them easier targets once replacements were sent to do the job the first two men had failed at.

As they bid farewell to the doctor, Matthew, whose hand was now muffled in a bandage, had Hudson count out a couple of thousand rand from his wallet, which Hudson folded into the doctor's palm.

When the doctor had gone Matthew spoke up. 'They must know you have some piece of information that helps narrow down where the Dakota could be. They must know that you wouldn't have come all this way just to start randomly searching the desert. Did you mean it when you said you knew where Gareth's plane was?'

'I was bluffing,' Brand said. 'I know the coordinates for the rendezvous at sea and now that we know where Venter and I hit the deck, I can trace a possible flight path, assuming Gareth and the other pilot were able to get their bearings and get back on track.'

Joao raised his bushy eyebrows. 'You looking for a plane?'

'Trust me, buddy, this is something you don't want or need to know about,' Brand said to him.

Joao shrugged. 'I've had enough trouble for one day. You can take my *bakkie*. I don't need to come with you, if you don't want me to save your lives again, but I'll have to charge you rent.'

*

Sonja found her aunt's house; it was hard to forget with its prime position and breathtaking view over the ocean. Ursula lived in upmarket Vineta, one of the earliest beachfront areas to be developed after Swakopmund reinvented itself from port to resort.

The house was also easy to find because it was still painted the same shade of pink as Sonja remembered from thirty or more years ago. She parked the Land Rover and got out, wishing now she'd brought chocolates or flowers, something other than beer. She walked along a flagstone path bordered with hardy cacti and succulents. With the wind and the sand not much greenery survived in Swakopmund. Sonja knocked on the door.

It opened a crack and a blue eye peered out at her. '*Ja?*'

'Tante Ursula?'

'I am Ursula, yes. Is that you . . . is that really you after all these years?'

'Sonja.'

The door opened wide and a diminutive woman with white hair piled in a messy bun looked up at her through funky red glasses with a beaded chain attached to them. Ursula wore a paint-spattered white cheesecloth smock. She looked like an older, shorter version of the kindly woman Sonja remembered from her childhood. The eyes still sparkled, though.

'Of course I know who you are, Sonja. My goodness, though, I didn't know if I'd ever see you again.' Ursula reached up, wrapped her arms around Sonja and drew her face down for a kiss.

Sonja pecked her aunt on the cheek, but stiffened a little in her embrace. She was not a hugger or a kisser, and even Sam had playfully mocked her reluctance to show affection in public. 'Hello, Tante. It's been a long time.'

'Too long, too long, much too long. Come in, my dear.'

Sonja followed her aunt through the doorway. While the house remained the same outside it was completely different inside. She remembered a place cluttered with photos of her aunt and uncle's travels abroad, and souvenirs they'd brought home with them from Europe, Asia and the Middle East. Her father had called his sister a hippy and Sonja had, in her earliest memories of her only other relatives, detected a faint resentment of her uncle from her father. Her uncle Udo, Ursula's husband, had been a parks ranger and therefore exempt from military service; Sonja thought that was where her father's disapproval stemmed from. Now the house made minimalist look like a junkyard. Everything was cool and white, cold almost.

'The house has changed,' Sonja said.

'*Ja*. You move with the times, hey? In the old days, when you were a girl, this place was like a hippy house, you remember? It was full of clutter – Persian rugs, fans from the Orient, and a shisha pipe that your father used to accuse us of smoking marijuana in.'

Sonja smiled. 'Hippy was the first word I thought of when I remembered the place, and you.'

Ursula laughed. 'Well, like I said, we all move on. I like being uncluttered now. It gives me a sense of peace. All the other stuff kept reminding me of . . . well, it kept reminding me of the past.'

'Of Uncle Udo?' Sonja said, regretting her words immediately.

Ursula smiled. 'Yes, of Udo. I do remember him, every day, but to be surrounded by so much of our early life became almost suffocating in a way. I knew that life needed to carry on, and Udo would have felt the same way.'

Sonja had a flashback to the last time she'd been in the house. Ursula hadn't been smiling, she'd been howling, and her mother had sat with her on the old sofa, covered in batik-printed sarongs, trying to console her, while Hans had stood behind them, in uniform, one hand tentatively on his sister's shoulder.

'I'm thinking the same thing as you,' Ursula said, breaking into her thoughts. 'His funeral was the worst day of my life. When they came with the news it took a while to sink in. I was in shock. But when I saw his coffin lowered into the sand, that was when I finally realised I would never see him again, he would never hold me again.'

Sonja looked out a big plate glass window, over the sea. 'It's a beautiful view.' Through an open door she saw an adjoining room with a drop cloth on the floor and an easel with a canvas on it. 'You're still painting, I see.'

Ursula touched her on the arm. 'I read about your boyfriend, Sonja. I am so very sorry. I tried contacting you, through Facebook. Emma said she passed on my condolences.'

'Thank you. As you say, we must move on. Life doesn't . . . stop.'

'I'll put the kettle on, shall I?' Ursula said. 'I'd offer you a beer or a glass of wine, but I'm out of both at the moment. I find it more enjoyable to drink when I'm socialising, rather than sitting at home by myself getting pissed.'

Sonja laughed out loud at the incongruous profanity. 'I've got a sixpack of oh-six-one in my truck.'

Ursula beamed. 061 was the area code for Namibia's capital. 'Tafel would have been better, but even Windhoek Lager is better than tea.'

Sonja walked out to the Land Rover, smiling again. She didn't want to talk about Sam with her aunt, though she wondered, now, if she'd subconsciously sought out the old woman because that was probably the one thing they had in common, apart from the bond of blood. She got the beers and took them inside. Ursula had opened the French doors that led from the lounge onto a sunny deck. She opened a market umbrella and set out a tray of *droëwors* and biltong and two beer glasses.

Ursula put four beers in the fridge and went back outside to where Sonja was leaning with two hands on the railing. Ursula poured them each a lager. '*Prost*,' her aunt said.

'To what shall we drink?'

Ursula shrugged. 'The future? Love? You tell me.'

Sonja shrugged and took a sip. 'My past doesn't really bear talking about, and I honestly don't know what my future will hold, Tante.'

'What about Emma?'

Sonja took another drink. 'She's all I have now. I was surprised to get your message from Emma about Sam. Thank you.'

Ursula laughed. 'Don't be so surprised. Just because you never send me an email or a letter or a Christmas card doesn't mean your daughter doesn't. We've actually been in touch for a couple of years now.'

'How did you find her?'

'She found me. Remember that thing called Facebook, Sonja?'

'I know it, I just don't like it. So, you know Emma's in Namibia?'

Ursula sat down in the shade, but Sonja stayed standing, her back to the sun and the ocean, enjoying the warmth and the smell of the sea.

'I do. She was planning on coming to see me after she had spent some time with you. It's you I wasn't expecting to see. I didn't think the Namibians would let you into the country.'

Sonja raised her eyebrows. 'You know about all that stuff in the delta, in Botswana?'

Ursula smiled. 'It's that thing called the internet again, Sonja. What I couldn't find online was a decent picture of you. It's why it took me a moment to recognise you. It seems you guard your privacy well – you were even wearing a scarf and dark glasses when you punched that paparazzi photographer in Los Angeles. I thought you looked a bit like Angelina Jolie in that picture.'

Sonja laughed. Her aunt was as smart and as funny as she'd remembered her, apart from the bleak time after her uncle was killed. 'I'm keeping a low profile here in Namibia as well, Tante Ursula.'

Ursula waved a hand in front of her face, as though shooing away a mosquito, and took a long draught of beer and licked her lips. 'Are you in trouble?'

'No. I was worried about Emma for a while. She sent me an SMS saying she needed my help. I panicked and crossed the border from South Africa, but it turned out she just wants to pick my brains about military uniforms. Her archaeological dig uncovered –'

'A man in a flying suit who appears to be the victim of an accident or military action during the bush war.'

'You don't miss anything, do you, Tante.'

Ursula waved towards her studio. 'My world revolves around painting and surfing the net. I have plenty of time to stay on top of current affairs. The story about the mystery airman got me thinking, about Udo.'

Sonja left the railing and took a chair under the umbrella. The sea breeze had taken the sting out of the African sun, but she could feel it starting to burn now. 'Really, why is that?'

Ursula looked out over the Atlantic; its glittering surface belied the cold dark waters beneath. 'Udo came across a stranded airman in the desert, in the Skeleton Coast National Park. It was a long way from where this latest body was found, but it got me thinking.'

'I don't remember hearing about that. I used to love his stories about his life as a ranger.'

Ursula sighed. 'And he used to love telling them to you, and embellishing the bits about his tangles with lions and rhinos and elephants. We were such a small family, and you may have guessed that I couldn't have children.'

Sonja nodded. Sometimes she wished she hadn't been taking the pill when she and Sam were living together. Maybe having a little piece of him would have dulled the pain. 'The airman?'

'Oh, yes,' said Ursula. 'It was only a few days before Udo died. He was patrolling the salt road, the one that runs along the Atlantic coast, in his Land Rover. He was heading north towards Möwe Bay and was between there and Terrace Bay when he found this guy staggering out of the desert. Udo called me from the park headquarters and told me about it. He said he was amazed the guy was alive. He was dehydrated and he had a head wound and he didn't know how long he'd been walking for.'

'The guy's lucky he came across Udo when he did. I don't imagine many vehicles use that road,' Sonja said. The coast was aptly named; it was littered with the rusting remains of numerous shipwrecks and the desert's relentless sands had been burying the sun-bleached bones of stranded mariners for centuries.

'*Ja*, you're right, and there were even fewer cars in the park during the war. It was a miracle. Udo told me the man said he had been flying a single-engine spotter aircraft that had suffered engine failure. He took the pilot to park headquarters where they patched him up. A military ambulance came and took him away.'

'Interesting,' Sonja said. 'Did it make the local newspapers?'

Ursula shook her head. 'When I next spoke to Udo on the telephone, two days later, he told me not to say anything about the mystery pilot. He said the man had been on a covert mission and Udo had been ordered by his superiors not to mention anything about it, to anyone.'

'What did you think about that?' Sonja asked.

Ursula shrugged. 'Nothing. It was the war. We all did as we were told.'

'Not you, from what I remember,' Sonja said.

Her aunt gave a little smile. 'I wasn't in favour of the war; your father was correct about me, I was no supporter of the government. The problem was that Hans thought I was against him and the soldiers; I hated the way things were, not the people in uniform.'

'I remember seeing you in the newspaper once, marching in protest about the South Africans siting their military bases next to schools as a tactic to prevent SWAPO from mortaring them.'

Ursula nodded. 'You're a soldier, Sonja, you know that even in war there should be honour, rules to protect the innocent.'

Sonja wasn't so sure about that. She had her own code that she tried to follow, but she'd done some things she would rather forget. There was nothing honourable about war. 'Udo never talked about the pilot again?'

Ursula looked out over the Atlantic again. 'No, and two days after our last conversation his Land Rover was ambushed on the salt road. According to the autopsy he was killed by a burst of fire from a Russian-made AK-47, the weapon of choice of the SWAPO guerrillas.'

'So tragic,' Sonja said, meaning it. Udo had served his country not by killing people but by trying to conserve its wildlife. She remembered him as a funny, kind, gentle man who, like his young wife, had probably been against the war.

Ursula reached across the table and put her hand on Sonja's. 'I loved him, Sonja, with all my heart, and I miss him every day, but I still have my life, I still carry on.'

Sonja nodded. Her aunt was getting frail, but there was still a light in her eyes, an innate goodness that kept her going, kept her optimistic. *Unlike me*, Sonja thought.

Chapter 16

Emma looked out the Perspex window of the Beechcraft, scanning the endless red rocky desert ground below them. 'Giraffe, eleven o'clock,' Natangwe said, pointing out the window.

Emma was surprised. Natangwe was loving flying and was pointing out animals and places he recognised continually. He was wide eyed and grinning most of the time, like a kid on an amusement park ride. Alex, however, was as white as a sheet and, once more, dry-retching into a white paper bag. *Poor guy*, she thought.

Natangwe stole a quick glance away from the window across the aisle to Alex, and then back over his shoulder to Emma. He winked at her. He was poking fun at Alex, which was mean, but she was enjoying seeing this playful side of Natangwe, who always seemed so brooding and intense.

Emma unbuckled her seatbelt and, bent at the waist, moved forward between the two young men and past Sebastian, who grinned at her, to the cockpit, where Professor Sutton sat in the co-pilot's seat next to Andre Horsman.

Professor Sutton looked back over his shoulder and held up a folded map. 'We're coming up to the area where your young man's lion was last recorded.'

Alex was not 'her' man, and the professor's condescending tone, as usual, didn't fail to annoy her. 'He's not well, I'm afraid.'

'He's not much of an asset, either. So much for those eagle eyes.'

Emma felt defensive of Alex now.

'No harm done,' Horsman said. 'The lions are pretty much on our estimated flight path in any case. I've plugged in the coordinates Alex gave me for the lion's last known location and we should be over it soon. It'll be a bonus if we help the desert lion conservation program as well as find our missing aircraft.'

Emma thought he was a good man. She had assumed he'd be some arrogant rich fat cat, but he'd been happy to help – unlike the stuck-up Sutton – and had a relaxed, easy manner about him. 'It sure would.'

'I'm taking her down, now that we're over those last mountains,' Andre said.

Emma rested a hand on each of the pilots' seats. It was quite thrilling, seeing the nose of the aircraft dip and the ground coming closer. Horsman levelled out and he and Sutton continued scanning the dry landscape below. Emma knew she should return to her seat and assist with the search, especially if Alex wasn't capable of even looking out the window for his own lions.

She was surprised, however, to find when she got back to her seat that Alex was sitting up, his laptop open in front of him and a map spread out on his knees. He wiped his mouth with the back of his hand. 'We should be nearly over the lion's last position.'

'So Andre just said,' Emma replied. 'You're looking better.'

He looked away from her, out the window. 'This is important, Emma. These lions are the last of their kind in the area.'

204

'Smoke ahead,' Andre said to them all over the intercom. 'Seems odd out in the middle of nowhere. I'm going down as low as I can to have a look.'

The Beechcraft dropped and banked sharply to one side as Horsman pulled their aircraft into a wide turn. Emma saw Alex's left hand clamp down on the armrest of his seat. She thought the ride was a buzz. They were so low now it almost felt as though she would be able to touch the rocky ground below, if she could open the window.

'Campfire,' Dorset said.

Emma saw three men dressed in bright traditional clothing look up and point at them. She caught a glimpse of a cooking pot and a couple of dogs barking up at them as well.

'There's . . .' Alex swallowed, 'there's been another fire down there. Can you take us around again, please, Andre, to have a look at that burnt patch about fifty metres from the men?'

'Roger,' the pilot said. They levelled out once more and then Andre pulled into the steep turning pattern again. Alex had a pair of binoculars out, his laptop and map at his feet now. He scanned through the porthole.

'They've burned something down there, an animal of some kind,' Natangwe said, relying on his bare eyes. 'I can see the skeleton. It's big, but not as big as a cow.'

'No,' Emma said, and put a hand to her mouth.

'It's the male lion,' Alex said, 'I'm sure of it.'

Emma caught his eyes and saw the inestimable sadness and frustration inside him. Alex took a hand-held GPS from his daypack. 'Can you please just circle a couple more times while I record this location, Andre?'

'Roger, just a couple more, then we need to get back on track. Fuel is getting low.'

'*Danke schön*, I very much appreciate it,' Alex said. He checked the latitude and longitude on his GPS and took out a notebook.

'The coordinates here are exactly the same as the last recorded location of the lion. There is no doubt that what we saw down there was its body, burned to cover the evidence of the crime.'

'Everyone, I'm climbing,' Andre said into the intercom. 'There are vultures up ahead and if we hit one of them we're in big trouble.'

Alex peered out the window on his side and Emma leaned over him. Below them, as their aircraft increased its altitude, they could see a cluster of vultures on the ground. Several more of the giant birds had taken flight at the noise of the Beechcraft's approach, but they were now settling into a circuit pattern, and, one by one, as if they were being guided by some natural air traffic controller, they were coming in to land again.

'There are cattle down there,' Natangwe said.

'I see them,' Alex replied. 'The vultures seem to be feeding on the carcass of a cow.'

'Probably killed by that lion,' Natangwe said. 'That's a big part of some herdsman's income gone for good.'

Alex shot him an angry glance. 'Natangwe, you don't understand what the project I'm working on is all about. We want to empower the herdsmen and show them they can make money from tourists coming to see the desert lions. We're showing them new and different ways to keep their cattle safe.'

'Doesn't seem to be working.'

Emma was worried the tension between them might spill over mid-air, which would not be good for anyone. 'Guys, we can talk about this on the ground. How about we concentrate on trying to spot the missing aeroplane and, while we're at it, shouldn't we be looking for the lionesses and cubs?'

The faceoff between the two younger men was put on hold as each, sullenly, looked back out his respective window.

They flew on over the rocky red expanse. It was like another planet down there, Emma thought. Alex's airsickness seemed to have abated and she went to the rear of the aircraft and opened up a cooler box. She handed out bottles of water and Cokes, and apples and pears to the five men.

'Andre,' she said as she handed him a bottle of water, 'can we use our phones on this flight, or is it like a commercial flight where they're banned?'

He nodded his thanks to her. 'Sure, you can use your phone up here, but I don't think you'll get much signal.'

'Thanks.'

Emma went back to the cooler box and took a juice and an orange for herself, and peeled the fruit while staring at the endless landscape below. She took her phone out and turned it on, but as Andre predicted there was no signal. She would check it again when they returned to Ondangwa to refuel, and send her mother a message from there.

Chapter 17

It was nearly dusk when Andre Horsman landed the Beechcraft on a game farm near Otjondeka. Andre had suggested this instead of heading all the way back to Ondangwa.

Emma, like the others, had agreed. Although they had found no trace of the missing aircraft, it had been an eventful day. Andre had said that they could refuel at the farm, owned by an old air force friend of his.

'I still need to get back to Ondangwa Airport and my vehicle soon,' Alex told Emma as they drove in the back of an open Land Rover game viewer through the gathering darkness to the farmer's house. 'I have to drive to where the male lion was killed and talk to those herdsmen.'

'Will they be in trouble?' Emma asked.

Alex shrugged. 'It's up to the Namibian police and the courts.'

Natangwe looked back at them from the row of seats in front. 'Nothing should happen to them. Man and lions have existed here for thousands of years.'

'Yes,' said Alex, 'and man very nearly succeeded in wiping them off the face of the earth.'

The farmer's name was Benjie van der Westhuizen. As well as sheep there was also game on his farm, and he pointed out springbok and mountain zebras as they drove to the house. 'I have some small guest chalets for hunters and tourists who come sometimes to the farm, you will be very comfortable in there,' Benjie told them.

'Do you have wi-fi or phone signal here?' Emma asked him.

'No phone signal. We normally have satellite internet, but regrettably it has not been working these last two days. I am waiting for a technician to come out and fix it, but we are a long way from anywhere.'

Emma felt frustrated by the lack of communication in Namibia. They hadn't picked up a signal anywhere. Her mother was due any time at the dig site and Emma now wished she had left a message somewhere for her, though she couldn't be sure that if she left a note at Namutoni, the nearest national park camp to the dig, her mother would even get it.

'I for one am enjoying being out of contact from the rest of the world for a while,' Professor Sutton said.

'I have my satellite phone,' Alex said, lowering his voice so that only Emma could hear. 'You can use that to send an SMS if you like, but not for calls unless it's a real emergency. I don't want everyone knowing as they'll all want to use it after a day or two and I will be in trouble from the donors.'

Emma patted his arm. 'Our little secret.' To Andre, in a louder voice, she said, 'How long do you expect we'll keep searching?'

He swivelled in his seat. 'Personally, I'll keep searching until I find that aircraft, but Benjie only has enough fuel spare for one more day's flying, and to top us up tomorrow night to get us back to Ondangwa.'

'So we'll be back at Ondangwa day after tomorrow?' she asked.

'Yes. From there I'll refuel and if we're still searching I'll have to relocate to somewhere further west, near the Atlantic coast, maybe at Purros; there's an airstrip there.'

'OK, cool,' Emma said. 'Professor, I'm just worried about my mother. I'm meant to be meeting up with her soon.'

Lights and a flickering fire beckoned them ahead and Benjie stopped the game viewer at a semicircle of six rondavels, round huts set around the blazing fire and a *braai* area. A bigger building, presumably Benjie's farmhouse, was a further hundred metres away. 'So this is where you will be staying. I hope it will be comfortable.'

'I'm sure it will be fine,' Sutton said.

They offloaded their bags and Emma, Natangwe, Alex and Sebastian took a room each, as did the two older men. Emma opened the door of her rondavel. It smelled a little musty, and vaguely gamey, which she thought might have something to do with the old zebra skin on the floor, but otherwise it was clean and tidy. She pulled the light switch and saw a double bed and a doorway that led to a toilet and shower. Emma opened her bag, took out her hairbrush and went into the en suite to straighten herself out a little. A few minutes later there was a soft knock on her door.

'Alex,' she said as she opened the door.

He put a finger to his lips. 'Not so loud.' He reached under his shirt and pulled the satellite phone, in its pouch, from the waistband of his shorts. 'Just an SMS, OK?'

She smiled. 'Yes, OK.'

'But you must take it outside somewhere, to get a satellite signal. It won't work indoors.'

'I was just about to go out to the fire.' She poked her head around the door and saw that none of the others had emerged from their rooms yet. 'All quiet. I'm ready, why don't we go somewhere out the back of the rondavels and try and get a signal.'

He nodded. 'OK.'

The darkness of the African night soon engulfed them as they moved away from the fire and the dull glow of the solar-powered lights in the rondavels. Alex turned on the phone, which resembled a clunky, old-fashioned mobile, and unfolded a similarly retro aerial and pointed it towards the sky.

Instinctively, Emma looked up. 'Wow.' She had thought she was getting used to the spectacular night skies in Namibia, but every time she gazed up at the stars from somewhere remote, like this, the sheer number of stars and the volume of light took her breath away again.

'I never get used to this sight,' Alex said.

'You just read my mind.' His face was bathed in the light of the phone's screen and she thought he looked unearthly, like a handsome ghost or a traveller from another galaxy. He was cute, and there was an innocence about him. Emma smiled as she remembered that he was worried he would be rapped over the knuckles for using a company phone for private purposes. Emma was no criminal, but she had partied pretty hard in Glasgow and been part of a few late-night pranks around town. 'Do you ever cut loose?'

He looked up from the phone's screen. 'What does this mean, cut loose?'

She almost laughed at his formal pronunciation. 'Have fun, go crazy, freak out.'

He pursed his lips and she wondered if she had offended him. 'I enjoy my work, my research.'

'That's not what I meant. Have you ever, like, got really wasted and done something ridiculous that you later regretted, but at the time you couldn't stop laughing about?'

Alex's face creased in thought. 'No, I do not think so.'

Emma exhaled then Alex started to laugh.

'OK, you got me. So, spill. What did you do?'

'I should not say. Besides, we have a satellite signal now. You may send your message to your mother.'

Emma shook her head. 'No, tell me, what happened?'

Alex supressed a little smile, then folded down the phone's antenna. 'Very well, if you do not want to send your SMS . . .'

She grabbed his hand with hers, stopping him from shutting down the phone, wrapping her fingers around his. 'Tell me,' she said, not letting go. It was very dark, but Emma thought he may have been blushing. 'Now.'

He sighed. 'It was when I was at university, on a year's exchange, in Munich. I drink only beer here in Namibia, and even then not to excess. However, all the students in my class were drinking schnapps, and shooters. I became very drunk.'

She didn't want to let go of his hand, and he didn't try to move her away. 'And . . .'

'And we were playing a drinking game – I forget now the rules – and I lost. I had to run through the campus, in the snow, naked.'

Emma had to move her hand now, to cover her mouth. 'Oh my God, that's priceless. I would have died of the cold.'

He raised his eyebrows. 'Not of embarrassment?'

'No, just the cold,' she laughed.

'Anyway, it would have been fine,' he continued, 'except I was caught, by one of our professors.'

'Oh, no. Was he hard on you?'

'She.'

Emma laughed out loud, then remembered they were trying to be discreet, and covered her mouth again. She still tittered when she tried to speak again. 'Was *she* hard on you?'

Alex coughed.

'What? What happened?'

He looked around, as if there were spies in the darkness. 'She was, how would you say in English? The opposite. She was quite *soft* on me.'

'No way! She liked you?'

'You could say that.'

'What did she do?'

'Emma, please, I don't want to go into details. It's not gentlemanly.'

She knew she should drop it, she could tell he was definitely as red as a beetroot now, but she wanted him to open up, and, besides, she was curious about how his story ended. 'Did your friends show up to rescue you?'

He scoffed. 'Hardly. They ran off, with my clothes.'

Emma smothered another laugh. *Poor guy*. 'So you were left there, naked, with one of your professors, in the snow.'

'She ordered me inside the nearest building. She was angry with me, but told me I would die of exposure if I stayed outside.'

'Well, that was decent of her. What happened next?'

Alex turned away. 'You should send your message, Emma, the others will be looking for us soon. Benjie will be starting the *braai*.'

He was right, she knew, but she was enjoying this. It wasn't his discomfort that amused her, but the story was weirder – and more exciting in a strange way – than any of the antics she'd got up to at Glasgow University. 'Was she attractive?'

He swallowed. 'Please, Emma . . .'

'She was, wasn't she? Did you fancy her?'

He looked away again, towards the fire, then back into her eyes. 'She was beautiful. Many of the male students talked about her, fantasised about her.'

Emma felt a stab of jealousy but, perversely, she still wanted to hear the rest of the story. 'What did she do, what did you do, Alex?'

He held her gaze. 'She said she wanted to warm me up, and I agreed that would be the sensible course of action.'

Emma had stopped laughing. She didn't want to think of sweet, innocent Alex, the man devoted to his research and his lions, involved in hot, furious, illicit sex with an older woman, or anyone – at least anyone other than her. To her own personal immediate embarrassment, which she hoped didn't show, she felt herself becoming aroused. Emma had flirted with Alex, keeping her hand on his when he was threatening to turn off the phone, teasing out his story, but now she didn't know what to do or say. She felt as though the physical gap between them, just a few centimetres, was like a force field.

Emma moistened her lips with her tongue. 'What did she do, get you a coat, wrap you in a blanket?'

He swallowed and she watched his Adam's apple bob, wanted to touch it. 'No.'

'How old was she?'

'Only thirty-four, just thirteen years older than me.'

Emma saw something other than lust or a jocular memory of a fling in his eye. There was pain there. Emma hoped she hadn't hurt Alex. She was going to tell him she didn't need to know any more, but he beat her to it.

'We had an affair, Emma. It was wrong, but we were in love, at least I thought we were. Andrea, my professor, tried to end it, but we could not stay away from each other. It lasted another three months but in the end her husband caught us out.'

'My *gosh*.'

Alex looked away, shamefaced. 'He threatened to report her to the university. She would have been dismissed, the scandal was too great. He wanted her back. She didn't want that; she wanted to live with me. I left Munich the next day, and flew back to Windhoek from Frankfurt. I never heard from her again.'

Emma put a hand on his arm. 'I'm sorry, Alex.'

He looked at her again, back into her eyes. 'I'm not the virgin you thought I was. I slept with my teacher, a married woman. I broke my own personal code of honour. It's why I like living out here, in the desert, away from people.'

Now he's just being maudlin, Emma thought. She gripped him harder. 'We all make mistakes. I have, and my mother certainly has, but we all have to move on, Alex.'

He shrugged. 'Maybe I don't want to move on. Maybe I'm happy out here, with the solitude and the wildlife. Did you ever consider that?'

'Emma? Are you out here?' It was Sutton, calling from the direction of the fire.

'Yes, Professor?'

'Ah, there you are.' He appeared, silhouetted against the fire. 'Farmer Van der Westhuizen is on his own, his wife is away visiting her mother and he gave his maid the night off, he was not expecting company. He's asking for help in the kitchen and I'm afraid I haven't cooked anything other than sausage and eggs, and that was when I was your age.'

And what, I'm supposed to know how to cook because I'm a woman? Emma thought to herself. The old man was insufferable. 'OK, Prof, I'll be there in a minute.'

'He's already burning the cooking oil. I fear we have a disaster in the making.'

Alex folded the antenna down on the phone. 'We can do this later,' he said, zipping the phone back into its case.

'OK,' Emma said. 'Prof, I'm all yours, but I must warn you I'm no gourmet.' Emma walked towards Sutton and the fire. She cast a glance over her shoulder and saw Alex staring up at the stars.

Emma strode past the fire, where Dorset had returned to his seat and was drinking what looked like a scotch and ice next to Andre Horsman, who also had a drink.

On the other side of the fire pit from the rondavels was a rectangular building with a thatched roof that housed the communal kitchen for the camp and an inside dining area, whose open sides were enclosed with mosquito mesh and chicken wire. Sutton, the silly old fool, had been exaggerating.

As Emma walked in she was greeted with the mouth-watering smell of fried onions. Benjie was dropping fist-sized chunks of meat on the bone into a heavy steel pot, browning each piece in the onions. 'Smells good.'

He looked to her and grinned. 'Just my personal specialty *potjie*. The meat is gemsbok neck. It's going to be delicious.'

'If you do say so yourself.'

He laughed. 'Modesty is not one of my strong points.'

Emma leaned against the door frame. The farmer was relaxed and friendly and clearly in his element. He didn't seem to be missing his wife or his maid. He began adding a selection of spices and condiments to his one-pot stew.

'How do you know Andre?'

Benjie added chopped tomatoes and white wine to the pot, then took a sip. She wondered if he hadn't heard her question, but after licking his lips, he said, 'The war.'

'Were you in the air force as well?'

'Yes. It hurts any military person, be they army or air force, if you leave men unclaimed on the battlefield. I was a part of the initial search for that missing Dakota. Truth was we didn't really know where to start looking.'

'Do you think we've got a chance now?'

Benjie put the lid on his pot and wiped his hands, finally satisfied with his *potjie*, which was simmering away. 'This is the best chance Andre's going to get to find that plane. Until you found that man in the ground no one knew where the start point was. If the Dakota crashed in a rocky part of the desert there will still be pieces of it visible; if it crashed in the dunes it might have been swallowed by the sand, but if it ditched in the Atlantic it's long gone. In any case, it's worth trying. Now, whatever your professor may have said to you, I don't need a woman in the kitchen, but you can pour yourself a glass of sauvignon blanc from the fridge if you really want to make yourself useful.'

Emma smiled. 'Best idea I've heard all day.'

Emma walked out of the kitchen only to find the path blocked by Sebastian Lord. He held a dewy bottle of white wine in one hand and two glasses in the other. 'I was just bringing the sous chef some sustenance.'

She smiled. 'Well, Gordon Ramsay has just politely ordered me out of his kitchen so I'm unemployed.'

'Sauvignon blanc?'

'Sure. You're a mind-reader.'

He passed her a glass. 'Here, hold this.' Sebastian filled her glass then his. 'Andre's got fingers in everything, including the wine industry. He's got a small vineyard outside Franschhoek and for some reason I find myself having to give them a lot of legal advice.'

She laughed and sipped the wine. 'Yum.'

'You want to join the party, or just chill for a bit?' Sebastian nodded to a bench made of an old railway sleeper perched on brick piles, outside the kitchen hut.

'Chilling sounds great. I've been spending all my time with the professor and Natangwe the last few days, but it seems like longer.'

Sebastian laughed. 'And your friend Alex?'

Emma shrugged. 'He comes and goes. He's a bit of a nomad. He researches lions and cheetahs so he's always on the move.'

Sebastian looked into her eyes. 'It must have been such a buzz, finding that guy in the ground.'

'It was.' She recounted the moment when she had realised she'd discovered a body, and liked the way she seemed to command Sebastian's full attention. 'Sorry, I don't want to bore you.'

'Impossible,' he said.

Emma thought she should ask Sebastian something about himself. 'So, you like to travel?'

He nodded. 'Lots of businesspeople will tell you how much they hate being away from home and travelling for work, but

I say, what's not to like? I get to see the world, stay in nice places and meet plenty of different people. I was an air force kid and I spent my time growing up in places such as Bloemfontein and Louis Trichardt, so I think it makes me appreciate Paris and Rome more.'

He was funny and sexy and interesting, she thought. Emma cast an eye back to the fire.

'Sorry, I'm monopolising you,' Sebastian said.

She looked back at him. 'No, no. I love travelling, too, though I haven't done enough of it. And I'd like to see Bloemfontein and Louis Trichardt as well.'

Sebastian laughed. 'I'd be happy to show you.'

'Is your father a pilot?'

Sebastian looked up at the night sky and took a breath. 'Was. He flew Bosboks, bushbucks, small observation aircraft. He was shot down over Angola and killed.'

'Oh my God, Sebastian, I'm so sorry.'

He looked at her with his dark eyes and blinked. 'It's OK. I was a baby. My mom remarried and my stepdad, who was also in the air force, was a good guy, but Uncle Andre kind of looked after me like I was his own kid. Your folks?'

'Now *that's* complicated. But the short story is that I lost my dad as well. And my mom kills people for a living.'

Sebastian's eyes widened. 'Serious?'

Emma sipped her wine and Sebastian topped her up. 'I kind of wish I wasn't, but yes. She's, like, a military contractor, security and stuff.'

'Cool. A hot chick with a gun; doesn't get much better than that.'

'And how would you know what my mum looks like?'

Sebastian smiled. 'I'm guessing you take after her.'

Emma felt herself blush, and gulped down some more wine. She was getting tipsy, but she didn't care. She asked Sebastian about Paris and Rome and Hong Kong and New York, and other places she wanted to visit one day. In turn, he wanted to know why she was interested in conflict archaeology and what brought her to Namibia. By the time he opened the second bottle of white wine Emma had taken him up on an offer to visit the vineyard where it had come from, when she came to Cape Town after spending time with her mother.

Time passed quickly and Emma was a little unsteady when Benjie ordered them all to carry the tables and chairs out of the indoor dining room and set them up by the fire for dinner.

Emma made a conscious effort not to appear as though she was devoting all her attention to Sebastian, but every time she looked across the fire to Alex he seemed to look away.

Alex stood up as soon as he had finished eating. 'Excuse me. I'm tired, I'm going to turn in. Goodnight.'

The group said their goodnights and Emma started to feel bad about the way she had teased Alex, and about Sebastian, but Sebastian distracted her by asking her where in the world she would most like to work as an archaeologist. Unlike Alex, he was actually interested in her, and could hold a conversation.

'Hey,' Alex yelled as he re-emerged from his room, 'I've been robbed.'

Chapter 18

Hudson Brand saw the woman walk into reception at Etosha National Park's Okaukuejo Camp, and while he immediately knew he had seen her before it took him a few seconds to realise who she was.

She joined the queue for accommodation just as Brand finished paying the daily park entry fees to a woman in national parks uniform at the second queue. He went to the woman and removed his baseball cap. 'Mrs Chapman, isn't it?'

She looked at him, startled, and he noticed that her blue eyes were bloodshot. Her blonde hair – that was what had thrown him at first; he remembered it being auburn – was long, tied back in a ponytail, and looked like it needed a wash. There were perspiration stains on her bush shirt. 'Who? No,' and then Brand saw a flicker of recognition in her eyes before she looked down at the ground. 'Sorry, you've got the wrong person.'

Brand was used to hunting people as a private investigator; he could look at a photograph and memorise the features, even picture the person with different hair, or glasses, or some other minor disguise. There was the strong jawline, the high cheekbones; she was prettier in the flesh, though unkempt now, as though she hadn't slept and had been in the same clothes for days. He smelled her body odour, plus stale alcohol. 'Sonja.'

She looked up at him instinctively, though he'd doubted she would fall for such a simple trick. Her eyes tried to ward him off. 'Sorry, I thought you were Sam Chapman's wife. I was with him, the day before he died.'

She opened her mouth as if to speak but no words came out. He saw her defiance crumble, her lip start to tremble. She turned on her heel and walked out of the air-conditioned reception building, into the midday glare. Brand followed her outside. He caught up with her and she turned to face him when she heard the door close behind him.

'It's Sonja Kurtz. Sam and I never married.'

'I'm sorry for your loss, ma'am. Sam was a good man.'

'Can you possibly imagine how much I hate those words, "sorry for your loss"? I didn't lose him, he fucking died.'

Brand gave a small nod. He should leave her be, but he knew something of her background and he had seen that faraway, hurting look in her eyes in other people he'd known, as well as in the mirror more than once. 'I know the words don't help, nor does the booze or the pills, or whatever. Time is all, and even that's not a permanent cure. I didn't mean to offend, but, like I said, I did know him, briefly.'

She nodded. '*Ja*, I remember now, you sent an email.'

'Yes, ma'am. Hudson Brand. I was guiding your husband and his film crew while they were shooting in the Kruger Park. I left him with the section ranger and an anti-poaching patrol the afternoon he went with them. I wanted to go with them, but it was against national parks regulations.'

She took two deep breaths, as if to calm herself. 'I wanted to go with him as well. I still keep thinking that if I'd been with him he would still be alive.'

Brand nodded. 'I had the same thought for a while, but with respect, ma'am, we both know that's bullshit. We've both been through that before.'

Her eyes seemed to focus on him then, as if she were seeing him for the first time. She looked down at his right forearm and saw the tattoo of the buffalo head over crossed arrows. 'Three-two battalion. You were in Angola. But what do you think you know about me?'

'Friend of mine, Steve Oosthuizen, served with me in the battalion and couldn't ever shake off the life. He served with you as a contractor in Afghanistan with your mercenary crew, Corporate Solutions. We're in email contact every once in a while and when he found out I was going to be guiding Sam he mentioned he knew you, told me of your background, your relationship. Later, afterwards, I saw your picture in a newspaper story about the funeral; the article said you were married.'

She looked away again, as if to another place far away. 'The media always gets things wrong. We didn't marry because I wanted to be *independent*.' She said it as though it had been one of the greatest mistakes of her life.

It seemed like the utterance of each word progressively sapped her strength. 'Steve's given up contracting, for good, he says,' Sonja said.

'I'm pleased for him, and for Linda, his wife. He's been pushing his luck for too long. How about you?'

Sonja sniffed and knuckled her eye. 'Damn dust. I'd forgotten how dry this place is. How about me what?'

'Are you still in the game; still contracting?'

'I don't know what I'm doing,' she said, 'other than looking for my daughter. You sound American.'

He told her his story in a couple of sentences. 'Is your daughter missing?'

She seemed to regain her composure. 'No, she's working on an archaeological dig near here. I've come to visit her. Now, if you'll excuse me, I must go sort out somewhere to stay and try and find out where the dig site is.'

Brand was surprised by the coincidence. He normally liked to play his cards close to his chest, but he didn't want Sonja Kurtz walking away from him.

'Wait,' he called. She stopped and looked over her shoulder. 'That's the darnedest coincidence. I'm here with a friend to investigate a dig as well. How about that?'

Sonja turned and regarded him through narrowed eyes, instantly on her guard again. 'You're a safari guide. What interest do you have in archaeology?'

Brand decided to come clean with her. 'I'm a private investigator in my spare time. I've been hired by the father of the pilot of the aircraft that was carrying the man whose body was found at your daughter's dig site.'

'My daughter found that body,' she said, unable to conceal every trace of a mother's pride. 'What do you know about the man she unearthed?'

'What do I know, Ms Kurtz? I know that man should have been me; almost was.'

Now he had her full attention. 'All right, I'm listening, Mr Hudson Brand, whoever you are. Do you know where the dig site is? I want to check into this camp and then go look for my daughter, this afternoon if I can, or if not, first thing tomorrow morning.'

'You didn't ask why the man the dig uncovered should have been me,' Brand said.

'And you didn't answer my questions. Do you know where the dig site is? I don't care about you, just about seeing my daughter.'

She's a pistol, Brand thought. She reminded him of a cat gone feral, once sleek and attractive, now ragged and hissy. 'We've got a rough idea and I know a guy who works as a guide around these parts who knows most of what goes on in and around Etosha.'

'Good. You find out where the dig is and I'll get myself a room.'

'OK,' Brand said. He gave her the number of the chalet he was sharing with Matthew, and told her he would see her there soon.

Brand left Sonja and drove Allchurch to their bungalow. Brand recognised the layout of the camp, which had remained largely unchanged since he'd visited a couple of times during leave periods from the war in Angola. Back then, during the insurgency in South West Africa, Etosha had been all but empty, but now it seemed to be groaning at full capacity. The old chalets he remembered had been refurbished. Inside he found the two-room hut had been decorated in cool neutral colours and furnished with a double bed in one room and twins in the other. There was a desk with tea and coffee, and air conditioning. Allchurch still looked pale and he poured himself a glass of water from a pitcher and lay himself down on one of the single beds.

'I'll come and check your wound and change the dressing in a minute, but first I've got to make that call.' He had told Allchurch of his discussion with Sonja Kurtz on the short drive to the room. If Matthew minded someone else joining them at the dig site he was in too much pain to express an opinion.

Brand went back outside, into the sun. He got out his phone and scrolled through his contacts until he found the number for Otto Stapf. Brand had met Oom Otto when he was warden of Etosha, shortly after he had bailed out of the Dakota and joined 32 Battalion. On one of his leave periods he had made an attempt to find out if the Dakota had ever been discovered, but Otto told him the search had been called off, with no trace found.

'Oom Otto, it's Hudson Brand. I don't know if you remember me, but I was –'

Otto cut Brand off. 'Hell, but I thought that was weird when the media reported that they had found your body out near the King Nehale Gate. How are you, Hudson?'

'Fine, alive and well, same as the last time you saw me.'

Otto laughed. 'Yes, I thought it was just typical newspeople getting their facts wrong.'

Hudson dispensed with the small talk. 'I'd like to go see the place where I was supposedly buried. You don't happen to know where that dig is, do you?'

'I do.'

Brand held his phone in the crook of his shoulder as he took down the directions to the dig site, which was beyond the northern border of Etosha National Park on the Andoni Plain, outside the King Nehale Gate. 'Got it, thanks. I owe you a Tafel.'

Brand was about to walk back into the chalet when a Land Rover Defender pulled up. Sonja Kurtz climbed out looking even more pissed off than before. 'Let me guess,' he said, 'no accommodation?'

She nodded. 'I can't believe how busy this place is. During the war there was no one here.'

'I remember,' Brand said, devoid of nostalgia. 'Where are you going to stay?'

She shrugged. 'They say the camping ground is full, but they've given me an overflow space. I'll sleep in the truck.'

Sonja looked tired. 'Well, at least come in and enjoy the air con for a while.'

They went into the chalet. Matthew Allchurch had got off his bed and moved to the small sitting area. He started to stand as they entered. 'Hello.'

'Don't get up,' Sonja said, and her eyes fell on his hand, the bandage spotted with blood. She went to him. 'That looks like it needs to be changed.'

'I'm Matthew Allchurch, we haven't met.'

'Sonja Kurtz. Do you have a first-aid kit?' she asked Brand.

Brand had thought her to be on the skids, incapable of much since the loss of her partner but he figured that the sight of Allchurch's injury, and her insistence on changing the dressing before even knowing the man's name, was a sign of her military training kicking in. He knew that it wasn't just loud noises that triggered the responses; it could be smells, sights, little things like blood spots on a bandage.

'Yes, ma'am.' He went to his room, to his duffel, and took out the kit he travelled with, plus some extra gauze, dressings, and antibiotics the doctor in Outjo had left with them. Sonja was already undoing the dressing, quickly, yet gently.

She held Matthew's hand up to the light coming in through the window. 'Hmm, doesn't look too bad. You'll live.'

'Not too bad? I've lost half my finger.'

'Your little finger,' she said, as if it didn't matter. 'Believe me, I've seen worse.' She took the items from Brand and laid them out. 'Get me a bowl, Brand, some warm water and a towel.'

'The doctor said to keep it dry,' Allchurch said.

She looked at him. 'I *have* done this before.'

Brand set the water and towel down on the coffee table beside her. Sonja cleaned the dried blood from Allchurch's hand, and around the wound. Allchurch winced as she started to peel the dressing from the top of the remains of the finger. 'Men. Such pussies. Brand, get some liquor.'

Allchurch's eyes widened. 'The doctor in Outjo said –'

'I'm the doctor now. Besides, the alcohol is for me, not you.'

Allchurch laughed and she peeled away the rest of the dressing. 'As I thought, it looks OK. Still painful, though, I bet.' He nodded and sucked air between gritted teeth. Brand set down three glasses and unscrewed the cap on a bottle of whiskey. 'Five fingers for me, four for Matthew.'

Brand couldn't quite stifle his laugh. Even Allchurch managed a smile. Sonja gently dabbed antiseptic cream around where the doctor had stitched the digit, then carefully re-bandaged Allchurch's hand. 'As good as new. Almost.'

She sat back in her chair and took her drink, downing the generous measure in two gulps while the men sipped theirs. Sonja looked at the glass, then at Brand. 'Where are your manners, Mr Brand?'

Brand topped up the glass. He figured it wasn't her first drink today. 'Hudson.'

She closed her eyes, raised the glass to her mouth and tilted her head back, momentarily calm. 'So, we are going to be travelling together?'

Brand nodded and gave her a rough idea of where the dig was. 'My contact said the archaeologists' camp is easy to find; there's nothing else out there on the plains.'

'That's what I like about this country, what I'd forgotten, I think, the emptiness of it.' Sonja finished her second drink as Brand was nearing the end of his first.

What the hell, Brand thought. He topped them both up. He was getting a taste for the booze as well.

'I'd cook, but my hand . . .' Allchurch said.

'I've got some biltong and chips, or I can drive you to the camp restaurant,' Brand said. He looked at Sonja.

'Not hungry,' she replied, and took another drink.

Allchurch stood, and seemed steadier now. 'Actually, I think a walk would do me some good. Are you coming, Hudson?'

He looked to her, and she gave a little shrug. 'No, I believe I'll stay here.'

'Suit yourself,' Allchurch said, and let himself out of the chalet.

'A civilian?' Sonja asked after Allchurch was gone.

'Army lawyer.'

'Pretty much the same thing.'

Brand filled Sonja in on Matthew's long quest to discover the fate of his missing son.

'I'd do the same if I were him.' She leaned back into the chair and put her feet on the coffee table. Her boots were filthy, the socks, once khaki, were grey. He noticed the stubble on her legs.

'Do you have a tent?' he asked.

'No, I'll sleep on the back seat of the Landy.'

'Can't be comfortable.'

'Issue you four-poster beds in 32 Battalion, did they?'

He remembered being so tired, and the weather so warm in Angola, that sometimes he would just lie down in the grass at night and fall asleep, and pick the ticks off himself the next day. He wondered what her daughter was like, what she would do when this dishevelled creature showed up at her dig site. 'Say, are you OK?'

'What do you mean?' She'd said it as though he'd insulted her, the verbal equivalent of a slap.

'I mean, are you all right for money, food, whatnot?'

She reached for the paper bag of biltong on the coffee table, helped herself to a handful. 'I am now.' She shovelled the dried meat into her mouth and drained her third glass of whiskey. Then she stood, holding on to the arm of the chair to steady herself. 'I should go. The camp ground shower block awaits.'

'Do you have any soap? Shampoo? Want to borrow some?'

She looked down at him and he could see her eyes boring into him like offensive weapons, but he wouldn't look away from her. He recognised her, not just as the girlfriend of a man he'd known briefly, but as a fellow soldier in trouble. He'd been that person once, dirty, drunk, throwing up in his bed, surly to friends, angry at the world. This was not America, or Australia, or England, where military veterans got counselling and pensions for post-traumatic stress disorder. This was Africa, where the white – or, in his case, coloured – veterans of the war were told that border fighters didn't cry and, besides, there was no money and no one to help in any case if you couldn't sleep because of nightmares, if you drove your girlfriend crazy, if you cried out at night or jumped when a car backfired. When you put a gun to your head, or gassed yourself in your car, there was no national outpouring of protest, no collective shame at the way young men had been sent off to fight a war with no choice.

'What are you suggesting? That I stink?'

He stared back at her. 'Maybe that you just misplaced your wash bag.'

She looked as though she was going to bite him, but she backed down, sighing. 'I don't even have a bar of soap, let alone shampoo. And these are the only clothes I have.' She sniffed towards her underarm. 'You're right, I do stink.'

'Do you want to have a shower here?'

Again there was the moment's resistance, the wild animal wary of accepting food or kindness from a human. 'I suppose so.'

'I can lend you a T-shirt if you want to rinse out your shirt or whatever.'

'Want me to move in?'

'Just offering is all,' Brand said. 'I thought maybe you'd want to look good for your daughter.'

'OK,' she seethed, 'now you're just being insulting.' Sonja got up, walked past him into the double room and snatched a towel from the bed. She came back to him, poured another hefty measure of whiskey and took it with her into the bathroom.

Fifteen minutes later she reappeared with a towel wrapped around her, knotted above her breasts. Brand tried not to look anywhere other than her face, but it wasn't easy. 'I'll take that T-shirt now.'

'Coming right up.' He got up and fetched her a green one from his duffel.

Sonja went back into the bathroom and re-emerged wearing

his oversized shirt, and the towel now wrapped around her waist as a skirt. In her arms she carried her wet clothes. 'I washed them in the shower.'

She dumped the clothes on a chair and picked it up. Brand opened the door for her as Sonja took her things outside and hung them over the chair to dry. She walked back inside, retrieved her empty glass and waggled it at Brand.

'You sure you don't want to go easy for a while?'

'Do you have a gun?' she asked him.

'What if I do?'

'If you do, I'll find it. Pour me a drink.'

*

The sound of screaming woke Brand. At first he thought he was having one of his regular nightmares, about Angola.

He sat up, head throbbing, and swung his legs off the bed. He still had his boxer shorts on, though he had no recollection of undressing. The last thing he remembered was Matthew coming back from dinner and making some comment about him and Sonja being too drunk to talk straight.

Allchurch was awake as well in the single bed next to him. 'That sounds like someone being mauled by a lion.'

Brand burped. 'I'll go check on our house guest.'

He groped his way along the wall of the room until he found the light switch, then went out into the corridor. The cries continued unabated and, still drunk from the scotch, he followed them to her room. He knocked on her door, but all he heard was incoherent screaming. He let himself in.

Sonja was sitting up, her hands in her hair, eyes screwed tight, screaming at the top of her lungs.

'Hey, hey, wake up.'

She seemed not to hear him so he went to her, tentatively. Hannah, an old girlfriend, had tried to wake him from such a nightmare once and he'd awoken, fully, to find her screaming, his hands wrapped around her neck.

Brand grabbed Sonja on the arms near her elbows. 'Sonja, wake up.'

She bucked in his arms and, as he'd half expected, lashed out at him, but he held her firmly. 'No!' she screamed. 'No, Sam, no!'

'It's me, Sonja, Hudson Brand.'

Her eyelids fluttered and she looked at him, not focusing immediately, but her screaming stopped. 'Who are you?'

'Hudson Brand, Sonja. We met last night. Do you know where you are?'

She shook her head, trying to clear her mind. 'Home. No. Namibia. Etosha.'

'Yes. You're fine. You're safe.'

'I am?'

'Yes.' He had an overwhelming urge to hug her and tell her she would be fine, that one day the wound would close over with only the scar remaining. Instead, he said: 'Get some more sleep now. It'll be light in a couple of hours and we'll go find your daughter.'

Brand waited until she lay back down and closed her eyes. He lingered a moment, looking down at her. He smelled the fresh scent of her, now that she was clean, then turned off the light and closed the bedroom door.

Chapter 19

Benjie, the farmer, said that he would put the word out among his employees to try to find who had stolen Alex's camera, iPad and satellite phone. Emma could see, as they boarded Andre's aircraft on the grassy farm airstrip, that Alex was still fuming.

'I never got to tell my mum where we were,' Emma said.

Alex buckled his seatbelt as Andre started the engines. 'It's not the phone I miss, it's my camera and iPad. I had some important pictures of lions on the camera, and my whole database on the tablet.'

'Surely you've got back-ups somewhere else.'

'Yes, on my laptop back at Ondangwa, but my last three weeks of work were all on the iPad.'

The theft had put something of a dampener on their *braai* the evening before, and the novelty of the prospect of flying over endless expanses of rocky desert was fast wearing off, at least as far as Emma, Alex and Natangwe were concerned. Emma had expressed her worry that her mother would not be able to find her when she arrived at the dig site, probably tomorrow, but Sutton had assured her they would be back at Ondangwa by tomorrow midday at the latest, perhaps even earlier.

'Unless, of course,' he had said to her that morning over breakfast, 'we find the missing Dakota and there happens to be somewhere close by where Andre can land. Then, I think you'd agree, we would be mad not to set down and inspect the crash site.'

'Sure,' she'd replied half-heartedly.

Dorset Sutton was seated in the co-pilot's seat, a map spread across his knees. Sebastian was just behind them. She and Sebastian had been the last to turn in, sitting around the fire drinking yet another bottle of wine. Eventually, Dorset had opened the door to his rondavel and asked them to keep their voices down as he was trying to sleep. Emma had put a hand over her mouth to try to stop herself from laughing, but Sebastian had suggested they call it a night.

'I'll walk with you,' Sebastian had said to her.

She was sleeping in the farthest hut from the fire, and had told Sebastian she was fine, but she didn't stop him accompanying her.

'I've really enjoyed chatting to you,' Sebastian had said as he'd lingered by her door.

Emma had looked up into his eyes. 'Me too. You're very tall, you know that?' He was very tall, six-three he had told her, compared to her five-seven.

'Not quite freakishly, but not far off it.'

'No, not freakish at all.' She had giggled. 'In fact, I really like tall men.'

'What a coincidence,' he had said with a grin, 'I really like girls who like tall men.'

Emma had thought, then, that he might kiss her, but instead he just smiled his perfect smile again and said goodnight. She had turned in, listening for a knock at the door, her heart pounding in anticipation of what she might do if she heard it. In the end, the alcohol overtook her and Emma had slept well, though she'd awoken with a thick head and a dry mouth.

She wondered what would happen next, if they didn't find the missing aircraft. Would they go back to the dig site? Would Sebastian fly back to Cape Town and out of her life?

'Wake our friend up,' Dorset said into the intercom. 'We're just coming up to the limit of our search yesterday.'

Emma reached across and shook Natangwe. 'Hey, wake up.' She pointed to the headset in his lap and motioned for him to put it on. Groggily, Natangwe responded.

'What's up?'

'Time to put those super eyes to work again.'

He nodded.

Emma turned to Alex and he gave her a thumbs-up to acknowledge he had heard Sutton's message. He returned his gaze out of his window.

Below them, the landscape was changing. From their briefing from Andre that morning, just before they boarded, Emma knew they would be flying over the northern part of the Palmwag Conservancy. This, they had been told, was old cattle land, arid and marginal, that had been given back over to wildlife. It had become progressively drier and more desert-like the further west they headed. It stretched almost all the way to the Skeleton Coast National Park, which ended at the Atlantic Ocean. The landscape transitioned from rugged red sandstone and granite hills to a mix of sand and rock. To the south, on their left, Andre pointed out the wide green corridor of the Hoanib River whose flow to the sea had been blocked by a line of dunes.

'Gosh, it's like a real desert down there now,' Emma said to no one in particular.

'What were you expecting, tropical rainforest all of a sudden?' Dorset said from the front into the intercom, without looking back at her. 'Eyes peeled, everyone.'

She wondered why the professor had to be so arrogant. People said he was a brilliant archaeologist and a great mentor, but more and more she thought him just a bully. 'What time do you think we'll be back at Ondangwa, Andre?'

'Should be early this afternoon,' he replied. 'We'll have gone as far as we can by then while still leaving enough time to get back to refuel.'

'Down there, three o'clock!' Natangwe cried.

'What is it?' Sutton called back through their headphones.

'Something that doesn't belong down there in the middle of nowhere. Manmade.'

Andre banked the Beechcraft. 'Circling around.'

Emma was on the port side of the aircraft, so she craned over to Natangwe's side. He pointed out the window. 'Down there, see?'

She scanned the desert for anxious moments, not seeing anything, and then it jumped out at her. 'A big lump of something, but what is it?'

Natangwe shrugged. 'Don't know, but it doesn't look like an aeroplane.'

'Sure,' said Andre, who sounded disproportionally excited by the obscure find. 'Some debris as well. What's that doing out here in the middle of nowhere? It could be something that's fallen off an aircraft.'

'There's no road down there, though those marks look like tyre tracks,' Sutton observed. 'Someone's been into the dunes there.'

'I'm GPSing it,' Alex said. The thieves had either overlooked his hand-held GPS, or thought it not worth stealing.

'I've plugged it into the on-board sat nav system as well,' Andre said. 'Let's get back on course and I'll take her down even lower. Everyone on full alert from now on.'

It seemed Andre had throttled back, and that the landscape passed more slowly below them. Sutton, Emma saw, was now

235

looking through a pair of binoculars. She looked at the golden sand below and saw the twin furrows where a vehicle had been.

'There's something down there, where the tracks end,' Sutton said. 'Go around again, Andre.'

They circled the area and Emma could see what the professor had spotted. It was like looking at a geophysics survey of a dig. Undulations and irregularities in the land that indicated past dwellings or excavations couldn't be seen at ground level, and usually not from the air; only sophisticated ground location radar machines, rolled across a site like lawnmowers, could pick up such irregularities. But here, because the surface was sand, the still-low morning sun was casting shadows over berms and other unusual shapes.

'There's something irregular there for sure,' Sutton said. He sounded, Emma thought, positive but not jubilant. For all his faults he was a man of science and would need proof before he broke out the champagne.

'It could be that the plane bounced and began to break up on impact,' Andre said as he banked around for one more turn. 'That would account for the wreckage being spread over a bigger area. That certainly doesn't look like a whole aircraft down there. Let's have another look, Natangwe.'

Natangwe raised a hand and Emma fist-bumped him. Alex looked back at them and then out of the window again.

'What do you think, Andre, is there anywhere we can put down there?'

Andre looked around, through the cockpit windows. 'No, I'm afraid not, Dorset. We've got some fuel left, so we can go back to Benjie's farm now and maybe look at organising some vehicles. We're only about a hundred and fifty kilometres from his place.'

Emma had a mixed reaction to the news. On the one hand she wanted to be part of the expedition to discover the downed

Dakota, if this was, indeed, what they were looking at, but on the other hand her mother was due to arrive at the dig site tomorrow and she'd so far had no way of telling her where she was.

'This is amazing,' Natangwe said.

'Ah, Andre,' interjected Alex.

'*Ja?*'

'Any chance we can go all the way back to Ondangwa? I need to get to my vehicle so I can go to where that lion was killed.'

Sutton replied: 'Alex, you heard what Andre just said. We're going to try and get some vehicles from Benjie. We'll pass right by where your lion was killed. I'm sure we can stop off there on the way.'

Emma thought the older men were acting impetuously. Surely the best course of action would have been to return to Ondangwa and organise a proper expedition from there. There was no denying that their excitement was infectious, though.

'I guess so,' Alex replied.

Emma sighed. She hoped that by the time they got back to the farm Benjie would be in contact with the outside world again and she could get a message to her mother. She just hoped Sonja wouldn't do anything crazy if she got to the original dig site and found that Emma wasn't there.

*

'Sonja?' a strange voice called. 'Sonja?'

She tried to open her eyes but it was as though they were glued shut. When she did pry one apart, then the other, the morning light coming in through the chink in the curtains stabbed her like twin stilettos through the eyeballs.

'Who is it?' she managed to croak. She rolled over; her nose twitched and she started to gag. By the side of the bed was a plastic bucket with a layer of vomit in the bottom. Sonja dry-retched. *What happened?* she asked herself.

237

TONY PARK

'It's Hudson Brand. Wake up. I've got coffee. Can I come in?'

Sonja pulled down the sheet and looked at herself. She wore a man's green T-shirt with a stain dribbled down the front. She slapped a hand to her forehead. Below the T-shirt a towel was wrapped around her. It had fallen open. *If he did anything I'll kill him.*

'Wait.' She coughed. There was a glass a third full with scotch.

Sonja looked around the room, which was suffused with golden early morning light. On a luggage rack were the clothes that she now remembered washing. She went to them, unsteadily hopping on one foot as she pulled on pants and shorts. The shorts were still damp, but at least they were clean. 'Come in.'

He opened the door and grinned at her. She wanted to punch him, but her mood softened a little when she smelled the steaming mug he held out to her. She took it. 'How come you're smiling?'

'Well,' he drawled, 'I didn't start drinking before midday yesterday.'

She sipped the coffee, burning her tongue in her haste to get the drug into her. *Smart arse.* She hated sober people and their supercilious judgemental ways. Still, she mused, Brand had matched her drink for drink once she had arrived at the chalet. Not many men could drink her under the table, and if she hadn't, as he had correctly pointed out, had a head start, she bet it would have been him feeling like she did now, and her doing the grinning.

'What time is it?' Sonja blew on the coffee.

'Seven. You said last night you wanted an early start.'

The events of the previous evening – most of them – slowly came back to her. 'How did I get to bed?'

'I carried you.'

She regarded him through slitted eyes. If he had tried something . . .

'Relax,' he continued, holding up his hands, palms out to her. 'Nothing happened. One minute we were having a

238

conversation – about what I can't remember – and the next you were on the floor.'

She looked to the bucket by the bed. 'You?'

He shrugged. 'You were having a nightmare. When you finally snapped out of it you started to be sick. I took you to the bathroom, got the bucket for afterwards.'

Sonja looked down into the cup. 'I should say thank you.'

'I'm guessing you don't do a lot of that.'

She looked up at him. 'Don't patronise me. Thank you. That was kind of you.'

'If you want to go back to bed I can put Allchurch off another hour or so. Understandably, however, he's keen to get on the trail of his missing son's aircraft.'

She shook her head. 'No, I'll be ready to go in five minutes. A hangover's a self-inflicted wound, no excuses. We'll stick to the timings. Get out while I change out of your shirt. I'll clean it later.'

He touched the brim of his baseball cap and backed out of the door.

Sonja took off Brand's T-shirt. For the first time since she'd met him, the first time she'd been sober, she noticed his smell. The shirt had been clean, but there was a lingering smell of man about it, wood smoke, gun oil and leather boots. She bunched it in a ball and tossed it on the bed then put on her own shirt. She went to the bathroom and pulled her hair back in a ponytail, fixing it with the elastic she had miraculously found in the pocket of her shorts. She went back to the bed and got Brand's shirt, then held it under the running tap and washed away the sick stain with hand soap as best she could before wringing it out.

She regarded herself in the mirror. Her eyes were clear, well mostly clear, and her clothes were wrinkled but at least not stinking any more.

Sonja took Brand's shirt and went back out into the small living room of the chalet. Brand's client, Matthew Allchurch, was there. He looked well rested and not as pale as the previous day. His bandage was clean, with no blood spotting through. 'You look better,' she said.

'So do you. Good morning.'

Sonja walked past him and out to the pastor's Land Rover. She got in as Brand was loading his and Allchurch's bags into their *bakkie*. Sonja turned the key and noticed the fuel warning light had come on. She got out and, reluctantly, went to Brand. He was in the driver's seat now and put down the electric window.

'Yes?'

'I need cash.'

He pursed his lips. 'Are you asking me nicely for a loan?'

'Yes. This is me being polite.'

Brand undid the flap on the breast pocket of his safari shirt. He pulled out three hundred rand. 'That's all I've got.'

She took it from him. 'That will do, for now.'

'Yes, don't worry, I'll get some more at the next ATM in case you run out.'

He deserved a smile for that reply. She turned and went back to the Land Rover. She felt his eyes on her as she walked and she let the smile linger a little longer. Back in the Landy she started the engine and turned on the air conditioning. They drove to Okaukuejo camp's fuel station. While the attendant was filling the Land Rover Brand spread a map across the bonnet. Sonja and Matthew joined him.

He traced a line north-east from where they were. 'Namutoni's the nearest camp to the dig site, so we'll head that way, through the park, then out through the King Nehale Gate. The dig's east of there.'

With the refuelling done they headed past the stone tower, out the gates and into the wilds of Etosha National Park.

On paper the drive to Namutoni was about a hundred and fifty kilometres, but the maximum speed on Etosha's dusty internal road network was sixty. Added to that, they would inevitably be delayed by animals crossing the road and tourists pulling up in the middle of the road to watch them.

Sonja didn't mind. She was looking forward to seeing Emma, and for a while at least she could pretend she was ten again, driving these same roads, her nose pressed against the window of her parents' old Ford, eyes straining to spot a lion or, her personal favourite, a cheetah.

Etosha was starkly beautiful, its open golden grassy plains and swathes of bare earth studded with limestone rocks a complete contrast to the lush bush and web of waterways that made up the Okavango Delta in Botswana, where Sonja and her family had lived after Namibia gained independence. Her father, by then an alcoholic, had taken them into self-imposed exile, fearing that the brutal things he had done during the war against the now-rulers of his homeland would come back to bite him.

Off to her left, as she hung back to stay out of the *bakkie*'s dust cloud, she caught glimpses of a band of white nothingness on the horizon, partly masked by a curtain of shimmering heat haze. This, she knew, was Etosha Pan, the vast salt lake, dry at this time of the year, from which the park took its name. This was hard, barren country, yet an amazing number of animals, birds and other creatures survived here. Natural springs and manmade water-holes supported big herds of braying zebra and the clown-faced gemsbok, which the English called the oryx. Lions had it good during the dry season, reclining lazily by a waterhole and waiting for the herbivores to come and drink. They passed the Rietfontein Waterhole and, judging by the cluster of a dozen or more rented four-by-fours, Sonja guessed there were cats in residence.

But she and her travelling companions in the lead vehicle were not here as game-viewing sightseers, so they pushed on.

Sonja consoled herself with the thought that when she did meet up with Emma, and when her daughter was done with the dig, they would travel back through this wondrous place, enjoying the wildlife and each other's company at a slow, enjoyable pace.

Sonja was feeling good, and at the moment the realisation dawned on her the guilt pounced, like a waiting predator. She should have been here with Sam and Emma. The dying faces of the Vietnamese she had killed flashed into her vision and she had to grip the steering wheel tightly to stop the tremor from taking over her body.

'Get a fucking grip, Kurtz,' she said aloud, and lifted a hand off the wheel and smashed it back down.

She exhaled. Ahead, Brand had slowed, and Sonja used the simple process of lifting her foot from the accelerator and changing down through the gears to bring her back to the here and now. *What is he stopping for? I want to see my daughter.*

A brown arm poked out of the driver's side and Brand waved her forward. She checked behind her and eased the Landy to the right, so that she pulled up beside him. Instantly she saw her, a lioness, her huge muscles expanding and contracting as she slunk across the road. Behind her dawdled four tiny cubs. One stopped in the middle of the road and stared straight up at Sonja. The little cat's golden eyes found a chink in the scar tissue around her heart. She sighed. 'Go on, move along.' As if heeding her command the cub ran off, desperate to catch up with its mother.

The next two little ones played a game designed by mother nature to teach them to hunt: one tackled the other on the road and the cub on the receiving end, a brother perhaps, slapped back with a paw that would one day be the size of a dessert plate. The final cub squeaked and joined in the play chase briefly before they all caught up with their mother, the little ones immediately swallowed by the long grass. Sonja watched the lioness's shoulders rippling under fur the same golden colour as the environment she hunted in. *Perfect killer, perfect mother. At least I got one out of two right*, Sonja thought with no false modesty.

Perhaps inspired by the lion sighting Brand later took a turnoff to the left, towards Okerfontein. Sonja grimaced. 'Bloody sightseeing.' The loop road would add time and distance to their drive. Sonja's impatience, however, softened when they came across a black rhinoceros. She thought again of Stirling Smith. Sonja had been hard on him, perhaps no harder than he deserved, but maybe she ought not to hold grudges for so long. Stirling's heart was in the right place, helping to conserve endangered desert rhino.

What, she wondered, would her life have been like if she had stayed with Stirling and lived out her days as his partner? They would probably have managed a string of safari camps and, one day, sick of pampering spoiled rich foreign tourists, given it all up for the seclusion of a conservation job, living in the middle of nowhere on canned baked beans and two-minute noodles.

Pah. No, she had made the right decision, even though it had cost her the love of a good man and a large chunk of her soul. Sonja's had been a life lived to the fullest. She had been a good soldier and a better contractor – a mercenary, Stirling had called her. She didn't like the word; it had Rambo connotations. She was a professional, most often protecting rather than shooting, but when she had to use the tools of her job, be it an American-made M4 or a trusty Soviet Kalashnikov, she did so with professionalism and skill. She had nothing to cry over, but the bodies and the wounds she had seen in her life had left her a different person, not a better one.

With Sam she had hit the jackpot; he'd been funny, sensitive, rich, and a wildlife lover. Sonja thought about Hudson Brand in the vehicle ahead of her. He was attractive, clearly loved Africa's wildlife – with the zealot of a convert as Sam had – yet there was more to him. There was a hardness in those dark eyes, a reflection of her own. He knew what it was like to fire a rifle in anger, to see comrades fall, and to wake in the middle of the night with the same tortured dreams she had.

'Who are you?' she asked the empty interior of her dusty Land Rover. 'And where are you taking me?'

They followed the edge of the pan for a while then returned to the main wide road that led to Namutoni Camp. Sonja remembered it from her childhood, the whitewashed German colonial fort like something out of *Beau Geste*, the neatly manicured lawns and its oasis-like swimming pool. She followed the men into the camp and got out with them at reception, grateful to stretch her legs.

'How about those lions?' Brand said.

'How about my daughter?'

He nodded. 'I'm just going to check the directions with the people here at reception.'

Brand went inside. Matthew Allchurch sat in their borrowed truck, with the passenger-side door open. Sonja went to him. 'What do you hope to achieve? Do you want to find your son's body?'

He looked up at her, blinking in the strong Namibian sunlight. 'You're nothing if not direct.'

'I try not to waste time with small talk.'

'Well,' he said, cradling his bandaged hand in his good one, 'I suppose you're right. Also, I want to know what he was doing on his last flight, and why.'

'You suspect he was doing something illegal, perhaps immoral?'

Allchurch gritted his teeth, perhaps in pain, perhaps in annoyance at her inference. Either way she didn't care. 'I know my son. He wouldn't deliberately break the law, nor the conventions of warfare.'

She scoffed. 'You'd be surprised what men are capable of in wartime. "I was only following orders" is an excuse to unleash the barbarian that lives within.'

'What about you?' he asked, seeming to gain a moment of satisfaction, or confidence, in turning the tables on her. 'Don't tell me you've never done something you regretted?'

Sonja shrugged. She could see the faces of many, not all, of the men she had killed, and a female suicide bomber in Iraq, into whose head she had put four bullets before the woman had time to press the detonator. 'I sleep all right.'

'Not from what I heard last night.'

'Touché,' she said. 'I hope you find your son, and find out that he was a good man, but be prepared for the worst.'

He licked his lips and reached for a water bottle. 'Thank you.'

Brand came out of the office and strode across to them, quickly.

'Found out where they are?' Sonja asked.

'No. They're gone.'

Chapter 20

Sonja Kurtz stood by the excavated grave in the middle of the grassy plain with her hands on her hips, feet apart, and death in her eyes. 'Don't just stand there daydreaming, we need to get moving.'

Brand was beginning to regret bringing her along. He didn't want to have to wrangle with this wildcat now that she was angry. He looked around, trying to remember that night nearly thirty years ago when he had nearly died.

There had been a full moon, and all he recalled was the flatness of the landscape. The Andoni Plain hadn't changed any since then. He remembered walking, the shock making him shiver, his wounds bleeding, until he collapsed by the main road several hours later.

'Brand, are you listening to me?'

He ignored her, although he knew she was right; standing here was not helping. He looked again around the site, hoping fresh clues might jump out at him, but his mind was too full of the past and how close he'd come to death in that bizarre fall through the sky.

Kurtz was a good tracker, as it turned out. She'd talked briefly of spending part of her childhood in the bush in Botswana, and she must have learned a thing or two then. She had already identified the shoe prints of six people, five men and a woman – her daughter.

'Emma told me in a message there was a young African man working with her on the dig, and her supervisor, a Professor Sutton. She also mentioned meeting a lion researcher, another man. Two others, men not wearing boots or *takkies* like the other four, were also here.'

Brand shook himself out of his reverie and looked at Matthew Allchurch. 'Any idea who else would be interested in the discovery of this body?'

'Police maybe?'

'No sign of them here.' Sonja cast about, still scanning the sandy soil. 'So who are our two mystery men?'

Allchurch took out his phone and inspected the screen. 'No signal here.'

'Who were you going to call?' Sonja asked him.

'Horsman?' Brand asked.

Allchurch nodded.

'Who's Horsman?' Sonja asked. Hudson filled her in.

'He's as obsessed with finding Gareth's aircraft as I am,' Matthew said.

Sonja looked down at the ground then up at Matthew. 'Is he well off?'

'Very. Import-export business and a big share portfolio. He lives in a mansion in Constantia.'

'Likes his shoes?' Sonja asked.

'As a matter of fact he does. He has them hand-made somewhere in Italy.'

'Wears loafers, stands about five-ten or five-eleven?'

'Yes, I'd say he's a shade under six foot.'

'He was here,' Sonja said. 'Question is, where did he go, with my daughter and the others?'

'I only saw him the day before yesterday,' Allchurch said, 'in Cape Town. I had a feeling he might try to find Gareth's aircraft, though he said nothing to me about flying up here.'

'He must have caught a flight earlier than ours,' Brand said.

Allchurch shook his head. 'No, he's got his own aircraft.'

Sonja looked around again. 'Well, he didn't land here.'

'Ondangwa,' Brand said. 'It's not far.'

Sonja nodded. 'I know it. They will have his flight plan. Who's the other guy, his private pilot?'

'No,' Matthew said. 'He's a qualified pilot and he flies himself, but he often travels with his business partner, his nephew, a guy called Sebastian. They're like father and son.'

'Who wears dressy riding boots, like those Australian R.M. Williams?' asked Sonja.

Allchurch thought a moment. 'Yes.'

'How the heck did you pick those tracks?' Brand asked Sonja.

'Sam had them; he did a documentary in Australia years ago. He loved those boots.'

Brand rubbed his jaw with his thumb and forefinger and saw Sonja look to the horizon. *Time to move on.* 'We're jumping to a lot of conclusions here, folks, like that Horsman has taken everyone from the dig on a joy flight.'

'To search for Gareth's Dakota,' Allchurch said.

'I don't care where they've gone, or how,' Sonja said. 'I'm going to find my daughter.' She marched to the Land Rover and was about to get in when she stopped and cocked an ear. 'Hear that?'

Brand's hearing was good; it had to be living as a trails guide leading walking safaris in the African bush, but Kurtz's was better. It took him a couple more seconds. 'Chopper.'

'I don't hear anything,' Matthew said.

Sonja shielded her eyes with her right hand and looked east, then north. 'It's not coming from inside the park. Look, there it is.'

Brand caught sight of the distant speck. Sonja started to open the door of her truck, but stopped. Brand kept his eye on the aircraft. It was coming towards them low and fast. He thought of the ambush on the roadside, and the men who had tried to kill them. 'Get in your vehicle and drive, as fast as you can,' he said to Sonja.

'Why? Is there something you're not telling me?'

'Just drive.' Brand ushered Allchurch into Joao's Isuzu *bakkie*. The older man had gone pale again.

'You don't think it's the same people, do you?' Allchurch said, the panic raising the pitch of his voice.

'Same people as who?' Sonja persisted.

Brand opened the driver's door and got in. 'People who tried to kill us yesterday. Drive!'

Brand turned on the ignition and put the *bakkie* in gear. 'Dammit!' Kurtz had reached into her vehicle and was now standing with what looked like a nine-millimetre pistol in her hand. He took out the Uzi the Portuguese baker had given him and placed it in his lap.

'Make me a smokescreen,' she yelled to him.

Brand knew the smartest course of action might be to drive as fast as he could back to the national park's gate. But Kurtz was just standing there, like an ice maiden. 'For crying in a bucket,' he said.

'What?' Allchurch asked. 'Let's just get the hell out of here.'

'Hold on.' Brand dropped the clutch and put his foot flat to the floor on the accelerator. As he did so he turned the wheel hard to the right. The Isuzu began to spin in circles, the rear sliding in the loose sandy ground. Immediately a tornado of dust began to rise into the clear blue sky, obscuring both vehicles. Through the dust, though, Brand caught a glimpse of Sonja doing something at the front of the Land Rover, then climbing up onto the four-by-four's roof.

'She's crazy,' Brand said.

Brand looked out of the window and up into the sky. He could see the helicopter hovering, and sitting in the door was a man with a rifle. Brand kept the smokescreen going, hoping Kurtz knew what she was doing. Above the whine of the vehicle's engine he heard the *pop-pop* of gunshots.

Matthew was gripping the arm rest of the passenger-side door, a look of sheer terror on his face. 'I don't want to get shot again!'

'Me neither,' Brand said. A bullet tore through the roof of the Isuzu. Matthew screamed. *Lucky shot*, Brand thought, but it would only be a matter of time before their luck ran out. There was no cover for kilometres around them and if they tried to make a run for it the helicopter would simply track them until the gunman hit both of them through the roof. Brand looked around him but couldn't see Kurtz through the dust storm he had created. He had no idea what she was up to. 'I've got to take a shot at these guys and we need cover.'

Brand stopped the Isuzu and, before their natural smokescreen could settle, he ordered Allchurch out. 'Get underneath. You'll be safer there. It'll be harder for the bullets to penetrate.'

Allchurch yelped with pain as he bumped his injured hand while shimmying under the vehicle. Brand made sure the other man was safely under and was about to start sliding himself under when he saw a flash of headlights. Sonja jumped down out of her Land Rover. 'Get under my truck, now.'

'Why?' Brand asked.

'Just shut up and do as I say.'

Brand wasn't used to taking orders from anyone, but another speculative burst of fire through the dust brought this argument rapidly to a head. 'What are you going to do?'

'Draw their fire, make them use up some of their ammo.'

'No way,' he said. 'Stay with us, we'll make a stand.'

'General Custer made one of those and went down in history as a loser. Be ready to open fire on the chopper from the driver's side of the Landy. Both of you stay on that side under the vehicle. Got it?'

Brand nodded. Sonja strode through the settling dust to the Isuzu, climbed in and started the engine. Matthew squealed from underneath, but Sonja simply drove off, leaving him ashen, his eyes wide in his face through a mask of dust. 'Driver's side!' she yelled out the window.

Brand grabbed him by the arm and half lifted, half dragged him to the Land Rover. 'Come on. Let's do as she says.'

'Like we have a choice,' Allchurch coughed.

As the two of them crawled under the bigger four-by-four Brand noticed for the first time a coil of rope and metal cable stuffed under the nose of the vehicle. He had no idea what Sonja had been up to while he had been making the dust screen, but he had a feeling he was about to find out – if she survived the next five minutes.

From his vantage point under the driver's seat he could see the *bakkie* bouncing across the plain at high speed, lurching as it hit uneven ground. Like a lion or a leopard the helicopter pilot and gunman had been unable to resist the lure of running prey. The chopper had swung away from the dissipating cloud and was now bearing down on the Isuzu.

'Gutsy lady,' Allchurch said. He was huddled so close to Brand they were almost touching.

'Yup.' Brand saw the line of bullets bringing up fountains of dust on either side of the Isuzu as Sonja zigzagged. It would only be a matter of time, he realised, before the gunman and the pilot steadied themselves, anticipated her next swerve, and put a bullet through the engine, or Sonja herself.

'She's coming back,' Allchurch said, and Brand could see he was right. Sonja tracked a wide arc around the plain and began heading towards them. 'I thought she was leading them away from us.'

The opposite, Brand realised. He craned his neck and watched the Isuzu flash past the front of the Land Rover, about fifty metres away. Allchurch rolled over behind him to follow Sonja's high-speed progress. The chatter of gunfire was almost unceasing, stopping only to allow the gunman to reload.

About thirty rounds, Brand counted. He reckoned it was a military assault rifle, probably, like the two goons who had taken them on previously had used. Someone did not want him and Allchurch in Namibia.

Brand continued counting bullets while Matthew gave a running commentary. 'She's heading away from us again,' Matthew said, but the note of his relief in his voice didn't last long. 'Oh, no, she's turning, coming towards us now on the other side.'

Brand checked that the Uzi was cocked and ready.

'My God, Hudson, she's coming right for us!'

'Twenty-seven, twenty-eight, twenty-nine,' Brand counted as the bullets pinged into the Isuzu and thudded into the ground closer and closer to their hiding place.

'Shit, she's going to hit us!' Brand felt Allchurch snuggle into his back, and he, too, braced for impact.

With a bang and a screech of metal the Isuzu T-boned the Land Rover, hitting it at right angles. Allchurch screamed. Brand coughed dust. The collision would have looked serious from the air, as it had from Matthew's point of view, but Sonja had hit the brakes at the last minute. Another bullet clanged into the stricken *bakkie*. Brand saw the shadow of the helicopter pass over them, and dust and grit from the rotors' downwash sprayed in under the Land Rover. The pilot was flying low.

Brand suspected Sonja was still alive and had faked the crash to make it look like she had taken a bullet, but alive, dead or wounded, he knew what she expected of him. She had put herself out there as a target for five murderous minutes, and it was his turn now to take the heat. If she wanted fire from the driver's side of the Landy, then that's what he would give her, even if she wasn't alive to do anything about it. He wasn't going to cower under the vehicle like a dog while the gunman took pot shots at them.

'Stay here,' he said to Allchurch. Brand rolled out from under the truck and pushed himself to his feet. He came up firing short three-round bursts from the submachine gun to conserve ammunition, aiming for the gunman where the side door had been removed from the helicopter. He saw the man's open mouth as he screamed instructions to the pilot while trying to reload.

The pilot backed off, but Brand held his ground, pumping four more rounds in the direction of the gunman and pilot. In his peripheral vision he glimpsed movement from the front of the Land Rover, but deliberately did not look that way. Instead, he walked, coolly and calmly, to the rear of the vehicle, the Uzi still tracking the helicopter, which hovered just out of range.

'Come on boys, don't be chicken now,' Brand said.

The pilot lowered the nose of the chopper and it raced towards him, like a bull at a matador's cape. The gunman, Brand realised, must have reloaded. Brand squeezed off two aimed single shots at the pilot. He was a good shot, but even so hitting a man in a moving aircraft with a short-barrelled weapon was harder than it seemed in the movies.

'That's right, come to papa,' Brand said as the chopper bore down on him.

Brand skipped around the back of the Land Rover to the Isuzu. Looking into the cab he saw that the airbags inside had deployed, but there was no sign of Sonja. As the chopper turned broadside he opened up with two bursts as the gunman above replied, more than in kind. Brand dived onto the bonnet of the *bakkie* and slid across to the other side. He glimpsed more movement off to his left and briefly saw the face of Sonja Kurtz appear above the front bumper of the Landy. She nodded and winked to him, and he knew then exactly what he had to do.

Brand darted from the point of impact between the Isuzu and the Land Rover out into the open ground away from the two vehicles, following the tracks that Sonja had made when she had deliberately rammed the Landy. As he ran he imagined the gunman taking a bead on him and the chopper pilot steadying his machine above the two four-by-fours, giving his passenger a stable platform for the coup de grâce.

He stopped and turned and saw the gunman moving the barrel of his R5, peering at him through the sights. Brand fired twice more and had the satisfaction of seeing the rifleman duck and flinch; one of his shots must have come close.

Five metres below the hovering helicopter Sonja was standing on the Land Rover's roof carrier. In her right hand she swung a length of rope, weighted at the end with a heavy steel shackle, the kind used when recovering a vehicle stuck in sand or mud. Sonja let go the rope at the top of an upswing and the shackle sailed up and between the chopper's right skid and its fuselage. The shackle dangled for a moment, swinging in mid-air about a metre from the rear of the Land Rover. Sonja darted to the end of the roof carrier but couldn't reach it.

Brand lowered the Uzi, as if to change magazines. He wanted the pilot focusing on him, and didn't want the man to lose his nerve, even if the gunman had temporarily ducked out of the firing line. The rifleman raised his weapon again, sensing victory. There had been several times in Brand's life of peace and war when he thought he was about to die, and this was surely one of them. It would happen, if Sonja didn't do something soon.

The helicopter was drifting slowly further away from the Land Rover. Sonja backed up three paces then ran, launching herself off the rear of the truck. She reached for the swinging metal shackle and managed to grab it. Her weight caused the helicopter to buck and the pilot reacted instinctively, starting a climb. Sonja's feet touched the ground and she hauled on the rope. At the other end from the shackle she had made a loop which she had attached to the snap hook on the steel cable winch mounted on the front of the pastor's vehicle. Sonja, Brand saw, was furiously trying to pull through enough slack so that she could get the winch snap hook over the skid.

The pilot, however, was punching out, climbing rapidly. Brand ran around the crashed Isuzu to Sonja. 'You're certifiable!' he cried over the whine of the engine.

'He's getting away. Don't let go,' she said.

Brand grabbed the shackle and Sonja started to climb the rope. He marvelled at her strength and reckless bravery. When the gunman stuck his head out the open door Brand used his free hand to put two rounds in the man's general direction, causing him to duck back inside.

Sonja was almost at the helicopter. Brand held fast to the rope as Sonja hooked an arm up over the skid. She used her free hand to yank the winch cable over the skid, and Brand could only imagine the stresses on her lean body as the pilot pitched and rocked the machine to try to shake her off. The rifleman plucked up the courage to look out again, this time with the barrel of his R5 leading the way. Hudson fired, but the hammer of the Uzi clicked on an empty chamber. He swore.

Sonja, meanwhile, had the snap hook of the winch cable in her hand now. As the rifleman took a bead on her she opened the spring-loaded link and snapped it back onto the steel cable.

The first bullet looked to Brand as if it would surely go through her head, but just as he saw the muzzle flashes Sonja unhooked her arm from the skid. As she fell she grabbed the rope and the end of the snap hook. The linkage whizzed down the wire as her body weight carried her down, as though she were abseiling. A burst of bullets followed her.

Sonja landed hard enough to dent the bonnet of the Land Rover, then rolled off the truck as another burst of bullets cleaved the air where she had been.

Brand reloaded. 'Matthew, get out and run!'

Allchurch crawled from under the Land Rover, stood, and ran for the treeline. Brand fired at the chopper on the move as he ran to Kurtz, who was struggling to get to her feet.

'Are you OK?'

'Leave me,' she ordered. She took a deep, obviously painful breath. 'Keep firing.'

She pushed him aside as the Land Rover started to roll. The helicopter pilot was climbing, pulling the winch cable taut and, in the process, dragging the truck forward. Land Rover handbrakes, Brand knew, were famously inefficient.

Brand ran to the passenger side of the Land Rover and got in. 'The pilot's turning. He's going to give the gunner a clear shot at us.' Sonja had successfully lassoed the flying chopper – an impressive feat – but it now looked like all she had done was turn them into a tethered target. Brand leaned out the window and aimed and fired as best as he could until the fresh magazine was emptied.

He thumbed the release button and the magazine dropped into his hand, but when he felt in the pocket of his trousers there was nothing. 'Must have lost my last one when I was on the ground. You got a spare gun?'

'Kind of got my hands full here, Brand.' Sonja started the engine, rammed the gear stick into reverse and stood on the accelerator. The Land Rover fought the helicopter in a tug of war. Her tactic had caught the pilot off guard and he was struggling now just to keep his machine in the air, rather than focusing on giving his gunner a good shot.

The helicopter dropped and Brand saw the concentration and pure fear on the pilot's face through the cockpit window as the aircraft's blade slashed the air in front of their windscreen. 'If one of those blades hits us we're finished.'

'He's finished, too. Get out, Brand. At least one of us needs to survive this so we can kill the bastards that set us up. Find my daughter if it's you. Save her, Brand, her name's Emma.' Sonja battled the helicopter. The Land Rover's wheels spun on the loose ground, fighting for purchase.

Brand looked up. 'He's moving above us.'

'Watch out right!' Sonja yelled.

Brand turned just as the pilot dropped the helicopter and the tip of the skid that wasn't attached to the truck smashed through the right rear passenger window. Sonja braked hard and even more of the skid pierced the cab of the vehicle. Brand ducked to avoid having his skull caved in and swore.

'Oops, sorry,' Sonja said, and let slip a maniacal laugh. She put the truck into first gear and dropped the clutch as she accelerated forward. She pulled the Land Rover off the helicopter's impaled skid, but the chopper pilot, showing great skill, matched her speed. Sonja went up through the gears. Brand knew she couldn't outrun the helicopter and sooner or later the gunner would put some lucky rounds through the roof.

'What are you going to do?' Brand asked her.

'This is your last chance. Get out. Now.'

'No.'

'All right, then put on your seatbelt.'

Sonja veered to the right and wound the speedometer up to eighty kilometres per hour. It seemed much faster on the uneven ground as they bounced up and down in the cab. Brand buckled up. 'Weave, you're spending too much time in a straight line.' Brand stuck his head out of the window and saw he was right. The chopper pilot, still matching their speed, had drifted to the left. The rifleman on board was lying on the floor of the chopper, the barrel of his R5 aimed right at them. Brand ducked as three rounds stitched the bodywork no more than a metre behind him. 'Zigzag, damn it!'

'No,' she said, her voice ice cool. 'See that dip up ahead, with the slight rise on the other side?'

He peered through the dust cloud the chopper's rotor wash was stirring up. It was hardly more than an indentation. 'Seen.'

'When we hit it, hold on. Shit's going to happen.'

Sheesh, Brand thought. Everything about this woman was messy. 'Well, I'm out of ammo, so this better be good.'

She glanced across at him and grinned. 'Oh, it'll be good all right. Now hold the fuck on.'

Sonja revved the engine until it was screaming, then popped up into fifth gear. They were pushing a hundred now, and the depression and dip that had looked quite mild to Brand from a distance loomed up at them like the Grand Canyon. He looked at her and saw she was still smiling, loving this, embracing and enjoying the prospect that she could very well die in the next few moments. Brand knew that ironic thrill that the presence of death could bring.

As soon as their front wheels dropped into the dip Sonja did two things she shouldn't have – she accelerated, coaxing the last of the power out of the Land Rover's engine, and she hauled the steering wheel to the left as hard and fast as she could.

With lightning-fast reflexes, the pilot swung his machine out on the same side, as far as the winch-cable tether would allow. The gunner opened up on them and he must have reloaded, because Brand reckoned thirty rounds punctured the Land Rover from stem to stern.

They started to roll. 'Shit!' Brand said. He braced his hands on the dashboard as Sonja turned the steering wheel in the opposite direction, overcorrecting and guaranteeing that the big, brick-like vehicle would turn over.

Brand felt a stab of pain in his left arm and everything seemed to go into slow motion as the horizon swam and tilted in front of him. He was vaguely aware of a shadow passing over them, then the helicopter swung back into sight and he saw the pilot's mouth open in an unheard scream of terror. The flier was too slow, this time, to stop the rolling vehicle from pulling the chopper down. Its rotors sheered off as they hit the ground, flying in different directions, and then the fuselage ploughed into the dirt. Fire, noise, dust and the agonising screech of twisting metal erupted around them.

*

Sonja coughed. Flames crackled and the tortured frameworks of the helicopter and four-by-four pinged as they expanded and contracted. She spat, undid her seatbelt, and fell onto Brand.

He yelped, which was a good sign. He'd looked motion-less, dead maybe, blood flowing from his head, but he said, 'Goddammit, get off of me.'

She pushed down on him, levering herself up. The Land Rover had come to rest on its left-hand side. She put a boot on Brand's arse and reached up, opened the driver's side door and hauled herself, somewhat painfully, out of the vehicle.

The heat from the burning helicopter washed over her. She jumped down. 'You need help?'

Brand answered. 'No, I can manage.'

'Good.' She had work to do. Sonja surveyed the scene of devas-tation around her. The chopper's tail boom had snapped off and the main cockpit was engulfed in flames. The pilot's body burned like a Roman candle. *Shame*, she thought, he'd been good at what he did, but not good enough. Like all men he was greedy for the climax. She would have stood off and got her gunner to concentrate on the Land Rover's wheels or engine bay instead of trying to get close enough to see the whites of their eyes.

Sonja heard a low moan and turned. Thirty metres away was a prone form.

She pulled the pistol from her shorts and held it up as she approached him. The man was on his back, his face a mask of blood, his arms blackened and his clothes smouldering. He must have been shot out of the bird like a champagne cork when it blew up. The man might have thought himself lucky to be alive. He was wrong.

Sonja looked him up and down. There was no sign of his R5 assault rifle and he seemed clean, but all the same she patted him down. The man winced. 'Shut up.'

He spluttered, then summoned: '*Poes.*' Satisfied he wasn't carrying a sidearm Sonja stood and kicked him, hard, in the ribs. The man screamed.

'No one calls me the c-word, mister.' He convulsed and blood oozed from his mouth. Internal injuries, she thought. He'd die without emergency medical care and there was no chance that was on its way. At least she knew now that he spoke Afrikaans. Sonja kicked him again. 'Who sent you to do this?'

He coughed again. '*Fokof.*'

Sonja put a foot on his right arm, and when he grabbed at her leg with his left she shot him in the forearm. The man screamed again. 'Settle down. It's a through-and-through, you'll survive.'

She shifted her foot to his wound, making him cry out more. She was straddling him now, looking down his body. She put the pistol back in the waistband of her shorts and pulled her Leatherman out of its pouch. She squatted, increasing the pressure on his arms, and eliciting more crying and swearing.

The noises stopped with a sharp intake of breath as she hooked the wicked serrated saw blade into the waist of the man's charred jeans and ripped up, hard and fast, exposing his underpants.

'No.'

'Yes. Tell me your name and who you're working for, or you'll bleed out through the hole where your manhood used to be. Call me *poes* . . .'

'Please, no. I can't tell. I don't know their names.'

'What about yours?' She wrenched down his underpants and grabbed the shrivelled little white thing. She pulled on it and rested the blade under it. 'What's your name?'

'Viljoen. Cobus Viljoen.'

'Good.' She held his prick still and increased the pressure on the blade. 'Now, who are you working for, Cobus?' She looked over her shoulder, meeting his eyes.

'I can't tell you.'

'Yes, you can, and you will, or you'll die.'

'You're going to kill me anyway.' He spat to the side.

'Maybe, maybe not.'

'Kurtz!'

They both turned to look at Brand, who staggered towards them. He held a hand to his left arm and his fingers were stained with sticky, drying blood. 'For crying in a bucket, what the hell are you doing, can't you see that man's wounded? We've got to call the police.'

'Fuck the police,' Sonja called back to him. 'He's going to talk or I'm going to cut his cock and balls off.' She started to move the knife.

'No!' rasped Viljoen. 'Help me, man, this bitch is crazy.'

Brand held his hands up as he approached them. 'Now, now, let's everyone stay calm and there's no need for cussing.'

'Jesus, man, get her off me.'

'Or blaspheming,' Brand said to the man.

Sonja smiled. 'Shut up, Hudson. I just want to see him bleed.'

Brand looked to the man and Sonja focused on her work.

'Now, Cobus,' Brand said. 'Is that your name, did I hear right?'

'Yes, yes,' he wailed in a high pitch. 'Cobus.'

'I believe the lady asked you who you work for. Not too hard, is it.'

Sonja looked at Brand and, when Viljoen said nothing, shrugged. She started to saw, and held on to him tightly as his body convulsed. She felt the hot blood start to wet her fingers, but she knew she had only just pierced the skin.

'Russians! All right, for Christ's . . . I mean, for goodness sake, I was paid by a Russian gangster, all right?'

Brand held up a hand to her and Sonja smiled at him. The terrified man underneath her couldn't see her wink to Brand, or his acknowledgement through a slight nod.

'Names?'

'One guy. His name was Miro, I was never given a second name. You killed two of our crew, Hannes and Eddie, in the BMW.' Viljoen spat blood again.

Sonja was getting impatient. 'And who, exactly, are your crew?'

He seemed reluctant to talk to her, a woman, so she cut a little more. 'Stop that! All right. We're in the import-export business, security, that kind of stuff.'

'What kind of stuff?' she pressed.

'We bring in drugs, mostly. Also hookers and strippers for South Africa – they come into Namibia on tourist visas and we ship them across the border into SA. They're Russian or from some other eastern European places; that's how we knew Miro. Please, please, please stop cutting.'

Sonja steadied the knife, but tightened her grip on him for good measure. She took pleasure in his flinch. 'What do you export?'

'Diamonds, stolen from the mines here or blood diamonds from Angola – they're easier to get. The Russians have contacts in Asia so they take lion bones, ivory and rhino horn when we can get it.'

The mention of rhino horn started Sonja seething. 'You kill rhinos?'

'No,' Cobus squeaked. 'I'd never kill a rhino. I love those things. Besides, it's too hard here in Namibia; the distances are too big. We move some horn out of South Africa occasionally, and stuff stolen from stockpiles.'

'And this Miro took out a contract on us?'

Cobus nodded vigorously. 'Yes, that's right.'

Brand stood over him. 'Your other guys followed us from Windhoek's airport. How did you and the pilot know we'd be heading here?'

Cobus shrugged. 'We were given the GPS coordinates from Miro. We were told to come here and waste anyone we found at the archaeological dig site.'

Sonja inhaled sharply. She stood up, grinding her foot into Cobus's arm. He screamed, but she didn't care. She left his flaccid penis, oozing blood, hanging outside his shorts. She turned to look down at him. 'Anyone?'

Cobus squinted up at her; she'd put the sun behind her head. He looked like a rat caught in its nest, blinking up at the unaccustomed light. This piece of filth would have killed her daughter if Emma had been there.

'What are you going to do to me? I need a doctor. I'll tell you anything else you want to know.'

Sonja shook her head in disgust at this whining, cowardly creature. 'So, I don't suppose you know who Miro is working with here in Namibia, who would want a harmless archaeological team wiped out?'

'No. No, I don't,' Cobus said.

Sonja drew her pistol and pointed it between his eyes. At that moment she heard another vehicle engine and scanned around her. It was Matthew Allchurch, in the Isuzu, its front end crumpled in, steam hissing from under its bonnet. He drove towards them. She looked down at Cobus once more. 'I don't believe you.'

'No! I promise you, I'm telling the truth.'

'Kurtz? Sonja?' Brand said from behind her, but his voice sounded far away. 'I think he's telling the truth, Sonja.'

Sonja looked around at Brand. '*Ja*, I think you're right.' She turned back to Cobus, raised her pistol again and shot him in the head, twice.

Matthew Allchurch stopped the *bakkie* and got out. He walked over to join Sonja and Brand. He looked down at the body, retched and threw up. 'My God.' He wiped his mouth with the back of his hand when he had finished and said shakily, 'Who are you?'

Sonja looked at him, the pistol hanging loose, comfortable, in her right hand, like a natural extension of her body. She felt calm now that it was over. She blinked twice at the lawyer. He and his generation had sent countless thousands of young men off to war, on the border of South Africa and hundreds of other shitholes around the world, happy to be fighting the good fight against international communism or whatever ideology or religion their governments told them was wrong today, but they rarely saw for themselves the consequences of armed conflict. 'Who am I?' It was a good question. 'I'm a mother trying to find her daughter before someone kills her.'

Brand put a hand on her shoulder and she flinched. She snapped her head around and glared at him. 'You don't think maybe we could have got some more info out of that guy Cobus?' he said.

'I think you were right, that he was telling the truth and didn't know anything else. What would you have done with him?'

Brand shrugged, but she held his eye. She wanted to see what kind of man he was. 'He was in a bad way, internal bleeding and all. You could see it. Even if we could have got him to a hospital within an hour – pretty well impossible since you killed the only helicopter probably within a hundred miles – he wouldn't have made it. I heard you tell him that he'd be OK, that he just had a through-and-through wound. You gave him hope to get him talking.'

She scoffed at him. 'So what would you have done, made him comfortable while we waited for an ambulance to get here?'

'Can't say I know for sure. Maybe the "mercenary's gift", the quick way out, was the best thing for him.'

'You think I was being kind to him? *Pah*. He would have killed Emma if he'd found her here – you heard what he said – and for that he deserved to die. No one fucks with my family, Brand.'

PART 3
REVENGE

The desert lioness stood in the cave, her body tensed, her ears twitching, always on the alert for danger.

She pushed. The first tiny cub left her womb, landing in the darkness and the dust. The lioness turned, inspected the little one, gnawed the umbilical cord in two and licked her baby clean of fluid. Twice more she went through the same timeless ritual before allowing herself to rest.

Her work was just beginning. The little bundles around her would be blind for some weeks yet, totally dependent on her milk. It was up to her now to keep them safe from predators and to hunt and eat enough for herself to keep the nourishment flowing for her babies.

The odds were against them all. The father of these cubs was dead, shot while raiding a *kraal* and killing a donkey. Here in the Etendeka Mountains, though, she had a chance. This was a protected area where no human should hound her.

She and her kind had been driven out of their homelands, persecuted for decades, but here in the cave was their future, their revenge.

Chapter 21

They had been driving for three hours through the heat of the day and not even the air conditioning in Benjie's Land Cruiser could outdo the heat of the sun's rays slanting in through the window.

Emma stared out at the red rock of the flat-topped mountains in the distance. Namibia's landscapes changed quickly and dramatically. They were beautiful, turning from red to purple with the movement of the sun, but Emma couldn't really appreciate the spectacle. Benjie's satellite communications system had still been down when they'd flown back to the farm. She had been unable to get a message to her mother. Benjie, who had lent two vehicles to Andre Horsman but had elected to stay behind, promised he would get word to Sonja as soon as the system came back online.

Sonja, Emma knew, would be officially pissed at her right now.

Alex seemed similarly annoyed. He looked back at her from his position in the front passenger seat. Sebastian was driving the Land Cruiser and Natangwe was beside her. 'I really should have gone back to Ondangwa and got my vehicle,' Alex said.

Emma sighed. This whole trip had, literally, been on the fly. It had seemed exciting at first, but now Emma couldn't help but feel they'd been kidnapped by two overly enthusiastic old men. She would never have picked Sutton for the adventurous kind, but who knew, perhaps in every professor there lurked an inner Indiana Jones. Emma just thought they were being damned irresponsible now. They didn't even have a satellite phone among them any more, since Alex's had been stolen – Sutton had one, but when Emma pleaded with him to let her use it to message her mother he discovered it had run out of credit and he had no way to recharge it. *Absent-minded old fool*, Emma said to herself.

Professor Sutton and Andre were in the other vehicle, a double cab Hilux *bakkie*. Sebastian was hanging back about a kilometre behind the others, to stay out of their dust cloud. Alex looked forlornly out of his window and Natangwe had his head back, snoring gently. Sebastian took his eyes off the road for a couple of seconds to glance back at her and wink. Emma felt herself blush.

As the day wore on Emma dozed on and off, and more often than not when she woke she could see Sebastian's dark eyes in the rear view mirror, watching her.

'It's getting late,' Sebastian said eventually. 'But we're nearly there.'

Alex was holding his hand-held GPS up to the windscreen, to acquire enough satellites to give him a reading. 'About four hundred metres to the north, though the reading may not have been accurate given the speed we were flying at.'

Sebastian nodded. 'Understood. The prof and Andre are stopping up ahead.'

They pulled up and the two older men were already out, a map spread across the bonnet of their *bakkie*. Sutton came over to them, rubbing his hands. 'Right. We've still got an hour of light left, maybe two, so let's get cracking.'

'Professor, once we have located the wreckage I can borrow a vehicle to go look for the lionesses, and the carcass of the male, yes?' Alex asked Sutton.

Sutton grimaced. 'Yes, yes, very well. That was the deal we made. Once we find the Dakota we'll need to set up camp and start mapping the site, so we won't need both vehicles all the time. We'll make camp here for this evening, whatever happens.'

'Then let us go,' Alex said. 'The quicker we do this the quicker I can find my lions.'

Alex climbed up on the roof of the Land Cruiser and began tossing down tools, tents, canvas-covered camping mattresses, a bundle of firewood, and a couple of tarpaulins.

'Alex, you stay here, sort things out, will you?' Sutton called up to him. 'And toss me your GPS, I'll follow it to the bearing you took.'

Alex nodded, dropped to his knees on the roof-rack and passed the GPS to Sutton. He stood again, picked up a shovel and waved it at Emma.

Emma held out her hands, and when Alex tossed the tool to her she caught it, then reached into the back of the four-by-four for a litre bottle of water.

Sutton consulted the GPS then pointed towards a steep slope to their left, a mix of sand and rock. He set off, with Andre at his heels. It looked like a daunting first leg.

Sebastian took another spade and a pick and fell in beside Emma. 'I can't believe Alex is still going on about *his* lions, as though he owns them. Guy's obsessed.'

Emma nodded, but even in doing so she felt like she was being unfair to Alex, somehow betraying him.

'Yes, but if we have a tent to sleep in tonight it will be Alex who puts it up for us.'

'Fair dues,' Sebastian said, then lowered his voice. 'Hey, I wonder if the prof will let us share a tent.'

The thought made her heart beat faster. 'As if.'

'I'll come and visit you, tonight,' he said quietly, then louder, 'OK, let's go find this aeroplane.'

He strode ahead of her, lean, fit, sure footed. He was like a male lion; no, she thought, reconsidering, more like a leopard. He was sleek, muscled, but sly and cunning as well. She shivered again, despite the heat from the mix of sand and rock beneath her feet, thinking of what they might do later on.

Emma was perspiring within a few metres, and realised just how unfit she was.

Sebastian turned round, grinning, not huffing or puffing in the slightest. 'Need a hand?'

'Bugger off.' He could be condescending sometimes.

The view from the top of the bank was spectacular and, at the same time, awesomely scary. Emma paused, catching her breath, and looked over thousands of square kilometres of nothing. In the far distance, to the west, beyond what at first appeared to be endless lines of dunes was a low-lying band of cloud that hugged the horizon. That was the Skeleton Coast.

'Amazing, isn't it?' Sebastian had turned so that the sun setting over the Atlantic burnished his face orange-gold. He looked so incredibly rugged and handsome.

'It is. It's like we're the only people on earth.'

Sebastian lowered his voice again and whispered into her ear: 'Right now we are,' and lightly kissed her cheek before he strode down the hill.

Emma set off after Sebastian, the professor and Natangwe. Andre, carrying a shovel, had taken the lead, and Sutton was calling out changes in direction to him, unable to keep up. For some reason Emma had begun to be suspicious of Horsman. She couldn't put her finger on exactly what it was about the South African that she didn't trust, but it was there, niggling away in the back of her mind.

Was the desire to find the men in his command who had been missing for so long the only thing driving him? Andre had been a military man, and from what Emma knew of such people, principally through her mother, they didn't even go to the supermarket without a plan. Sonja would make lists for a weekend away with Sam, of things to take, places to go, and sights to see. 'Time spent on reconnaissance is seldom wasted,' she would say to him, quoting Sun Tzu. Emma and Sam had discreetly rolled their eyes at each other behind her mother's back every time she came out with one of those military dictums.

No, there was more to Andre than the commanding officer not wanting to leave his men behind. This operation had been planned in haste, as if Andre feared that someone else might get to the aircraft before them. So what if that happened? Why would Andre want to be there first, and why was he not worried at all about their inability to contact anyone outside of Benjie the farmer?

'Here!' Andre yelled. He waved his shovel in the air, then seemed to almost disappear as he jumped off a rise, or perhaps into a hole the others couldn't see. Professor Sutton started running, madly gesticulating towards an object that Emma, squinting into the setting sun, now saw was definitely not part of the natural landscape. It was angular, jutting out of the sand. She broke into a jog, and savoured the charge of adrenaline that coursed from her heart.

Sebastian slowed to wait for her, then took her hand. Instinctively, she pulled back, but he held tight to her. 'It's uneven here. Let me help you.'

She relented. 'OK.' His touch was electric.

'That looks like the first thing we saw from the air. It'd make sense as it's still rocky here, that's why it's visible.'

Sebastian had to catch a breath. His excitement was infectious. Ahead of them Sutton had reached the object and was standing with his hands on his hips, silhouetted in front of the red ball of the setting sun.

They walked to him. 'What does it look like, Dorset?' Sebastian asked the professor.

The older man turned to them. 'It's not part of an aircraft, that's for sure.'

Emma wondered for a moment where Andre had disappeared to, but when she reached Sutton she saw Horsman's head and torso appear. He was waist deep in a hole in the sand that looked to be about three metres by three metres square. Around the edge of the hole were timber crates and what looked like faded cotton webbing straps. A piece of black plastic sheeting, half buried, snapped in the breeze.

'No, not part of an aircraft, but definitely from an aircraft.' Horsman was smiling and his eyes were wide.

'How do you know?' Emma asked him.

Andre bent into the hole again and when he stood straight he was holding a shroud of ripped and faded green or khaki nylon in one hand. 'Because of this. It's a parachute.'

'Is there another person in there, like Harry?' Emma asked.

'No, not a person,' Andre said. 'Have a look at the boxes scattered around here. They're military ammunition boxes, stencilled with the identification marks of the South African army. The Dakota was on a mission to drop cargo to a recce-commando patrol.'

'So the patrol was here?' Natangwe asked.

Andre shook his head. 'No, the patrol was actually offshore, operating in small boats. That's why all the ammunition and supplies were wrapped in plastic.'

'So why do you think the box ended up here?' Sutton asked.

Andre looked at him and shrugged. 'Jettisoned, perhaps? Maybe the Dakota had engine or fuel trouble and they wanted to lighten their load.'

'What happened to the cargo?' Emma asked.

'Locals must have found it some time ago, looted it,' Sebastian said.

Natangwe snorted. He dropped to one knee to inspect the stencilling on the side of one of the opened green boxes. 'People out here are poor, but what would they want with seventy-six-millimetre high explosive anti-tank rounds?'

'Come to think of it,' said Emma, 'what would a bunch of guys floating in little boats at sea want with tank shells?'

Andre coughed. 'Well, odd things happen in war. I know for a fact that sometimes these artillery boxes were used to carry other cargo; there were always plenty of empty crates around and they're sturdy, good for carrying stuff that needed to survive a parachute drop.'

'It still doesn't find us an aircraft,' Natangwe said.

'No,' Sutton agreed, stroking his white beard and looking up into the sky, 'but it tells us the Dakota passed directly over us. We're on the right track.'

Chapter 22

Irina Aleksandrova continued reading the printed dossier her head of security, Mikhail, had prepared for her as the Air Namibia flight from Frankfurt began its descent into Hosea Kutako International Airport.

Mikhail was based in Moscow, which was lucky for him. If he'd been in Ho Chi Minh City when the mad woman had kidnapped her and murdered Tran, then she would have killed Mikhail herself. As it was, she had learned a lesson. He had wanted to come with her to Vietnam, but she had assured him that she would need no close personal protection there. She had assumed she would be safe there, and that had been one of the few poor decisions she had made in her life.

She finished her champagne and the flight attendant moved swiftly to her side – it was first class after all – and took the glass away. Mikhail was behind her in business class, and it made her feel a little more relaxed to know he and Yuri would be with her. Irina liked operating covertly, alone, but there were some missions where force and numbers were needed. In Vietnam she had successfully set up a trading network with Tran and had done nothing to quell the rumours that she and he were an item or, worse, that she was a prostitute.

Irina smiled to herself. It was easy, now that she looked back on it, for the journalist, Coonan, to have come to such a conclusion. He was a man, and like too many in his profession he'd been driven by a need to report sensationalism and salaciousness. She was a single, attractive Russian woman living by herself in a condo in Saigon, and she'd made regular, scheduled visits to a wealthy Vietnamese organised crime figure. Occasionally, she'd also visited the brothel. What Coonan hadn't realised, however, was that she had never sold herself for money and that rather than going to the upmarket whorehouse to make money or receive her assignments, she'd gone there to collect cash. Madam Nhu's was owned by her company.

Where she had fallen down, she realised as she flicked through the dossier in search of the photograph, was that she had dropped her guard and allowed herself to be photographed, followed and, ultimately, kidnapped. She would never make that mistake again, and the woman who had brought her undone and killed her business partner would die.

She was less worried about Tran – he would be replaced by someone within his organisation or else Irina would find another Vietnamese outfit to deal with – than she was about the woman. Irina came to the page she was looking for and stared into the cold, blank blue eyes of Sonja Kurtz.

The photograph was blurry, an enlargement of a low-resolution file ripped from the internet, but it was clear enough for Irina to recognise the woman immediately, and to commit her strong features to memory. The picture was from an article about the funeral of the American environmentalist and documentary film-maker Sam Chapman. Irina had never heard of the man before her kidnapping but she conceded, now, that Coonan had come to the correct conclusion that the horn taken from the rhino on the night the Mozambican poachers had shot this Chapman had indeed been bound for Tran.

Irina thought about what she might have done if she were in Sonja Kurtz's shoes. *Probably the same thing.* While she could empathise with Kurtz, Irina could not afford to let her live. Mikhail's research had tracked her to the continent of her birth, to Africa, the same place Irina happened to be heading.

The Airbus touched down with a squeal of rubber and Irina looked from the file, whose salient points she had committed to memory, to the dry landscape that flashed by outside.

Irina felt refreshed from her sleep on the plane, one of the benefits of flying at the front of the aircraft, as she waited inside the terminal for Mikhail and Yuri to catch up with her. 'See to the rifles, Yuri,' she said to Mikhail's number two.

'Yes, Irina Petrovna,' Yuri said, addressing her by her patronymic name, Petrovna, as a form of respect for his superior.

Irina and Mikhail cleared immigration quickly and a car was there to take them to the general aviation terminal, where they waited in an air-conditioned lounge for Yuri to catch up with them. Irina had coffee and read a local newspaper, *New Era*. On page five was an article about the SWAPO government getting tough on foreign ownership of land. Irina shook her head. She had managed to buy six thousand hectares of bushland, once used for sheep and cattle farming. The government was ranting, again, about absentee landlords, pointing the finger at Germans and other foreigners who lived abroad but maintained their game farms largely for their own private pursuits instead of the greater good of the people of Namibia.

That was exactly why Irina had bought her land, and why she was here to add to it, so she could have somewhere to retreat to in solitude whenever she felt the need to go hunting or to entertain her business associates. The hypocrisy of the situation was evidenced by the fact that she had paid a hefty bribe to a local government official and party member to smooth the way for her purchase. If anyone outside their circle or in the media asked, then the local authorities would point to the endangered species breeding program that Irina was establishing on her farm as a model of conservation management that would pay dividends for the local community and the environment. In reality, Irina would be breeding trophy antelope and lions to be shot by hunters.

Irina was about to put the newspaper down when a headline caught her eye. *Rhino horn smugglers in court again.* She read the story; the two Chinese men who had been arrested at the very airport they had just passed through with fourteen rhino horns in their possession had appeared in court for a second time. Bail had again been refused and the men's advocate had entered pleas of not guilty. Irina folded the newspaper and passed it to Mikhail.

He read the article. 'Still no mention in public about where the horns came from.'

Irina pursed her lips. They had been using Namibia as a conduit for horns taken in South Africa for some time, but this seizure was not from one of their suppliers. 'Any ideas?'

Mikhail shrugged; it was a barely perceptible gesture thanks to the thickness of his neck and his massive shoulders. 'I was trying to find out while you were in Vietnam. If they were South African, or taken by Mozambicans, we would have heard, but our people know nothing of a shipment this size. It doesn't tally with what we know is in the market from South Africa, and what the police and army there have seized this year. It could be Zimbabwe.'

Irina mulled the figures over. 'Perhaps they're from stockpiles? We would have read online if there had been this many killed recently; there are only about eight hundred animals left in Zimbabwe.'

'You're thinking it's from the aeroplane.'

Irina exhaled. 'I don't want to get my hopes up. It would be a shame if the aircraft has already been found by some local people and looted.'

Irina's contact in southern Africa had alerted her to the internet news article about the discovery of the body of a South African flier on the plains just north of Etosha National Park. The man had been excited about the discovery and had put into place a plan of his own to investigate the discovery. He seemed to think it might be a clue as to the location of the missing transport aircraft crammed with rhino horn from Angola.

Her father had spoken of the lost Dakota every now and again, his tone full of the same reverence with which a treasure hunter might speak of a Spanish galleon full of gold doubloons. Her man in Africa had, in fact, been her father's business contact during the war in Angola.

Her father, Dimitri Petrovna, had been a colonel in the KGB, based in Luanda, Angola, and her uncle Sasha had been captain of a fishing boat, trawling the international waters off the coast of that country and the old South West Africa. The two brothers had worked hand in hand, not only to further the cause of international communism in the Third World, but also to line their own pockets. When the Berlin Wall came down and Russia adopted a free market economy, Dimitri and Sasha had the experience, the money and the connections to set up a business empire that soon spanned several continents.

Yuri arrived with the bulky baggage and it was loaded into a twin engine turboprop aircraft, which the three of them boarded. A little over an hour later they were landing at Irina's game farm.

It was good to be back in Africa. She could see why her father had loved it here, even though it had then been a war-ravaged country all but devoid of wildlife. It was the sky, Irina thought as she climbed into the open-topped Land Rover game viewer driven by Benjie, the manager of her farm. He had been a sheep farmer, but the German former owners of the property had been reluctant to invest the capital needed to keep the farm viable. Irina had inherited the farm, and Benjie van der Westhuizen – and his wife and two small children – as part of the deal.

Benjie was much older than her, having served in the same war as her father, but he was ruggedly handsome. He tipped his hat to her as he made sure she was seated. 'I suppose you'll want to rest,' he said to her as he climbed into the driver's seat. Mikhail and Yuri were in a second vehicle behind them, which would catch their dust. Irina liked to ride alone with Benjie. She enjoyed verbally sparring with him, and more.

'What makes you think I'm tired? You know I don't need much sleep.'

He glanced back over his shoulder as they took off. 'I remember. So, I take it we're going to the lodge?' Benjie asked into the slipstream.

The Land Rover bounced over the red dirt road and Irina had to hang on to the safety bar in front of her. 'Take me to Gemsbok Dam.'

Benjie glanced back at her. 'Just us?'

She laughed. 'No, you horny Afrikaner, all of us. I have a new toy I want to try out.'

Benjie looked up at the sun, riding high above them. 'It's nearly midday, Irina. We'll be lucky to find any game at all at this time of day.'

'Oh, you'll find them,' she said. 'That's why I pay you, to keep me satisfied.'

Benjie laughed, then drove off the road to the rutted track that led to Gemsbok Dam, the largest waterhole on the farm.

She knew they were close to the dam, but she was surprised when Benjie pulled over and switched off the engine after a few minutes of driving. He took the .375-calibre hunting rifle from its padded case on the rack across the dashboard, got out of the vehicle, and worked the bolt to chamber a round.

'Why are we stopping here?'

'It's the middle of the day. The animals will be surprised if we show up at the waterhole in the vehicles. They're more used to us going on game drives in the early morning and late afternoon. We'll walk in. It's only a kilometre or so.'

Irina climbed down. Mikhail and Yuri pulled up behind them and the following breeze blew dust over her, which Irina waved away. 'Get the case down,' she said to Yuri in Russian.

Yuri produced a set of keys and undid the padlocks securing the long aluminium case. Irina tapped him on the arm to move him aside and knelt in the dust. She opened the case almost reverently. Inside was a 7.62-millimetre Dragunov sniper's rifle. It wasn't a hand-crafted hunting rifle, it was a workmanlike piece of equipment, the Russian military's chosen weapon for its marksmen. Its utilitarian nature aside, it was still, Irina thought, a thing of beauty, with its futuristic – for its time – stock, enclosed handgrip and its long lines. She lifted the rifle from the case.

'Fill me a magazine, Yuri,' she ordered as she peered through the telescopic sights, aiming at a bush two hundred metres off. She pictured Sonja Kurtz in the crosshairs.

'There's 7.62 in the ammo box in the back of my Land Rover,' Benjie said to Yuri, pointing to where the bullets were. 'I brought some for the two AK-47s in case you wanted to fire them as well. Will that be OK for your Dragunov?'

Irina nodded. 'I would have preferred the special sniper cartridges, but that will suffice. We may use the AKs later.' Yuri deftly loaded ten rounds into the box magazine and handed it to Irina, who fitted it and cocked the rifle.

Benjie lifted a sand-coloured military-style hiking pack from the front passenger seat of the Land Rover, shrugged it on and took up his rifle. 'Shall we?'

'Have you seen lions lately?' Irina asked as they walked.

'Yes, at Gemsbok Dam, just two days ago. The pride is doing well. One of the lionesses was pregnant and I didn't see her with the group, so she's most likely left the pride to have her cubs.'

'That's exciting,' Irina said.

As they continued through the dry, thorny bushveld Irina felt the adrenaline pumping through her body, banishing any tiredness she might not have slept off in first class. Her father had first taken her hunting in Siberia when she was twelve. She had cried when she'd shot her first red deer, but her father had explained to her as he'd butchered the dead animal the importance of what he was teaching her. The meat from the deer had fed them and her mother waiting at home, and Irina's father had told her the skills that she was learning and would hone as a hunter – tracking, reading the wind and animal behaviour, and having the courage to overcome her emotions – would stand her in good stead when she grew up. He was right, Irina mused as she followed Benjie's footsteps, careful not to make too much noise. Sonja Kurtz was a hunter, a predator, and Irina would need all of her skills and more to corner her quarry and dispatch her.

Benjie raised his hand and Irina stopped. Benjie pointed ahead and to the right. Through the bushes Irina could see sunlight glinting on the surface of the waterhole. She put the butt of her rifle on the ground, resting the barrel between her legs, and lifted the binoculars hanging around her neck. On the other side of the waterhole was a magnificent male kudu. He was drinking while his two companions scoured the surrounding bush and the edge of the pan for danger.

'How old do you think he is?' Irina asked Benjie.

'Two and a half twists on his horns, a nice long mane under his neck – I'd say about six years old. He's in his prime.'

Irina had begun shooting for the pot, her family consuming everything she and her father shot, but in later years she had developed a taste for trophy hunting, lining first the walls of her dacha outside Moscow and more recently her Namibian safari lodge with the biggest and best examples of every species she could hunt.

'I want him.' Irina suppressed a smile. She didn't want to look too keen. 'I need to get closer.'

She turned to Mikhail and Yuri and motioned for them to wait where they were. Benjie led off and she followed him, her Dragunov held up and ready across her chest.

They did not have to walk far, only another seventy metres, until Benjie positioned them to the right of the three kudus, at the edge of the cover the thornbush provided. If they moved into open ground to close the distance between them the animals would see them and run.

'Do you need a support, a tree maybe?' Benjie said quietly.

Irina shook her head. She moved her left foot forward a little and bent her leg slightly, moving most of her weight onto that leg. She pulled the butt of the rifle hard into her right shoulder and slid her index finger through the trigger guard. Irina knew where to aim; the kudu was standing in a perfect position, its left side towards her. She placed the crosshairs on the spot just to the rear of where the bull's left front leg met its body, right over the heart. She breathed in and out, watching the sights rise and fall. After taking her next breath she exhaled half of it, until the crosshairs were back on the heart. Irina began to squeeze her whole right hand, not just applying pressure on the trigger, just as her father had taught her.

A musical tone sounded behind her and the kudu took flight, all three of them leaping high into the air and then bounding away.

'*Ty che blyad*?' Irina snarled.

'What?' Benjie asked.

'What the fuck is that?' Irina repeated, in English. The

ringtone got louder and Mikhail barrelled his way through the bush to her.

'You idiot,' she barked.

'Forgive me, Irina Petrovna. It's Miro. You said I must keep the satellite phone on at all times in case he called and –'

'I *know* what I said.' She snatched the phone from him and stabbed the answer button. '*Da?*'

Irina listened to the report from her man on the ground in southern Africa. Miro was a Serb, based in Johannesburg, who acted as her local contact with the South Africans who sourced rhino horn, diamonds and other local commodities for her, and assisted with logistics and shipping.

'Unacceptable,' she said into the phone. 'Find another helicopter and a pilot who will collect some reinforcements from the trawler.'

She ended the call. Mikhail took it back from her and raised his eyebrows.

'That idiot, Miro . . . The local hit men he contracted to kill Allchurch and Brand failed. He sent two more in a helicopter and Sonja Kurtz and the others brought down the chopper and killed them as well.'

Irina ran a hand through her hair. She was surrounded by incompetents. Miro had been a spymaster during the Cold War and he did, at least, have a good network of informants throughout Namibia. Irina knew that Brand, Allchurch and Kurtz would now start searching for the downed aircraft. She had to get there before them, and with enough firepower to protect her consignment if it turned out that the missing aircraft was found and the rumoured cargo was still present. She already had one of her fleet of shipping trawlers in the Atlantic, off the coast of Namibia, waiting to take the cargo on board. The crew were hard men, many of them combat veterans, and they would be her muscle.

'Irina!' Benjie hissed.

She turned and saw the guide and hunter raise his rifle. He was peering into the bush, and as she followed his eye line she heard a low menacing growl.

'What is it?' Mikhail said.

'Quiet. Back up, slowly,' Irina said to the bodyguards.

She tossed the phone to Mikhail and raised her own rifle again. Not a bird called, not an insect chirped. A tawny blur erupted from the khaki bush ahead of Irina and rocketed towards Benjie, whose rifle shattered the silence.

The lioness's head and forequarters came into view as she leapt at Benjie and her body seemed to rock in mid-air as his bullet hit her, but when the big cat hit the ground she kept coming at him. Irina took aim at the moving target and fired, twice.

Benjie went down, the lioness landing on top of him, her claws instinctively attacking, raking at the guide underneath her. Irina ran forward and fired twice more into the lioness.

'Are you alive?' she panted.

Benjie, white-faced and shaking, tried to crawl out from underneath the dead lioness. Mikhail and Yuri, at first tentative, caught up with Irina and helped her move the big cat off Benjie. When they had rolled the cat over Irina saw that the lioness's nipples were distended and she certainly did not look pregnant. Irina put out her hand and Benjie clasped it. She pulled him to his feet. 'Talk to me.'

Benjie seemed incapable of speaking at first. He coughed and turned to look at the dead cat. 'I . . . I heard her.'

'And you probably saved us,' Irina said. 'You're bleeding, Benjie. Mikhail, use the satellite phone to call an ambulance.'

Benjie looked down at his arms, only just seeming to realise that he was bleeding. The lioness had shredded both his forearms in her dying moments and blood was welling up from the deep lacerations. 'There's a first-aid kit in my pack.'

'See to him, Yuri,' Irina said, and started to walk away.

'Where are you going?' Benjie asked, his voice croaky. She looked at him. His face was pale, but Yuri was already dousing the wounds with saline and had a dressing out.

'You said yourself, the lioness probably had cubs.'

Mikhail had been connected to a medical air evacuation service and was giving them directions to the lodge on the game farm.

'Leave them,' Benjie said.

Mikhail ended the call. 'We must get him into the vehicle and to the lodge, Irina Petrovna. A helicopter is on its way.'

Irina turned to face the three men. 'What I *must* do, Mikhail, not that it is any business of yours, is to rescue this lioness's cubs. They'll die without my care. Don't you understand that?'

Irina turned and set off back into the bush.

She picked up the spoor of the lioness in the powdery dust between the thornbushes. It was easy to follow, and she traced the path the lioness had taken when it had come out to investigate them. She heard a soft squeak, a repetitive *ow, ow, ow*. She walked a little further then stopped and listened once more. She heard the noise again and moved towards it.

In a thicket of long grass she found them, three tiny cubs, their fur spotted and their fluffy ears seemingly too big for their bodies.

'Hello, my babies,' Irina said.

The cubs called still for their mother, but were too small to know that humans could pose a threat to them. Irina slung her rifle over her shoulder and, after a bit of running and chasing around the grass, managed to coral and then scoop up all three cubs.

Irina held the cubs close to her, nuzzling them as she walked back. 'There you are, let Mother look after you.' Two of the cubs, she noticed, were female. She would hand-raise the girls, find someone to care for them when she was in Russia and, eventually, she would buy a male lion to service them and begin her breeding program.

'And you,' she whispered to the tiny male cub, 'you will grow into a fine, big black-maned lion. You'll make a lovely trophy for a hunter one day.'

Chapter 23

Brand marvelled at the change in Sonja Kurtz.

She looked calm and collected as she reassembled the folding-stock variant of the AK-47 assault rifle that she had just finished cleaning and oiling. She was sitting cross-legged on the polished concrete floor of the family cottage he, she and Allchurch were sharing in Namutoni Camp, in Etosha National Park.

Strewn around them were the supplies they had gathered that day in Ondangwa. Joao, the Portuguese baker-cum-arms dealer, had met them in the car park of a shopping centre and transferred several bundles wrapped in blankets from the back of his truck into Sonja's Land Rover which, though badly damaged on the side where it had rolled over, was still moving. They had replaced a shattered windscreen on the Land Rover, but they had abandoned the Isuzu at the King Nehale entrance to Etosha when its radiator had given out. Joao had been less than impressed, but Matthew had promised to pay for all his repairs, or buy him a new vehicle.

It had been a busy day, starting with nearly being killed, and they were all exhausted, yet Sonja had given her orders and they would be wheels-rolling at six the next morning. Brand checked his watch. It was just after ten at night. Despite his tiredness he was still wired from the day's events. Allchurch was in bed, asleep, leaving the last of the packing to the two ex-military people. 'Want another beer?'

Sonja worked the cocking handle of the rifle backwards and forwards a few times then dry-fired the action before looking up at him. 'No thanks, I'm good.'

She had taken a nap in the afternoon, seemingly having no trouble sleeping on her own command, and she looked clear-eyed and alert. She had also showered, washed her hair, and taken her clothes to the camp laundry. Brand had cast an appreciative eye over her as she'd walked to the laundry clad only in a bikini top and a printed wrap she had bought from a roadside curio stall on the way back from Ondangwa.

The previous night Sonja had passed out, drunk, but tonight she had limited herself to two beers and no spirits. She stood, wrapped the weapon in its blanket again, and sat at the small dining table opposite Brand. She checked her phone. 'Bingo.'

'What is it?' he asked.

'It's the lion research people. They've finally sent through the GPS coordinates for where the dead desert lion is believed to be. We're officially in business.'

They had caught a lucky break, hopefully. After they had survived the attack at the dig site they had driven to Ondangwa, reasoning that the helicopter had most likely taken off from the nearest airport. They had driven to the general aviation section of the airport and asked in the terminal for the contact details of anyone who chartered helicopters. It turned out there was only one operator and it was the man who had been flying the machine that Sonja had downed.

It was one thing to know that they had been right about the helicopter departing from Ondangwa, but it brought them no closer to the people who had bankrolled the hit on their lives.

'Did you see that *bakkie* outside in the car park, the one kitted out with the roof tent and all that camping gear?' Sonja had asked him in the terminal.

Brand recalled the vehicle. 'It had *Desert Lion Researcher* or something like that on the side.'

Sonja had nodded. 'Emma said she had met a boy, a Namibian German, who was working with predators, both cheetahs and the desert lions.'

She had asked the woman at reception if she knew who the owner of the vehicle was. The woman had replied that while she didn't, the young man driving it had asked her to have security keep an eye on the truck while he was away on a charter flight.

'How many other people were on that flight?' Sonja had asked.

The numbers had matched the tracks of the people at the dig site, and when Sonja had shown the woman behind the counter a picture of her daughter on her phone, the woman had confirmed that Emma had been on the charter, which had left two days earlier, but had not yet returned.

'Was the aircraft South African?' Allchurch had interrupted. 'Owned by an Andre Horsman?'

The woman said she could not reveal the name of the owner.

'We could try and get the flight plan from the authorities,' Brand had said to Sonja. 'Might help if you had any contacts in the police.'

Sonja had moved away from the receptionist and the counter. 'That'll take too long. Get ready to see what she's hiding behind that counter of hers.'

Sonja had left them and gone into the ladies room in the terminal. A few minutes later a piercing alarm had sounded. The receptionist had rushed from her station to the toilets. Sonja later revealed that she had held her cigarette lighter up to the smoke detector. The ruse had given Brand time to do as

Sonja had ordered: he had moved behind the counter where the receptionist was based and checked her computer. It took him just a minute to find a log of departures for the past week. Two days earlier Andre Horsman, his aircraft, and five passengers, including Emma Kurtz, had taken off. The destination was listed as Rundu, in the far north of the country, but Brand reckoned that was the last place they were headed.

Sonja had got online on her phone and found the contact details for the Namibian Predator Project and called their office in Swakopmund. The coordinator there told them that their researcher, Alex Bahler, had sent an SMS from his satellite phone advising that he was leaving his vehicle at Ondangwa to go on a charter flight which was searching for a downed aircraft, and, at the same time, would allow him to search for the male lion that had been reported as dead. The coordinator asked Sonja to ask Alex to get in touch with the office if she located him, as they were beginning to become concerned about his whereabouts.

Brand watched Sonja checking their inventory of food, drinks, medical supplies and other equipment from a list she had drawn up. She was focused, meticulous and professional, the epitome of a good soldier. She tucked a stray strand of blonde hair behind her ear. She was also damned attractive. He found it hard to reconcile those little feminine touches, like fixing her hair, with the person he had seen execute a wounded foe. He wondered if this was part of his attraction to her, in some slightly disturbing way. He hadn't wanted to talk to any of his previous girlfriends about his time in the war and in Angola, and none had shown any particular interest. He felt that with Sonja neither of them needed to outdo each other with war stories, but there was a shared connection between them. Brand had had his fair share of nightmares and, like Sonja the night before, had tried to keep them at bay and still the shake in his hands with booze.

'Can I help?' he asked her.

She was packing foodstuffs in cardboard cartons. 'No, thanks.' She gave him the briefest of smiles and it seemed so out of character for her that he felt a jolt in his heart. 'I'm all good. It's keeping me from worrying about my daughter.'

He understood. 'I need some fresh air. I think I'll take a walk to the waterhole.'

'OK, see you just now.'

Brand let himself out of the chalet and took the wooden walkway that connected the accommodation to the floodlit waterhole just outside Namutoni's perimeter fence. He paused. Somewhere far off a lion called. As always he found that the sounds and smells of the African night helped soothe him. They were heading for danger, there was no doubt about it. Sonja Kurtz had saved his life and Matthew's, and he and the mild-mannered retired lawyer had narrowly escaped death on the road as well. In the morning he would give Allchurch one more chance to fly home. Brand doubted Matthew would turn back, but one thing he was sure of was that Sonja would march through hell's fires to find her daughter.

He took a seat on a bench under the thatch-roofed *lapa* and watched a lone bull elephant drinking from the waterhole. The massive pachyderm shone a ghostly white in the glare of the floodlight, his skin coated in a fine layer of Etosha's white talcum-powder dust.

He tried not to think about Sonja. Instead, he put his mind to understanding what was going on somewhere out there in the wilds of Namibia, and what his enemies were up to. The archaeology team's departure with Allchurch's contact, Andre Horsman, was linked to the attempt on their lives, of that Brand had no doubt. Horsman had been at Ondangwa during the war. Brand hadn't met him, but from the description Matthew had given him, Brand wondered if Horsman was the fair-haired man who had tried to kill him on the Dakota all those years ago. But if so, how had he survived the crash of the Dakota, and why didn't he know where the plane had landed?

Brand had the coordinates of where the cargo on the Dakota was to be dropped that night; he had taken them from the map in Venter's flight suit pocket after he had killed him. Brand had been surprised to see that the cargo was to be dispatched at a point in the Atlantic Ocean. He remembered running his hands over the loads and wondering why they were wrapped in plastic. This, clearly, was to allow them to float. That meant that a ship would be waiting to collect the contraband.

Horsman had told Allchurch that his son's mission was to drop supplies to a special forces unit operating in small boats off the coast of South West Africa near the Angolan border. Brand thought this was ludicrous. There was nothing on that coast that would warrant a raid by the South African recce-commandos. Allchurch, too, had questioned the mission, and had wondered if his son was instead flying a load of SWAPO guerrillas who were to be thrown to their deaths. Brand had been able to assure Allchurch that was most certainly not the case.

Brand came back to his theory that Horsman had not been the worried commanding officer back at base but the gunman on the flight, and that he'd somehow survived the crash. That also explained why someone was trying to kill him and Allchurch now. Horsman would have used Allchurch over the years to scout for leads to the whereabouts of the missing aircraft. Now that Horsman had the information he needed, Allchurch was surplus to his requirements, and the last thing Horsman needed was for Allchurch to be present at the discovery of the Dakota and its cargo.

But if that theory was correct, why, Brand wondered again, did Horsman not know where the plane had crash-landed? *Who rescued him, and why didn't they go searching for the Dakota back then?*

'Beautiful animal.'

Brand was startled. Sonja had come to the hide overlooking the waterhole without making a sound. 'Yes, it is.'

'I grew up around wildlife, in the Okavango Delta, but I never really appreciated the animals and birds. I was restless; I wanted to see the world and the British Army seemed to offer me the best way to do it. Crazy, hey?'

'No, I was the same,' Brand replied. 'My mom had lived in Angola and thought America would offer us a better life, but all I wanted to do when I was growing up was come to Africa – that and join the army.'

'We are alike, you and I,' she said.

He glanced at her, but she was looking at the elephant. She had made a statement of fact, not one of endearment. 'We should all just walk away from this.'

'For you and your travelling companion this is about finding a plane, or cargo, or a body; I'm going to find my daughter.'

'You're convinced that Horsman's up to no good?' Brand asked.

'Aren't you?'

He nodded again. They were thinking along the same lines, not trusting anyone. 'I don't believe in coincidences, like your daughter and her fellow archaeologists suddenly disappearing without any ability to get a message to you, and then the dig site being strafed by a helicopter gunship. Nice work with the chopper, by the way.'

'Why thank you. That's possibly the nicest thing that's been said to me in a long time.' She looked as though she was about to smile again, but frowned instead. 'That is, apart from "sorry for your loss".'

Brand winced, remembering that he'd said the same thing to her. However, he resisted the urge to say something comforting. It would be wasted on her. Better, he thought, to stay silent and let Sonja talk if she wanted to.

They watched the waterhole without speaking for a while, then Sonja said, 'I loved Sam. I don't know if I've ever actually loved anyone other than my daughter. When he died it was like having a piece of me amputated.' She looked at him, straight in the eyes. 'You know what that's like?'

'Yes.' He did, and it still hurt, all these years later. It was in Angola and, like Sonja, the woman he'd lost there was probably the only one he'd ever really loved.

The elephant moved off and was followed, ten minutes later, by a black rhino. Hudson saw it first as it emerged from behind a stand of tall reeds growing at one end of the waterhole, and pointed it out, silently, to Sonja, who nodded and smiled when she saw it. The rhino approached the waterhole cautiously, a few steps at a time, its head raised, listening for signs of danger. Eventually it reached the edge of the water and drank. Its reflection was mirror-sharp in the still, floodlit water. They watched the rhino for twenty minutes, until it turned and headed back into the bush.

'Thank you,' Sonja said.

'What for?'

'For not saying anything. Some people never stop talking; they seem to think that if they keep speaking, mouthing platitudes, that they'll make me better, like some stupid wizard muttering an incantation.'

He nodded.

'You can talk now.'

That made him smile. 'I'm an investigator. A tip a police officer friend taught me a long time ago is that if you want someone to talk, sometimes it's better to say nothing. People will eventually fill the silence.'

Sonja chuckled. 'So you were playing me?'

'No, no,' he assured her. 'I've felt your pain. There's nothing I can say that will make you feel better. I can tell you that killing more people, or drinking or smoking yourself to death won't ease the pain. You just got to take it.'

'*You just got to take it?*' She seemed to mull the words over, as if she were tasting them, savouring them. 'I like that, Brand. I kind of wish I'd brought a cooler box with some beers now.' She checked her watch. 'We've got to be up before dawn. I want to get out of Namutoni as soon as the gates open.'

'Agreed,' he said, though she made no move to stand. A hyena gave its mournful *woo-hoop* call, close by. 'Tell me about this friend of yours who works in the Palmwag Conservancy, the one who's going to help us.'

Sonja pursed her lips and Brand thought she was going to clam up again. All she'd told him and Allchurch, before going outside from the chalet to make a long call that afternoon, was that she had a friend who worked in the conservancy, which lay to the south-west, between where they were now and the Skeleton Coast. Sonja had told them, after the call, that her friend would be able to guide them to the place where the lion was killed, and that he would know if there was any suspicious activity on the Palmwag Conservancy or any of the adjoining wildlife reserves.

'Name's Stirling Smith,' she said at last, almost sighing as she spoke the words, as if it was a reluctant duty. 'We were childhood sweethearts, I guess you'd say. I left him, in Botswana, to see the world. I hurt him. He's involved with desert rhino monitoring and research, but he knows the lion people. He'll be able to guide us to the coordinates of where the male lion was killed.'

'The name sounds familiar,' Brand said. He had a feeling he'd seen or heard of the man, in connection with rhinos.

'He was in the news this week, commenting about those Chinese guys who were arrested at the airport in possession of fourteen rhino horns.'

Brand snapped his fingers. 'That's it, the SABC news and online.' Brand, like a couple of the more astute journalists who had covered the seizure, had been intrigued by the discovery of so many horns at one time. There hadn't been fourteen rhinoceros poached in the whole of Namibia in the last few years, so the horns had to have come from some other source. There had been speculation that they might have been transited out of South Africa, or perhaps from some other government stockpile. That had happened close to where Brand lived, near the Kruger Park; some horns had been stolen from the secure vault of the provincial parks board's offices. 'I'd be interested in talking to him about that.'

'Whatever,' Sonja said. She was reluctant, it seemed, to talk more about her former boyfriend.

As with before, he knew not to push it. Brand stood. 'Like you said, we should hit the sack.'

She stayed sitting, eyes scanning the darkness beyond the cordon of light. 'I saw movement out there, just now.'

Brand followed her line of sight and saw the slope-shouldered bulk of the hyena as it loped into view and headed straight for the water.

'I love these things,' Sonja said.

The hyena, in Brand's experience as a safari guide, rarely made it to guests' top ten animals though he, like Sonja, had a soft spot for them. 'They live in a matriarchal society where the highest ranked male in a clan is still subservient to the lowest female in the pecking order. They're extremely efficient predators. I've no idea why you might like hyenas.'

Sonja looked up at him and for a moment he thought he'd overstepped the mark, but then her eyes softened and her grimace cracked. She stood. 'I like you, Brand.'

She stood and exited the hide to the right, away from the walkway that led there. Curious, Brand got up and followed her outside. He found her, standing in the dark, out of the floodlight's reach, staring up at the sky.

'The stars are amazing here. I'd forgotten how clear the sky is; I used to lie on my back for hours as a child just staring at them, imagining . . .'

Brand stood next to her and looked up as well. 'Imagining space travel? Alien civilisations?'

'A country without war.'

He looked at her upturned face. There was just enough light to illuminate her features. They were strong, angular almost, but not unattractive. Before, in her grief and dishevelment, she had seemed fragile, but now that she had regained a semblance of normality – even if that normality was the guise of a trained killer – he found her confidence and sense of purpose attractive. Arousing.

Sonja lowered her gaze and looked at him, almost as if just noticing him. 'It was close today, with the chopper.'

'Yes, it was.'

'You've been there, on the front line, on the edge of life and death. In Angola?'

'And elsewhere.' It wasn't the time for war stories, though, he realised. If she was only just noticing him, as a man, then this was the first chance he'd had to look at her eyes. He was a sucker for eyes. Hers were beautiful. 'Damn close.'

'Exciting, wasn't it.' Her voice was low. He glanced down, saw the rise and fall of her chest, her bush shirt stretched across so that he could see the button straining against the stitched hole.

Sonja might, Brand thought briefly, kill him if he was misreading this, but at the same time he didn't care. He took the half step needed to close with her, a jolt of adrenaline firing out from his heart to the rest of his body like a car being jump-started. *No*, he told himself. He checked himself. She was on the rebound, still grieving over Sam Chapman.

Before he could move away her mouth was on his. It was more a collision than an embrace. Her lips were crushed against his and he felt her hands move up under his jacket, her nails, though bitten to the quick, digging hard into the muscles of his back through his shirt. He'd thought she had looked like a tormented feral animal when they'd met, but now she was like a lioness, snarling, biting, almost demanding as he felt her hands on his belt buckle. There was no doubt where this was headed now.

He shrugged off his jacket and tossed it on the ground, and while his hands were off her she undid his zip. Brand took her in his arms and kissed her hard. She ground herself against him, one leg hooked around him, and he felt the heat of her. She was breathing hard as he undid the button on her shorts and slipped a hand inside. She breathed in his ear. 'Yes. Now. Quickly.'

Brand lowered Sonja to the ground, on his discarded jacket, still kissing her as he wrenched her shorts down and over her legs. They were in the shadows, but otherwise exposed. The thought of someone coming to the hide for a late-night stroll both worried and excited him. Sonja seemed not to care. He pulled back from her and she clutched at him, raking his arms, then paused when he produced his wallet and the emergency condom he always carried.

She grinned, pure lust in her eyes. 'Boy scout?'

'Bad boy.'

She grabbed the front of his shirt and pulled herself back up to him as he fumbled with the foil wrapper and rolled on the latex sheath, one-handed. She reached for him, taking him in her hand, spreading her legs wide. Sonja guided him and grunted as he started to push. He held back but she grabbed him, harder, and pulled him into her. Brand needed no more encouragement and he was overcome by the primeval need to fuck, or to forget, or both.

Sonja kept kissing him, her tongue matching his thrusts, drawing him into her, taking his face in both hands one instant then digging the fingers of both hands into the flesh of his bottom the next, drawing him deeper into her body. Any thought of discovery vanished; he was consumed by her eyes, by the noises she made, by the taste and smell of her.

Her cries became quicker, shorter, higher-pitched, almost out of character with the steely controlled warrior he'd seen that day. 'Fuck, yes,' she said, too loud, and he smothered her mouth with his own. She bit him, on the lip, almost in protest at his attempt to silence her. He tasted blood and she sucked on the wound. Brand felt her muscles squeezing him and it was more than he could take.

Sonja locked her legs behind him and drew him in, even deeper than before, as her whole body clenched around his. He shuddered and held the violent, passionate kiss with her as he felt her gasps.

He was exhausted, and when the shaking had stopped and their heartbeats slowed a notch he rolled off her, landing heavily in the cool sand and grass. Sonja lay her head on his chest, her breath still coming in short, hot bursts.

Brand put an arm around her, but she shrugged him off, not resentfully, but gently.

'We need to get up before someone sees us,' Sonja said.

'Now you think of that?'

Sonja found her shorts and pulled them on, lifting her hips off his jacket so she could zip and button up. She got to her feet and looked around, then reached out a hand to him and he clasped it. 'Come on, up you get, old man.'

'Hey, go easy on the "old",' he said, though he felt every one of his considerable years right now.

When they were both standing he took her in his arms again and kissed her. She pulled back a little and looked up at him, then raised a finger to his lips. 'Shush, no talking now. I wouldn't know what to say.'

'You took the words right out of my mouth.' He bent and collected his jacket, shook it, then held it out to her.

'No, thanks, I'm still warm.'

He smiled. When they walked back to the hide, and the light, he could see that her cheeks were flushed, and it made her look better, happier, healthier. He was pleased. Brand felt the night air chill the sweat on his back and he shrugged on his jacket. It was still warm from her, and he liked the idea of keeping her close to him, feeling her, a little longer.

She walked ahead of him, leading the way from the hide to the chalet, not bothering with a torch. When they got back the unit was dark, Matthew having turned in. Brand opened the door and switched on the light. He wasn't one to feel awkward around women, but he knew Sonja was calling the shots this time.

Sonja went to her door, put her hand on the handle and turned to him. 'I'm going to take a shower.'

'OK.'

'Alone.'

He nodded. 'Fine.'

He walked towards the door of the room he was sharing with Matthew, but Sonja moved across the small living area to stop him. She put a hand on his chest. 'Hudson . . .'

'Yes?'

She looked up at him, and he looked into those eyes that he'd just devoured. 'Thank you.'

He said nothing.

'What happened just then; I don't know what it was, but it can't distract us from the mission.'

'Agreed.'

She stood up on her toes and he bent his head and kissed her.

'Get some sleep.'

She left him and went into her room. He watched her through the open door. He wanted to go in there and lie down again with her on the bed, but he knew he needed to let her be. She couldn't be forced; she would either come back to him or not, but she was right – for Sonja at least, the mission would always come first.

Chapter 24

They drove hard through the long, hot day, Sonja at the wheel most of the way, and when Brand took over she used her down time to sleep. She didn't feel the need to while away the hours with small talk.

Sonja was keyed up for the mission ahead. Although she didn't really know their enemy, there was no doubt that someone or some organisation was out to stop Brand and Allchurch finding the missing aircraft, and, by association, she was marked for assassination as well. At least that was how it seemed, but not everything was adding up.

They had, true to her plan, been the first vehicle out of Namutoni Camp when the gates opened at six in the morning. Sonja had taken them through the park at the maximum legal speed – she didn't want to get caught by rangers or traffic cops for speeding inside a protected reserve with a Land Rover full of assault rifles, pistols, hand grenades and ammunition. Their stops had been few and brief, only for the call of nature and refuelling.

Sonja watched her rear view mirror and scanned the air for tails, but if there were more hit men out there, they hadn't zeroed in on them yet. They would be careful next time, she reasoned. Brand had outgunned them on the road between Windhoek and Etosha and she had brought down their helicopter – Namibia was a small country with a low crime rate and incidences like these would eventually come to the attention of the local police. Sonja couldn't call in the cops even if she wanted to. They were on their own, but she was happy with that. Brand was a good man.

And that was a problem.

Perhaps she was aware of her feelings because she had been sober the evening before, at the Namutoni waterhole. *I like you, Brand*, she had said to him. It was a statement of fact, and she was sure, or at least she hoped, that he had read nothing more into it, but something told her he had, and that she had meant more than the mere words expressed.

It was crazy, she thought, as she glanced at him in her peripheral vision. She had only just met the man, and he had brought down a world of hurt on her – nearly got her killed in fact. Sonja reached for the map and flitted her eyes between the road and the paper.

'Here, let me navigate,' Brand said in that deep voice of his, just a trace of southern United States drawl still evident. He wasn't handsome in the clean-cut, chiselled way that Sam had been, but he was easy on the eye, if a little weather-beaten. He was a man who had been through hell, just as she had, and survived, but was still able to wink and smile every now and then. She thought that in him she saw, perhaps, hope for herself. He'd alluded to losing a woman in the Angolan war. Not losing, she reminded herself, more like having your heart cut out.

'I'm just looking for the next turnoff is all,' she said to him, not meaning to sound as petulant as it came out.

'I reckon it's about ten kilometres from here. Have you been to this part of Namibia before?'

She shook her head. 'No. This is new to me.'

'Amazing landscape, what with all these flat-topped mesas and valleys. It reminds me a little of Monument Valley.'

Sonja checked the mirror. Still no one behind them, and Allchurch was sleeping in the back seat. Matthew's supposed ally, Andre Horsman, was shaping up as their principal enemy and, in Sonja's book, that made him her number one target. If he had harmed Emma in any way there would be no mercenary's gift for him; he would die slowly and painfully.

'What are you thinking about?' Brand asked her.

'Killing people.'

He chuckled, but she silenced him with a glare. 'Lighten up.'

She was offended. '*Lighten up*? You're the one with the contract out on you – you and Matthew.'

'I've been thinking about that,' he said.

Brand had a sparse way of talking, as if he were a fisherman casting out a line, waiting for her to bite. 'Thinking about what?'

'If Horsman's the Mister Big of this operation, I can under-stand him wanting to rub out me and Matthew. We both know almost as much about the missing aircraft as he does, and if he's got a line on it, he wants us out of the way.'

'Yes,' she said. He was stating the obvious.

'But what about you? Why would he want to kill you as well? The guy you shot said he was told to wipe out everyone at the dig site, right?'

Sonja nodded. 'A vague order. What if we'd been escorted there by national parks officials or police? Would he have killed them as well?'

'Exactly,' Brand said. 'I think that guy Viljoen might have kept something back.'

Sonja thought about what Brand was saying. If he was right, if the gunman, Viljoen, had been told specifically to kill her, then there was more to this than met the eye. It also meant she had fucked up by not interrogating him in a more effective manner, and perhaps by killing him prematurely. 'But why me?'

In the back of the Land Rover, Matthew Allchurch awoke. 'Sorry, was I snoring? Where are we?'

Sonja checked the pastor's satellite navigation device. 'Close, ten minutes away from Palmwag Lodge.'

'OK,' Allchurch said.

'Say,' Brand said, looking over his shoulder, 'your pal Horsman – you said he was into import-export.'

'Yes, that's right. He brings in electronics from Asia, exports some South African specialty food products. There are South African shops around the world thanks to the diaspora.'

'What part of Asia? Wouldn't include Vietnam by any chance, would it?'

Allchurch rubbed his chin. 'Yes, I think so. I remember him talking about his last trip to the Orient; he went to Thailand and I'm pretty sure he said he was going to Ho Chi Minh City, or that he had been there.'

Brand looked at Sonja. 'Are you thinking what I'm thinking?'

'I am,' she said. Brand clearly didn't believe in coincidences, and neither did she.

'You haven't visited Vietnam lately, have you, Sonja?'

Brand was teasing her, she thought, or perhaps just fishing. 'Where I've been is none of your business, Brand.'

He held up his hands in mock surrender. 'Well, a friend of mine in the South African National Parks criminal investigation services told me a certain Vietnamese kingpin in the rhino trade had been assassinated recently.'

'That so?' Sonja tightened her grip on the Land Rover's steering wheel. She checked the sat nav.

'Yup. He asked me if I had any idea who might have been responsible. You know, people sometimes talk, especially people in the South African ex-military world, about taking the law into their own hands. Crime's bad in SA, but the whole rhino poaching thing really seems to bring out the vigilante side in some folks.'

Sonja gritted her teeth. 'Well, I wouldn't know anything about that.'

'From what I read in an article by that author and journalist, Ross Coonan, the guy in Vietnam was probably going to be the end user of the rhino horn that was taken the night your husband was killed.'

She glared at him.

'That same Ross Coonan was also killed in Vietnam, same time as the kingpin.'

Sonja was seething inside. The fact was that she *did* feel guilty about Coonan's death, even though she told herself, time and time again, that she had given Ross the chance to pull out, several times. She thought about what Brand was saying. If Horsman was involved with the rhino horn trade then maybe his partners in Vietnam had called on him to take out a hit on her. That, however, would assume someone had already tracked her down. She had entered Namibia quietly and illegally so she didn't see how that was possible, but another thought crossed her mind. If she was a target then so, too, was Emma; perhaps someone had located her daughter and knew that Sonja would come to Emma's rescue if something happened to her.

'You think they're still after us?' Brand asked her, breaking into her thoughts.

'Wouldn't you be?'

Brand nodded. 'I would. But hey, they must be running short of manpower now; we've taken out four of their guys.'

'And a helicopter.'

He smiled. 'Yes, and a helicopter.'

'If this is a war, Brand, it's only just beginning.'

'Yup.'

The GPS announced they were arriving at their destination, Palmwag Lodge, on the edge of the Palmwag Conservancy.

They turned off the main gravel road and stopped at a thatch-roofed access gate, where they signed in.

'What is this area?' Allchurch asked from the back.

'It's a wildlife conservancy,' Brand told him. 'Back in the day this was all cattle land, but the Namibian government took it over and set it aside for wildlife. The local communities around the conservancy benefit from tourism here, and it's a sanctuary for endangered animals such as the desert rhino, desert elephant and the desert lion.'

Sonja hadn't been to this part of her home country before. The lodge looked well set up, with a sign to a swimming pool and bar beyond the reception area. In the car park, near where she pulled up, was a Volkswagen Amarok four-by-four *bakkie* with a rhino conservation charity logo and the names of various corporate sponsors plastered on its sides. Stirling Smith walked out of the reception building, a map in one hand, and Sonja took a breath to still herself.

His clothes were dusty and sweat stained, his eyes soft and blue. He walked to her.

'Sonn.'

He always called her that. He didn't seem to know if he should hug her so she extended her hand between them. 'This is Hudson Brand, Matthew Allchurch.'

The men all shook hands and Stirling suggested they go into the lodge. They passed through reception and followed a path to the bar and swimming pool, where plump tourists were turning their pale European skin pink on sunbeds. Stirling led them to a table under a thatched umbrella-shaped *lapa*, and a waiter came over and took their order for a mix of Cokes and coffees.

'Thanks for seeing us at short notice, Stirling.' Sonja was determined to keep this businesslike. They had lost their virginity to each other, but that hadn't been enough to keep them together forever.

'No problem at all,' Stirling answered.

'As I told you on the phone, we're looking for some men who might be flying over this part of Namibia.'

He nodded vigorously. 'I'll stop you there, Sonn. I think I've got some news for you.' He unfolded a map of northwestern Namibia on the table. When the waiter arrived with their drinks they set them down on the stone pavers beneath them and Stirling arranged the map so they could all see.

'Our scouts and the conservancy's rangers are always on the lookout for suspicious activity, because of the presence of the rhinos. Here in the northwest of the conservancy,' he said, stabbing the map with his forefinger, 'our guys have seen an aircraft flying over the last couple of days, west, then east again, then back to the west.'

'What's up there?' Matthew asked.

'Not much,' Stirling said. 'Few tourists venture into that part of Palmwag. It's wild country, rocky desert, sand, dry riverbeds. The Hoanib River runs along the northern border of the conservancy and that's popular with four-by-four enthusiasts – mostly South Africans – and tour operators as it's a main thoroughfare for the desert elephants. However, people mostly access the Hoanib from Sesfontein or Purros to the north, using the main roads around the conservancy. Like I said, not many people drive through the Palmwag area itself.'

'To the west is the Skeleton Coast National Park,' Sonja observed.

'Yes, more endless tracts of nothingness. If your people are looking for a missing aeroplane they've got a lot of ground to search.'

Sonja knew, however, that their enemies were following the same track as they were. Brand stood to get a better look at the map and she knew he was mentally transposing the supposed route of the lost Dakota, from where the body of Venter had been found north of Namutoni to the drop point just off the coast in the Atlantic Ocean. He traced a line with his fingers.

'That'd be right,' Brand said, running a finger along the line that marked the northern border of the conservancy. 'They would have overflown that area.'

'You know where these people would be flying?' Stirling asked.

'More or less,' Sonja said. 'What's the quickest way to get there, and then on to the Skeleton Coast?'

'Straight line.' Stirling traced a path through the conservancy, from the lodge where they were now up to the northwestern corner of the reserve. 'The roads are pretty good for the most part. You could go on the outside roads to Khowarib and cut into the Hoanib at Sesfontein, but that's further by distance.'

'And can we cross into the Skeleton Coast Park up there?' Sonja asked.

Stirling shook his head. 'No. The nearest gate into the national park is a hundred and thirty kilometres southwest of here.'

'That won't do,' Sonja said.

'There's a track to the coast that follows the Hoanib River, but that passes through a private concession. Access through there is forbidden,' Stirling said. 'I can't be a party to helping you break the law.'

That was his problem, she thought. He was such a stickler for the rules that he cared more about not crossing lines on a map than he did for the safety of her daughter. It was pointless trying to argue with him, but at least it meant he would not try and accompany them, like a lost puppy. On paper he was the perfect partner – handsome, intelligent, clearly still in love with her, but when push came to shove he always backed away and played it safe.

'Of course not, Stirling, and rest assured we have no intention of breaking any rules.' Sonja glanced at Brand and noted his raised eyebrows.

'It's been unusually busy up in the Wilfriedstein and Sesfontein areas recently,' Stirling said, keen to turn the conversation away from illegal activities.

'How so?' Brand asked, sipping his Coke.

'Well, the desert lion people just had one of their animals shot up that way. Our guys thought that the aircraft flying overhead might be looking for the lion.'

'We believe there may have been a lion researcher on that aircraft; a Namibian by the name of Alex Bahler.'

'Ah, Alex,' Stirling said. 'I know him. Good kid, super dedicated. You say your daughter's on the plane too, Sonn?'

She wished he wouldn't use the diminutive of her name around strangers, but she didn't want to make a thing of it in front of Brand. 'Yes. She's with a team of archaeologists and they're looking for the aircraft that went down during the border war.'

Stirling rubbed his chin. 'Yes, so you said on the phone. Long way south of the border.'

'Long story,' Brand said.

Stirling nodded. Sonja thought he wouldn't want to know more, in case it embroiled him in yet more wrongdoing. 'And you think she's in trouble?'

Sonja didn't know how much to tell him, but she couldn't hide the fact that she had traipsed halfway across Namibia to get here. 'Yes. It's all too suspicious. We think there's valuable cargo on the missing plane and that the man flying that aircraft will stop at nothing to find it. If he does, he won't want to have witnesses around.'

'Wow. Sonja, if there's anything I can do, I'm here for you.'

Here being the operative word, Sonja thought, tucked away in his lodge or his research camp, sheltered from the real world of crime and death. 'You're doing more than enough to help us right now, by giving us intelligence. We don't want to put you or your men in harm's way.'

'In harm's way?' He sounded offended. 'My men and I caught two poachers last week and they were armed with rifles.'

Sonja was not easily impressed, and arresting a couple of poachers wasn't enough to make her fall at his feet, but at least it showed Stirling was not afraid to get into the field occasionally and get his hands dirty. 'I didn't mean to offend you, Stirling. What else has been going on lately?'

He seemed to relax a little in his chair. He blew on his coffee and drank some of it before replying. 'Well, we think those two poachers were spurred on by a big seizure of rhino horn that happened at the airport in Windhoek recently.'

'I read about that,' Brand interrupted. 'Where did that rhino horn come from?'

Stirling became animated, and Sonja could tell he was in his element talking rhinos. 'Well, the interesting thing, Hudson, is that we think it came from our area, but not from rhinos that were killed by poachers – we've only lost two in the last few years.'

'I don't understand,' Matthew said. 'Where did they get fourteen horns from?'

Stirling referred them back to the map. 'The two Chinese guys arrested were junior engineers on a road gang, working northwest of us, on the salt road. The only rhinos in this area are in the Palmwag Conservancy, around here, so the police asked me if I'd help them find out where the horns were from. We have DNA samples from all the rhinos we monitor, so it's reasonably easy to tell if the horns were from rhinos related to our ones.'

'And?' Hudson asked.

'They weren't. In fact, there are DNA samples from all the viable populations across Namibia and the horns seized at the airport didn't match any of them. The other thing was they looked very old, not fresh at all. My opinion was that they'd come from a stockpile somewhere, but when the police checked there were no reported thefts from the Namibian national parks stockpiles.'

'South Africa?' Allchurch said.

'No,' said Stirling. 'The last heist of stockpiled horn in SA was from the Mpumalanga parks board's strongroom, but these horns didn't match any DNA samples from the recorded horns over there either.'

Sonja listened, her mind processing the information. She looked at the map again. The tiny towns of Sesfontein and Wilfriedstein were very close to the projected flight path of the Dakota that Hudson had showed her on their map.

'So,' Brand said, 'no matches with rhino populations in Namibia and South Africa, and the horn was old. Close to thirty years old?'

Stirling shrugged. 'Hard to say, but it was all very odd. It was like these two Chinese guys had stumbled upon some hoard of buried treasure. I mean, fourteen rhino horns – that's worth more than a million, maybe two million dollars in today's money.'

'Hudson?' Sonja gestured to Brand with a nod. 'Please excuse us, Stirling.'

'Sure,' said Stirling.

She stood and walked away from the table. Brand followed her to the edge of the pool. 'Tell me, what was on that Dakota?'

Brand looked back at Stirling. 'You heard the scientist – those horns weren't from South Africa or Namibia. I always thought the cargo on the Dakota was ivory, which was the big commodity back in the late eighties.'

'But it could have been rhino horn.' Sonja felt her anger rising. This stupid pursuit of horns made of keratin, the same substance as human fingernails, had left a trail of death and sorrow throughout Africa, and cost the life of her soulmate. It seemed destined to plague her life.

'Yes,' said Brand. He ran a hand through his thick hair. 'It's possible. There were rhino in Angola, as with the rest of southern Africa, but most of them had been taken out by the end of the war. It's possible UNITA had a stockpile and they were offloading them to raise money for arms, or for the senior guys to line their own pockets once they knew Savimbi was finished.'

Sonja thought through the economics, and overlaid it with her knowledge of the time. 'Horns are smaller, lighter than tusks, and worth a lot of money, but the markets weren't as accessible.'

'You're right,' Brand agreed. 'China was locked off from the west back then, and the Vietnamese didn't have the cash-flush economy they do now.'

Sonja thought about the coordinates Brand had showed her, the ship waiting off the coast of South West Africa, just inside international waters. 'Russians?'

'Could be,' Brand said. 'When I worked for the Company, the CIA, we did what we did to further America's aims. Sometimes it was illegal, like the guys who used to run drugs out of the Golden Triangle – Laos, Burma and Thailand – to fund anti-communist rebels, or Savimbi selling ivory and diamonds to buy guns, but the deal I was investigating stank worse than that.'

'How so?' she asked.

'It was like, uber-secret,' Brand said. 'My CIA boss in Angola and Venter, the loadmaster on the aircraft, were running an operation that wasn't just black, it was criminal. We all pushed the boundaries, but I cultivated Venter because I thought that what was going on with those flights out of Angola was about people lining their own pockets by dealing with the commies.'

Sonja remembered something her father had said when she was a child about the Russians and the Chinese wanting to take over South West Africa and South Africa. 'My father used to say the

Russians were supplying FAPLA, the Angolan Army, and that half the Russian Navy was anchored in the port of Luanda. He used to say the South Africans should bomb them.'

'Maybe not half the navy,' Brand said, 'but the Russians and Cubans were backing the Angolans. Question is, if there were some dirty CIA guys and South Africans selling rhino horn to a Russian contact, why would they have to drop the stuff in the Atlantic off the coast of modern-day Namibia?'

Sonja thought it through. 'I think you just answered your own question. Not only were your people crooked, but the Russians on the receiving end were as well, and the Angolans who supplied them. The cargo couldn't go through Luanda, as it was coming from the opposition, UNITA, and that Dakota couldn't have overflown South West Africa to a safe drop zone off the coast without someone clearing the way inside this country.'

'Andre Horsman,' Brand said.

'Who was an officer in the South African Air Force, with the seniority to recruit an air crew who had flown Dakotas on maritime patrols and to clear flight paths, on the pretext of dropping supplies to supposedly secret recce-commando missions offshore.'

'Black OPs,' Brand said.

'Exactly. No one would question what Horsman was up to.' Brand was silent, looking as though he was searching his memory. 'What are you thinking?'

He looked up, then at her. 'I'm thinking what six bundles, each weighing about two hundred and fifty pounds – about a hundred and twenty kilograms apiece – of Angolan rhino horn might be worth on today's market in Vietnam.'

Sonja did the calculation in her head. She whistled through her teeth. '*Sheesh*, depending on which estimate you use, just over seven hundred kilograms of horn could be worth around nine million US dollars.'

'Worth killing for,' Brand said.

Sonja went back to Stirling, with Brand in tow. 'Stirling,' she asked, 'do you have any theories about where those fourteen rhino horns might have come from?'

'I've thought about that,' Stirling said. 'According to the police the men arrested weren't associated with the local Chinese running trading shops, and they'd only been in the area a short time, just a matter of weeks.'

'So,' Sonja said, her mind turning over, 'they must have been outsiders who saw the opportunity for a quick buck. Maybe they only just recently discovered the horn themselves.'

'Yes,' Stirling said. 'We work in well with the local Damara and Himba people and they value the presence of rhinos as an income-generating prospect. They're not into poaching, and if they catch any of their own people trying to hunt rhinos or elephants, they turn them in and deal with them via traditional justice. However, that's not to say they wouldn't try and sell some horns if they just happened to find them.'

People living in poverty could be tempted, Sonja thought. 'Where were the road builders working?'

'Inside the Skeleton Coast National Park,' Stirling said. He pointed to a spot halfway between Terrace Bay and Möwe Bay, the northernmost outpost in the park.

'What does "Möwe" mean?' Brand wondered aloud.

'Seagull, in German,' Sonja said.

Brand nodded. 'Looks remote.'

'Very,' Stirling agreed.

'Have you spoken to the police? Have these Chinese guys given up anything?' Brand asked.

'Negative,' Stirling replied. 'I did talk to the cops – they got me in to try to trace the horns' origins – but the detectives in charge said the road builders had clammed up. They claimed not to speak English and when an interpreter was brought in they refused to give any names or say when, where or how they got the horns.'

Brand looked at Sonja. 'What do you think?'

Sonja mentally sifted the pieces of information they had. 'We have a rough flight path, but searching the whole route by land would be impossible. We don't have access to an aircraft, but we do know where the Chinese guys were working. We can get to the Skeleton Coast and see if we can pick up the road gang and try and do some tracking. It *is* a remote area, but that means strangers, or tracks, will stick out more.'

'Still a hell of a job,' Brand said.

She put her hands on her hips. Stirling had given them some valuable information, but it was time to get moving again. She couldn't sit still. If the rhino horn had come from the downed aircraft then it meant someone had beaten both them and Andre Horsman to the Dakota. The haul of precious cargo might already be all gone – perhaps previous shipments had even been success-fully spirited out of Namibia and these two road workers were the unlucky ones who'd got caught. It didn't matter – Horsman would find the aircraft and he had her daughter with him. Sonja was worried that once he was finished using Emma and the others as cheap labour, or if he realised his prize was gone and he didn't need the archaeologists any more, he would kill her on the spot and bury her somewhere in the deserts of the Skeleton Coast. 'Got any better ideas, Brand?'

The guide shook his head, and looked to his client. 'What do you think, Matthew?'

Allchurch had brightened, having rested well in the Land Rover. 'I don't care about any rhino horn or whatever else is in that aircraft, I just want to find my son. I say we get moving.'

'Thanks, Stirling, we can take it from here,' Sonja said. 'Let's saddle up.'

'You've only got a couple of hours of daylight left and you can't drive through the conservancy at night,' Stirling said. 'Plus, your Land Rover looked to me like it's taken a battering. You're crazy to be driving out there with one damaged vehicle in the first place; most people go in a convoy of at least two in case something happens.'

'We'll get as far as we need to,' she said. She didn't like the way he always seemed to find an excuse not to do something and his petty rules annoyed her. She knew, however, that it would not be wise to drive at night in the bush as the chances of hitting a wild animal were high, and the conservancy's security staff might stop an unknown vehicle after dusk. Also, he had a point about the mechanical state of the pastor's Land Rover.

'Let me come with you, escort you at least until you get to the border of the Palmwag Conservancy.'

Sonja didn't want Stirling tagging along, for a number of reasons.

'I had a quick look under the Land Rover when we pulled up,' Brand said. 'Stirling's right. We're losing more oil than even a Landy should leak. We took some damage, Sonja. I'd like to have a better look at it before we leave.'

Sonja was getting impatient. 'We'll take extra oil and water and keep topping up. I can't sit around here twiddling my thumbs while you play mechanic.'

'Two vehicles are always better than one in the bush, you know that, Sonn,' Stirling said. 'I can carry extra fuel, water and oil and, if I do say so myself, I'm pretty good with vehicles. My Amarok's out front; I'm already packed from being out with the rhino scouts, so I can leave now if you want. Maybe let's all grab a quick shower first.'

'Sounds like a plan,' Brand said.

Surrounded by these men, Sonja felt outmanoeuvred. She was used to calling the shots, not following orders – at least she had been before she met Sam. As much as she'd loved Sam she knew that in being with him she had sacrificed some of the control she had always exercised over her own life. She didn't like other

TONY PARK

people telling her what to do, even if they were being sensible, but she realised she needed to control her emotions now, and conserve her strength.

'All right,' she said at last. 'Stirling, you can come with us if you want to. We'll all shower up and Brand, you drive the next shift while I get some shut-eye.'

*

'Emma?' the voice was low, deep.

She wasn't asleep. Her heart started pounding. 'Go away, Sebastian,' she hissed through the barrier of ripstop canvas.

'Let me in. Or I'll blow your tent down.'

Emma sat up and unzipped the sleeping bag that had also come from Benjie's stock of camping gear. It smelled of someone else's sweat, but it was cold in the desert and she welcomed its downy warmth. She was wearing only a shirt and a pair of boy briefs. 'Sebastian, it's late.' Despite her words, she reached over and undid the tent zip, just a little.

'Hi.' He grinned at her through the gap. 'Can I come in? It's bloody freezing out here.'

'No.'

'Come on,' he persisted. 'We had fun chatting over dinner, didn't we?'

'That doesn't mean I'm going to sleep with you, Sebastian.' He had some hide, assuming she would just lie back and open her legs for him. The problem was, however, that she was attracted to him.

'I know. How about we just hang out?'

Shit, she thought. He was a smooth worker. She would like to kiss him, but she didn't trust him, or herself for that matter, to keep it at that. She had no protection, in any case. 'You don't hang out in a tent.' The moment of silence between them was interrupted by the noise of another zip nearby opening.

'It's Sutton,' Sebastian hissed. 'He must be getting up to take a piss or something. My tent's past his. He'll see me here.'

'Bloody hell.' Emma got to her knees and quickly undid her zip all the way. Sebastian stumbled in, half tripping over the sill of canvas. He landed next to her and started to giggle. Emma clamped a hand over his mouth. 'Shut it!'

She peeked outside and saw Professor Sutton stumbling out of his tent, dressed only in a pair of boxer shorts, his flabby white tummy hanging over his waistband. It wasn't a pretty sight. Emma took her hand off Sebastian's mouth, and zipped up again, as quietly as she could.

'That was close,' he whispered. 'Fun.'

It was *not* funny nearly being caught by the professor. She hardly imagined an old fogey like Sutton would have approved of her becoming involved with Sebastian. However, she couldn't deny that it was exciting. 'You can't stay, Sebastian.'

He sat up and placed his hand behind her head, wrapping his fingers in her hair. She wanted to tell him to stop, but her throat seemed constricted, as if she'd lost the power of speech. He kissed her and she felt her body melt into his.

Emma broke from him, and took a breath. 'I'm not easy, Sebastian.'

'I know that.' He caressed her cheek with the back of his fingers, then drew her to him again and lay back, pulling her down on top of him on the sleeping bag.

She had the power to roll off him, to end it now, but she didn't want to. She felt his hands on her, running down her back, tracing the curves of her body. She felt his biceps, and ran her fingers through his hair.

Sebastian lifted his head and kissed her again. His lips were soft, but he moved his hands behind her head and on her back like he was claiming her. She wanted to resist, but at the same time she craved the release of giving in to him, and the heat building inside her body. She met his tongue with hers. He grabbed her bottom and squeezed and Emma moaned.

She shifted, straddling him and sitting across his groin, feeling his erection pressing against the thin barrier of her pants. As he massaged one of her breasts she reached down, grabbed each of his lapels and ripped them apart. A couple of buttons popped off and one hit her in the belly.

'Wild thing,' Sebastian said, taking each of her nipples between fingers and thumb.

'I've always wanted to do that.'

'I hope you can sew buttons back on,' he said.

Emma knocked his hands from her breasts and punched him in the chest. 'Sexist pig.'

He laughed and in one quick movement rolled her over so that he was on top of her, pinning her wrists. Emma struggled a little. This was turning her on. 'Kiss me.'

'Ask nicely,' he replied.

She poked her tongue out at him and he relented. As he kissed her, deeply, his hand moved to her pants. She gasped when he touched her; it was like an electric shock the first time, but she forced herself to relax and he found the right spot.

Emma closed her eyes. She wanted Sebastian, now, but it was Alex's face she saw above her. She hated herself for feeling guilty, and wanted to be able to just give in to her desire. She had resisted Sebastian's advances up until now. Sebastian was full of himself, for sure, but his assertiveness and self-assurance were appealing, in a primitive, alpha male kind of way. And he was good with his hands.

As if sensing she was having second thoughts Sebastian tried a different tack. He took his mouth from hers, kissing her chin, lightly, then made his way down her neck, between her breasts, leaving a trail of kisses all the way down. Emma moved her fingers to Sebastian's head and grabbed a handful of curls. She moaned again.

Sebastian didn't go straight to her, but kissed the inside of her thighs first instead. She found herself getting even more turned on as he began tracing the outline of her through the sheer cotton of her pants. She felt herself getting wetter and was sure he could tell. He drew the fabric up between her lips and started kissing then sucking them. It was driving her wild. Emma grasped his hair and tried to draw him to her clitoris, but he held off.

He hooked his fingers in the elastic waistband and she lifted her hips, eagerly, as he pulled the flimsy garment down her legs. She opened herself to him and felt incredibly exposed as he moved his mouth back to her. This time he delved into her with the tip of his tongue and she tried but failed to stifle a moan.

She looked down at him and caught his eye in the pale moonlight. He smiled at her. 'You're beautiful,' he whispered, then returned his attention to her, licking the length of her until he came to her clitoris.

Emma felt her breath start to quicken as he formed an 'o' around her most sensitive spot and drew her into his mouth, sucking on her. At the same time he began touching her. She wanted to cry out, to urge him on, but he needed no direction and she didn't dare make a sound. *My, he's good.* All thoughts of anyone else had left her mind. She was totally focused on Sebastian and what he was doing to her.

Emma pushed back onto him, hungry for his touch, for more of him. She wrapped her legs around Sebastian, giving herself over to the waves welling up inside her. 'Yes,' she hissed. She raised a hand to her mouth and bit down on it, but couldn't stop a high-pitched cry from escaping as her body surrendered to his touch.

'Emma? Are you all right?' Alex called softly from outside her tent.

Chapter 25

Emma had awoken in the chilly pre-dawn hour, alone in her tent. She had been angry with herself for letting Sebastian in, and angry with Alex for interrupting them.

She had told Alex, through the tent canvas, that she was fine, and when he had moved off she had given Sebastian his marching orders. The moment had passed and she'd felt terribly guilty, mortified at what she would have said to Alex if he had caught her and Sebastian having sex.

Now, as their four-wheel drives churned up and over one sand dune after another, she felt hot and bothered. Sebastian was in front and Alex was on one side of her, Natangwe on the other. None of them was much in the mood for talking.

'I think we should call this search off for the time being,' Alex said, breaking the silence. 'We should go to the police in the nearest town, or to the ranger's post in the Skeleton Coast Park, and report what we've found.'

'Yes, we should,' Sebastian agreed, 'but we've got no phone contact and the nearest police are hundreds of kilometres away. We've come this far, we'd be crazy not to push on until we find the aircraft.'

'You are not taking this seriously, Sebastian,' Alex protested.

Emma was annoyed at both of them. Sebastian was being his usual flippant, disrespectful self and Alex was finding excuses not to do anything. 'You're both right and you're both wrong, but we may as well keep on going,' she said.

They were all hot, tired and sleep deprived after the cold night in the desert. She wanted this trip to be over, but she still wanted to discover the missing aircraft. Emma found, too, that for the first time in a very long time she was missing her mother. She and Sonja had never had a good relationship when she was younger but now, knowing that they should have already been together, she felt an almost physical pain, a kind of longing inside her for her mother.

'It's all academic anyway,' Sebastian interjected. 'Sutton and Horsman are two men on a mission. They're not going to do anything until we find that aircraft, or run so low on fuel that we have to turn back to the farm for resupplies. I don't think there's anything we can do that would convince those two old farts to stop the search.'

Emma gave a little laugh. Sebastian did have a way of lifting the mood. Alex was checking his GPS and seemed to be cross-referencing it with a map spread across his knees.

'Where are we?' she asked.

He checked the device and the map again and placed his finger on an empty patch of Namibia. 'As far as I can tell we just crossed into the Skeleton Coast National Park. We are breaking the law.'

'Fun, isn't it,' Sebastian said from the driver's seat.

'We're not likely to bump into anyone,' Natangwe said. 'Maybe a few Himba.'

'The professor must know what he's doing,' Emma said, feeling less than sure of herself as she uttered the words.

'The professor should know that there is no way he can start digging around in a national park. I've had enough of this,'

Alex said. 'Sebastian, catch up to them. I'm going to talk to Sutton. This is not correct.'

'Stop being so bloody German,' Sebastian said.

'Sebastian, that's out of line,' Emma countered. Things were getting hot inside the vehicle.

They crested a dune and Sebastian slowed. Sutton and Horsman had stopped a little way down the opposing slope and were out of their vehicle.

'Wow,' Natangwe said.

Emma drew a breath and opened the door of the Land Cruiser. The hot air hit her like a shock wave, but she paid no attention to the heat. Below them, in a valley between two dunes, was the tail of an aircraft.

'The Dakota,' Sebastian said. 'Woo-hoo!'

Emma held a hand to her eyes to cut out the sun's glare and scrutinised the valley. She made out pieces of wreckage, mostly covered with sand, that had created little mounds in the otherwise uniform undulations of the desert. She made out a wing tip, the blade of a propeller, some distance behind the tailplane. It appeared the left wing, or part of it, had come off in the crash.

Shifting her eyes back to the left she made out a ridge that marked the line of the fuselage; just the top edge of the main body of the aircraft was visible, the bare metal glinting where decades of sand and wind had blasted away whatever paint had been applied to the Dakota.

Sutton and Horsman were back in their vehicle, driving slowly down to the wreck. 'Come on, let's go,' Sebastian said, climbing back into the Cruiser.

Emma opened her door, but paused when she saw Alex just standing there, away from the vehicle, making no move to get back inside. 'Are you going to walk?'

He said nothing, so she moved around the car to him.

'You two can walk down the hill if you want,' Sebastian said. He started the engine and leaned into the back to close Emma's door.

Emma was excited to find the aircraft, but she was concerned about Alex. 'What is it?'

Alex stood there, looking down into the valley. 'I have a very bad feeling about this, Emma. There is more wrong with this than Sutton and Horsman entering a national park without authorisation. The haste with which this whole operation was organised, the secrecy, it's just not right. You must feel it as well.'

She did, but this was not the time to abandon ship. They had beaten what were apparently miraculous odds and found an aircraft that was nearly completely buried in the desert. It was an amazing discovery.

'Too much does not add up,' Alex continued, fuelling her doubts.

She started to walk down the hill. 'You're overreacting.'

'Am I?' he asked.

She stopped and looked over her shoulder. He was standing there, still, at the brow of the dune. Below them the two vehicles were approaching the wreckage, stopping a respectful distance away from the first piece of visible wreckage. Emma could see the others getting out, and Sutton's impatient red face looking up at them.

'We're not getting the full story here, Emma.'

She was torn. 'So what do you want to do, Alex? We're stuck out here.'

'I'm going to take one of the vehicles, as Sutton said I could, now. Come with me, Emma.'

He *was* overreacting, she told herself again. There was something not quite right, dishonest even, about Horsman, but Sutton, for all his bombast and chauvinism, was a respected academic, not a thief. If there was some sort of treasure on board the Dakota then Horsman might want to take the lion's share. She wondered who the rightful owners of the cargo would be, so long after the war. In any case, there were too many of them, all witnesses, for Horsman to get away with a major crime.

'Come on, Alex.' Emma started to walk and looked back up the slope at him. He stood for a moment, hands on hips, seeming to deliberate whether or not to follow her down to the crash site. She was getting impatient now and felt that Alex was being silly. He couldn't just run away. Emma stopped again. Reluctantly, Alex began to trudge after her.

Sutton and Horsman had stopped just short of the ridge of bare metal that marked the spine of the aircraft. Emma could see now the sharp bend in the middle which hadn't been visible from the top of the dune. The fuselage had buckled on impact. She realised, with a mild sense of dread that mixed with the adrenaline coursing through her, that they might find more dead bodies on board.

'We should remember,' Professor Sutton said, glancing around to make sure they were all in earshot, and reading her mind, 'that there will most likely be dead men on board this aircraft. As excited as we all are, I think it appropriate we take a minute's silence before we begin.'

'Quite right,' Andre said.

They bowed their heads. Emma looked at Alex out of the corner of her eye and saw that he was not taking part. He was looking back at the two parked four-by-fours.

'Show some respect,' Sebastian hissed under his breath.

Alex just glared at him.

'Right,' Sutton said, looking up and at all of them. 'Let us begin. For the students, I need hardly remind you that –'

'I'm going to take one of the vehicles,' Alex said, interrupting him.

Dorset looked like Alex had just insulted his mother. 'Excuse me?'

'You said, Professor, that I could take a vehicle to go check on the carcass of the desert lion. I am taking you up on that offer now.'

Andre stepped between them. 'Guys, please. Alex, how about if you just help us for the rest of today, and then maybe head off and check on the lion tomorrow? Would that be OK?'

Alex glared at Horsman. 'No, sir, it would not be *OK*. I am a conservationist, a scientist,' he shot a glance at Dorset as if to challenge his ethics and credentials, 'and I object to the way you have illegally entered one of my country's national parks. You have found your aircraft and now I think the most appropriate thing is for you to report its location to the Namibian national parks authorities. This is what I am also proposing to do when I leave here.'

Horsman raised his hands in a placatory gesture. 'Alex, calm down, please. Can't you understand that there are probably deceased airmen under that sand over there? I have been searching for them for half my life. I can't rest until I know they've been found and given Christian burials.'

Alex cleared his throat. 'With respect, these men, if they are here, have lain undisturbed for decades. A day or two more, after which they can be properly exhumed, will not harm them, or you.'

Sutton looked to Horsman. 'He's right, you know. We should tell the authorities. *I* should tell the national parks people because I'm the senior archaeologist here. I have a good relationship with the Namibian government. I've conducted digs all over the country. It may take us some time, but I'm sure we can come back here with full approval. I'll travel with Alex personally.'

Andre put his hands on his head, grasping at his scalp in instant and obvious anger. 'No! No one is leaving this site.'

'I am going, and there is nothing you can do to stop me,' Alex said. 'Professor Sutton, if you wish to accompany me I think that would be appropriate. Better still, we should all go and report to the park authorities before there are any repercussions. If we are found here without authorisation the rangers might call in the army, or arrest us as trespassers or suspected poachers. I'm sure none of us wants to be charged.'

'No!' Andre yelled. 'I'm in charge of this mission and no one's going anywhere without my say-so.'

'Andre, please –' Sutton began.

'No,' Horsman interrupted the professor. 'We start digging, now.'

Natangwe, who had been quiet up until now, stepped into the cluster of men. 'Alex is right. He and I have not always agreed on things, but in this he is correct. This land belongs to the people of Namibia, not you.'

Emma looked around and saw that Sebastian had moved to the double cab Hilux *bakkie* that Sutton and Horsman had been driving.

'Natangwe, are you coming with me?' Alex turned and walked to the Land Cruiser.

Emma could see that the keys were still in the ignition. She had been blinded by the excitement of searching for, then finding, the Dakota. She hadn't thought through the legal ramifications of what they were about to do. She knew she might never come across a find such as this again for the rest of her life, but she didn't want to see Alex and Natangwe leave.

'Stop,' Horsman said, not yelling now.

Perhaps it was the change of tone that made Alex, and then Emma, turn to look at him. He had produced a black semi-automatic pistol from somewhere and was pointing it at Alex.

'Are you mad?' Alex asked, his hand on the open door of the Cruiser.

'If you get in that vehicle I'm going to shoot you.'

Emma couldn't believe what she was seeing. She had begun to wonder about Horsman's motives – if he was simply interested in retrieving his missing men, or whether he was motivated by something more – and now it was horribly clear it was the latter. This was crazy, though, she told herself.

Emma had been around guns before. 'Andre, please put the gun down.' Horsman looked to her and the pistol followed his eye line. Emma shivered and put up her hands. 'Let's talk about this, OK?'

'I knew you were a criminal,' Alex said. 'Did you steal my satellite phone as well, to stop me from letting my people know where we all were?'

Emma looked to Andre and saw the smug smile play across his thin lips. 'There's a shovel in the back of the Cruiser. Get it out, Alex, and start fucking digging.'

Alex glared at him, but moved slowly to the rear of the vehicle and opened the double doors.

'Please, we don't have to carry on like this,' Emma said, beseeching Andre. 'The gun's scaring us. I know this is important to you, but please don't harm us.'

Horsman shifted his eyes to her. 'I'm not going to hurt you, Emma, as long as you and Alex and Natangwe do as I tell you to. We're going to uncover the Dakota, retrieve what's on board and then you'll all be free to go.'

Emma swallowed; somehow she doubted that. Alex was shifting bags in the back of the truck to get to a shovel and Sebastian was out of sight. She sensed something was brewing. She needed to keep Andre's focus on her for now. Emma moved her hands to her eyes and started to shrug her shoulders up and down, as if she was beginning to sob. 'Please . . . please don't hurt me.'

'Shut up, stop that,' Horsman said.

Through lidded eyes she could see he was still mostly watching her, the pistol pointed at her head, but he was glancing around as well. Emma needed to put more into her act. She dropped to her knees and started shuffling towards him. 'Please, I don't want to die, Andre. I'll do anything you want.'

Behind her Emma heard a yell and felt a *whoosh* of displaced air rush past her left shoulder. She looked up to see Andre fending off the shovel that Alex had hefted at him like a spear. Alex barrelled past her, brushing so close that he knocked her over, perhaps deliberately, and she toppled to the sand. As she rolled she saw Alex slam into the older man and punch him in the face with one hand. With his other, Alex held Andre's gun hand pinned to the ground.

Emma expected Sebastian to reappear at any second. She dragged herself to her feet and started to move towards Alex and Andre. She heard a cry and a thud and looked towards the vehicles to see Natangwe falling to the ground. Professor Sutton was watching on, open-mouthed. Sebastian strode past him and Emma towards the melee and Emma saw that he had a military-style rifle – she thought it might be an AK-47 – grasped in his hands.

Sebastian pointed the barrel of the rifle in the air and fired a three-round burst. Emma shrieked at the noise.

'Get off him, Alex, now, or I'll put a bullet through the back of your thick head.'

Alex looked over his shoulder to see Sebastian aiming at him down the barrel of the AK. 'You bastard.'

'Off him, now,' Sebastian repeated. 'You've got until I count to three, and if you're not off by then I'll shoot Emma, then Natangwe, then Sutton, then you.'

Emma couldn't believe what she was seeing. She checked the others and saw that Natangwe was sprawled face first on the sand and Sutton was on his knees, his hands clasped together on the top of his head in a position of submission. *Coward*, she thought. Sebastian had obviously clubbed Natangwe from behind with the rifle; perhaps Natangwe had been trying to help Alex. 'My God, Sebastian, why?'

Sebastian glanced at her and shrugged. 'Money, of course. What else is there in this screwed-up world?'

Alex rolled off Andre and glared up at Sebastian. Andre got up and pointed his pistol at Alex, silently daring him to try something again. When Alex didn't move Andre delivered a swift kick to the younger man's ribs. Alex convulsed but didn't cry out. Andre joined Sebastian at his side.

Sutton was still kneeling, just outside the circle.

'It must be worth a good deal, whatever it is inside that Dakota, for you to kidnap us all and then murder us once we've finished digging it up,' Emma said.

Sebastian laughed. 'We're *not* going to kill you, Emma. That's the last thing I'd want to do.'

'You were quite happy to a moment ago,' Alex said, sitting up in the sand.

Sebastian swung the barrel of his AK-47 back to Alex. 'You push me and you'll regret it. Yes, Andre and I need you all to excavate the cargo on the aircraft, but when you're done we'll leave you here, with some water. You'll be found eventually, or you'll try and walk out – either way you'll have a sporting chance. By the time you do get to safety Andre and I will be long gone from this bloody continent, somewhere we can't be extradited from.'

Emma said nothing, but she didn't believe Sebastian. 'Is that the only reason you brought us here, on your search, to dig up the aircraft?'

Sebastian sighed. 'No. If your friend Natangwe over there hadn't been stupid enough to tell the media about the body you found then we would have pulled strings with the mining company and the government and called off the dig. The company would have alerted Andre as soon as Sutton reported finding the dead guy. We would have called in the cops to take care of the body and, in the meantime, we would have carried out the search by ourselves.

With outsiders interested, I'm afraid we needed to take you three out of the limelight for a while as well and, as you just pointed out, you've saved me some digging.'

Natangwe had been knocked out by the blow to his head, but he was on his hands and knees now, shaking his head groggily as he came to.

'You were lucky that the mobile phone signal was so bad when we were at Ondangwa and in the air,' Emma said. 'If other people had found out where we were going someone would already be searching for us.'

Sebastian shook his head. 'You know what Andre's day job is? Importing electrical gadgets from Asia.'

Horsman walked to the Land Cruiser and reached under the driver's seat. After a bit of fiddling he removed a black metal box. 'A simple jammer, usually used by people in secure offices who don't want their staff talking on their cell phones. No one knows you're here, Emma, so you'd better do as we say.'

Emma regarded Sutton. The old professor was still on his knees with his hands on his head. He looked dejectedly down at the ground.

'Get over there, join the others,' Sebastian said to Natangwe, motioning with his assault rifle.

'What's in the Dakota?' Emma asked, looking from Andre to Sebastian.

'What do you think?' Andre replied.

Sutton looked up at them, then across to Emma and back to Andre. 'Something bulky and valuable, physically useless, but prized more than diamonds, gold or drugs in southeast Asia today.'

'You're getting warmer,' Sebastian said.

'Rhino horn?' Emma asked.

Sutton nodded to her. 'A stockpile from Angola, probably hoarded by the Portuguese government in the old days, if I'm not

336

mistaken, and smuggled out in the dying days of the border war in some illicit deal.'

'Very good, professor,' Andre said. He looked to all of them. 'Look, people, we're not going to kill anyone or hurt anyone any more than has been done already, as long as you all stay calm and help Sebastian and me get what we came for. If you want to help us carry the stuff out, then perhaps we can negotiate a deal, a small fee for services rendered and a promise not to go to the police. We can all do well out of this discovery, though Emma, you won't be able to hit the lecture circuit to tell the next generation of archaeologists about your big find, unfortunately. What do we say, people?'

Alex coughed. 'We say, go fuck yourselves.'

Sebastian spun, raised the AK-47 to his shoulder and pulled the trigger. A bullet punched through the door of the *bakkie* and Alex reeled away in shock. 'Get your shovel and start digging.'

We're finished, Emma thought.

Chapter 26

The drive across the Palmwag Conservancy took them through breathtaking countryside.

The landscape changed from the flat-topped mountains and plains covered in red rocks interspersed with single stems of dry yellow grass to vast, flat open expanses of desert. Despite the inhospitable nature of the terrain life still managed to manifest itself; they saw mountain zebra, stocky animals with pendulous dewlaps under their necks; small bands of gemsbok, or oryx; the occasional lone springbok and even a trio of giraffe when they paused in a dry riverbed for coffee and tea from Thermos flasks.

Though she took it in, Sonja had too much else on her mind to appreciate the stark beauty around her. Each passing hour fuelled ever more gruesome scenarios about what might have happened to Emma, and Stirling's attempts at small talk had become annoying.

He was beside her, in the passenger seat of his own vehicle, dozing, thankfully. Sonja had ridden with Brand and Allchurch for the first half of the long journey – it had taken them most of the day, driving as fast as the rough roads would allow, to cross most of the conservancy – but after their brief lunch stop Brand had pulled her aside.

'Stirling's beat,' Brand had said. 'He's been out in the field for days with his men, and you heard how they were tracking rhino at night. He nearly went off the road half an hour ago; he needs someone to take over at the wheel for a while.'

'You do it,' Sonja had said back to him.

Brand had lowered his voice. 'Matthew's my client. People have been trying to kill us, Sonja. If they spring another ambush somewhere I need to be next to him.'

She looked at Stirling now, head back, a silvery thread of drool running from the corner of his mouth, out for the count. She couldn't help it, she smiled. He looked so innocent, because he was. Stirling didn't break laws, didn't kill people, and loved nothing more than spending time in the wild with animals.

The fact was, though, that the country of her birth was peaceful, stable, and safe, a haven for people as well as animals. Sonja was smart enough to know that part of the prickliness she felt towards Stirling was based on jealousy; she resented the fact that he was happy here, in this beautiful country where she could never legally return.

'Maybe you and Emma could come and stay at our camp for a while, once we find her,' Stirling had said, his last attempt at conversation before he had nodded off, defeated by his own tiredness and her abruptness.

She took her eyes off the road briefly. He was still so hand-some, suntanned from his time in the desert and lean from the frugal, healthy life he lived. He was too good for her, always had been, she mused. *Yet Sam had been like that as well.*

Sonja saw brake lights ahead. Brand was slowing for some-thing. They were in a dry riverbed, steep rocky walls rising on either side of them. Instinctively she scanned the ridgelines on both sides. This was what the military called a chokepoint, somewhere an enemy could rain fire down on them while they had to slow down to negotiate a natural obstacle. Sonja laid her right hand on the nine-millimetre Glock nestled between her thighs, and willed her heartbeat to slow to its normal rate.

She exhaled, however, when she saw Brand start to move again, one brown arm pointing out his window and off to the right. Sonja looked in that direction and saw, lounging under a tree, the massive pale grey dusty bulk of a desert elephant. Leaner than their comparatively better fed cousins in other parts of Africa, the desert elephants had adapted to their harsh environment. This one raised his trunk to sniff their scent, and flapped his massive ears to create a breeze over the web of veins that circulated his blood through his twin natural air conditioners. Sonja kept pace with Brand, driving slowly past the elephant. They were in a rush, but even she could not begrudge them the chance to take in this magnificent sight.

'Stirling, wake up.'

He didn't respond, so she reached over and pinched his arm.

'Ow! What was that?' He blinked and rubbed his eyes, then furtively wiped away the saliva from his mouth. 'What's wrong?'

'Nothing.' Sonja stopped the truck and pointed out the window. 'See for yourself.'

'Hey, a desert elephant!'

'You should be a wildlife researcher.'

'Ha, ha,' he replied dryly. Stirling sat there in silence, just staring at the old bull, a smile playing across his face. 'Tell me you're not moved by that.'

Sonja sighed. She needed to stay focused on the mission, not on elephants and not on Stirling Smith. 'I'm moved by the need to find my daughter.'

'Sure,' he agreed. 'I see elephants quite often in the course of my work, once or twice a week, but I still never really get over the excitement of seeing one, or the magic of it. Sorry.'

She bit her lip. 'You don't need to apologise, Stirling. It's who you are, it's why you're so . . . so . . .' She wished she hadn't spoken.

'So what? So *soft*? That's what you think of me, isn't it, Sonja?'

Curse him, she thought. 'No, Stirling, so nice is what I was going to say. It's not an insult.'

'Nor a compliment.'

'Stop fishing for one,' she said. 'No, it's not a compliment, but not an insult either, it's just who you are.' She left the engine running but opened her door. The elephant shook his massive head and blew a stream of dusty air out of his trunk, but she ignored him and walked around to Stirling's side. 'Get out.'

'Why?'

'Your turn to drive. I'm going to sleep.'

*

This is not archaeology, Emma thought as she hefted another shovel load of sand, *this is grave robbing*.

The skin on her hands was already raw where blisters had formed and broken, and when she paused to brush her hair from her face, as briefly as she could before Sebastian barked at her to get back to work, the salt from her perspiration stung the open sores. Her back ached and her shoulders and arms were bright red from the sun.

Sebastian stood on a rise above them, the butt of the AK-47 resting on his thigh, like some road gang prison officer. She couldn't believe she had been stupid enough to almost fall for him.

'Shame it didn't work out between us,' he had whispered to her as he'd frisked her, and then Natangwe and Alex, before ordering them to pick up shovels and get to work.

'Bastard,' she had hissed at him, and he had laughed.

'Emma, can you help me, please,' Professor Sutton croaked, bringing her back to the present. He had uncovered a sheet of riveted aluminium, part of the fuselage that had apparently peeled off when the Dakota had crashed. 'I need to shift this.'

She trudged through the sand to him. The aircraft was emerging, slowly, like an intact fossilised dinosaur. Andre had directed them all to concentrate on the port side, the left, along the rear third of the fuselage. This, Sutton had told Emma and Natangwe, was where the cargo door would be. It seemed Andre had dropped all pretence of caring about the fate of the pilots who, if they had been killed on impact, would be entombed up front in the cockpit.

'Professor,' Emma lowered her voice even more, 'we need to escape or overpower Sebastian and Andre. You know they're going to kill us, don't you?'

Sutton frowned and looked around to make sure they weren't being watched too closely. Sebastian was barking orders at Natangwe and Andre had taken up a shovel and was clearing away sand forward of the tailplane, not far from where they were. 'They'd be mad to massacre us all,' he said quietly, between grunts.

He was a naïve old man, she thought. 'I spoke to Natangwe earlier. He's going to try to get away tonight. They'll have to let us sleep sometime. He's going to try to get to the road that runs through the Skeleton Coast Park, north to south, and flag down a passing car.'

'There will be no traffic at night, and he might wait all day in the blazing sun with no water or food and not see a single car. We're far north of the normal tourist route.'

He was scared. Emma helped him drag the bodywork aside.

'Stop talking, you two,' Sebastian called to them. 'Back to digging.'

Emma picked up her shovel and walked to where Andre was. His shirt was soaked with sweat; there was no denying he was doing his share of the excavation, but then he was motivated by an all-consuming greed. Emma saw the khaki fabric ride up his back, revealing the butt of the nine-millimetre pistol sticking out of the waistband of his cargo trousers. She knew how to cock and fire a pistol, and strip and clean it. She glanced over her shoulder and saw Sebastian staring down at them – it felt like his eyes were targeting her in particular, through his sunglasses. Would Andre have a round in the chamber, she wondered, or would she have to rack the pistol, as her mother had shown her on the firing range?

Emma moved closer to him and started shovelling sand. She would have to position herself so that Andre was between her and Sebastian; if she could get to Andre's weapon then she would have time to cock it, if necessary, and get a shot off at Sebastian before he could react; Andre would be her shield.

Alex caught her eye and she wondered if he could tell what she was thinking, or if he'd had the same thought. He motioned with his eyeballs towards Sebastian and Emma looked up at their guard.

'Yes, I'm watching you, Emma,' Sebastian called, then laughed. He raised his AK-47 into his shoulder and pretended to fire, kicking the end of the barrel up in mock recoil. 'Don't try me. Just keep working.'

Andre attacked a mound of sand at the side of the aircraft mercilessly, huffing and puffing with each shovel load. Sutton moved next to him. Andre was distracted with his digging and Emma took her chance to edge slowly down the fuselage towards the tailplane. Sutton was now just behind Andre, between her and Sebastian. Emma hoped he might shield her movements. She worked her way closer to Andre, scooping aside half-loads of the sand that was amassing around Andre's ankles. She had to duck to avoid the return swing of his shovel.

'I can see inside,' Andre panted.

'Where?' Sutton asked, closing in on the other man, trying to see over his shoulder.

The bulk of the two men close together shielded her from Sebastian, although in her peripheral vision she could see him moving. Alex had left his position by the side of the fuselage, shovel held up at waist height. Emma sensed Alex was moving to intercept Sebastian and further screen her.

Emma dropped her spade and closed on the older men, reaching between them. Her fingertips were just centimetres away from the grip of the pistol when Andre lurched forward and Professor Sutton's sizeable bulk fell on top of him, propelling them both into the cavity which had just been exposed.

Sebastian fired two shots. 'Stand back.'

Emma withdrew two steps, her opportunity missed as Andre angrily elbowed Sutton off him. Sebastian had, mercifully, fired into the air, but he now pointed the barrel of his rifle at Alex who had dropped his shovel and raised his hands.

'Everyone take a deep breath,' Sebastian said. 'Alex, go join Emma. The pair of you, sit down by the tail where I can see you, hands on your heads.'

Alex moved to where Emma was and they both sat down, but Alex seemed intent on placing himself between her and Sebastian.

'Very gallant, Alex, and very stupid of you, Emma, to try and take Andre's pistol.' Sebastian went to Sutton, who was on his feet, dusting himself off, and pushed the academic to one side. Andre was looking into the Dakota's cargo hatch, his torso out of sight. Sebastian strode to him and pulled the exposed pistol from his belt.

'Hey!' Andre spun around and was confronted by Sebastian, waving his pistol at him.

Sebastian slipped the gun into his own shorts. 'I'll hold on to this. Watch your back next time.'

Andre snorted with indignation.

'Sutton, get in there with Andre and see what you can pull out.

You two,' he motioned to Alex and Emma with his rifle, 'don't move or you'll go to heaven together.'

Andre had disappeared inside the partly buried aircraft and Sutton squeezed his bulk through the gap in the sand after him. 'It's here,' Andre called from inside the Dakota a couple of minutes later.

Sutton backed himself out into the fresh air, coughing and sneezing.

'What is it, Professor?' Emma asked.

Sutton took off his glasses and rubbed the lenses on the tail of his shirt, then put them back on. He sat down, heavily, in the sand. 'Boxes, wrapped in plastic, with parachutes attached to them.' He held his hands, palms up, as if to say he had no further idea. 'And it still smells in there, terribly.'

Emma shivered despite the overpowering heat.

'Come back in here, Sutton,' Andre said, his face animated in the doorway.

Sutton seemed not to hear the other man at first, then turned to him, his expression blank. 'I think I'll just sit a moment, if it's all the same to you. I'm feeling a bit faint.'

'Bahler, get in there.' Sebastian waved his AK-47 at Alex and then at the Dakota, to reinforce the command.

When Alex stood up, Emma did too.

'What do you think you're doing?' Sebastian asked her.

'I'll help.'

Sebastian shrugged. 'Many hands and all that. Try anything, though, and you'll be joining the dead pilots inside there.'

'Your threats are becoming more comical by the second,' Emma said.

Sebastian laughed. 'Just behave. I told you, if you play nice then we're all going to get out of this alive. The sooner we move the cargo, the sooner Andre and I can get away and you can go back to your mommy.'

Emma seethed at his mention of Sonja. 'She'll kill you, you know, if she ever finds you.'

'*If* being the operative word. She's a pre-menopausal ex-mercenary and from what I hear, a bit of a basket case. I'm not overly worried.'

Emma glared at him through slitted eyes. She thought – no, fantasised – briefly about what her mother might do to a man who spoke to her that way, and bit back her reply. She followed Alex through the crawl space into the interior of the Dakota.

Inside, the darkness was strobed by a head torch Andre had produced from somewhere. He turned back to them and grinned like a demented cyclops. 'Here it is! Still here after all these years. Help me undo the cargo straps and we'll carry it out.'

Emma sniffed. Sutton was right, the air smelled of something old but rancid. The odour was coming, she imagined, from whatever was left of the pilots up the front in the cockpit, beyond the dust, the sand that had blown in through the shattered windows, and God alone knew whatever other desert-dwelling creatures lived in this crypt.

'Hey, we need some more light in here,' Emma called out.

'Sutton,' Sebastian barked, 'go get a couple of torches out of the Land Cruiser and the Hilux.'

Emma felt her way around in the darkness. As Professor Sutton had said, the cargo seemed fairly ordinary at first touch. There were bulky crates or, rather, plastic-wrapped bundles, each about a metre by two metres. On top of each one was a dusty, spongy bag, which the prof had identified as a parachute. Emma traced a fabric cord from the top of the parachute she was touching upwards to a steel wire cable that ran along the inside of one wall of the fuselage. Emma had done a parachute jump once in LA. She'd been attached to an instructor, in a tandem jump, but he'd later explained to her that if she wanted to jump by herself but didn't have the confidence to do a freefall jump she could jump with a static line parachute. This was the same sort of rig, she realised, with the line running from the 'chute to a fixed cable inside the Dakota. When the cargo was pushed out the door the line was pulled tight and that then pulled the parachute from its bag, which was tied to the top of the bundle.

Andre had gone to the front of the aircraft, to the cockpit, but was now coming back to the rear.

'What did you see up there?' Emma asked him.

Andre swallowed. 'Nothing. None of your business, in any case.'

'The pilots?'

'Get to work,' Andre said.

Alex was running his hands over the cargo. 'These boxes are tied down with cargo straps. I've tried working the buckles, but they're corroded. They won't budge. I need a knife.'

'Very funny,' Andre said. 'Back up, both of you.'

Emma and Alex retreated aft, towards the light streaming in through the open hatch and the semi relief of the dry, hot desert air. Emma coughed and sneezed, as Sutton had, from the dust. Andre pulled a Leatherman from the pouch at his belt and unfolded a serrated blade. He cut quickly through a series of straps on the bundle closest to Emma and Alex. 'Shift this one out, while I free the others.'

The light behind them was blocked by a head and torso silhouetted by the sun. 'Natangwe, is that you?' Emma asked.

Natangwe ducked his head and entered the fuselage. He held a hand to his head. 'Sebastian says I must come help you move the cargo.'

'Your head's still bleeding. You might have concussion,' Emma said.

'That's the least of his problems,' Alex said under his breath.

'Stop whispering down there.' Andre continued sawing through the old restraint straps.

347

Emma and Alex got their hands on the bundle nearest them and tried sliding it. 'There's some sort of roller system underneath,' Emma said, hearing the protesting screech of no longer lubricated wheels.

'You push, I'll pull,' Alex said.

With Natangwe's help they half rolled, half dragged the bundle to the window of light. Alex knelt on the floor of the aircraft. 'Hey, look at this.' He held up a strap, with buckle still attached, that Andre had not cut. It had been left by the side of the roller system.

Emma looked down and picked up another restraint, then cast her eyes upwards. Hanging from the wire cable that ran the length of the fuselage was a folded and stitched canvas line, the same as the one attached to the parachute on the bundle they had been rolling.

'That must be off the bundle we found further back in the desert,' Alex said.

'Less talk, more work,' Andre said. He moved to them. 'Let's get this one outside.'

With Andre, Natangwe and Alex all lifting together there was no room for Emma to get a handhold in the confines of the fuselage. She didn't care. She had no interest in helping Andre and Sebastian get rich, and hastening her own death. She was under no illusion that they would let her, Sutton, Natangwe and Alex go with a promise not to tell the police about what they had found.

Emma backed slowly into the darkness, towards the still buried nose of the Dakota. As she moved, feeling her way past the remaining cargo bundles, the musty, foul smell she'd first noticed became stronger. She swallowed hard and steeled herself for what she might find. The sole of her boot landed on something metallic. She carefully lifted her foot and then dropped to one knee. Feeling on the deck she closed her fingers around the object. It was a bullet casing. She held it close to her face so she could make it out in the gloom. 'Nine millimetre,' she mouthed to herself. The discovery made her heart beat faster.

Andre was cursing and the three men were heaving and grunting. The cargo bundle had to weigh more than a hundred kilograms at least, she reckoned. They were making slow progress, with both Andre and Natangwe scooping away sand from inside the aircraft that was blocking the way out. Emma crept further forward. She ran a hand along the interior wall of the fuselage and inspected her fingers. It wasn't just dusty; her skin was black. There had been a fire in here, which may have contributed to the crash. On the floor she noticed a spent fire extinguisher, which reinforced her theory. In other circumstances this piecing together of a historical puzzle might have been exciting and fun; now it was a matter of life and death.

Seeing the spent extinguisher she realised it could have made a good weapon, to blind Andre or Sebastian with so that she could steal one of their guns. No, she countered, after this many years the pressure in the extinguishers would have dropped. She wrapped her fingers tightly around the bullet casing and slipped it into the pocket of her shorts.

The further she walked the darker it became and the more she relied on touch. She stepped on something soft and reached down to pick it up. The fabric was cotton, dry, crumbling in her hands, and there was a pad attached; it was a bandage of some kind. As well as a fire there had been people shooting on board and later a wound was dressed. Emma stood and walked with her hands outstretched. She was stopped by something metal. She ran her hand over it and felt canvas and padding of some kind. It must be a seat, she thought; the pilot's or co-pilot's. She kept feeling and then gasped, fighting back a scream. There was something firm but yielding.

Emma needed light. Sebastian had frisked her, Natangwe and Alex, but perhaps out of some vestige of decency he had not run his hands across her breast. Even though her phone had not worked for days, thanks largely to Andre's portable jamming device, she habitually kept it in her bra; it was the only place she had found she could keep it without forgetting it. She reached into her shirt and turned it on, praying there was some battery power left.

As she fully expected, the jammer was not needed out here in the desert as there was no signal. Her battery was in the red. She opened messages and tapped a quick SMS to her mother, telling Sonja they had been kidnapped by Andre Horsman and Sebastian Lord and were being forced to excavate a lost aircraft full of illegal cargo. *I'm scared they are going to kill us, Mum. If you can't find us somewhere in the Skeleton Coast National Park, west of Palmwag, then please know I love you, always.*

She choked back a sob and then selected the light app on the phone. She shone the weak beam ahead of her and took another sharp breath. The dead pilot's skin was still largely intact, mummified by the heat and dryness surrounding his metal sarcophagus. His lips were stretched in a gruesome smile, his teeth visible.

Emma was trembling, scared, although she knew the man could not harm her. She leaned closer to him, playing the light over his tormented features. There, at his temple, she saw the neat hole in the dry skin. Emma leaned around him and saw the exit wound on the other side of the skull.

The other pilot's seat was empty.

Emma played the weak light from the phone down over the pilot's chest, arms and bony hands.

'Come on you bastards, push,' Andre called from the back of the aircraft.

Emma knew she had to be quick. At the pilot's waist was a canvas webbing belt. She leaned over the body, gagging again at the ancient but still present smell of decay, and ran her fingers along the belt. 'Yes,' she whispered quietly as she felt the holster at his side. She leaned further over and saw the flap that would cover the pistol, but when she lifted it she found that it was not fastened and, to her dismay, there was no gun in the holster.

'Shit.'

Emma dropped to her hands and knees and started feeling around her. She squeezed between the two pilot's seats and felt below the pedals and, almost retching in the process, around the dead pilot's legs. She found another bullet casing, but nothing else. She backtracked and moved to the dead man's side. Her phone flashed twice and the battery died. Blinded, she kept feeling away.

'Aagh!' The scream escaped her without warning as she felt something brush her face. She recoiled, then summoned the strength to reach out and touch it. She felt dry, papery skin on lifeless fingers. The pilot's arm was hanging down. She felt on the floor beneath his fingers and her hand brushed the angular shape of the man's pistol.

Chapter 27

Sonja rolled out her improvised bedroll, a couple of blankets and a pillow, on the sandy dry riverbed they had chosen as a campsite for the night. They had driven as late and as far as they could, to the western boundary of the Palmwag Conservancy. From here they would soon enter the dunes that bordered the Skelton Coast. It would be hard enough in daylight with a GPS, impossible at night.

She went to the campfire that Stirling had lit and was tending and took the black metal kettle off the flames. She poured water, now boiling, into four tin cups, and added two-minute noodles and flavouring. She passed the mugs and forks to the men and sat down on the ground, cross-legged, in front of the fire.

Sonja wouldn't admit it to the others, but she was feeling dejected. The enormity of the odds against them finding Emma and her colleagues was weighing on her. She was in no doubt that her daughter was in dire danger, if she wasn't already dead, but the more she thought about the vast empty tracts of desert around them the less sure she was that they had even a hope in hell of finding Emma.

'We should be able to pick up the road construction crew early tomorrow, once we hit the Skeleton Coast,' Stirling said from across the flames, trying to sound positive.

Sonja looked at him and nodded. If they could find out – even though the Namibian police had been unable to – where the Chinese road workers had found the rhino horns, it might lead them to the wreck. That was, of course, if the horns had even come from the missing Dakota. The Chinese road workers had provided no information to the police about how or where they had bought the rhino horns, according to Stirling, but Sonja was certain that if she could get to them they would talk.

Brand had been chatting to Allchurch in the gloom, but he came to the fire now and sat down beside her, eating his noodles in silence. When he had finished he said, 'Thanks. Great meal.'

She smiled. 'Fuel.'

'Yup, you got that right. Matthew's gone to sleep in the back of the truck. His hand's OK.'

Sonja nodded. Allchurch still seemed like a burden to her, but if he could fire a weapon he might be of some use to them. And even if he couldn't shoot, if they could ambush the people who had Emma there would be four armed bodies for their enemy to confront; that might be enough to scare them into submission. However, she could not be optimistic; these people had already had two serious attempts at taking out Brand and Allchurch, and her, and Sonja did not think they would roll over without a fight.

She would be ready. She was mentally prepared for the mission ahead and, having stayed away from hard drink for a brief period at least, in better physical shape than she had been.

'Stirling, are you coming with us tomorrow?' Hudson asked across the fire.

Stirling set his tin mug down. 'I've been thinking about that. I wasn't going to, as you'll be illegally entering the Skeleton Coast Park, but I've decided I'm coming along with you.'

'It's not up to you to decide,' Sonja said. 'It's my mission, not yours.'

'I know this country,' Stirling said.

'I was born here.'

'Yes,' Stirling agreed, 'but not in this part. Also, I know many of the parks people in the Skeleton Coast. We get together for regular coordination meetings. I can help smooth things over if you get caught by the rangers.'

Sonja wasn't convinced that Stirling would be able to get them out of trouble.

'Sonja's right,' Brand intervened. 'Thanks for the offer, Stirling, but I'm sure between us Sonja and I will be able to find the route and talk our way out of any trouble we find ourselves in. We'll play dumb tourists; probably just get a slap on the wrist.'

Now that surprised Sonja – Brand taking her side. She wondered if the handsome American had an agenda of his own. 'I'm going to bed.'

Stirling looked up at her as she stood. 'So am I coming or not?'

Her childhood sweetheart was and always had been indecisive and over-cautious. 'That's up to you. We've been in a lot of *kak* on this trip, Stirling – people have tried to kill Brand and Allchurch twice, and me once. It's probable they'll try again if they can target us. Are you sure you want to take the risk of being shot, just to tag along?'

'I wouldn't be *tagging along*. I told you, I know this part of Namibia better than any of you, and if your daughter's in trouble I want to help out.'

'You're not coming.'

'You said it yourself, Sonja,' Stirling said, 'someone's out to get you guys. If you've got a spare gun I'll help even the odds. What do you say, Hudson?'

Brand rubbed his chin and looked at Sonja. 'Well, we do have an extra rifle.'

Sonja ran a hand through her hair. 'OK, whatever. Stirling, if you want to get yourself killed in your first firefight, then by all means join us. You don't know what you're in for, but if you think you can handle it, then I don't care.'

Stirling stood. 'Sonn, I know you think I'm a coward, but I've faced down a charging lion and I shot a rogue buffalo that would have killed one of my guests if I hadn't fired quick enough.'

'It's different killing people,' she said.

'I'm sure. Look, all I'm offering is to guide you and to be there if you need me.'

She put her hands on her hips. 'But *why*, Stirling? I've only ever treated you like shit. I left you when we were young and you let me down once before.'

'You were breaking international law, starting a war that didn't need to be fought,' he countered.

He was right, and that pissed her off as well. She waved a hand in the air. 'I'm going to bed. You can all fight for the right to come with me and die if you want, but I'm getting up at oh-dark-hundred tomorrow to go find my daughter. Whatever the rest of you do – well, I just don't give a fuck.'

She left them, annoyed, but not blinded by anger. She took several deep breaths, calming herself. She went to the Land Rover, took out the rifle she had earmarked for herself, a cleaning kit and a small tin of oil. She sat, cross-legged, on her bedroll and closed her eyes. There was enough moonlight for her to see clearly what she was doing, but she needed to be able to strip this weapon, reassemble it, and fill the magazine in complete darkness. The soldier's simple task settled her, as meditation might some hippy. She was at one with the night, with the cold metal parts in her hands, with her mission.

She would find her daughter, and if anyone tried to stop her, she would kill them.

*

Emma and the others worked into the night, unloading the bundles from the Dakota and then unwrapping them in the glare of the Land Cruiser's headlights, in which Sebastian stood, silhouetted, watching over them with rifle in hand.

Emma wondered what would happen next. Even if Sebastian and Andre killed them all and emptied the two vehicles of all of their gear and loaded the roof carriers, there was still nowhere near enough room for all of the cargo they had recovered from the Dakota.

The sweat that had soaked her clothes through the afternoon had chilled her as soon as the sun set. Andre attacked the last of the bundles with a knife, slashing off the now brittle plastic wrapping, and then used a crowbar to open the wooden crate within. 'Yes!' He punched the air.

His elation had become tiresome. He had already opened all the other crates and this one, like the rest, was full of the same illicit cargo: rhino horns, perhaps hundreds of them. Emma sat down in the sand and Alex and Natangwe took a seat either side of her. Sebastian watched them like a lion selecting his prey. There was no way she could talk.

After she had discovered the dead pilot's pistol she had nearly been caught with it. Andre had stumbled back into the Dakota, his headlamp picking her out in the darkness of the fuselage, but he had been too insistent on her getting back to work to notice her stuffing the pistol in her shorts and hurriedly pulling her T-shirt down over it.

In the rare breaks they had between shifting the bundles she had checked out the pistol. It was caked in dust, and when she had pushed the magazine release button, as her mother had shown her, instead of the mag sliding slickly into her palm she'd had to claw at it to free it, breaking two fingernails in the process.

On another break she fingered the rounds out of the magazine and was dismayed to find there were only three. The pilot must have been firing at someone inside his own aircraft the night he went down; that accounted for his right arm dangling over the side of his seat and the pistol lying on the floor, not to mention the bullet hole in his skull.

The events of the night the plane crashed occupied her mind less than the prospect of what she would do with this ancient pistol that was so dirty it would probably explode in her hands if she was even able to cock it and pull the trigger.

'Alex,' she whispered out of the side of her mouth when Sebastian briefly took his eye off them in order to check on the haul of rhino horns.

'Yes?'

'Can you get to the back of the Land Cruiser?'

'I don't know, why? What do you want?'

'There's a plastic storage crate there, I noticed it when we were packing. There's a toolkit in the crate and I noticed there were some plastic bottles as well – gear oil, engine oil, brake fluid, that sort of thing.'

Alex exhaled. 'What do you want with oils?'

Sebastian looked back at Alex and Emma, pointing the barrel of the AK-47 at them as he resumed his watch. Emma stayed silent until Andre called out that he needed help to move the latest box to where the others were, and Sebastian switched his focus to Natangwe.

'Natangwe, go help him,' Sebastian said, and tracked him with the rifle as he moved.

'I've got a gun,' Emma whispered to Alex.

'Seriously?'

'Keep your voice down.' Emma saw that Sebastian was still watching Natangwe and Andre. The professor was resting, sitting in the sand about five metres from Alex and Emma. 'I found it in the Dakota; there's a dead pilot up in the cockpit and it was his. But it's filthy and might not even work unless

357

I can clean it. Hell, it might not work at all, but it's our only chance.'

'Do you know how to use it, how to clean it?' Alex whispered.

'Yes, my mother taught me.'

'What every young girl should learn from her mother.'

Emma liked that he could joke at such a time, but this was no time for laughing. 'How can we get to the Land Cruiser?'

Alex pursed his lips. 'You notice how Andre and Sebastian have collected the rhino horn in one place?' It was stacked about ten metres behind the Hilux, which in turn was in the dark, the same distance past the Land Cruiser.

'Yes.'

'Why didn't they just get us to load all the horns into the vehicles?'

Emma hadn't thought Sebastian and Andre's orders through; she was tired and she had a headache, which she guessed was due to dehydration. They had worked all afternoon in the blazing heat and Sebastian had allowed them only one half-litre bottle of water each, while he and Horsman had drunk steadily through the day. She focused on Alex's question. 'There must be someone else coming, perhaps in a bigger vehicle.'

'Yes.'

'You think they might want to keep us alive as slave labour until then?' Emma asked.

'Perhaps. I can't really see Sebastian letting us go, can you?'

Emma looked at the handsome man she'd almost given herself to. 'No.'

'Sebastian,' Andre called from where he and Natangwe had moved the last crate. 'I'm going to answer the call of nature.'

'OK,' Sebastian replied. 'Natangwe, get over there with the rest.'

Natangwe walked over and sat down on the sand beside them. Sutton shifted closer to them, sliding along on his bottom. 'What are we going to do?' Natangwe asked.

Emma didn't have an answer, but she heard the hopelessness in this normally proud, opinionated, intelligent young man's voice. 'I don't know.'

'Hey, no one speaks unless they're spoken to,' Sebastian called to them. He walked closer, swinging the AK-47 from side to side, checking each of them. Emma felt her heart pounding.

Sebastian took a pace closer to them, though remained out of striking reach of any of them. He must have realised, Emma thought, that if he got too close and the men made a move on him he could only hope to hit one of them before the others overpowered him. But, she wondered, would any of these men have the guts to try something or, for that matter, would she be as brave or as reckless as her mother would undoubtedly be in such a situation? *What would Sonja do?* Emma asked herself. She would wait, she would analyse, she would plan, and she would act.

Sebastian confronted Alex down the barrel of his rifle. 'Everyone's going to walk out of here alive as long as no one does anything brave or stupid.' He took a few steps back from them and looked out over the dunes in search of Andre, who was taking his time on his toilet break.

'I've got a pistol,' Emma said quietly.

Natangwe nodded. 'I know, I saw you with it.'

Emma felt slightly miffed. 'It's almost inoperable. I need oil or something to clean it with, and I don't have much ammo.'

Natangwe seemed to ponder the predicament and then, checking that Sebastian was still looking the other way, quickly reached into his pocket. He unfolded his hand, briefly, revealing a Swiss Army pocketknife to the other two. 'I also found this in the aircraft. It must have fallen out of someone's pocket during the flight. It looks old.'

Emma frowned. 'It'd be hard to kill or maim Sebastian with that.'

'I could if I got close enough,' Alex said through gritted teeth. Sebastian turned his attention back to them and Alex stared back at him.

'You need to get into the truck, right?' Natangwe said out of the side of his mouth.

'Shut it,' Sebastian called.

Emma gave the slightest of nods. Natangwe stood up and started walking towards Sebastian, who raised his rifle again, into his shoulder. 'Stop, or I'll shoot you.'

'I need to go to the toilet as well.'

'Do it here,' Sebastian said.

'I will not. Never.' Natangwe looked down at Emma. 'Not in front of a woman.'

'*Sheesh*,' said Sebastian. 'All right, go behind the Land Cruiser, but make it quick.'

Emma followed Natangwe's movements out of the corner of her eyes. Sebastian was looking at her now, though, so she stared back at him defiantly, hoping he wouldn't look too closely at Natangwe. No one spoke and the tension hung in the air around them, like the cool fog from the Skeleton Coast that had begun creeping towards them from the Atlantic. Emma shivered.

'Hey!' a voice called out. They all looked in the direction of the noise. It was Andre, running back towards them down the face of a dune, brandishing a shovel in the air like a weapon. 'What the hell do you think you're doing?'

'What is it?' Sebastian called.

'This little bastard is letting the air out of the rear tyre.' Andre grabbed Natangwe by the collar of his shirt and pulled him up, but then jumped back in alarm as Natangwe slashed the air just centimetres from the older man's chest, the blade of the pocket-knife flashing silver in the gloom.

Sebastian fired a shot. 'Drop the knife!'

Natangwe held out the knife, but slowly lowered his arm.

'Toss it to Andre.'

Andre scooped the pocketknife from the sand and walked to Sebastian, who gave him back the pistol he'd taken for safe-keeping earlier that afternoon. Andre walked to Natangwe. 'Get down on your knees, boy.'

Natangwe looked ready to explode. 'Don't call me that.'

Andre levelled the pistol between Natangwe's eyes. 'Get down on your knees or I'll shoot you here. I don't need all of you alive.'

With eyes locked on Andre, Natangwe slowly lowered himself to his knees. Keeping the weapon trained on Natangwe, Andre walked around behind him and pointed the pistol at the base of Natangwe's skull.

'No!' Emma screamed. She felt Alex's arm tighten around her, trying to shield her from what was about to happen next. 'Don't shoot him, Andre, please.'

Andre and Sebastian both looked to her. Andre brought his hand up and then savagely clubbed the butt of the pistol down on the back of Natangwe's head. Sebastian strode across, reversed the AK-47 in his hands and slammed the stock into Natangwe's neck and back three times, each vicious stroke ending in a thud and a diminishing convulsion on Natangwe's part. Emma noticed that Natangwe didn't cry out in pain or for mercy once.

Emma stood and broke free of Alex's grasp as he tried to stop her. She ran at Sebastian, who turned his rifle on her. She stopped.

'All right. Everyone, just chill the fuck out,' Sebastian said, running a free hand through sweaty hair. 'Natangwe was stupid, and he's paid the price, but I'm not going to kill him unless I have to. Alex, get up and help Emma change the tyre.'

Alex stood and walked to Emma, putting an arm around her.

'Get your hands off her.'

'Don't make him angrier than he is,' Emma whispered.

Reluctantly, Alex removed his arm and Emma shivered. She liked it better when he was holding her, even though it had only been for a few seconds each time. She quickened her pace and knelt beside Natangwe.

'Get away from him.' Sebastian backed off a few metres so he could cover all of them and not be rushed by anyone.

'I need to check on him.'

'He'll live,' Sebastian said to Emma.

Emma cradled Natangwe's head in her lap. He was conscious, but only just. He blinked up at her, and tried to speak. 'Shush,' she said. 'You were very brave.'

'Yes,' Alex added out of the side of his mouth as he opened the rear of the four-by-four under Sebastian's watchful stare. 'You did well, Natangwe.'

Natangwe coughed. 'Thank you.'

'Set him down, Emma,' Sebastian said. 'Help Alex, and if either of you tries anything I'll shoot Natangwe.'

Emma seethed at Sebastian, her hatred burning her from within, but she told herself to stay calm and tried again to think what her mother would do in this situation. Sebastian, she realised, would have already been dead if she were Sonja. Alex found a wheel spanner and a jack, which he tossed out onto the sand.

'This is a small bottle jack, it will be useless in this sand,' Alex called to Sebastian. He pointed up at the driver's side of the Toyota's roof carrier. Bolted to it was a high-lift jack, secured with a padlock. 'We need that one.'

Sebastian held the rifle's pistol grip with one hand and reached into his pocket with the other. He took out the vehicle's keys. 'Don't try and be a hero, Alex; it'll cost you your life.'

Alex nodded and caught the keys. He made slow work of finding the right key.

Emma could see Alex was deliberately distracting Sebastian.

'Hurry up,' Sebastian called.

Emma leaned into the back of the truck and started rifling through the crate. There was gear and engine oil, and brake fluid and automatic transmission fluid for the gearbox, but they were all in one and five-litre plastic bottles. There was no way she would be able to smuggle one of those past Sebastian. She moved the bottles in the crate around, frantically trying to find something she could use, or an empty container to decant some oil into.

'Get out of there, Emma,' Sebastian called. 'There's nothing you need in there. Alex has the jack.'

'Emma,' said Alex, 'find the crank; we need it to lower the spare wheel down from under the Toyota.'

'Yes, very well,' Sebastian agreed. 'Find that thingy as well.'

Emma's hand closed around a small aerosol can that she'd missed on her first search of the crate. She took a quick look; it was a lubricating spray called Q20. It was, she thought, the kind of stuff used to loosen rusted bolts and stuck door hinges. She had seen her mother using a similar spray on a pistol once, though Sonja had warned her not to clean ammunition with it as the liquid would destroy the primer in the rounds. Some girls learned how to bake from their mothers, Emma had learned about guns. She shifted the crate and found the collapsible rod that lowered the tyre. She had watched Sam change a wheel on his four-by-four in Los Angeles one time; it was, he had told her, about the most adventurous thing he had done since meeting her mother in Africa.

Emma looked out the side window and saw that Andre was busy guarding Professor Sutton, who had been ordered to open some tins of food and heat the contents over a gas stove.

Emma withdrew herself from the rear of the truck and, when Sebastian was looking away, holding his hand out for Alex to toss him the keys, she dropped the can of spray onto the sand next to Natangwe. Without even knowing what the contraband was, Natangwe raised his T-shirt and, wincing in pain, slipped the can behind the waistband of his trousers.

Emma got down on her knees and inserted the long rod of the crank into the hole in the rear bumper, as Sam had shown her, and jiggled the end around until it mated with the socket above the spare wheel. She started to wind. It was stiff at first, but with a screech of metal, the chain came free and the spare started to drop.

Alex hefted the heavy high-lift jack to a position next to where Emma was.

'All OK?' he asked her.

'I think so,' she said quietly. 'I've got some lubricating spray but Sebastian's never going to take his eyes off us. I don't know when I'm going to get a chance to clean the gun.'

'Where's the spray?' Alex whispered.

'In Natangwe's trousers.'

'Stop winding the tyre down.'

'OK,' Emma said.

'The spare wheel's stuck,' Alex called to Sebastian.

'Well, get underneath and try to shake it free. There's some lubricating spray in the back of the vehicle,' Sebastian said.

'Shit,' Emma whispered.

Alex made a show of rummaging in the rear of the Toyota. 'Get it back off Natangwe, pass it to me,' he whispered.

With Alex blocking the view Emma knelt and retrieved the spray from a still groggy and slightly bewildered Natangwe. She passed it to Alex. He lifted the can high and shook it. 'Found it.'

'Emma, you get underneath and spray the chain. I'll try to keep cranking.' Alex passed her the spray and, with his back to Sebastian, winked at her.

'Just get a move on,' Sebastian called to them.

Emma got down on her hands and knees and dropped to her belly. The sand was cool on her exposed skin. She leopard-crawled under the Land Cruiser.

It was dark, but Sonja had taught her to strip and reassemble a nine-millimetre Glock blindfolded at the indoor shooting range in Los Angeles. '*This is ridiculous, Mum,*' she remembered saying to Sonja, but she sent her mother a silent thank you now as she slithered deeper into the gloom.

Emma reached around and pulled the pistol from her jeans. She looked it over. It was a different make from the Glock; the word 'star' was engraved on the metal slide and embossed on the black plastic grip. '*Most pistols have the same basic components,*' she heard her mother saying in her head.

The magazine release button was close to her thumb and she pressed it. Again, though, the magazine seemed stuck. She sprayed some lubricant on the button and the end of the magazine. 'I'm spraying now,' she called out for Sebastian and Alex's benefit. Above her she heard the rattle of the crank as Alex pretended to make hard work of turning it. His movements, while slight, dislodged bits of dried mud and road grit, which pattered down on her. She coughed as she breathed in the grit, and the strong fumes from the spray made her eyes water in the confined space under the vehicle.

Emma wiggled the magazine out and doused the pistol all over again with spray. 'Keep trying,' she yelled for effect. She pulled back the slide, 'racking it', her mother had called it and, holding it rather than letting it go, she found the pin that released the locking mechanism. She used the index finger of her right hand to push it out, and extracted it with her left hand.

When Emma eased the pressure on the slide she found it was reluctant to move, which was not a good sign. Again she hosed the weapon with spray.

'This shouldn't take this long,' Sebastian called. 'Get a move on, Emma.'

She cursed under her breath. Emma lay on her back on the sand and placed the parts of the pistol on her belly, in order to keep them free of grit and sand. With each movement of the slide backwards and forward the pistol's working parts seemed to free up a little more. Emma took the slide all the way off and pulled the spring and barrel from inside.

'Shit,' she said.

Alex dropped to his knees. 'What is it?'

'I just dropped the bloody barrel in the sand.'

'Stay calm,' Alex said in a low voice, 'you are doing fine.'

Emma took a breath, felt for the missing component and wiped it on her shirt. She liberally sprayed lubricant all over it to blast away the sand, and down the inside of the barrel as well. She used the tail of her shirt to wipe the pistol inside and out as best as she could. For good measure she reapplied a couple of squirts to the components as she reassembled the weapon.

'Almost there,' she called out.

'Hurry up,' Sebastian chided again.

'Pass me some water.' Alex rolled a bottle under the truck to her. Emma took the magazine and thumbed out the three bullets. These she cleaned with water and then dried thoroughly with her shirt. She quickly reloaded and then slammed the magazine back into the handgrip.

'Done,' she said. For good measure, Emma sprayed the chain above her to make it easier for Alex to lower the spare wheel. As she reversed out, sliding on her back and then rolling over at the last minute to secrete the pistol again, she heard the spare wheel thud into the sand.

Alex got down on his knees and helped drag her out. He squeezed her hand. 'Great job.'

'I don't know if it will work. The ammunition may be too old.'

His eyes met hers in the glow of the fluorescent work light connected to the vehicle's cigarette lighter plug. The light hung from the roof carrier. 'There's only one way to find out if the pistol and your bullets are in working order.'

Emma looked across at Sebastian, who waved the barrel of the AK-47 to cajole them along. She had given herself to that thief, this creep, and the thought now filled her with nothing but revulsion.

Sebastian was staring at them and, on impulse, Emma put her hand behind Alex's head and drew him to her. She kissed him on the lips.

A flash leapt from the muzzle of the assault rifle and a shot sailed over their heads. Alex wrapped his arms around Emma. After a couple of seconds, which she needed to calm herself, she gently broke from the embrace.

'Yes, there's only one way to find out.' She picked up the tyre lever. 'Bring it on.'

Chapter 28

Sonja stopped the Land Rover and got out when she could see the shimmering blue strip of the Atlantic Ocean, which appeared on and off on the horizon through the shifting curtain of wind-blown sand that stung her arms, legs and face.

She stood with her hands on her hips. Brand and Stirling joined her, one either side. Sonja looked around, taking a moment to appreciate the all-consuming emptiness of the landscape, and the enormity of the task she had set herself.

Brand scanned left to right through a pair of binoculars. 'Can't see any sign of the road gang.'

Stirling put his hand up to shade his eyes. 'No. Which is odd, as I thought they would have been in this area.'

'We need to keep moving,' Sonja said, leading the men back to the vehicles. The occupants of the three vehicles they had passed that day had seen no sign of a party of archaeologists on land, and no flyovers. Sonja hoped they might pick up some spoor once they hit the salt road, the main route that ran north–south along the edge of the Atlantic.

She drove through the dunes down towards the coast. As she approached she saw that the Atlantic was living up to its fearsome reputation. Walls of cold water, greener up close than from a distance, smashed themselves to smithereens on the shore, creating volcanic geysers of white spume.

Once at the salt road Sonja turned right, heading north towards Möwe Bay. They drove for an hour, Sonja leading and pushing the Land Rover up over the hundred mark; the salt road was smooth, wide and solid. With each kilometre, however, her anxiety increased.

She slowed and did a U-turn, Brand and Allchurch tailing them, and drove back to a section of the road where there had obviously been some recent widening work. They got out of the vehicles again and Sonja dropped to one knee to inspect the tracks of vehicles and heavy machinery.

'These tracks are full of sand. The gang must have got this far, then packed up and left. Dammit.'

'Nothing we can do about that,' Brand observed.

He was right, but she *had* to do something. Sonja walked away from the road towards the water, which was about two hundred metres distant. The others followed her. As she walked the stiff onshore breeze shot chilly needles of water from the breaking waves at her face. The cold air helped clear her head.

'Desolate place,' Brand said, looking around.

At the water's edge was the rusting hull of a ship that had been wrecked. From its size Sonja guessed it had been a fishing trawler. It was these metal remains, as much as the bones of animals, whales and even humans that gave the coast its name. Brand had stated the obvious.

'Beautiful, though, in a striking way,' Stirling said. 'I think if I'd worked in the Namibian national parks service I wouldn't have minded being out here, away from it all.'

'My uncle . . .' Sonja stopped, turning instead to Brand. 'Tell me again what year the Dakota came down.'

'1987,' Brand said.

Sonja processed the information and thought about her conversation with her Aunt Ursula in Swakopmund. She thought about what she was doing at the time of Uncle Udo's funeral, how old she would have been. Same year. 'And the date?'

Brand closed his eyes and thought for a moment. 'Sixteenth of November. Hot.'

'What is it, Sonn? What are you thinking?' Stirling asked.

'I need your satellite phone, Stirling.' Sonja went back to the Land Rover, with Stirling a few paces behind.

Stirling found the phone. He turned it on, flipped up the large antenna and sat it on the bonnet of the Land Rover so that the phone could acquire its satellite signal.

Sonja drummed her fingers on the front fender of the truck while they waited for the phone to wake up. 'My Uncle Udo was a ranger here on the Skeleton Coast during the war. He was killed in a SWAPO ambush, but just a few days before that he rescued a pilot whose aircraft had come down in the desert. He died two days after you nearly did, Brand.'

The two men looked at her, absorbing the new information. The satellite phone beeped. Sonja took out her own phone, switched it on and found her aunt's number in her contacts list. Committing it to memory, she put her phone away, took up the satellite phone and dialled.

'Hello, Tante Ursula, it's me, Sonja,' she said.

Sonja quickly dispensed with the pleasantries and asked her aunt if she could remember, or check, the date on which Udo had found the flier. Ursula said she would check Udo's diary. Sonja heard a beeping noise and looked at the phone's screen. 'Shit, battery's nearly flat.' She turned the phone off. 'I'll give her fifteen minutes then call her back,' Sonja said to the men. 'Stirling, do you have a car charger for the phone?'

Stirling looked sheepish. 'Well, yes, but when I got the phone out just now I saw the charger wasn't in the bag where it's supposed to be. One of the scouts or the young research students who used it last must have forgotten to put the charger and cable back; they're probably still in whatever vehicle they used.'

She put the phone down, ran her fingers through her hair and walked away from the vehicle, back towards the water. Sonja thought of Udo, patrolling this lonely road. It would not have been a bad life, she thought, being away from people most of the time and able to return to his beautiful, artistic, fun-loving wife when he was on leave. But the bloody war had intervened, or had it been something worse, something more evil than men fighting for a cause?

The men had sense enough to leave her alone this time, and when she checked her watch and confirmed it had been a quarter of an hour, she went back to the Land Rover and phoned Ursula again.

'What happened to you?' Ursula asked. In response Sonja explained she had waited to conserve the battery.

'All right, I will be quick then. This sounds like it's important.'

'Just tell me, please, Tante, the date that Udo found that airman, and, more importantly, if he made some reference as to where it was. I'm putting you on speaker phone so I can make notes. And please, speak English so my friends here can understand you.'

'*Ja*. OK. The date was the seventeenth of November.'

Sonja had taken a green hard-backed military notebook out of her back pocket and was writing.

'Day after,' Brand muttered.

'Does he record the time he found the man, Aunty?' Sonja asked.

'Yes. It was in the morning, at 9.17.'

Sonja made a note. 'Is there a location?'

'I'm checking. Udo says he was on patrol from Möwe Bay to Terrace Bay when the man walked into the road and flagged him down. He says the man was wounded and seemed to have lost a lot of blood. He appeared weak and there was blood on him, on his face and uniform. He says: *Asked where he was from, what unit, and all he would say was, "Get me to a doctor, now". His accent and uniform were South African. He spoke to me in English.*'

They waited, and Sonja transcribed her aunt's words. She would review them, although she already knew they were in the rough vicinity of where Udo had been patrolling that day. In this area that could equate to hundreds if not thousands of square kilometres. 'Anything else?'

'*Ja*, but it's just a whole collection of numbers. Shall I read them to you, Sonja?'

The phone was beeping again. 'Yes, please, Aunty, but quickly.'

Ursula read out the numbers and Sonja's heart leapt when she heard the letters 'S' and 'E' interspersed within them. 'That's *lekker*, Aunty. Is there anything else?'

'No, that's all. I hope this helps you. Is Emma all right? Are you with her?'

'We're going to find her.' The phone beeped once more and died.

'Latitude and longitude,' Brand said, looking over Sonja's shoulder at the numbers she had written in her notebook.

'I'll get the GPS,' Stirling said. He unclipped it from the inside of his vehicle and brought it to them, along with the paper map, which he unfolded on the bonnet of the truck. As Sonja read out the numbers he punched them into the handheld device, then set the reference as a new destination. They waited until the GPS calculated distance, direction and time.

'Seventy-three kilometres north of here,' Sonja said, holding her hand over the small screen to reduce the glare. 'And look, the point is almost exactly on the salt road. My uncle knew how to read a map.'

Matthew had got out of the car and joined them. 'What's going on?'

Brand filled him in, quickly, and showed him the approximate locations of where they were, and where Udo had picked up the airman, on the paper map.

'Could this pilot that your uncle found have been my son?' he asked Sonja.

'I've no way of knowing. In his diary, according to my aunt, there's no mention of a name, nor even a physical description, which you wouldn't expect anyway, just a reference to the man being wounded and covered in blood, and that he'd come out of the desert.'

Brand looked away from the coast to the dunes to the east. 'It's too much of a coincidence for it to be another aircraft. The Dakota was heading for the sea, but it must have crashed in the desert less than a day's travel from the coast. The guy was wounded, so he must have been moving slowly. I left the aircraft late at night. Even if the guy your uncle found had started moving at night, he was only found just after nine the next morning. He couldn't have travelled far; maybe twenty kilometres at the most. It's not easy to walk in sand, particularly if you're hurt.'

'But how would we know where to look?' Allchurch asked.

'That's easy,' Sonja replied. 'If the aircraft went down in the desert there are only two logical directions to head.' She ran her finger along the paper map so the men gathered around the bonnet could all see. 'There's little civilisation to the north or south. If you went east you'd eventually cut one of the north–south roads, such as the road between Palmwag and Purros, but if the man walked to the salt road then he obviously knew the Dakota had gone down close to the coast.'

'West would be the most logical, then,' Brand interrupted. 'He'd have known that someone from the parks service would be patrolling the coastal road, even if he had to wait a while.'

Sonja nodded. 'So, if we get to the point where my uncle rescued the man all we have to do is turn east into the desert.'

Sonja went to the driver's-side door of the Land Rover, but Matthew Allchurch, looking elderly and somewhat frail, stopped her. 'Sonja, please, I know we must go quickly, but I just wanted to say that I will do anything I can to help you find your daughter. Your uncle rescued someone from that flight, but my son never came home. I need to know what happened to Gareth. Someone survived that flight, and if they're still alive, somewhere, I need to find them as well.'

She was impatient, but Allchurch's words, the soft longing in his voice, touched her. Sonja reached out and put a hand on his forearm. 'I know what it's like to lose someone you love, Matthew. We will find out what is going on with this bloody wrecked aircraft, and why people are willing to kill to get to it, and to cover their trails. You know my priority is my daughter, but we will discover the truth, and I hope that truth can bring you some peace.'

He blinked, and she saw his eyes begin to glisten. If she were a different person she might, she thought, put her arms around him and draw him to her. Allchurch needed to move on, but so did she. Sonja was not given to public outpourings of emotion and, more than that, she knew that if she gave this kind, sad, wounded man a hug, she might just break down in tears again herself. Now was not the time for that.

Chapter 29

Irina put the Dragunov sniper's rifle down, satisfied it was now perfectly zeroed for long-range killing, and took an AK-47 from the groundsheet laid out on the dry yellow grass at her feet. She cocked the rifle and brought it to her shoulder.

'Ready,' she called.

Behind her, Mikhail held a remote control device designed to activate electronically a series of pop-up targets that he had placed randomly in the open space in front of the firing point that morning, while Irina had been having her breakfast. She was adamant that she did not want prior warning of where the targets would be.

Irina walked forward, the rifle still up. In her peripheral vision she picked up movement, twenty metres forward and to the right. Irina swung the barrel of the rifle and fired two shots, a double tap, and the green target cut in the shape of a man went down.

She advanced, all senses alive. She was channelling her anger at the incompetence of her men into this shoot. Benjie was out of action in hospital, recovering from the sixty-five stitches in his mauled forearms, and the local contractors Miro had hired had failed her dismally.

Horsman had called her that morning from the site of the crashed Dakota. At least they had found the long-lost aircraft. All of the rhino horn was offloaded and awaiting transport. Irina had to explain that the helicopter that would have been used to come and collect the valuable cargo had been downed, and that the person responsible for destroying it, Sonja Kurtz, was out looking for them as she spoke. She warned Horsman to be vigilant and to sit tight until she arrived in another helicopter. He should keep Kurtz's daughter and the others alive, as hostages, in case Kurtz got to them first.

Irina was about to prepare herself for the next attack when the sound of far-off engines made both her and Mikhail turn. She checked her watch. 'Good, they're on time.'

The twin engine Bell 412 helicopter swept in low over the tree line, heading straight for them. She had told Miro she would be on the rifle range that morning and that he should bring the men to her for some weapons practice. She kept her own AK-47 in her hand as the helicopter, a modern civilian variant of the Huey helicopter that had carried American soldiers into battle during the Vietnam War, rocked back on its tail, the pilot flaring the nose for landing. Irina turned her back to the hail of dust and debris that washed over her and Mikhail, and took shelter in the lee of the two Land Rover game viewers which she and Mikhail had driven from the lodge.

The helicopter settled, and as the pilot let the engines cool, the rotors still turning, Miro climbed down from the co-pilot's seat. The sliding rear door opened and six men, all solidly built, followed him out, heads bent beneath the blades.

'Irina Petrovna,' Miro said, smiling to hide his nerves. 'All is in order.'

She said nothing. She appraised the men. A couple of them, whom she recognised, nodded to her in greeting and she returned the gesture, almost imperceptibly. They were crew from the fishing trawler cruising off the coast in the cold waters of the Atlantic. Like her father, Irina recruited from the ranks of the services and these men had all served in the Russian Navy. She had asked Miro to find men among the crew who had trained to fight on land: naval commandos. These looked like hard men, and the two she had recognised immediately, she knew, had seen active service in Chechnya. The eldest, Sergei with his bushy grey moustache and shaven head, had been in Afghanistan. He bowed to her.

The pilot shut down the engine and he, too, got out of the machine and walked to her. He held out his hand. 'Quentin Swanevelder.'

Irina shook his hand. 'Thank you for coming at such short notice. Miro has briefed you on our mission?'

'He's briefed me that as well as illegally flying out to your ship and picking up these *okes* we're flying into the desert to pick up some cargo and then back out to the trawler, under the radar, in every sense of the word. There may also be people with guns trying to stop us.'

'You have no problem with this?' she asked.

'The pilot of the other helicopter you chartered was my *boet*, like a brother to me. We served in the same squadron during the bush war, and later in Angola with a mercenary outfit. If those same people who killed him try and stop you and your men, I'll help you get them.'

'Good,' she said. 'You passed over the lodge on your way in?'

'Yes, I saw it. Impressive place.'

Irina pointed along the gravel road behind them. 'Take the nearest Land Rover to the lodge. Mary there has prepared food. You can freshen up.'

'I'd prefer to stay with my helicopter.'

Irina stared him down. 'I'd prefer you not to be here.'

Swanevelder looked as though he might reply, but thought better of it and, instead, nodded and went to the nearest vehicle. The key was in the ignition and he drove off.

Irina walked along the rank of men. Most of them bore tattoos, some done in prison. All of the men here had willingly participated in Irina's criminal activities. Her trawlers regularly smuggled contraband – drugs, arms, women – so moving several crates of rhino horn would not concern them. This could, however, end in a firefight, and some of them might not have fired a weapon recently.

She stopped in front of Miro. '"*All is in order*"?' she said to him in Russian, mimicking him. 'You're told to get rid of two men, a safari guide and an old lawyer, and they kill your hit men.'

'I can explain –'

'Shut up. You then send a helicopter with a man on board with a machine gun and because a woman joins these two men they are able to kill the pilot and the gunner and destroy an aircraft *I* paid good money for. Do you think no one will notice the downing of a helicopter and the deaths of four people in Namibia, Miro?'

'Irina Petrovna, I am sorry. I should have seen to matters myself.'

She raised the AK-47, gripping it with both hands, and levelled it at Miro. 'That is the first thing you've got right in a long time. Get down on your knees.'

He put his hands out to her. 'Please.'

Irina raised the rifle to her shoulder. 'On your knees!'

He complied, looking up at her, his mouth slack.

'All of you, listen to me,' she said to the sailors. 'The stakes in this operation are too high for failure. This is the most valuable single movement of cargo any of you will have taken part in. There are other people looking for this stuff and they are armed. If I tell any of you to do something, I expect my orders to be obeyed. The rewards will be good, the punishment for failure not so good. Miro?'

He looked up at her. 'Yes, Irina Petrovna.'

'Stand up.' She lowered her rifle. He looked, she thought, pathetically grateful for his life.

'I will not disappoint you again.'

'I know you won't, Miro.' She smiled for him. 'Go to the Land Rover and get the rifles for the men.'

'Yes, Irina Petrovna.'

As Miro began to walk the short distance to the Land Rover, his back to them, Irina raised the AK-47 to her shoulder again, flicked the safety, and pulled the trigger twice. Miro was pitched forward, one bullet in his back, the other in his skull.

'Mikhail, hand out the rifles,' Irina said. Her underling gave a half-smile. While he was issuing weapons and ammunition to each man Irina took the satellite phone out of the console between the Land Rover's two front seats. She dialled.

'Yes,' said Andre Horsman on the other end of the line.

'The helicopter and the men are here now. We will be with you within two hours,' Irina said.

'Good. You have the money?'

'Of course.' What she had was eight men armed to the teeth and ready to kill. What she did not need was a greedy South African who, once this operation was done, would be of no use to her. Never again would she get hold of a shipment of rhino horn this size. Tran had wanted to corner the market, to build up a stockpile and name his own price. She would succeed where he had failed.

'Can you get here sooner?' Andre asked.

Horsman was scared, she could hear it in his voice. If Brand and Kurtz beat them to the crashed Dakota there was a very good chance they would be able to rescue Kurtz's daughter and the other archaeologists. *Yes*, Irina thought, *I could be there sooner, but I'm not going to be.* 'You'll be fine,' she said instead.

'I know I'll be *fine*,' he said, the anger bubbling up, 'but we want to get out of here before the others arrive.'

'I know, I know.'

'You still want me to keep the girl alive?' Horsman asked.

'Yes. Even if Kurtz doesn't get to you first she won't stop looking for her child. I need leverage over her and I need to get the cargo to the ship. The girl is insurance.'

'All right. And the others?'

'Kill them.'

*

Andre walked back into sight. Emma had watched him take the satellite phone with him when he had trekked over the nearest dune. They had worked through the night, digging in shifts, moving sand and heaving and sweating to try to move the heavy cargo bundles out of the aircraft.

Andre and Sebastian had allowed them a break to eat some more canned food for breakfast. Their guards had been keeping a close eye on them so communication between Alex and Emma had been limited to quick, whispered messages. They were all tired and Andre and Sebastian had both stayed up all night following their previous attempt to take Andre's gun. Emma and Alex had decided to hold off making their move until, inevitably, one of their captors decided to take a rest break.

'Alex, Natangwe, break's over, get back to work,' Andre said. Emma, the two young men and Professor Sutton had been sitting with their backs to the fuselage of the Dakota, hiding in what shade they could find. 'Sebastian, have a rest.'

Sebastian had been sitting on a folding camping chair under the roll-out awning on the side of the Land Cruiser, covering them with the AK-47. Sebastian nodded, handed the rifle to Andre and crawled into the back seat of the Cruiser and lay down, his boots sticking out.

It was already oppressively hot. The wind had died and Emma

swatted away a fly. Professor Sutton was sweating profusely. He mopped his forehead with a sodden handkerchief.

'Come on, get up,' said Andre, motioning with the barrel of the AK.

Alex got to his feet and dusted down the back of his pants. 'What are we digging for?'

'I need holes deep enough and big enough to fit half of the crates. I just made a call; I was expecting some more transport to come and collect the stuff, but they're not going to make it any time soon, so we're going to load what we can into our two vehicles and come back later for the rest.'

'Where does that leave us?' Emma asked. Alex went to the back of the Land Cruiser under Andre's watchful gaze and pulled out two shovels. He tossed one to Natangwe, who was already on his feet and caught the tool with one hand.

'You might have to ride on the roof.' Andre laughed, but no one else did. 'Start digging.'

Alex looked to Emma as he stabbed the ground with the blade of the shovel. She caught his eye. Emma knew what he was thinking; Alex and Natangwe were digging their own graves, and those of Emma and Sutton. The time for her to act had come.

Emma felt the hard bulk of the pistol pressing into the small of her back. There was no better time than now. Something was in the offing, which was why Andre had given the young men the order to dig. Also, for the first time Sebastian was lying down, off guard, in the back of the truck. He had swapped Andre the rifle for the pistol, and with luck would soon be asleep.

Emma reached behind her back.

'What are you doing, Emma?' Sutton whispered beside her.

'Stay calm, Professor, don't move. Don't draw attention to me.' She watched Andre and then flitted her eyes to Alex. He saw her and must have sensed what she was up to, because he threw his shovel down on the sand, in the shallow pit he had dug so far.

'Fuck you, Andre,' Alex said in a voice laden with threat, but not loud enough to rouse Sebastian from inside the truck.

Andre stood under the awning, his head touching the fabric. He swung the rifle so that it was pointed at Alex.

Emma used the distraction to pull the pistol from the small of her back. She glanced back at Sutton. The professor's eyes and mouth were wide open. Emma brought the pistol up, wrapping her left hand around her right as she walked towards Andre, who was still looking at Alex.

Emma counted off the metres as she closed the gap and slid her right index finger through the trigger guard. The pistol was already racked, cocked for just this eventuality, a round already in the chamber. She had carefully eased the hammer back into place after she had quickly cleaned and reloaded the pistol under the truck. Her mother had taught her how to carry with 'one up the spout', but also advised her never to do so unless she found herself in hostile territory in a war zone.

Just as Sonja had shown her, Emma readied the pistol by using her right thumb to pull back the hammer. She raised the pistol and pointed it at Andre, lining up the centre of his torso.

'*Not the head, not the heart, not an arm or a leg,*' her mother had taught her on the shooting range. '*You don't shoot to be clever or to wound, you aim for the centre mass of the target to put the target down. Two shots, always – the double tap.*'

Emma had joked with her mother, asking her if she had any advice for dealing with men. Her mother had replied by putting nine rounds into the heart of a paper target, plus one into the head and another into where the balls would have been. '*I've been doing this all my life, with targets and men. You aim for centre mass.*'

Andre was not stupid. He glanced around to check on his other captives and he saw Emma coming towards him. She felt a stab of pure fear and suddenly panicked, thinking she would not have the courage to pull the trigger.

Emma stopped and steadied her aim. In slow motion she watched Andre swing the rifle towards her. Off to the left she saw Alex bend and pick up the shovel and run towards the older man. Natangwe was on his heels, holding up his own tool like a club. Sebastian was sitting up in the back seat of the truck.

Andre's mouth was open as if he was screaming something, but Emma heard nothing except the pounding of her own heart in her ears. She closed her right hand as though she was making a fist. The pistol bucked in her hand, harder than she remembered, and the noise of the shot seemed to bring her back to the present as it restored her hearing.

Andre pitched backwards like he'd been punched in the chest, his rifle flying up at a crazy angle. His finger must have been wrapped around the trigger because a burst of rounds stitched holes in the canvas awning above his head.

Emma pulled the trigger again, but this time there was no jolt in her hand, no noise. She pulled it once, twice more, but there was nothing but a dull click.

She heard her mother, in her mind, a memory from their time on the shooting range. '*Weapon fires, weapon stops!*'

Emma looked at the pistol, panicking, then she heard Sonja again in her head. '*Weapon fires, weapon stops!*'

Her mother yelling in her ear, over and over again on the range, trying and succeeding in rattling her. Sonja had taught her the drill for what to do if she had a jam or a misfire. The bullets in this pistol were more than thirty years old. Something had gone wrong.

'*Cock, lock, look,*' Sonja said.

'*Cock, lock, look,*' Emma mumbled to herself. She pulled back the slide on the top of the pistol, thumbed up the locking device and tilted the pistol over. Emma saw the bullet stuck in the chamber. She shook it, as she'd practised with her mother, and the dud round fell out. That left her only one more. She could see it, sitting there, seemingly so tiny and inoffensive, a little piece of brass, copper and lead.

In front of her, Andre was on the ground, and, worryingly, Alex was falling, pitching forward as though he'd been shot, though Emma couldn't recall hearing another bullet fired. Professor Sutton, she saw in her peripheral vision, had dived to the ground to save his own skin. Natangwe had been behind Alex but now he was ahead of the white man, one palm outstretched and the other hand holding his shovel, which he now grabbed again with two hands. Emma realised Natangwe had pushed Alex out of the way for some reason.

As Emma ran towards the men she released the lock with her thumb and the slide slammed forward again, chambering her last round. She brought the pistol up.

Alex crawled to Andre, who, even though he was wounded with blood spitting from his mouth was trying to bring his rifle to bear. Alex punched Andre in the face and wrenched the AK-47 from his hand.

Sebastian was the danger now, but when Emma tried to take aim at him she saw that Natangwe was in the way, blocking her shot. Natangwe launched himself into the Land Cruiser through the open rear door.

A gun fired and Natangwe toppled backwards out of the Toyota. Alex was starting to stand, but now he risked getting in the way of Emma's shot. 'Get down, Alex!'

She saw him look back at her and realise that she would be able to get the first shot off. He dived forward in the sand, holding the AK up so it was in front of him when he hit the deck.

Emma could see Sebastian clearly. He was shifting his aim towards her. *God, I thought I wanted him.* Emma squeezed the trigger. There was a noise like two claps of thunder and then everything went black.

Chapter 30

'Now that's a truck,' Stirling Smith said as they pulled up behind a converted Mercedes Unimog four-wheel drive lorry fitted with a camper on its back. A young couple had flagged them down. They looked relieved as they walked towards the Land Rover.

'Let me handle this,' Sonja said. 'We need that truck.'

'OK.'

Ten kilometres short of the point where Sonja's Uncle Udo had picked up the injured airman the pastor's Land Rover, being driven by Brand ahead of them, had started to slow down. Brand put on his hazard lights and pulled over to the left and stopped.

Sonja stopped behind him and got out. 'What's wrong?'

Brand popped the bonnet. 'It's gone into "limp home" mode and the temperature gauge just red-lined.'

Sonja lifted the bonnet and saw the problem immediately. A fine jet of coolant was escaping from a hose. Stirling and Brand joined her and she pointed out the problem. 'It must have been nicked by a bullet fragment or some bodywork when the guy in the chopper was strafing us.'

'What do we do?' Stirling asked.

'Keep the radiator water reservoir topped up and try to find a replacement.'

'Out here?'

Stirling's scepticism had been well founded, and Sonja was just as surprised and relieved as he was when they saw the Unimog, although it appeared this vehicle was in trouble as well.

'Hello,' said the young man by the Unimog. He was sunburnt, wearing a headscarf instead of a broad-brimmed sunhat, and shorts and a tie-dyed T-shirt. His female partner wore harem pants and a tank top. 'I am sorry, my English is not so perfect.'

'*Sprechen Sie Deutsch?*' Sonja asked.

'*Ja, ja,*' he said with relief.

Sonja spoke with the man for a couple of minutes in German, with his girlfriend or wife, hands on hips, interrupting every now and then, unable to control her anger.

Brand, who had been behind them in the slow-moving Land Rover caught up and lowered his window. 'What's up?'

'They've run out of diesel,' Sonja said.

'You're kidding, right?' Brand asked.

'Check out the girlfriend,' Sonja said out of the side of her mouth. 'She's been telling him to fill up since Swakopmund.' The woman continued to berate her partner in German.

'I'd laugh if that kind of mistake wasn't so serious out here. Too bad. We could have used that truck.'

'We're taking it,' Sonja said.

In German, she told the young man that she wanted to arrange a swap, her Land Rover for his Unimog. She would use the spare jerry cans on the Land Rover and Stirling's Amarok to put fuel in the truck's tank and the young couple would take the Land Rover back to Swakopmund, slowly, topping up the radiator as they went, and Sonja would return the Unimog when she was finished with it.

The young man erupted in an angry outburst, his girlfriend following suit.

'I take it that didn't go down too well?' Brand said when the red-faced couple had exhausted themselves.

Sonja looked at him and raised her eyebrows. 'It was always going to come to this.' She reached behind her, pulled her pistol from her pants and pointed it at the young man. In German, she told the couple to offload their personal valuables from the truck.

The woman started wailing and Sonja tried to soothe her. 'Stirling, Hudson, get the fuel cans down and tip the diesel into the Unimog's tank.'

'Yes ma'am.' Brand said.

Sonja kept an eye on the couple as they unloaded their belongings from the Unimog and stacked them near the Land Rover. The woman was still sobbing, and Sonja assured her that as long as they did what she asked no one would be hurt and she would bring their truck back to them in one piece. She mentioned, too, that she was on a mission to rescue her daughter.

The woman was angry, and told Sonja through her tears that their life savings had gone into the campervan. She swore she would contact the police as soon as she got to Swakopmund.

'Get on the ground, face down,' Sonja ordered the couple.

'Are you going to kill us?' the man asked.

'No, not unless you're stupid. Hands on the back of your heads.'

When they had complied Sonja put her pistol back in her shorts and took out her notebook. She wrote the name, address and phone number of her Aunt Ursula on a piece of paper, ripped it out and knelt and forced it into the young man's hands.

'Stand up. That's the details of my aunt in Swakopmund. Unlike me, she's nice. She'll put you up if you tell her what happened. She won't be surprised, but she'll confirm I'm borrowing your truck to rescue my daughter. Drive the Land Rover slowly, and keep an eye on the temperature gauge. There's enough fuel in the tank to get you to Henties Bay at least, if not Swakopmund. You can fill up there.'

The men had finished refuelling the truck and Matthew Allchurch, with his one good hand, had dragged their personal equipment and bag of weapons from the Land Rover. The other two loaded the Unimog and Sonja climbed up into the cab. It took a few goes to start the engine, with Brand under the bonnet hand-priming the empty fuel system, but eventually the big engine coughed to life with a belch of black smoke.

'Go see my aunt. She'll take care of you until I get back,' Sonja called as she left the Unimog and got into the Amarok with Stirling. Brand and Allchurch climbed up into the camper.

Sonja watched the countdown of kilometres until they reached the point mentioned in her uncle's diary. They stopped. It was an empty stretch of road flanked by the angry Atlantic on the left and a windswept sandy plain rising to dunes studded with dry grass to her right.

She had no way of knowing if Udo's coordinates had been correct – it must have been little more than a guess on his part in any case – but she had nothing else to go on. Sonja turned ninety degrees to the right and watched the GPS to confirm she was heading due east. The survivor of the Dakota crash would have headed due west to the coast, so this was the best she could do. Stirling gunned the Amarok's engine and released the clutch.

In the wing mirror she could see Brand and Allchurch turn off the road and follow them. She had no idea how far inland the aircraft would have crashed. Also, she was acutely aware that if Uncle Udo had been slightly off in his calculations they might miss the crash site completely, even though they might pass very close to it.

As they approached the slope of the first dune Stirling stopped and engaged the low-range setting on the gearbox. He took off in second, building up speed and momentum before the gradient increased. To her satisfaction the Amarok ploughed on, taking the incline in its stride. However, when they crested the top of the dune she saw it was just the first of a seemingly unending series of sand ridges that stretched to the horizon and probably beyond.

They stopped an hour later. It was becoming oppressively hot. Sonja got out of the truck and walked back to the Unimog, where Brand had also alighted and was spreading a map out on the sand.

Brand pointed at a spot on the map. 'I put us here.'

Sonja agreed, but knowing where they were didn't bring them any closer to finding Emma. 'About fifteen kilometres inland. That's still a long walk for a wounded man, through this kind of country.'

Sonja lifted the binoculars hanging around her neck to her eyes. The landscape around her was beyond harsh; it was cruel. It looked like nothing could survive here, though Sonja knew from the lessons of her youth that these empty sands did contain life, and that myriad small creatures gleaned enough water from the freezing mists that rolled in each evening to survive. Emma could be alive out here somewhere; she *must* be alive.

As well as seeing nothing she could hear nothing except the susurration of the wind shifting the sand.

'With the fuel we put into the Unimog I estimate we can make it as far as Wilfriedstein,' Brand said, drawing her attention back to the map. 'I led a safari there once, in search of the desert elephants. There's fuel there and a mock castle that was built by a crazy German guy as his farmhouse years ago; it's been turned into a bed and breakfast. It's a good place to stay.'

'If we don't find Emma and the others we can refuel there and resume the search.'

'Perhaps we can organise an air search?' Stirling suggested. When Sonja didn't reply, he went on, 'Sonn, we can't go on covering things up from the police.'

Sonja frowned. The fact that he was right didn't stop him from irking her. She knew that the smart thing, the 'normal' thing to do would be to go to the Namibian police and explain her fears to them, based on the attacks that had been made on her and the others. However, given her record in the country, Sonja suspected she would probably be arrested on the spot.

'We'd have to convince them Emma was in trouble in any case,' Brand said, 'and who knows if they'd even have a chopper or an aircraft available to mount a search. Best we deal with this ourselves.'

'Brand's right,' Sonja said. 'We have to keep looking. Mount up and let's –'

A sharp sound like a bullwhip being cracked made Sonja stop and put her hand up. There was nothing in nature in this environment that made that sound.

'What was that?' Allchurch began.

'Quiet!' Sonja strained to hear another sound, and her heart lurched when it came. Three shots, in rapid succession. She pointed. 'That way. Slightly northeast.'

Brand nodded. 'Agreed. Let's get there, now.'

'I need a gun,' Matthew said.

Sonja spared him a brief appraisal, then nodded her head. 'On the move.'

Sonja went to the driver's side of Stirling's vehicle. 'Stirling, get in the back and open the green bag. Get the weapons ready.'

Stirling nodded and Sonja got in the front, started the engine, and swung in an arc towards where the sound had come from. She cared nothing for his cursing as she floored the accelerator and screamed down the side of one dune to give her the momentum to tackle the next. In between being thrown about the cab Stirling readied their arsenal, slapping magazines into the rifles. Even if he didn't have the stomach to kill a man she knew he could handle firearms, thanks to his training and experience as a safari guide.

Brand, on the other hand, would be with her, at her side, when she went into battle. The sound of the bullets terrified her, not because she felt they posed a threat to her own safety but because of what might have happened already. She could think of only one scenario in which gunshots were being fired at the crash site. Whoever had kidnapped Emma and the others had no further use for them.

Sonja tried to get her head around the tactical situation. She pulled the pistol from her belt and set it on the dashboard where it could be easily reached. She couldn't drive into the middle of an ambush, yet whoever was firing would hear the noise of their vehicles coming a long way off. Sonja pounded the steering wheel.

'What is it?' Stirling asked from the rear seat. 'Sonja, are you OK?'

She wanted to scream at him, *No I am not fucking OK, I think my daughter might have just been executed.* She was so scared she couldn't think straight.

Stirling put his hand on her shoulder and gripped it. 'Sonja, let me take over.'

She looked at him, blinking. Without asking she did as he said. Sonja stopped and got out.

'Get your rifle,' he said to her.

She reached into the back of the truck. The smooth wood and the warm, slightly oily feel of the metal parts helped calm her. This was the tool of her trade. It would either save Emma or avenge her. Sonja was smart enough to know that all the killing she had done since Sam's death had not brought him back, nor even helped quell her grief, but nor had it hurt. She removed the magazine, checked it, replaced it and yanked back the cocking handle.

The metallic chatter was the soundtrack to her life. This was how she prepared for work. She felt her fear settle and her eyes focus. Sonja got back in and Stirling set off.

'There's a big dune coming up,' Stirling said.

'I see it.'

'I'll drop you at the base. You'll have to walk up.'

Sonja nodded. 'I understand.'

It was how she would have planned it, although she would have had to order Stirling to drive towards where the guns had been firing. She would have put him in harm's way, but instead he was volunteering to do it himself.

'If you see them from the crest of the dune, stop there, Stirling. Don't get too close to them.'

Stirling looked at her. 'I'll do what I have to, Sonja. You can move off to one side and wait at the top of the dune and pick them off from up there.'

Stirling had taken the initiative, but he was no warrior. Given the nature of the terrain there would be open ground that she would have to cover, and whether she went on foot or in one of the vehicles she would be exposed to fire.

'No, Stirling. That would be a good plan if we were approaching in darkness, but we have to drive straight there. I'll drive and let you out and you can wait for me to get to the crash site.'

Stirling shook his head. 'No. I'm in this.'

He had shown his mettle, through his words at least. Across the rush of the wind Sonja heard the *pop-pop* of more gunfire. 'Faster, Stirling, faster!'

Sonja looked back and saw that the Unimog was catching up to them, accelerating to keep pace with Stirling as he rushed downhill then attacked the slope of the next big dune. Sonja wrapped her hand around the pistol grip of her assault rifle. She checked behind her again and noticed that Brand and Allchurch had swapped places and Brand was sitting on the sill of the passenger-side window. He had his rifle out of sight, but Sonja knew it would be ready.

As they crested the dune Sonja took in the scene below her. There, stark and surprising in the nothingness of the desert, was the broken carcass of a wrecked Douglas DC-3 Dakota. There were two four-wheel drives and a number of stacked crates, but what concerned her most was the clutch of people, two men crouched around what looked like another one or two people lying on the sand in the shade of a Toyota Land Cruiser.

Off to one side was another man, who, judging by the broken puppet angle of his arms and legs, was clearly dead.

'No!'

Stirling, startled by Sonja's cry, mistimed a gear change and the Amarok stalled.

'Get this thing moving!' she screamed at him.

Chapter 31

Brand told Matthew to swing out from behind the stalled Amarok and they raced down the dune. Brand had his rifle at the ready.

However, as they approached the wrecked aircraft Brand could see there was no apparent threat. In fact, one of the men was waving them in. 'Hurry, Matthew.'

When they reached the crash Brand got out and assessed the scene. There was a young woman, who from her features and the hair not covered by a blood-soaked bandage was clearly Sonja's daughter. He glanced up at the crest of the dune; having lost momentum Stirling had sunk in the sand and was trying to free himself. Sonja was out of the vehicle and running down the dune.

A young white man, bare-chested, came towards him. 'We need help, please. We have two people injured and need to get them to a hospital.'

'Alex Bahler?'

The man looked surprised. 'Yes, how did you know?'

'We'll get to that,' Brand said. He knelt between the two casualties. 'This guy's losing too much blood.' He lifted a shirt soaked wet and red, clearly Alex's, that had been pressed against the man's thigh, and blood welled up rapidly. Brand replaced it. 'Shit, femoral artery's been nicked. I need an extra hand here.'

An older man, bushy white hair protruding from under a floppy bush hat, knelt beside him. 'Let me help.'

'Put your hand on this shirt, here, keep the pressure on his artery.'

'Got it,' the man said, as Brand removed his hand.

'What's this kid's name?' Brand asked.

'Natangwe,' said the man.

Brand lightly slapped the wounded man on the cheek. 'Natangwe, Natangwe? Can you hear me?'

Natangwe opened his eyes.

'Talk to me, man. Can you hear me?'

'Yes, yes, I can,' he said weakly.

'You're going to be OK, buddy. We're going to get you out of here.' Brand knew it was important to reassure the patient, but he felt less than confident of his words. He looked to the other casualty, Sonja's daughter. 'What about her?'

'I don't know,' said Alex. Brand saw the pain in his eyes as the man took the woman's limp hand. 'She is breathing, but unconscious. The bullet didn't enter her skull.'

Brand put his fingers to Emma's neck and checked her pulse, which was strong and even. Her breathing was regular, as Alex had said. He peeled the bandage away from her head. Like all head wounds it had bled profusely, soaking the bandage, but the bleeding had all but stopped now. She had been lucky; the bullet had grazed her temple, though there was no way of telling yet what damage had been done. She was still out cold.

'Hopefully it looks worse than it is,' said the man with his hand on Natangwe's wound.

'And you are?' Brand asked.

'Professor Dorset Sutton,' the older man said.

'Hudson Brand.'

'Brand? H. Brand?'

'Yes.'

'That's the same name as the man we uncovered at a dig site near Etosha National Park.'

'Long story. Right now, we need to do something about Natangwe and Emma here. They need proper medical care. Matthew?'

Allchurch jogged to him, carrying the small first-aid kit from the Unimog. 'This is all we've got.'

Brand unzipped the kit, but the dressings in it were more for minor cuts and burns.

'I'll check inside the Dakota,' Matthew said. 'There might be a better kit in there, even if it's old.' Matthew disappeared into the dark hole of the open cargo door.

Sonja arrived at the crash site, breathing hard, but then put her hand on her mouth in horror as she saw her daughter lying on the ground. Stirling had freed the Amarok and arrived just after her. Sonja sprinted to Emma, dropping to both knees.

Brand went to Stirling. 'Have you got a decent first-aid kit?'

'I never head into the bush without one.' He went to the back of his *bakkie* and came out with a military medic's bulky field pack.

Sonja cradled her daughter's head in her lap. 'Emma! My baby, talk to me.'

'Sonja,' Brand interrupted. 'This young guy . . .'

'Natangwe,' Alex said.

'Yeah, Natangwe. He's hit real bad. How are your medic's skills?'

Sonja was wide-eyed. 'Brand, this is my *daughter*.'

'Yes, I know,' Brand said. 'She's unconscious, but her airways, breathing and circulation are fine. It might just be concussion.'

'*Just* concussion? She's been fucking shot in the head, Brand.'

'Sonja, I know she's your daughter but there's nothing we can do for her right now.' He leaned closer to her and lowered his voice. 'Natangwe, here, however, is bleeding out. He's going to die unless we do something soon.'

Sonja, still holding Emma's head, looked across at Natangwe, who groaned in pain. His eyes were heavily lidded and he looked like he might pass out at any second.

'Get out of the way, both of you,' Sonja said to Brand and Sutton.

Brand shifted himself to one side and Sonja gently laid Emma's head in the sand. 'Watch her,' she snapped at Alex. He took her position.

Sonja moved to Natangwe, brushed Sutton's hand out of the way and put her knee on Natangwe's groin, near where his wounded leg met his body. She put her weight on him.

Brand lifted the bloody shirt and took another peek at the wound. 'Pressure on the artery has slowed the bleeding right down.'

'We need a new, better dressing.'

'Coming,' Stirling called. He dropped his medical pack next to Sonja and unzipped it. 'Some serious dressings here.'

Brand moved in and sorted through the bag. He ripped open a bulky padded wound dressing and quickly replaced the sodden shirt with it. He tied it tight.

'Natangwe, can you hear me?'

He blinked up at Sonja. 'Yes.'

'I know you're hurting, but I need you to press down here, on your groin, where my knee is, as hard as you can. Can you do that for me?'

'Yes.'

She put her hand on his body and pressed down. 'Harder, Natangwe.'

'Here, I'll do it,' Alex said.

Sonja wiped her bloody hands on her shirt and looked at Brand. She raised her eyes and Brand knew exactly what she was trying to communicate. Natangwe would be dead soon if they didn't get him to a surgeon.

'We have to get him to a doctor,' Brand said. 'Stirling, where's the nearest town?'

'Wilfriedstein,' Stirling said. 'The Castle hotel there will know where the nearest doctor is.'

'Andre,' Alex said, pointing with a jab of his thumb, 'the dead guy over there had a satellite phone.'

'Get it,' Sonja said.

Alex went to Andre and patted down his body and found the phone. He punched some buttons. '*Scheisse.*'

'What's wrong?' Sonja asked.

'He put a security lock on it. I can't get it working.'

'Mum?' a faint voice said.

Alex, Brand and Sonja turned in unison.

'She's awake!' Sutton cried out. 'Thank God, she's awake.'

Sonja and Brand knelt either side of Emma and Sonja lowered her head and kissed her daughter. 'Can you see me, my girl?'

Emma blinked a few times. 'Yes. My head. Ow, my fucking head.'

Sonja coughed, choking back what looked to Brand like a mix of tears and laughter.

'Mum, you've gone blonde.'

Sonja took a breath to still herself, but didn't seem able to speak.

'How did you find us, Mum?'

Sonja exhaled. 'I'll tell you later.' She hugged Emma, holding her close to her breast. 'I'm just so glad you're alive. We have to get out of here.'

'How's Natangwe?' Emma asked.

'We need to get him to a doctor, as quickly as possible.'

'Mum,' Emma winced as she touched her head wound, 'there are people coming for the stuff from the aircraft. They're on the way. The others were waiting for them and they were just about . . . they were just about to . . .'

Emma started crying and Sonja hugged her. Brand noticed the two partially dug holes and the shovels. He could tell exactly what had happened – at least he thought he could. Now that he could afford to shift his attention from the casualties he noticed the legs of a second dead man protruding from the Land Cruiser. He stood and walked to the first body, bending to confirm he was dead by checking his pulse. The man was his age or a bit older, his complexion fair. Brand thought of the blond-haired man who had tried to kill him on board the Dakota that night.

The man in the vehicle had been shot between the eyes. 'Natangwe do this?'

'No.' Brand turned. It was Sutton, the professor, who spoke. 'Emma got them both. She's a bloody heroine. Deserves a medal for bravery, she saved us all. They were going to kill us.'

Sonja looked up at the professor, as did Emma, who cuffed the tears from her eyes.

Sutton looked at Emma. 'I'm so sorry, for being so beastly to you on the dig, and since then. It's my way. I'm a silly old fool, drunk on my own power and standing. You've shown me the meaning of real courage, Emma. I was sitting there, praying we wouldn't die, and you and Natangwe put your lives on the line for all of us.'

'I killed them, Mum,' Emma said softly. 'But Natangwe's the hero, he saved my life.'

Brand saw the way Sonja hugged her daughter tightly. 'You did the right thing. But really, we must leave now.'

'Andre and Sebastian,' Sutton said, gesturing to the dead men, 'didn't load their vehicles because they knew someone was coming to pick up the cargo. They were going to use their trucks to get away. Emma's right. I fear whoever is coming to collect is on their way now.'

'All right,' said Brand, taking charge, giving Sonja time to comfort Emma. 'Professor, you'll drive one of the four-by-fours, the other we'll disable.'

Stirling had moved to the cargo crates and was prising open the lid of one of the wooden boxes in the unwrapped bundle with a discarded shovel. 'Hudson, this is rhino horn,' he said. 'Masses of it.'

'I figured it might have been ivory at the time; no one was that het up about horns in those days. The guys shipping it wouldn't have imagined what it would be worth today.'

'No,' Dorset chimed in, 'but they know now, which was why they were prepared to kill for it. We can't leave it here, to be picked up by Horsman's partners.'

'Andre Horsman?' Brand asked.

'Yes, that was the man's name,' Dorset said.

'I met him once. A long time ago.'

'Andre?' Matthew said, overhearing them.

Brand nodded. Matthew walked quickly to the dead body on the sand, which he had so far avoided or not looked at closely. He stood over Horsman. 'He was the commander of my son's squadron,' he said quietly, almost to himself. 'I thought he was my friend. He was using me, all this time, waiting to see if one day my efforts to find Gareth would pay off – for him.'

'It looks that way,' Brand said. 'He knew I was still alive, but he never came after me. I was on the front line for the rest of the war, far from him. If he checked up on me, which I'm sure he would have from time to time, he would have worked out pretty quickly I was too poor to have ever found his missing cargo.'

'Then he sends me to you,' Matthew said, 'to get you to come here with me, so he could get us both in the same place.'

'And kill us,' Brand said.

'All of us,' Sonja reminded them. 'Come on, let's get out of here. Brand, I don't give a fuck about all this rhino horn. What do you want to do with it?'

Stirling picked up the box he'd been inspecting and tossed it into the back of the still-open rear of the Amarok. 'We're taking it with us.'

'Why not burn it?' Allchurch said. 'The cursed stuff killed my son.'

'Shoot, I didn't think, Matthew,' Brand said. 'When I sent you inside the aircraft, did you . . . was Gareth in there?'

'No,' Matthew said. 'There's a body in there, a skeleton, but I checked the identity discs. It was the pilot, Danie Bester. I know his parents. I'm afraid there's no sign of Gareth.'

'I'm sorry.'

Allchurch looked up, his face animated. 'No, don't be. I've been thinking about what Sonja said, about the man her uncle picked up on the salt road. We don't know who it was. It could have been Gareth.'

'Possible, I guess,' said Brand without conviction.

Stirling was working up a sweat, tossing boxes into the back of the truck.

'You sure you want to take all this stuff?' Brand said.

'We can't leave it here to be stolen, and it will take too long to burn it. Also, if we can hand it over to the Namibian authorities it will be great PR, showing how they've stopped all this falling into the wrong hands.'

'As long as your PR stunt doesn't cost Natangwe his life,' Sonja weighed in. 'You've got until we've loaded Natangwe, then we're going. You can catch up to us if you need to, you'll travel faster than the Unimog, but you'll have to take your chances.'

'I'll help you,' Sutton said to Stirling. 'I don't want these criminal bastards getting a cent from the defenceless creatures that were killed for this horn, even if they are long dead.'

Alex had fetched a blanket from the Unimog campervan and together he, Emma, Sonja and Brand gently slid Natangwe onto it and then lifted him. They eased him into the camper, which was equipped with two single beds, and made him as comfortable as they could.

Alex took a seat on the bed across from Natangwe. 'I will ride with him, if that is all right.'

'Sure,' Sonja said. 'Just keep pressure on his artery. He's lost a hell of a lot of blood.'

Brand looked out the door of the camper. Stirling and Sutton were still tossing crates of rhino horn into any spare piece of space in the Amarok. They had filled the luggage area and were stacking boxes on the rear seat and floor of the double cab.

'Move it,' Brand barked. He'd seen good men die, Sonja's husband among them, over this stupid stuff, and he had no intention of losing Natangwe because Stirling wanted to stage a bonfire of his own in Windhoek or hand over the horn to the authorities at a press conference so he could garner more support for his rhino conservation NGO.

Sonja climbed down from the truck and strode past Brand and the others to the Land Cruiser. She leaned into the back of the vehicle, where the other dead guy was. Brand didn't know what she was doing – perhaps searching his pockets for ID or other intelligence. He busied himself by dragging the body of Andre Horsman under the canvas awning. When Sonja finished what she was doing she backed out of the Land Cruiser and walked past Brand with not so much as a goodbye, then climbed back up into her vehicle. 'Leave this vehicle, it's got no spare wheel, take the Hilux instead,' she ordered them.

The Unimog started with a puff of black smoke and Sonja drove off, heading east towards the closest town, Wilfriedstein. It would be cross-country driving most of the way, a hard journey, but it was their best chance of getting away from whoever was coming to collect the horn, and of getting Natangwe to medical care.

Brand got in the Hilux with Matthew while Stirling and Sutton, kindred spirits for the moment at least, were still loading boxes of horn into the Amarok, though there was still an intact bundle left. Brand kept an eye on his rear view mirror and saw, with some satisfaction, the other two moving off before he lost sight of them. They had abandoned the final bundle load of horn, still wrapped for airdrop from the Dakota all those years ago.

The desert stretched out in front of them. Brand thought about the attack on them on the Andoni Plains. 'Matthew, keep an eye out above. They used a chopper once before to try to get us, so they've got the money to hire another one.'

*

Irina sat in the co-pilot's seat next to Swanevelder. They flew low, nap-of-the-earth the pilot called it, less than a hundred feet above the undulating contours of the inhospitable land below them.

When Swanevelder had returned from the lodge the Russian seamen had boarded the helicopter, this time all armed and dressed in an assortment of green and camouflage bush clothing that Mikhail had sourced for them in advance. Ironically, given the trade she was in, Irina had plans to start her own anti-poaching patrols on the game farm and had bought uniforms and military-style combat vests for her future force. She envisaged a day when she would breed her own rhinos to supply the Asian market, either covertly or overtly if the authorities ever decided to legalise the trade in rhino horn. When Swanevelder had asked Irina where Miro was she had replied, simply, that it was a day when casualties could be expected.

Swanevelder checked his GPS. 'Coming up to your coordinates.'

Irina scanned the emptiness in front of her, seeing nothing at first.

'There,' said the pilot, pointing dead ahead. 'See the glint? Sun reflecting off metal.'

'Circle,' she ordered him. 'There were supposed to be two vehicles; I see only one.'

They flew around the crash site and Irina knew immediately that something was wrong. There were no people milling around, no signal from Andre or his sidekick, Sebastian Lord. 'Put down a hundred metres away. We'll walk in.'

When her troops were out Irina formed them into a skirmish line either side of her and, rifles up and at the ready, they advanced on the crashed aircraft while Swanevelder kept the chopper's engine and rotors turning.

'Andre!' Irina called, but there was no answer.

'Check the inside of the aircraft and the vehicle,' she ordered the men closest to her. 'The rest of you keep a lookout.'

'Irina Petrovna,' Mikhail called from the vehicle. 'Come, see this.' Irina flicked the safety catch on her rifle to safe, assured at least there was no danger to her. Under the awning attached to the Land Cruiser was the body of her South African partner, Andre Horsman. 'Look inside.'

Irina stuck her head in the back. It was already starting to reek of flesh putrefying under a desert sun. The body of Sebastian Lord was propped up. A piece of cardboard nestled in his lap. Painted on it in dried blood were the words: *You're next. SK.*

'Ah!' Irina walked out into the open, flicked her safety catch to automatic and emptied the magazine of her AK-47 into the air in one long burst. Her men burst from the crippled aircraft or ran for cover until they worked out it was just her venting her rage.

When she had no more bullets and the rifle hung loose at her side, smoking, while a pile of hot brass lay at her feet, Yuri summoned the courage to come to her. 'Irina Petrovna, there is only one container of rhino horn left. They must have taken the others.'

'There are tracks leading east,' Mikhail said, pointing to the blurred furrows in the sand that led away into the dunes. 'They will be easy to follow from the air.'

'We must catch them,' Irina said.

Mikhail pointed to the remaining bundle of rhino horn. 'What about those?'

'We'll get them on the way back. How long ago did they leave?'

Mikhail looked around and sniffed the air. 'Bodies decompose fast in this heat, but I would say these men were killed this morning.'

'Back to the chopper, everyone!' Irina waved both hands, including her rifle, above her head, and Swanevelder gave her a thumbs-up out of the window, signalling it was safe for them to approach.

Once back on board Irina pointed out the tracks in the sand to the pilot. 'Follow them.'

'They won't get away from us,' the pilot assured her.

Irina clenched her teeth for a moment, then nodded. 'They had better not.'

Chapter 32

They drove out of the Skeleton Coast National Park and back into the northwest of the Palmwag Conservancy, the landscape changing from dunes to rocky desert.

Using a combination of memory, the GPS and dead reckoning, Stirling directed Sonja towards the Hoanib River and finally, to his relief as much as hers, they found the dry watercourse. If they followed the Hoanib east it would take them to a turn-off to the remote outpost of Wilfriedstein, between Sesfontein and Purros.

'I think we're losing Natangwe, Mum,' Emma called from the back of the camper. 'He's really weak.'

Sonja was taking a turn driving and she pulled over and climbed into the rear compartment. Natangwe was barely conscious.

'This is the second dressing,' Alex said, pointing to the blood-soaked pad on Natangwe's thigh. 'We're keeping pressure on the artery, but the blood keeps flowing. I think it's getting worse.'

'Emma, do you have any tampons?' Sonja asked.

'No, mum, not on me.'

'Tea bags,' Sonja said. 'Alex, search the cupboards.'

Sonja kept pressure on the sopping dressing while Alex ransacked the internal storage cabinets.

'Got some,' he said, shaking out the contents of a packet.

Sonja lifted the pad and packed the wound with half a dozen teabags. 'These act as a mild coagulant, and absorb plenty of blood. Fresh dressing.'

Emma passed her another and Sonja tied it in place. The dressing stayed dry, for now, but Natangwe's eyes were closed.

Sonja slapped Natangwe's face. 'Natangwe? Natangwe, can you hear me?' Alex and Emma were right, he was slipping away. 'We've slowed the bleeding but he's lost too much. He needs saline, something to keep his fluid volume up, otherwise he's not going to make it.' It was time to stop pretending otherwise.

'Take some of my blood, give him a transfusion,' Alex said.

Sonja did a mental inventory of the medical supplies they had on them and had inherited from the owners of the campervan. 'I don't have anything to collect the blood in. Besides, you might be different blood types; you could kill him if you're not matched correctly, and he's not capable of telling us his blood type, even if he knows what it is.'

'I'm O negative,' Alex said.

Sonja nodded. 'Universal donor. You can give your blood to anyone.' She ran a hand through her hair. 'The only thing we can do is set up a patient to patient donation. Tell me, Alex, honestly, have you been tested for HIV-AIDS? Hepatitis?'

Alex nodded. 'I have been. I am clear.'

Emma put a hand on his arm and looked to Sonja. 'Is it safe, Mum?'

Alex took Emma's hand. 'Natangwe put himself between you and Sebastian. He took a bullet for us, Emma. He was ready to die for you and me, so this is the least I can do for him. If it buys him a couple more hours until we can get to a doctor, then it is worth trying.'

'Emma, help me,' Sonja said. 'Get some sterile wipes and clean their arms – Alex's wrist, where his artery is, and Natangwe's elbow, where I'll find a vein.' Sonja rummaged through the well-stocked first-aid kit and found two IV lines. It was a shame the German couple hadn't packed saline solution as well. However, she could rig something up. She snipped the cannula from one of the tubes and was able to attach it to the end of the other line and fasten it in place with tape. The line was just long enough to connect Alex's left arm, if he was lying on one bunk, to Natangwe's right.

Brand had caught up to her and stopped his vehicle. He climbed up into the cab. 'Everything OK?'

'Only just. Alex is giving Natangwe a transfusion; without it I think Natangwe might not make it.'

Brand looked at the two men, the line between them, and the bloodied rubber gloves Sonja was now snapping off. 'Gutsy move all round, but we still need to get him to the doctor.'

'Brand, can you ride with me?' Sonja asked.

He nodded. 'Matthew should be OK for a while.'

Brand climbed aboard the Unimog and they set off again with Sonja driving as fast as she dared given the delicate situation in the back. The two men were OK, she told herself, as long as neither one of them rolled out of his bunk, and Emma was sitting on a cushion on the floor between them, reassuring them both. Sonja glanced at her daughter, whose head was still bandaged, and saw the way Emma stroked Alex's brow while still being positive and tender with Natangwe. She was so proud of Emma, and so angry that greedy men had put her only child's life at risk. She shivered when she thought of how close she had been to losing her. If the bullet fired by Sebastian had been a fraction of an inch closer to the mark, Emma would have been dead.

'You OK?' Brand asked her from the passenger seat.

'Just thinking about Emma.'

Brand glanced over his shoulder. 'Great kid. You should be proud.'

'I can't take much of the credit. My mother and an expensive boarding school raised her. I was lucky to see her even during the holidays, and when I did she didn't want to know me.'

'Just a teenage thing, I guess. You seem to have made up for it.'

Sonja sighed. 'I hope so, Hudson.'

He did a double take, theatrically turning his head from the dry, alternately rocky and sandy bed of the Hoanib, to face her. 'What?'

'What do you mean, "what"?'

'Did I just hear incorrectly, or did you call me by my first name?'

'It won't happen again.'

'I kind of liked it.' Hudson paused. 'Did you want to talk about the other night, or should we discuss strategy?'

Sonja knew he was making fun of her. 'God, was it only two nights ago?' She had been running on adrenaline, and their lovemaking at Namutoni, while still vivid in her mind, seemed like an age ago.

'I had a good time, did you?' Hudson said.

'That's not the point.' She slowed to take a bend, gearing down, trying to make the turn as gentle as possible on the young men behind her. Sonja glanced back into the cabin again. If Emma could hear their conversation she gave no sign. She seemed totally besotted with Alex. Sonja wondered if they were in love.

'What happened, happened, Brand.'

'We're back to Brand again, I see.'

'The way it should be.'

Sonja brushed a strand of hair from her face. 'I can't get involved with another man. Not now. Maybe not ever again.'

'Because of Sam?'

She looked at him. 'Because of my fucking life. Look at us. Someone tried to kill my daughter, kill us. I'm a magnet for this kind of shit.'

'I'm not looking for a wife, Sonja. I've got too much baggage of my own.'

Sonja stared out the windscreen again as she drove, deliberately not looking at him. 'I think the best times of my life were when I had no baggage, just a backpack.'

'That's not true,' he said.

She glanced at him again. Who was he to tell her what was right or not right in her life? 'How would you know?'

Brand gestured to the back with a flick of his head. 'What about her?'

'She's not *baggage*, she's my daughter. She's growing up – grown up. Soon she won't need me at all.'

Brand took up his AK-47 and unloaded it, removing the magazine and working the cocking handle to eject the chambered round, which he deftly caught with his free hand. Sonja could do that trick. 'Come see me in South Africa, when this is all done.'

They'd be lucky to survive. They had two wounded and a truck full of rhino horn, and the people after them didn't leave witnesses. Sonja wasn't scared of a fight – she was only concerned for Emma's safety – but she realised she was worried about what might happen if they did survive and Hudson Brand came courting, or whatever it was Americans called it. 'I don't think so.'

*

Green reeds in the bed of the Hoanib told Brand there was still water there, not far beneath the surface, and just before they came to the turnoff to Wilfriedstein they started coming across shallow pools. They also saw a desert elephant munching contentedly on the riverine vegetation.

Time was of the essence but even Sonja couldn't avoid instinctively slowing to a crawl as they passed the great creature, whose body, white with desert dust, was splotched black here and there where he had been cooling himself, hosing himself down with water.

Alex was sitting up. He smiled at the sight of the desert elephant. His face was pale from the loss of the blood he'd donated to Natangwe, but the other man looked better now. Alex had a bandage around his arm.

Wilfriedstein revealed itself anticlimactically. A herd of goats, tended by a young boy, and a few straggling cattle told Brand they were getting closer to habitation. They had left the bed of the tributary and were on a rough dirt road.

The town itself was one street, dusty and listless in the midday heat. Sonja barrelled past the modest collection of shops – a general dealer, a Chinese trader's shop selling cheap consumer goods, a shebeen and a pharmacy. At the town's limit, past a mechanic's shop where men worked on a couple of cars outside a mud hut, she executed a U-turn and stopped at the stores. The other vehicles followed and pulled over. Sonja told Emma to go to the pharmacy and buy whatever bandages and dressings they had, as well as packets of painkillers. 'And find out where the local doctor is.'

Brand got down from the Unimog and headed for the shebeen.

'A little early for celebrating?' Sonja called to him.

'Whiskey, for anaesthetic, surgery, molotovs.'

'Roger that,' she said to him.

'And I'm going to the cops,' Brand said.

'OK. You're on your own then. Do me a favour, don't mention me.'

Brand went to the small police station and found the door locked. A man with several layers of filthy tattered clothes and bloodshot eyes, presumably homeless, sat on an upturned dustbin. 'No police,' he said.

'Where have they gone?' Brand asked.

'Bus crash,' the man replied.

With the shopping finished and no prospect of immediate help or sanctuary from the law they turned back to the other side of town and the side street that led to the town's sole filling station and the castle beyond. 'Emma checked on the doctor – he's out of town, not due back until tomorrow,' Sonja reported.

Brand thought about that. Natangwe needed help. 'So we refuel and keep going, maybe north to Opuwo – they'll have a clinic there – or we stay here and call in an aerial medical evacuation.'

Sonja nodded, weighing up the pros and cons as they pulled up next to the single island of fuel pumps shaded by a small tin roof. A woman sitting in the shade of a square mud-brick building across the road held up her hands and shrugged her shoulders.

'No fuel?' Brand called.

'No electricity,' she replied.

'They can't run the pumps. Shit,' Brand said.

'I think that solves our dilemma,' Sonja said. 'We stay here, make a stand, and call for a casevac for Natangwe.'

'The castle's just up the road,' Brand said.

He'd been here once before and Schloss Hähner, for all its quirkiness, still had the look of an oasis in the desert, right down to the towering palm trees and manicured emerald lawns at the gate. They parked and an African man in white shirt and dark trousers came up to them.

'I am very sorry,' he said after they had exchanged greetings.

'What's wrong?' Brand asked.

'We are closed for the next two days. We have no water. There is a problem with the mains, and as you may have heard at the filling station, there is no electricity. We have a generator, but we are out of diesel . . .'

'And you can't refill because the filling station is closed because there's no electricity.'

'Exactly,' said the doorman with a smile.

'We need a phone, urgently,' Brand said. 'We have a man who has been wounded and needs aerial evacuation.'

The smile left the man's face. 'I am sorry. We have no landline. We rely on cellular phones here, but we need a booster to get signal. I am afraid the booster is not working . . .'

'Because there's no electricity. Shit.'

'We can't keep running and at least Natangwe's stable – for now,' Sonja said.

Brand looked at Sonja. 'I vote we stay here at the castle. We can take one of Stirling's jerry cans of diesel and get the generator running.'

Sonja nodded. 'Good place for a last stand.' She took the doorman aside and explained to him that despite the lack of water and electricity they still wanted to stay the night. When the man tried to politely decline her request, twice, Brand heard Sonja raise her voice. In the end, he complied.

Sutton and Stirling arrived, followed by Matthew, who was bringing up the rear alone in the Hilux. 'You know there's no fuel at the filling station. I can't go on.'

'We know,' Brand said. 'We'll park the vehicles in the court-yard and entryway to the castle. We need to block that entrance.'

Emma, Alex and Dorset lifted Natangwe down from the Unimog and carried him inside the hotel. Stirling reversed his Amarok as far into the courtyard as he could, and Brand backed the Unimog in until its rear bumper was almost touching the Amarok's front. Matthew was able to park the Hilux halfway under the castle's ornate arched entryway.

Brand collected the rest of their arsenal and marched inside the B&B, ignoring the protests of the doorman. He found a staircase that led to the roof and walked up, the doorman in tow.

'Really, sir, I'm concerned by all these firearms, and . . .'

Brand put the rifles down, along with a rucksack full of spare ammunition. 'Look, what's your name?'

'Isaac.'

'Listen, Isaac, I suggest you and whatever staff are here take the rest of the day off. We've got some people coming to visit us and they're not exactly going to be the most polite guests of all time.'

Isaac looked down at the pile of rifles and swallowed hard. 'It is my duty to stay here and care for the hotel, even though we are empty. I will, however, tell the non-essential staff that you will not be needing them today. What about dinner?'

Brand could tell Isaac still wasn't getting it. 'We might not be alive in time for dinner.'

'I see.'

'Go, Isaac.'

'I must stay.'

'Suit yourself.'

Brand stuffed as many banana-shaped thirty-round magazines in his cargo pants pockets as he could. He tucked in his bush shirt and dropped another two down the front. He left a spare AK and a pile of three magazines on the roof and took the other two rifles downstairs.

First he went to Stirling and handed him a rifle. 'You good with this?'

Stirling stared at the AK-47, rotating it in his hands, a pained expression on his face. At last he looked up at Brand and met his eyes. 'I've never killed a man, but yes.'

'Let's hope it doesn't come to that.' He handed Stirling three loaded magazines.

Alex and Emma had put Natangwe on a leather lounge in the bar and dining room area. Brand went to him and gave him the nine-millimetre pistol. 'You know how to use this, son?'

Natangwe blinked at him. 'Sort of.'

'I'll show him,' Emma said. 'Mum taught me.'

Brand had seen Emma's handiwork, the legacy of her mother's

training. He handed Alex an AK-47 and fished four magazines from the backpack. 'You know how to use a rifle?'

'Yes, sir,' Alex said.

Brand gave the remaining rifle and half the spare ammunition to Emma, and handed Matthew some more magazines. 'This,' he said, waving the end of the barrel of his own rifle around the room they were in, 'is our last point of defence. Matthew, Alex, I want you two on the roof with me. Professor Sutton, have you had military service?'

'Before these young people were born, but yes.'

'Good,' Brand said. 'There's an AK and ammo for you on the roof as well. Emma, you stay here and look after Natangwe.'

'No way,' Emma said, her voice rising. 'I'm not a bloody nurse. You need me up on the roof, with you. I'm probably a better shot than any of you.'

Brand squared up to her, noting that Emma had the same forged steel look in her eyes as her mother, not to mention her beauty. 'I saw what you did back at the crash site. You don't have to convince me you can shoot.'

'Then why leave me down here, out of the action?'

It irked Brand to have to explain himself. Of everyone present only Sonja could match him on combat experience; he knew what he was doing. And he now cared for Sonja, so he cared for her daughter as well – though he couldn't tell the girl that. 'We need someone, a shooter, in reserve. If we lose a man up top, or the enemy masses on one part of the fort, I need a firefighter to hose that hotspot down. I figured it'd be a tie between you and Alex as to who could move the fastest, but I know you're a good shot. Plus, you got a good man down, here in the bar, and the way I hear it he took a bullet for you. I'd say that means you owe him some watching over.'

She looked to Natangwe, who rested with his eyes closed, then back to Brand. 'But –'

'But nothing, Emma,' Sonja said. 'Hudson is correct. You are our strategic reserve. Alex?'

'Yes, Frau Kurtz?'

'I'm not a Frau. Check the kitchens and talk to Isaac. Find us some food while we still have time. Tell Isaac I'll pay.'

'Of course.'

'Emma, go help him,' Sonja added.

'Yes, Mum.'

Brand gestured with a flick of his head for Sonja to join him outside in the bright sunlight of the courtyard. It was a nice hotel, and he hoped it stayed that way. 'When the bad guys come, you're in charge, here at the castle.'

'What do you mean?' she asked him.

'I mean that whether they come on wheels or by chopper they're either going to come down that road,' he pointed towards the small fuel station, 'or land on the road to get here. I'm going to be there to try to stop them.'

Sonja shook her head. 'I'd already thought of that. *I'm* going to be outside the castle.'

'Your place is inside, with your daughter.'

She put her hands on her hips. 'I don't have a fucking *place*, mister. The best way I can protect my daughter is to kill as many of these bastards as I can before they get to you and your ragtag army.'

'I'm not going to argue with you about this,' Brand said.

'And I'm not your wife, Brand.'

'No more "Hudson"?'

'No more anything. I'm younger than you, faster than you, and the last time I saw combat wasn't thirty years ago.'

'I killed a rhino poacher in Kruger last year,' Brand said. As he said the words he felt foolish for letting her draw him into such an argument, and for making such a statement. He felt off balance around her.

'*Pah*!' she said. 'That's nothing. You do what you want. I'm going to be outside the castle walls and on the move when they arrive – if they arrive.'

Brand could see from her eyes there was no point arguing with her. She probably *could* move faster than him, though he hated to admit it. 'All right. We'll be ready for you, covering you when you fall back.'

She gave a curt nod. 'Good.'

'Tell me, how's Stirling going to hold up, if we get in the shit?'

Sonja's face softened and she looked, he thought, as concerned as he was. 'He's no killer, Hudson. I'll talk to him.' She looked up at the sun, unfiltered by even a skerrick of cloud. 'Damn, it's hot.'

'Only going to get hotter,' Brand said. 'Appreciate it, if you talk to him.'

Sonja nodded. 'I'll do it now.'

Chapter 33

B rand said he was going to move the Hilux, to better block the entrance to the old fort. Stirling was standing in the doorway of the restaurant and bar, leaning against the door frame.

Sonja knew she didn't have time to stop for a shower, but she felt disgusting. She sat on a chair in the courtyard of the fort, put her AK on a table, unlaced her boots and kicked them off. She emptied her pockets, stood, went to the edge of the swimming pool and dived in. She swam a couple of laps, fully clothed, and when she came back to the same end where she'd started, Isaac was waiting for her with a pool towel.

'Thank you.'

'A pleasure, madam.'

Sonja walked across the small square of well-tended grass to where she'd left her things. As she put her foot down she felt a stab of fire in her toes. 'Ow, fuck!'

'What is it?' Stirling asked, his hand at her elbow.

Instinctively she shrugged away his offer of assistance, but the burning pain wouldn't stop. 'Ouch!'

'Here, stop struggling.' Stirling got down on one knee. 'It's a bee.'

She felt foolish. 'Let me sit down.'

'No, stop. Don't move. It's still there, between your toes.' He shooed the bee away, but the pain remained. 'The stinger's still in you, I'll get it out.'

Sonja reluctantly put a hand on Stirling's shoulder to steady herself. 'Hurry.'

'Patience, patience.' Stirling had taken out his wallet and from it he'd taken a credit card.

At least he knew what he was doing. If he'd grabbed the stinger with his fingers, or, worse, a pair of tweezers, he would have squeezed in more venom from the stinger while trying to pull it out. Instead, he used the edge of the plastic card to brush the stinger out from between her toes, sweeping away from the puncture point to stop any more poison being forced into her.

'Lean on me and we'll get you to your chair.'

She did, reluctantly. Her toe still throbbed mightily as she sat down. 'I sometimes get a reaction to bee stings.'

'No need to sound so embarrassed. You *are* only human, Sonja.'

He was making fun of her, and that made her angry.

Stirling looked into her eyes. 'I'm not making fun of you, Sonja.'

How, she wondered, had he known what she was thinking? She wanted to look away from him, but she found herself looking into his face, still youthful, still full of innocence. He'd lived a good life, devoting himself to the environment and wildlife he loved. He was handsome and sweet and she had to put her anger aside and make sure he was ready to kill.

*

The pilot, Swanevelder, pointed at the cluster of flat-roofed build-ings ahead. 'Wilfriedstein. Don't blink or you'll miss it.'

Irina raised her binoculars to her eyes. It was the first town they had come to, and unless Brand and Allchurch and the others had cleverly hidden in a dry riverbed or ravine, this was where they would be heading. The blood they'd seen on the sand told her Brand's group had at least one person wounded, so they would be looking for a doctor.

'The fuel station is near the castle bed and breakfast,' Swanevelder said. 'If they're still here, that's where they'll be, or if they've passed through someone down there will know. There's not so much through traffic that three vehicles full of white people wouldn't be remembered.'

'We will set down in any case,' Irina said. 'Circle the castle.'

'Roger.'

The pilot brought the Bell over the town then executed a wide turn. Irina lowered the binoculars and picked out the orderly, angular walls of the castle ahead amid the more ramshackle later developments. It was also the only green space in town, surrounded by tall palms and with little chequers of watered lawn. First, though, they passed over the filling station, which was so small Irina didn't notice it until Swanevelder pointed out the above-ground fuel tanks.

'I can't see any vehicles there,' she said.

They carried on, over the short dirt road between the pumps and the station. 'Nothing in the castle's car park, either,' Swanevelder said.

Irina was about to concur when she saw the irregular shapes at the gateway to the fort. 'No, wait. Look, a vehicle is parked in the gate of the castle and two inside the courtyard. That must be them – no tourists would park like that.'

Swanevelder nodded. 'They've used their trucks to block the entrance. Looks like they're getting ready for a siege.'

'And we are about to give them one. Though it'll be the quickest siege in the history of warfare.' Irina looked over her shoulder to her marine troops. 'Lock and load,' she said in Russian. 'Prepare for battle.'

'How do we do this?' the pilot asked.

Irina looked back into the cargo area and motioned for Mikhail to put on the spare set of intercom headphones. When he had them on he gave her a thumbs-up. 'Swanevelder, you land by the filling station. Mikhail, you're in charge of the ground force. Close on the fort, disable their vehicles. I will use the helicopter to command and control and I'll use the Dragunov to take out as many of them as I can, or at least make sure they keep their heads down. They will have posted people on the roof of the castle – that's what I would have done. But they'll soon move inside once I start firing. I'll give you cover while you rush the front. Do not burn any of the vehicles – I want all that rhino horn intact.'

'Understood,' Mikhail said.

*

Brand was striding down the dirt road from the castle to the filling station, just a couple of hundred metres away.

He'd only pretended to agree to let Sonja be on the outside; she needed to be with her daughter. Brand tried to convince himself that it had nothing to do with an urge to keep her safe, but seeing her distracted by Stirling had sent a jolt of relief through him and given him the chance to head off.

He heard the deep *thwap-thwap* of a helicopter's blades. He sidestepped off the road and dived for cover in the shade at the base of a palm tree. The chopper circled overhead.

When the aircraft had its rear to him he got up and sprinted through the trees and the rubbish at the side of the road to the filling station hut. The attendant was still sitting on a plastic chair out the front.

'I'd clear out if I were you, sister,' he said to her.

She looked at his rifle, and then up to the sky, nodded, got up, and walked away towards the cluster of shops that passed for the town of Wilfriedstein. Brand watched the helicopter continue in its arc. The logical place for it to land would be right here, on the road. The castle hotel's car park was too tight, he reckoned, and surrounded by trees, but here it was a little more open. He needed to take out as many of them as he could as they were getting off the helicopter. But how? He had no explosives, no rocket-propelled grenades and no anti-aircraft missiles; besides, he was unwilling to shoot down the helicopter in case the pilot was an innocent. There was even a slim chance that it could be the medical evacuation aircraft, though it would have put down by now if it was.

Sonja would have to stay in the castle now, which was one consolation. Brand felt better being outside, on the move. Sonja would do as good a job as he in organising the garrison, and she would be close to her daughter.

Brand looked around him for a suitable spot with enough cover and concealment. Then from inside the hut he heard a distinct click and a whirring noise. The motor on the air compressor outside the hut burst into its puttering song, bringing the pressure back up to a useable level. The electricity in Wilfriedstein had just come back on.

He darted across to the pumps under their simple metal awning. Fortunately they were the old style that didn't require the operator to use a security tag to get them going. Brand pulled out the nozzle from the petrol pump, reset the meter, and pulled on the lever. The pump clattered to life and fuel jetted from the nozzle. He flicked the catch on the handle that would allow the attendant to leave the pump running while he or she was checking the oil or cleaning a windscreen.

Brand surveyed the land around him. Running alongside the road that led to the castle was a depression, a natural or hand-dug drain for the little rain this part of Namibia could expect during the wet summer. Brand pulled the pump's nozzle as far as the black rubber hose would allow and set the handpiece in the ground, with the spout facing along the ditch, towards the fort. The chopper was coming around again.

Brand ran back across the road to the attendant's hut. He tried the handle, but it was locked. He flicked the safety catch on his AK-47 to fire and shot the lock off with a single round and kicked open the door. Inside he found a one-litre glass Coke bottle and a rag. He returned to the pump, filled the bottle and soaked the rag in petrol, then ran down the road and crossed over once more. He took up a position fifty metres towards the hotel, behind a stout palm tree.

The helicopter pilot swooped around then aligned his machine with the course of the road. He came in, flaring the nose up to bleed off speed, his tail rotor dipping close to the ground. Brand slitted his eyes against the wall of grit, grass, sand and twigs that the big rotors washed towards him. The sliding rear cargo doors opened and he could see that the interior was crowded with men dressed in green fatigues. Each seemed to have a rifle.

As the skids touched the ground the men inside started piling out. Each took two or three steps then hit the ground on his belly. These were trained military men, Brand realised. Another person, slightly built, perhaps even a woman, opened the co-pilot's door, jumped out, and then got back into the empty rear compartment. As soon as that was done, just seconds after touchdown, the Bell helicopter was lifting off, nose down as it climbed away.

The men who had deplaned were on their feet now, moving, no doubt looking for the nearest cover. Brand knew the drill they were following – he'd learned it himself. They would run for no more than three seconds, not enough time for a sniper to draw a bead on them, then hit the deck and crawl to a piece of cover.

They would work in pairs, one covering his buddy while the other got up and repeated the basic manoeuvre.

They were all moving now, though, to get off the exposed piece of road where the chopper had just dropped them. Brand thumbed the safety catch on his AK-47 to automatic and squeezed the trigger. A man yelled something in Russian and Brand guessed that one of the ten rounds in the long burst had hit its mark as one of the green-clad figures stumbled and pitched forward.

The rest of them, Brand saw, had done exactly as he hoped. The man who had yelled out had presumably identified the fire as coming from ahead and to the right of them. The troops had broken left and were seeking cover on the opposite side of the road to him. Brand put down his rifle and picked up the bottle filled with petrol. He took out his Zippo, lit the petrol-soaked rag stuffed in the neck, stood and threw the Molotov cocktail across the road, aiming for the fuel-filled ditch.

Brand's movement and the fiery arc of the burning wick attracted the attention of at least one, maybe two, of the Russian gunmen. Bullets slammed into the trunk of the palm and whizzed over Brand's head as he dived again for cover. The fusillade was stopped, however, when the bottle struck the ground and burst into flames with a thump and a *whoosh*. The Molotov had missed the ditch, but the fire spread through the dry grass within seconds and the fuel-filled drain erupted into a wall of fire. Two gunmen stood, their uniforms ablaze. They ran, screaming, trying to escape their terrible pain. Level-headed comrades stood and tackled the men to the ground and rolled them in the sand. Men yelled to each other and in the confusion, Brand stood again, fired another long burst at the Russians to keep their heads down, and fell back towards the fort, running as fast as he could, parallel to the road.

*

Sonja watched Brand's escapades from the roof of the castle, through binoculars. 'That's three out of action at least; two men on fire and another wounded on the road.'

'He did well,' Stirling said.

Sonja looked at him. 'He did. But this is a long way from over. Alex, Professor, Matthew,' she called to the other men on the roof, 'get ready to put down some covering fire. Here comes Brand!'

When the electricity had come back on Sonja had sent Alex to call the police on the hotel telephone, but before he could get through, the power had cut out again. They were still very much alone.

Hudson was running to them, but the Russians were emerging from the smoke and flames of the grass fire Brand had started, advancing on the castle in a ragged extended line formation.

'Wait until they get closer, or until they start firing on Brand before you open fire,' Sonja told them. Stirling was down on one knee, his rifle pointed between the fort's stone crenellations.

Sonja heard the deep bass thump of the helicopter again and looked up to see it approaching them. 'Stay close to the walls everyone. Keep your heads down.'

The helicopter slowed, however, and settled into a hover. Sonja heard the *pop-pop* of shots, partly muffled by the chopper's engines, and saw two puffs of dust erupt just ahead of Brand's pumping legs. He zigged left then zagged right, but the next two shots were even closer. Brand sprinted to the mud-brick building and barrelled his way through the closed door, splintering the timbers with his shoulder. Sonja raised her AK-47 and fired a burst at the helicopter, but if her shots passed close they had no effect.

'Everyone,' Sonja called, 'two aimed shots at the helicopter. Fire!'

The rifles on the roof all swung towards the aircraft, and the volley of deliberate fire must have either had some impact or whizzed close enough for the pilot to take evasive action. He tilted his machine and dipped away.

Brand emerged from the hut and ran towards them. Sonja noticed one of the Russians stop and raise his rifle, aiming at Brand. She fired two quick shots at the man and he moved to cover behind a palm tree. 'Run, Hudson!'

'What do you think I'm doing?' he yelled back.

Bullets smacked into the rendered walls of the castle, dislodging sheets of plaster, and Sonja and the others on the roof popped out from behind their stone walls to return fire. 'Keep moving along the wall, on your hands and knees, under cover,' Sonja said. 'Don't let them draw a bead on you.'

Brand came running up the steps from the courtyard to the roof of the building. Below them the fire from the Russians eased off, but was soon directed elsewhere. Sonja heard the *ping* of bullets striking metal. Brand turned and ran to the wall above the entrance to the courtyard and peeked over the edge. 'They're shooting the shit out of the trucks. Tyres are going down and the engines are taking fire. They're closing off our means of escape.'

'Select your targets,' Sonja called. The Russians had gone to ground and were concentrating their fire for the time being on the trucks, but she knew they would rush the castle soon. 'Wait until they're between fifty and a hundred metres out. Aim for the centre of the body. Don't miss.'

'Chopper's moving behind us,' Brand called.

'*Scheisse*!' Alex yelled as a bullet smacked into the wall next to him.

'Are you hit?' Sonja asked.

Brand rushed to the younger man, who was lying on his back, his face white. Another round slapped into the roof of the castle by Alex's feet as Brand knelt by him. 'Talk to me, boy, you OK?'

Alex held up his arm and Brand saw the hole in his shirt. A bullet had passed through the fabric of Alex's sleeve. 'It missed you. You're fine. Shit.' Two more rounds bracketed them. Brand turned on his knee and fired a burst of three rounds towards the helicopter, which hovered, side on, about two hundred metres from them.

The shooter temporarily switched targets, putting five or six quick rounds into the engine area of the Amarok parked in the courtyard. It fitted with the strategy of trying to bottle them into the castle.

'Someone up there's a good shot. We're sitting ducks here,' Brand called to Sonja.

As if to reinforce the point Sonja was forced to drop to her belly in the lee of a wall when two rounds searched for her. 'Agreed. We've got to take this downstairs.'

'They're coming!' Sutton yelled. He held his AK-47 over his head, firing blindly over the stone wall at the men below who had begun advancing.

'Don't waste your ammo,' Brand chided the professor.

'Five of them down there, on the move,' Stirling reported.

Brand grabbed Alex by the arm and hoisted him to his feet, but directed his instructions at all four men. 'Get downstairs, find a window and start shooting.'

Sonja fired at the helicopter and the pilot moved off to change position. She used the break in suppressive fire from above to rest her rifle on the wall and take aim at the advancing force. She found a man, tracked him as he moved and waited for him to find cover behind a palm tree. Sonja watched the man who'd been closest to him. When he dropped to one knee behind a low wall, Sonja knew the first man would get up. She aimed to the left of the tree. The man had held his rifle in his right hand, so he would come out from around the tree on that same side, she was sure of it. As the man emerged Sonja squeezed the trigger. The round took the man in the chest and pitched him backwards.

Sutton had led the charge downstairs, followed by Alex, Stirling and Matthew. Just Brand was left on the roof, with Sonja.

He, too, took aim at an advancing Russian, and fired, but missed. The helicopter was settling into a new position. Sonja saw the figure sitting in the back and the long barrel of a rifle, probably a Dragunov or similar, she thought, coming to bear. 'Come on, let's go,' she said to Brand.

Brand ran down the stairs, and when Sonja was halfway down she turned and scanned the skies for the helicopter. Temporarily denied any targets the pilot had returned to the drop-off point by the filling station and landed. Sonja crept back up onto the roof. Below her the defenders were trading bullets with the advancing Russians, who seemed to have gone to ground. Sonja put down her AK-47 and looked through her binoculars. The pilot sat in the helicopter, its rotors still turning, but the passenger who had been firing at them got out and went to the side of the road, to the burned grass, where the three earlier casualties were lying.

Sonja studied the person. The build was too slight to be a man's. The woman had left her rifle in the helicopter. She went to the prone figures. One of the men who had been burned was still alive. He reached up to the woman with a blackened hand and smouldering clothing. She reached behind her, and Sonja wondered whether she had a first-aid kit on her belt until she saw the pistol in her hand.

Sonja watched, transfixed, as the woman fired a shot into the man's head. His body convulsed. She moved, methodically, to the next man and then the third, dispatching each of them in the same way. Sonja couldn't tell if the men had been conscious or not. She swallowed hard. She was no stranger to death, but these people were all on the same side. The woman looked up towards the castle, and Sonja adjusted the focus so that she could better see the face of this cold-blooded killer.

The features were instantly familiar, the high, broad cheekbones, the full, wide mouth. And there was something about the woman's defiant stare, as if she were searching out Sonja herself, knowing she would be watching, and deliberately challenging her with a look.

'Irina Aleksandrova.' Sonja lowered the binoculars, blinked, then raised them again. The woman was still looking up at her.

Irina was in charge. The pieces dropped into place and Sonja realised how ready she had been to misread the information she and Ross had gathered. Irina was not a hooker, nor a bystander to organised crime. She'd had a regular thing with the Vietnamese gangster, Tran, but it was not for sex, or not sex alone. The gunman in the helicopter that had targeted them at the archaeological dig site had talked of being contracted by Russians. Irina was not an innocent pawn, she was the head of a crime syndicate; she hadn't been killed in Vietnam because she'd been running the whole operation from the beginning. In Sonja's mind, if Irina was in bed, in a business and literal sense, with Tran, then that also made her an accessory to Sam's death.

Sonja reached for her rifle but by the time she was back in a firing position Irina had returned to the helicopter and it was lifting off. In anger, Sonja fired a burst of three rounds at the chopper, but it was long range for the AK-47 and she doubted her bullets found their mark. If they did, they did nothing to slow the pilot or the machine, which headed straight towards her as soon as it was off the ground.

Irina must have switched from her sniper's rifle to an assault weapon, because as the helicopter's shadow swept over her just as she reached the bottom of the stairs, Sonja was chased inside the castle by a long burst of automatic gunfire.

*

'I know who's in charge of the Russians,' Sonja breathed as she entered the bar and restaurant area, which was thick with cordite smoke.

'Does it matter right now?' Brand asked.

'It's a woman by the name of Irina Aleksandrova. She wants me dead, and she was part of the operation that was cornering the market in rhino horn in Vietnam – the same crew ultimately responsible for Sam's death. I had her for a while, in Saigon; I was using her for information.'

'So that *was* you in Vietnam who killed the rhino horn kingpin.'

'Tran Van Ngo, yes. That woman was his business partner.'

'I take it you didn't part as besties,' Brand said as he reloaded and cocked his weapon.

Sonja checked her own ammunition. 'You could say that. By the way, good work down there by the filling station, even though I told you I was going to do that. What's the status?'

'The assault's stalled. We're about evenly matched now, and they know they'll take losses as they cross the open ground out there to the fort. I suspect they'll try to outflank us, use the shooter in the chopper to keep us indoors.'

'We need to take out the chopper,' Stirling said.

'Easier said than done,' Brand said.

'They're coming again!' Alex called.

Emma was by his side now as they all returned their focus to their windows. The Russian ground troops were trying to advance. Brand took aim and fired and saw the man drop, though he couldn't tell if he'd hit him, wounded him, or just scared him.

Bullets shattered glass and ricocheted around the walls of the bar and restaurant. Pictures and glasses were smashed. Natangwe groaned from his place on the leather couch.

'Maybe we can call a truce,' Stirling said. 'They have men wounded; maybe we can negotiate with them.'

'*Negotiate* with them? I just watched Irina execute her three wounded men. She's not going to do a deal with us, Stirling. If we can't hold out until some cops or someone else show up she's going to try to kill us all. But I won't let that happen.'

Brand took two shots at a moving man, then looked to her. 'What have you got in mind?'

'They want that fucking rhino horn, so I'm going to get rid of it.'

'No!' Stirling said.

She glared at him. 'Yes. I hate that stuff, Stirling. It caused Sam's death – it's caused too many deaths. I don't care what it's worth, now or in the future.'

He stood there, and Brand could see his mind turning over. 'Yes, you're right.'

'Hudson, Irina's going to try to stop me if she thinks I'm going to destroy the trucks.'

Brand nodded. 'Roger that. We need a diversion.'

'If you set fire to those trucks inside the gate of the castle you might kill us all – what if they blow up?' Sutton said.

'Two guys moving, out in the grass,' Alex interrupted, then loosed off a couple of shots.

Brand went to the window, then ducked to one side as a storm of bullets passed through and shattered the remaining shards of glass. 'They're outflanking us; that's their buddies putting down covering fire.'

Emma and Alex sniped from adjoining windows. 'They're moving too fast,' Emma called.

'I'm going topside,' Brand said.

Brand heard the chopper above and made for the staircase to the roof. He took two steps at time, but spun around when he got to the top, hearing footsteps and huffing behind him. 'Professor.' The older man looked up, still wearing his slightly ridiculous floppy hat and sunglasses. 'What are you doing up here?'

'I want to help, I have an idea.'

Brand put a hand to his eyes to shield them from the glare of the lowering sun and looked for the chopper. He could hear it, but still couldn't see it. He blinked and saw a speck. 'Bastard's coming in out of the sun.'

Brand sprinted for the crenellated wall furthest from him to try to get some cover from the shots he knew would be coming from the helicopter any second now. When he got there he turned to see Sutton standing in the middle of the flat roof, waving his arms, rifle in one hand.

'Get down!'

Sutton laughed. 'You wanted a diversion.'

Bullets started heading their way and Brand realised Sutton was clearly visible to the Russians on the ground, even though the chopper wasn't in range or at an ideal angle for the sniper on board to get a sight picture.

Brand was half hidden by the masonry work and from this vantage point he could see a Russian break cover, standing behind a tree so that he was hidden from the people inside the castle, but exposed from above. Brand aimed, squeezed the trigger and the Russian fell back.

Sutton was laughing, but on his belly now, crawling to the fortifications. 'Good show! Took your time, though, eh, Yank!'

Brand shook his head. The old man was crazy, but when he took his glasses off for a second to wipe away some grit or perhaps even laughter-induced tears, Brand saw a flicker of real joy there.

'Haven't had this much fun in years.'

'Chopper, get down!'

Brand nestled himself into the corner where the wall met the roof line, his AK up and ready in case he could get a shot off. Sutton, on the other hand, was moving his arms and legs like a kid making a snow or sand angel as the Bell passed low overhead. Brand fired a burst of eight rounds at the helicopter, which peeled off. He could see the head of the gunman sticking out, although now he could see quite clearly that Sonja was right – it was a woman. The chopper banked and turned before Brand could loose off another burst.

'So what's your idea, Professor, other than trying to get yourself killed just then?'

Sutton, lying still now and catching his breath, put his glasses back on and looked to Brand. 'I think we need another diversion. Sonja's right to want to destroy the horn, but we can't have ourselves trapped here in the castle with a couple of burning trucks blocking the gate.'

'You're crazy, right?' Brand asked.

'Assuredly. But I'm also right. And the other thing I know is that those Russians aren't going to scale the walls and they're moving too fast and too professionally for your fledglings downstairs to take them out. You need to lure them into a trap.'

Brand put two and two together. 'You want to move the trucks – open the gates so the Russians can charge in, and then take them out when they enter the gate.'

'Exactly.'

'But who's going to move the trucks?'

'Me. I'm old, Brand, expendable. I checked them earlier, during a lull. There's a tow cable in Stirling's Amarok. I'll attach it to the Unimog, which is running, even if the radiator's full of holes. I'll at least be able to create a diversion by driving away. I checked the Amarok just now, it won't start and the Hilux is completely finished. I'll shunt the Hilux out of the way and tow the Amarok out into the open. You just make sure you and the others are lined up and ready to kill those bastards when they rush the gate.'

'What happens if the Russians kill you and simply tow the rhino horn down to the helicopter? You'll have handed them what they want.'

Sutton nodded. 'I thought of that. As soon as I'm clear of the castle I'm going to torch the Amarok with the horn in it. Stirling's wrong; it's not worth saving. It's better to get rid of the stuff.

433

Worse case, if the Russians do kill me and get hold of the horns they might just leave you alone.'

Brand thought the old man was crazy, but if he wanted to throw his life away that was his business. 'OK. Good luck.'

Sutton got up and made for the stairs. One of the Russians obviously saw movement on the roof, for he fired off a couple of rounds. He looked at Brand, who stared back at him and gave him a small salute.

'Hudson!' Emma called from the courtyard.

'What is it?' Sutton disappeared down the stairs and Hudson leaned over the internal parapet to see Emma.

'They're around us now. We lost sight of them.'

'They're going to be coming through the main gates soon. Get everyone to take up position in a doorway, in the bar, in the hotel rooms. Stay out of sight, and when they storm the entryway, let 'em have it.'

'That's the plan?' She sounded as incredulous as the plan deserved.

''Fraid so. Tell your mom.'

'Will do.'

Brand jogged down the stairs. It was eerily quiet now. The Russians were working their way around the castle to get into position for the final assault. The helicopter was standing off, also waiting for the last push, its engines just a mosquito-like drone in the distance. All of the castle's defenders were taking up positions around the internal courtyard. Emma had even moved Natangwe to the doorway of the bar. He sat in a chair, his gun hand propped up on the padded leather armrest. He gave a weak smile. *Gutsy kid.*

Brand moved to the trucks and found Sutton between the Unimog and the Amarok. Sutton was securing a wire tow cable from the tow ball at the back of the bigger truck to the double cab's recovery shackle below the bumper bar.

Alex was watching on. 'Have you called for the aeromedical evacuation chopper now that the power's back on?' Brand asked Alex.

'Done,' Alex said.

'Good work.' He turned to the professor. 'Ready to go?'

Sutton stood straight. 'Ready as I'll ever be.'

'That Unimog's shot up pretty bad. You won't get far, Professor.'

Sutton blinked at him. 'I don't need to go far. I just need to get far enough away to open your trap and to stop the Amarok from setting fire to the castle and harming someone when I torch the fuckers.'

Brand had to laugh at the obscenity. 'Right.' He looked at the old wooden cases piled in the rear cargo area of Stirling's truck. There was a fortune in there.

Sutton got into the Unimog and started the engine as a hail of gunfire erupted from the other side of the car park.

Chapter 34

Sonja leaned around the trunk of the stout palm tree in the castle's courtyard and fired two three-round bursts in quick succession in the direction of where the gunfire had come, covering Hudson as he ran back through the now open entryway.

The Russians had opened fire as Dorset rammed the disabled Hilux out through the entryway and pulled away from the hotel, the Unimog towing the Amarok.

'Where's Emma?' Brand asked her as he made it to the tree and flattened himself behind it.

'In the bar, with Natangwe.'

Brand nodded. 'Good.'

Sonja removed the magazine from her AK-47, checked the remaining rounds, and refitted it. 'Ready?'

'Ready as I'll ever be,' Brand said, imitating the professor.

Sonja braced herself against the tree. Brand broke cover and took the stairs to the main tower two at a time. At the top she saw him peek over the fortifications and look around. Then he looked back down at her, touched his eyes with the first two fingers of his left hand and pointed in the direction of the open gateway.

Sonja knew he was asking her silently if she could see any movement from ground level. She shook her head. It was eerily quiet now; no one else was shooting. The noise of the Unimog's engine was fading away, so at least Dorset hadn't been killed. At any moment she expected the *whoosh* and roar of Sutton setting fire to Stirling's vehicle. Even the helicopter was keeping its distance, its engines just a distant hum.

Brand's rifle barked twice.

'What is it?' she called up to him.

'Son of a bitch.'

'What?'

He jogged to the edge of the tower and looked down at her. 'I can see them, the Russians, they're running down the road back to the filling station. They could be regrouping, or maybe they've had enough.' He trotted down the stairs.

Sonja joined him at the bottom of the staircase. 'Where's Sutton?'

'He's about halfway down the road to the garage. The Russkies ran right past him. He's waving a white flag – a pillowcase or something out of the window. Damn it. What the hell's he up to? He was supposed to burn the horn.'

Sonja tried to process the dramatic change in events, and their fortunes. The Russians were brave, but also foolish trying to attack such a fortified position. Perhaps they'd seen the opening of the entryway to the castle for what it was, a chance for the defenders to slaughter the remaining attackers, and lost their nerve. She looked around. Alex and Stirling emerged from their positions around the courtyard.

'Alex, while it's quiet take that fuel can you took from Stirling's *bakkie* and get the generator started.' Alex nodded and left.

Sonja went into the bar to check on Emma and Natangwe. She allowed a couple of seconds for her eyes to adjust to the gloom of the bar, which was cooler than outside. Natangwe was propped in his chair, just inside the doorway. Sonja looked around. 'Where's Emma?'

Natangwe looked up at her, his eyes red. 'She . . . she didn't tell you?'

'Tell me what?' Sonja felt her heart start to quicken.

'She went out. She said Professor Sutton wouldn't be able to tow the *bakkie* away with no one behind the wheel.'

The noise of the generator roaring to life filtered through from the courtyard and lights flicked on inside, illuminating Natangwe's pained face. Sonja turned on her heel and strode back across the courtyard towards the entrance.

'Where are you going?' Brand called down from the roof. Alex appeared in the doorway.

'Emma's with that idiot, Sutton.'

Stirling was closest to the entryway. He ran outside, turned right at the car park and headed down the dirt road, rifle in his hands, his long legs pumping. Alex also ran to the gate, but Sonja pushed past him and followed Stirling.

'Stirling, wait, be careful,' she called after him.

Her heart was pounding now; she could feel the vein in her neck throbbing, hard enough to hurt her. She didn't know what was going on, but Sutton was halfway between the castle and the filling station. Sonja heard the thud of the helicopter's blades. She looked up as she ran; the chopper had turned and was coming straight towards them, using the dirt road as its axis.

'Stirling, take cover!'

In the open side door of the helicopter Sonja could see Irina Aleksandrova. She was holding a long-barrelled sniper's rifle, a Dragunov. Irina was tracking Stirling, who was still ahead. Sonja raised her AK-47 to her shoulder, took aim and squeezed the trigger.

Click.

Sonja swore. There was the noise of gunfire and as she yanked back the cocking handle and pulled off the magazine to clear her rifle she glanced up and saw Irina shifting her aim. Sonja shook the jammed round clear of the breech and was about to take aim again when she was knocked off her feet. 'Bloody hell.'

Hudson Brand rolled onto his back, half on top of Sonja, and loosed off fifteen rounds at the helicopter as its shadow passed over them.

'Get off me, for fuck's sake,' she yelled at him.

'Thank you would do,' Brand said.

Sonja pushed him off her, replaced her magazine and cocked her rifle. 'Get up, Brand, get moving.'

'Yes, ma'am.'

'Moving!' Sonja called. She stood and began running through the grass on the edge of the road, towards the filling station. Through a cloud of dust generated by the two vehicles she could see Sutton in the Unimog, towing the Amarok. They were driving into a whirlwind stirred up by the helicopter, which looked like it was about to land on the road in front of them.

Brand gave three rounds of covering fire in the general direction of the Russians, whom Sonja glimpsed making for the helicopter. She thought Stirling had found cover on the other side of the road but to her left she saw a booted foot sticking out of the grass. 'No!'

Sonja darted across the road and hit the ground next to Stirling. She rolled him over. The tactical situation was going from bad to nightmarish and Emma was being driven to the enemy by her professor, who seemed like he was foolishly going to try to negotiate with Irina.

'Moving,' Brand yelled.

Sonja knew she should cover Hudson, but she was searching for a pulse. Nonetheless, she heard gunfire, from her side of the road, not Brand's. Sonja raised her head and looked for the source.

'I've got you covered, Hudson!' It was Emma. Sonja exhaled with relief that her daughter had obviously got out of the Amarok, but some return fire from the Russians made Emma drop to the ground.

'Stay down, Emma!'

'Coming to you,' Brand called.

'Get Emma,' Sonja replied.

She went back to Stirling. His breathing was shallow and ragged. She slapped his face. 'Stirling? Stirling, can you hear me?'

Brand and Emma ran to her and dropped to their knees. Emma took up a firing position behind a palm tree and kept watch on the activity by the filling station. Sonja felt a mix of pride and annoyance. 'Emma, where did you go without telling me?' As she spoke she used her Leatherman to cut open Stirling's shirt. He'd taken two bullets in the belly and one in the chest and dark blood was welling. Hudson helped her, taking field dressings out of his pocket and pressing the pads against the wounds.

'I got in Stirling's truck to help Professor Sutton – he came looking for someone to help. I thought he was only going to move the trucks fifty metres or so. I hopped into the Amarok and we'd just started to move, out the gate, when Matthew appeared next to me, opened the door and dragged me out. That's when the gunfire started and I ran to the nearest tree and hid.'

'That's the best thing you could have done,' Sonja said. 'I'd forgotten about Matthew.'

Alex jogged to them and also dropped down into the grass. 'Emma, my God, I was going crazy looking for you. How is Stirling?'

Sonja didn't look up from tying a dressing around Stirling. 'Not good.'

'I'm also worried about Natangwe; he's drifting in and out of consciousness,' Alex said.

Brand looked to Emma. 'What are they up to down the road?'

'The chopper's landed,' Emma said. 'Professor Sutton's nearly at it. He's still driving. Some woman's out of the helicopter and waving at him. He's . . . shit!'

*

Dorset Sutton saw the Russian bring his rifle up to his shoulder and Irina Petrovna Aleksandrova swinging her Dragunov sniper's rifle in his direction. The woman peered through her telescopic site at him, then lowered her weapon. She put a hand on the barrel of the other man's AK and pushed it down as well.

Dorset ducked down below the level of the dashboard. On the floor of the truck he wedged a small plastic cooler box he'd found in the cab onto the accelerator pedal. He grabbed his AK-47 from the passenger seat.

The helicopter loomed large in the windscreen as the truck trundled on. Sutton moved between the front seats, raised the rifle to his shoulder and fired. The burst blew out the windscreen of the Unimog and stitched a line of bullet holes through the Perspex windows of the helicopter. Sutton saw the pilot slump over his controls, then he turned and scrambled through the access way between the cab and the bespoke camper behind. Bullets followed him, zinging and ricocheting around him.

Moving between a couch and a galley kitchen he grabbed the handle of the rear access door to the camper and turned it at the moment the front of the truck ploughed into the helicopter.

Turning rotor blades sheared off, bounced and flew into the bush, and the Unimog reared up onto the cockpit. The gunmen who had been waiting to either board the chopper or shoot up the oncoming truck were not as lucky. One was crushed by the Unimog and two more were incinerated as the rampaging vehicle smashed into the engine and ignited the Bell's fuel tanks. The explosion sent a mushroom cloud of oily black smoke into the air and a fireball in every direction.

As Dorset opened the rear door, the force of the blast behind him propelled him like a human cannonball out of the campervan and onto the bonnet of the Volkswagen Amarok being towed behind. Winded and dazed, it took him a couple of seconds to work out that on the other side of the windscreen that his right

441

shoulder had just painfully shattered was not Emma Kurtz, but Matthew Allchurch.

Dorset raised his arm, the pain welling up, and pantomimed the turning of the ignition key with his right thumb and forefinger together. Matthew, however, seemed to be a step ahead of him as the engine started up before he'd even finished signalling. Dorset had lied to Brand about the vehicle being disabled; it was fine. Dorset, his training from half a lifetime ago kicking in, fought through the pain that threatened to overwhelm him and rolled off the dented bonnet. He pointed the barrel of his rifle at the tow strap that linked the Unimog to the Amarok and pulled the trigger. With the strap all but severed he opened the passenger door.

Bullets raked the *bakkie* and Sutton ducked, saving his life as another round whizzed over his head, then fired two snap shots at a Russian who had survived the impact of truck and helicopter. The man fell backwards.

'Nice shooting,' Matthew said as Sutton hauled his aching body inside the Amarok.

'Thank you. Now, if you don't mind, I think reverse gear is in order.'

*

Brand stopped the compressions on Stirling's chest and Sonja rocked back on her heels. Stirling had started breathing again, though his chest was gurgling with blood. At least he was alive, thanks to Hudson and her giving him CPR.

Alex came to them. 'Is there anything I can do?'

'Pray the evac chopper gets here soon,' Sonja said. 'Stirling's barely alive, Natangwe's bleeding out again and the professor and Matthew were probably just fried.'

Brand stood and looked at the wreckage of the burning helicopter and truck.

A ringtone sounded and Brand pulled his phone out of his pocket. 'Hello?'

No one answered his greeting, but Brand could hear a voice on the other end, far off, as though someone had accidentally turned on their phone by sitting on it. *'Now if you don't mind, I think reverse gear is in order,'* the voice said. It was Dorset Sutton.

*

Matthew reversed hard and fast away from the burning wreckage. 'Go past it,' Sutton said, 'to the main road, and turn left.'

Matthew looked to him. 'Why not go back to the castle?'

'We have to draw any remaining enemy away from the others. We'll see if we can find the local police and lead them back here.'

Matthew stopped, put the truck into first, and glanced at his phone to make sure his call to Brand had been answered. Then he accelerated past the helicopter, the Unimog and the fire, which was spreading to the bush on either side of the road and threatening the filling station. He drove to the main road and turned left, then slowed down.

'Faster, Matthew, we need to find the police.'

Matthew stopped the truck near the small cluster of shops. Locals were nervously milling around, moving into the road to watch the pyre in the distance. A few started to move towards the strange vehicle.

'What are you doing? Drive, Matthew. Hurry.'

'No.'

'Why not?'

'Not until you tell me what happened to my son.'

Dorset shook his head. 'I have no idea what happened to your son. How should I?'

Matthew put the car into first again, moved off and began to turn around.

'What are you doing?' Dorset asked him again.

'We're going back to the castle. Hudson wants to talk to you, wants to take a good look at you again and ask you some questions.'

Dorset raised his AK-47 and pointed it at Matthew. 'I told you to drive out of town, now keep going.'

Matthew stopped the truck again. 'No.'

Dorset curled his finger around the trigger. 'Get this bloody vehicle moving or I'll kill you, here and now.'

Matthew stared at him. 'Do it. You think I haven't been half dead since my son disappeared all those years ago? I'll make you a deal. I'll drive; I'll be your hostage or whatever you want me to be and I'll help you get away with the rhino horn in the back if you just tell me the truth about my son.'

A trio of local youths, two brandishing sticks, was closing in on them. 'Bloody drive. I'll tell you what you want to know.'

Matthew stared at him. 'Gareth.'

Sutton sighed. The men were shouting now, wanting to know what had happened to their town. 'All right, I was on the Dakota. Gareth survived the crash. Now, if you want to know more, can we please go?'

Matthew accelerated and weaved between the mob.

*

Brand put the phone on speaker. Alex had moved away from where they were treating Stirling and was calling the aeromedical evacuation service again, to get an update on the helicopter's arrival. There was no movement at the destroyed chopper and no more gunfire; all of the Russians must have been killed or seriously wounded.

'Status?' Brand called to Alex.

'They're on their way. The dispatcher says they should get to us in about twenty minutes, same with the police. They had to respond to a bus crash first.'

Sonja stroked Stirling's face, though he was unconscious. 'Hang on, Stirling.'

Brand looked away, back to Alex, and Emma, who had run to the castle and back and brought with her a blanket. 'All right,' Brand said, 'let's load Stirling and get him back to the castle with Natangwe.'

They lifted him onto the blanket and Brand, Sonja, Alex and Emma each grabbed a corner and carried him. Brand held the phone up as they walked.

'*What happened to the other pilot, Bester?*' Matthew asked.

'*He wanted to turn around, after Brand started the fire on board, and fly back to Ondangwa. He got cold feet, even though he'd taken a couple of shots at Brand. I told him to carry on to the drop zone, over the ocean. He refused, so I shot him in the head.*'

Brand shook his head and said a silent prayer for the dead and the dying.

*

Dorset looked at Allchurch. He would have to kill the man at some point, and perhaps it was better to do it now.

No, he thought, reconsidering; he might need a hostage. His plan was to make for the border, to cross the Kunene into Angola, at a drift where the river was low. On the other side he knew an ex-special forces and BOSS – Bureau of State Security – man who ran a fishing camp on the Atlantic coast. He'd find a way to ship out the rhino horn from Luanda. He didn't have the whole shipment, but what he and Stirling had been able to load into the Amarok would be enough to set him up for life, and make up for the near thirty years he'd spent trudging around the Namibian deserts on archaeological digs searching for the Dakota.

His situation was bad, but it could have been worse; at least he was alive, unlike Danie Bester, the pilot he'd killed on board the Dakota, and Jacobus Venter. He'd survived the war in Angola and escaped prosecution by South Africa's Truth and Reconciliation Commission by hiding behind the false identity of archaeologist Dorset Sutton. He had, in fact, studied archaeology at university in South Africa after his compulsory military service. He'd been recruited by the security service to spy on subversive students supporting the African National Congress, and had completed his degree in the process. A fake overseas degree and his real knowledge had helped him into a lecturer's job some years after democracy had come to South Africa and eventually he had landed a professorship. Since then he'd been developing a special interest in Namibia's archaeology to cover his search for the Dakota. Dorset had set up the pipeline for ivory, rhino horn and diamonds out of Angola to the Russians, via Irina Aleksandrova's father. He knew the daughter and had been in regular contact with her over the years. Dorset also knew of Andre Horsman, but the ex-air force officer had never met Dorset, who ran the smuggling operation from behind a series of cut-outs. Dorset had long watched Horsman's ham-fisted attempts to find the missing aircraft. If the youngsters, Emma, Alex and Natangwe, hadn't killed Andre and Sebastian then Dorset would have; leaving them to do the dirty work had preserved his cover a little longer. He'd shown himself to Irina as he lay on the roof of the castle waving while she flew over in her helicopter. She had landed, as he'd hoped she would, and called off her men as she waited for him to deliver the goods to her – then he had taken her out of the picture. With less than a full aircraft load of horn there would have been fewer profits; now with Irina and her contact Tran Van Ngo dead Dorset could set up and have complete control over a new market in Vietnam. All he had to do was get away.

They were out of Wilfriedstein, though Allchurch was slowing down again. 'Faster,' said Dorset.

Allchurch glanced at him. 'Why don't you just kill me now, be done with it? I know you're going to.'

Dorset nodded. 'You're right, I should. But all the others know I'm a criminal now, since I've driven off with the rhino horn. What difference does it make if I let you live? I won't be coming back to Namibia or South Africa again.'

'You murdered Danie Bester and I'm assuming you murdered my son as well. There's no statute of limitations on that, no jurisdiction where you can hide from that.'

'Well then you're right, Matthew. You just signed your own death warrant.'

Allchurch stopped the Toyota on the side of the road and opened the door. 'We're one and half kilometres out of town, Sutton. Far enough for there to be no witnesses. You can kill me now if you want. Just tell me how my son died.'

*

Brand held up his phone and they listened to Dorset and Matthew's conversation. 'I have to go and try to get him,' Brand said.

Sonja picked up her AK-47 and turned to Emma. 'You and Alex stay here with Stirling and Natangwe. The paramedics can help you load them, OK?'

'Yes, Mum,' Emma said.

Brand took a spare magazine for his rifle from the cargo pocket on the side of Stirling's blood-soaked pants. 'Sonja, I can do this myself.'

'I'm coming. I can't be here when the cops come.' She looked to her daughter. 'Emma, you'll have to think up some story. OK?'

Emma nodded.

'Mum,' Emma said as Brand started to walk away. He looked over his shoulder. Sonja had stopped. Emma went to her and wrapped her arms around her. 'Mum, I love you. Please stay safe.'

'I love you too, my girl.'

They ran out of the castle's gate and split left and right, onto opposite sides of the road, and jogged towards the blazing skeletal remains of the melded chopper and truck. Brand had his rifle in his shoulder as he picked out bodies in the ground, watching in case one moved.

'No survivors my side,' Sonja called to him over the crackle of flames.

'Nor mine.' He smelled burning meat, remembered Angola, and swallowed hard.

'No sign of the woman, Irina?'

'No,' Brand said. By the side of the road were the three men the gangster had executed. Brand had no history with the Russian woman, but he felt an instinctive hatred for someone who would treat her men like that.

Sonja spied something on the ground. She bent and retrieved a charger, a pressed metal clip with five rifle rounds attached to it for ease of loading. Someone must have dropped it; Sonja put the spare ammunition in her pants pocket.

'What's Matthew saying?'

Brand had the phone in his pocket, but had plugged in his hands-free cord and earpiece. 'Nothing. There isn't even an engine noise. I think they've stopped. The last thing he said was he was a kilometre and a half out of town.'

'Then let's get a move on.'

Brand and Sonja turned left when they reached the main road, passed the filling station and started running up the road.

'Shit,' Brand said.

'What is it?'

'Dorset's telling Matthew to get out of the truck. I think he's going to kill him.'

Chapter 35

Matthew got out and stood by the side of the road. He thought about running, but he knew he wouldn't get far before the bullet drilled into his back. In any case, he needed to know.

The white-haired professor, the picture of the harmless, wise academic, moved to the driver's side of the truck and raised the rifle to his shoulder with the practised ease and the stance of a killer. Matthew took a breath. 'At least tell me.'

Dorset tensed, his finger curled through the trigger guard; Matthew knew from his brief time in the army that one only did that when one was ready to shoot.

'Tell me,' Matthew said again, louder, emboldened by the crystal-clear certainty that his own death was imminent. He thought of Helen, of how her sadness would just be multiplied because of his foolishness, trying to lay Gareth to rest. 'Tell me how my son died.'

Dorset blew a breath out of his mouth, seemed to sag a little in his marksman's stance, and licked his lips. 'It was a different time, you know?'

Matthew nodded slowly. 'I know. I investigated shootings of civilians, of soldiers killing each other; most of them I helped sweep away. We were fighting for our survival.'

Dorset laughed. 'Don't patronise me, you know that's not true. We were fighting against an ideology that crumbled of its own accord, fighting for one that disappeared a few years later when our politicians sold us out.'

'Sold us out?' Matthew countered. For whatever Sutton had been, he wasn't stupid. 'Don't lapse into clichés. You were part of the system, propping it up, but you took a different path, turned to crime.'

Sutton rocked his head from side to side. 'Yes, true. I was in the intelligence service, and the longer I spent in Angola the more I realised how little intelligence there was. The smart ones were feathering their own nests.' He glanced up, as if to heaven. The dry easterly wind began its daily torment, whipping up dust and grit and snatching at the professor's clothes. 'I tried to save him.'

'Save him?' Matthew asked. His lips were cracked, his hand ached, and he almost wished he were dead. Only Gareth was keeping him alive.

Dorset lowered the rifle, just a little. 'The fire that Brand started had spread into the wiring, something to do with the fuel pumps. The bottom line was that we were running out of fuel and there was nothing Gareth could do to keep the engines going long enough to ditch in the sea – though I had no desire to be rescued by a bunch of Russians – or to get back to Ondangwa. We tried lightening the load, jettisoning some cargo, but it was too little too late, and I didn't want to lose all of the rhino horn.'

Matthew nodded. 'I see. So it was all about the money.'

'Of *course* it was. You know it wasn't about saving Angola, or even saving South Africa.' Dorset sounded angry now, losing it. 'Gareth said he would have to put the aircraft down. He reckoned we were close to the coast, that we could make for the salt road and someone would find us, even if it took a couple of days. He had seen me kill Bester, but he was calm. I thought . . . I thought . . .'

'You thought you could corrupt him, buy him?' Matthew asked, feeling the dread rise up inside him. For a moment he wanted just to turn and walk up the road, knowing Dorset would put a bullet in his back and end the pain.

'I did, but I was wrong.'

Matthew felt the relief, but knew it was false. 'But he survived the crash.'

Sutton looked around him, as if for ghosts. 'Yes. He was injured, but I fared worse. I thought he might try something so I sat behind him, my pistol covering him. When we crashed I was thrown into the front of the cockpit and through the windscreen like a bloody javelin. I was battered and bruised and sliced and almost killed. I was unconscious.'

Matthew tried to imagine the scene, the smoking aircraft in the dunes where they had seen it, Gareth the only person conscious, his co-pilot executed beside him. 'He should have killed you.'

The professor nodded. 'Yes, you're probably right, but he didn't. He carried me, for God knew how far – it's taken me this long to work it out – over his shoulder, through the desert. I came to on the edge of the salt road. It was blistering hot, we were being sand-blasted by the wind, and he was hurt as well, a fractured wrist I think.'

'But he saved you?' Matthew pictured his son, young, lean, fit, outraged at the betrayal by those around him of all he'd thought he was fighting for.

'Yes. I tried to reason with him, to get him to go along with a story I made up.'

Matthew felt tears welling up inside him, for the first time in many years. 'But he wouldn't.'

Dorset lowered the AK-47. 'No, he wouldn't. Matthew, I'm going to offer you a deal. No, forget that, I'm just going to leave. I have a *bakkie* load of rhino horn, enough to see me living in comfort for the rest of my life. I'm leaving, and you can leave too. Go, and know your son was not corrupt or immoral or a war criminal. The only mistake he made was to save my life.'

'You killed him, just like you killed Roland Pretorius.'

Dorset shook his head. 'No, Matthew, I didn't kill Roland, but I read about his death. I imagine Andre killed him, or had him murdered before he could get to you and tell you about the smuggling operation and Andre's role in it. Goodbye, Matthew. I'm giving you this chance, a chance I didn't give Gareth. He was young and he was fit, but I was a spy for the old regime, the Bureau of State Security. I'd killed plenty of men, some with my bare hands, men who would bring down our civilised, perfect society. Gareth had a gun, but I got it off him.' Sutton started to get into the *bakkie*.

Matthew pictured the scene: the two men in the desert, so close to being rescued, beating the odds, and then one of them turning on the other because Gareth, the young, principled pilot who thought he had joined the air force to protect his homeland, had been dragged into a cesspool of greed and corruption and was threatening to do the right thing. Dorset had taken his son's sidearm and killed him on the edge of the Skeleton Coast. 'What happened to my son's body? Did you bury him?'

Dorset glanced away for the briefest of seconds. 'No. I heard a hyena, and there were lion in the area. My guess is the desert lions ate him.'

'You bastard.' Matthew reached for the pistol stuck in his trousers in the small of his back.

Dorset saw the movement, and quicker than Matthew would have thought possible, the old grey-hair had the AK up again and pointed at him.

Matthew fumbled with the pistol, not even able to remember if it was still loaded, let alone cocked. *I am going to die, just like my son did, at the hands of the same man.*

The shot echoed across the open land around them.

*

Sonja reached across to Brand and put her hand on his rifle, forcing him to lower it. They had stopped running as soon as Sutton and Allchurch had come into view, both of them out of breath and, if Sonja was honest, she at least was feeling her age. Brand had raised his weapon to take a shot at Sutton.

But Brand hadn't fired, someone else had, and Dorset Sutton was now on his back, in the dust. Matthew was running towards them from about three hundred metres away.

As they had run, between ragged breaths, Hudson had told her his theory about Sutton. He'd told Matthew he had been expecting to find that Andre Horsman was the man on board the Dakota who had ordered his death and had tried to shoot him when Venter, the loadmaster, had been unable to kill him. But Brand had checked the body, and although Horsman was blond and the right age, there was something about his build that wasn't right.

Someone had walked out of the desert onto the road and been picked up by Sonja's uncle. If it wasn't Andre, then who was it? Brand had told her that it was the way Sutton had carried on when Irina and her pilot had flown in for the kill that had made him think he was the one. Sutton had exposed himself to Irina more than once, not just recklessly, but blatantly.

'I think she knew him,' Brand had said to her. 'I told Matthew, and I said we would confront Sutton after we'd finished with the Russians. I was willing to risk losing the rhino horn to buy us some time, and if I was right about Sutton, that he was in cahoots with the Russians, then it would have only been a matter of time before he turned on us, in the castle. But then Matthew took it on himself to go and kick Emma out of the *bakkie* and try to take on Dorset alone. Crazy bastard.'

They both now dropped to one knee, their training mirroring each other's, rifles up, covering Matthew, seeking a target, but there was none. Someone had shot Sutton, but neither of them could see who.

'Three hundred!' Brand yelled, and Sonja focused on the range and saw the figure emerge from the scrubby thornbushes at the side of the road and make for the *bakkie*. 'On the road, lone rifleman.'

'Seen,' Sonja replied. She raised her AK and saw the slim woman with the overly long sniper's rifle. It was Irina. Sonja took aim, quickly, and fired a double tap.

Irina dropped but crawled to the vehicle, unharmed. Matthew looked back and, missing his footing, sprawled into the dirt.

'Moving!' Brand yelled.

Sonja cursed to herself. She wanted to be the first to close the distance between them and Irina, but Brand was on his feet and sprinting, not too slow for an old guy. Sonja laid down a burst of six or seven rounds in Irina's direction. The range was too far for the AK-47 to be accurate, but Sonja kept the bitch's head down.

Brand dived for the ground. Sonja knew he would be crawling to a fire position. She counted to three. 'Moving!'

Matthew was on his feet again, hands and face bloodied. She waved at him with her free hand, motioning for him to seek some cover in the bush. Sonja, however, stayed on the road to narrow the distance between her and Irina as quickly as she could.

Brand was firing, covering her run, but before Sonja had covered half the distance she'd planned, Brand called out, 'Stoppage!' His weapon had jammed.

Sonja saw the barrel of the Dragunov laid across the roof of the truck. Irina was taking aim. Sonja zigged to the left as the bullet kicked up the dust where her foot had just been. It was her turn to trip and fall.

'Cleared,' Brand called. He stood and pumped four rounds at the *bakkie*, but Irina was already in the vehicle and on her way. A cloud of dust obscured her escape.

Sonja got up and ran, passing Brand.

'She's gone,' Hudson said.

'She dropped her rifle,' Sonja called into the wind.

Sonja passed Matthew, ignoring his cries of thanks or whatever he was saying. Irina had dropped the Dragunov when she'd climbed into the truck, probably because she was out of ammunition and didn't want to be caught on the road in Namibia with a military sniper's rifle. Sonja got to Sutton's body. She kicked him, confirming he was dead, and picked up his AK-47. She removed the magazine and saw he had one round left. She thumbed it out. Next she quickly removed her own magazine and saw she had only two bullets. Sonja remembered the clip of five bullets she had picked up near the burning helicopter. She took them out of her pocket and saw they were Russian 7.62x54r rimmed rounds, which could not be used in an AK-47. They were for Irina's sniper rifle and she must have dropped them in her dash to escape the exploding chopper.

'Stay calm,' she told herself. She picked up Irina's rifle, took out the magazine, which was empty as she had assumed, and loaded the five bullets she had been able to salvage. Irina was getting away from them, already three hundred metres away and moving fast, too far to stand a good chance of stopping her with an AK-47. But the road was not as good here as in other parts of Namibia, and she was entering a bend. Her change in direction also meant that the dust cloud she was leaving was being blown away from her, giving Sonja a clear view of the fleeing *bakkie*.

Sonja refitted the magazine to the Dragunov and looked around her. There was nothing to rest the rifle on except for the dead guy. She lay down behind Sutton and rested the rifle barrel on his chest. Tucking one leg up into her body she was able to raise herself enough to get a good, stable view of the *bakkie* through the telescopic sights.

The east wind was pushing the grass over at a forty-five-degree angle; Sonja allowed for it, cocked the Dragunov and squeezed off a round.

'Go right, lead her by another metre,' Hudson said from behind her.

Sonja gave a small nod, took the correction under advisement and lined up ahead of the moving vehicle. She took a quick glance behind her and saw that Brand had a small pair of binoculars up to his eyes.

She returned her concentration to the vehicle and squeezed the trigger.

'Irina veered, just then. You hit the truck somewhere, but she's still going.' Frustrated, Sonja fired twice more, but Irina kept moving.

'One shot left,' Sonja said. She felt rather than saw Brand drop to the ground next to her, on one knee. The next thing she felt was his hand on her back. She would have flinched, normally, at a strange man's touch, but Brand wasn't strange.

'You'll be fine.' Brand raised the binoculars to his eyes.

Sonja took aim, just ahead of the blue gas bottles fixed to the rear of the *bakkie*'s cab. She breathed, in and out, as her dead father had taught her all those years ago, when this staggeringly beautiful country had been in the grip of a terrible war.

In.

Out.

In.

Sonja made a fist around the rifle's grip, feeling the strength return to her eye, her hand, her heart. The round left the Dragunov, cleaving the dry desert air. A moment later it hit the gas bottle on the back of the truck, and the vehicle exploded.

Chapter 36

Sonja waited for the police to leave the hospital in Windhoek before she walked in, wearing a new floppy bush hat and dark glasses.

Her hiking boots squeaked on the polished linoleum floor as she strode along the corridors, following the directions Emma had SMSed. Her daughter intercepted her.

'How's Stirling?' Sonja asked.

Emma bit her lower lip. Sonja saw that her eyes were red. 'Mum, they just don't know. We convinced the staff we're the closest thing he has to family so you can go in there.'

'And Natangwe?'

'Stable,' Emma said. 'Thank God. The doctors said Alex's transfusion saved his life. Alex is off organising transport and stuff for us.'

'OK. Good girl. I hope you understand, I couldn't be here when the police arrived. I had things to do — I've transferred some money from the States for those poor Germans whose truck I took. They've been staying with Ursula and she leant them a car; she explained why I needed their vehicle and they seem happy they're going to get enough to buy a new one. Also, I had to anonymously report the location of an abandoned Land Rover in Swakopmund to the police so a certain dirty old pastor can claim it.'

'Dirty old pastor?'

'I'll explain later,' Sonja said.

Emma laughed. 'Well, we spun the police quite a story here. Also, I told them about Benjie van der Westhuizen, the farmer friend of the guy who kidnapped us. The detective in charge called a little while ago – they sent someone to check on Benjie's farm, but it was abandoned. Looked like he'd left in a hurry; all they found were three little lion cubs. The cops are sending some wildlife people to collect them.' Her face turned serious. 'Mum, sit down with me for a minute, please.'

Sonja instinctively looked up and down the corridor, checking for danger, then sat on one of the tatty vinyl-covered chairs Emma motioned to. She took off her glasses. 'What's wrong? Are you all right?'

'I'm fine, Mum, all things considered. It's you I'm worried about.'

'Me? There's nothing wrong with me other than a few cuts and bruises.'

'That's not what I meant, Mum. I mean, all this, where you've been, the talk about you being in Vietnam . . . I want to know if it's finished now.'

Sonja took a breath and looked down at her fingers for a while, then back at Emma. 'It is.'

'Really?'

Sonja nodded. 'I thought I could get over Sam by killing the people responsible for his death, Emma. I know that must sound terrible.' Emma said nothing, but reached out and took Sonja's hands in hers. Sonja swallowed hard. 'I realised these last few days that as much as I loved Sam I can't live in the past, I have to move on, and I have to make sure you're all right.'

Emma squeezed her hands. 'Thanks, Mum, but you have to look after yourself, too. You're still grieving for Sam, or at least you have to *let* yourself grieve for him. And he wouldn't have wanted you to – I don't know – stagnate, or become a hermit or whatever. He was so full of life; he would have wanted you to get on with yours.'

Sonja freed one of her hands and rubbed her eyes. 'You're right. I do want to get on, and . . .' She felt the sting of tears and the first sob rise from deep inside her. As much as she hated the idea of crying in public she felt suddenly incapable of stopping, and when Emma wrapped her arms around her Sonja felt herself unable to do anything other than let the tears soak her daughter's T-shirt.

'It's OK, Mum, it's OK. You can cry for him. It's natural.'

Sonja had spent a life suppressing her grief, or drinking it away. When, at last, she sat up and dried her eyes, as weird as it was she felt as though a burden had been lifted from her. She still felt sad, still missed Sam, but there were other people she needed to check on, and perhaps care for.

Emma hugged her. 'OK?'

Sonja sniffed, nodded, and composed herself, gently breaking away from Emma's embrace. 'Better.'

'Oh, and Mum, seriously, you have to stop this mercenary shit.'

'Whatever.'

Emma put her hands on her hips. 'Don't "whatever" me.'

Sonja gave a small laugh. 'Go find your boyfriend and tell him you love him – that kind of nonsense.'

'Mum!'

'Go.'

Sonja got up and walked into the private room with Stirling's name written on cardboard fixed to the door. She hated hospitals, the faint smell of piss and disinfectant, the flowers, the relatives wishing they were somewhere else, the air of slow death. Stirling was hooked up to monitors and a respirator, a tube draining red gunk from his lungs. Sonja put a hand to her mouth. 'Stirling.'

She went to him and sat on the side of the bed. Sonja reached out and brushed his cheek with the back of her fingers. It had been decades since she'd done that. She took his hand, the cannula and IV drip protruding from above the wrist, in hers.

'Hi.'

Sonja turned her head and saw Brand standing in the doorway, holding his baseball cap. 'Hi.'

'I spoke to the doctor before, told him I was Stirling's brother. Well, half-brother. He said it's fifty–fifty whether he'll make it. It's good you could come.'

She nodded, unable to say another word. Her throat felt constricted.

'There's a flight in three hours, back to Cape Town. I want to get Matthew on it,' he said.

'Of course,' Sonja said. 'And you?'

'If there's room. Not sure if there's much reason for me to stay in Namibia.'

Sonja closed her eyes. She was so damned tired. It felt like she hadn't slept in a week, not since she and Brand had been together in Namutoni. She remembered the feel of him, his big arms around her, and how well she'd slept afterwards. She said nothing for a minute, then, remembering her conversation with Emma, imagined how Matthew would be feeling. 'It's terrible Matthew couldn't find his son.'

'He's coming back,' Brand said, 'when things die down here. He wants to bring his wife and they're going to hold a small service, on the Skeleton Coast, where we turned off the road to look for the Dakota. That's probably the closest place to where Gareth died.'

'That's something, I suppose.' So much death, Sonja thought, so much grief.

Brand put his hat on. He came to the bed, pulled a piece of paper from his pocket and handed it to her. 'OK then, adios, that's my cell phone number if you need me.'

Sonja felt torn. 'Do you have to go?'

'Do I?'

'Bye.' Her reflex to push away was too strong.

Brand turned and walked out of the room into the corridor. Sonja looked into Stirling's face and thought about what they had shared, what they might have shared if she had never left Africa, how her life would have been. She wished that she'd had it in her to be content to stay in the bush, to marry Stirling. Her life would have been so easy.

Sonja sat for a while longer, watching Stirling. The harsh Namibian sun stabbed its way through the chinked armour of the venetian blinds and cast prison bars on the white hospital bed linen.

She took out her phone and the piece of paper Brand had given her. Sonja entered his number and tapped out a message on her keypad. *Here's my number, if you need it. I meant what I said. I like you.* Her thumb hovered over the send key for a few seconds as she debated deleting or changing the message.

In the end she pressed send. Sonja looked at Stirling again. He was so handsome, so good, so pure. Brand was like her, fucked up, broken, a borderline alcoholic, rough around the edges.

Her phone beeped and she checked the screen.

Me too.

Epilogue

O nce her three cubs were walking nicely and could see – they were blind for the first week of their lives – the desert lioness led them out of the cool of the cave and onto the baking red stony plains.

She needed food to keep her milk flowing and the little ones were always hungry. They travelled in the cool of night and laid up in what little shade they could find during the day. Twice she had tried to catch a springbok, but hunting was difficult for a single mother being tailed by three noisy offspring.

When the rocks gave way to grasslands she came to a fence and wriggled under the lowest strand, using a ditch excavated by a warthog. The scent of the animal was fresh. She was wary, eyes and ears searching for signs of humans.

In time she came to a building. She lay down in the scant cover of a tree and watched and waited until nightfall. All was quiet. She had spied a pair of warthogs tending to the watered lawn in front of the farmhouse and noted where the portly pigs retreated to for the night, a burrow in a nearby anthill. She motioned to her cubs to stay put and crept closer to the warthogs' den.

Her plan would be to either dig the warthogs out or to wait until dawn when they emerged, still half asleep, of their own accord. But a noise stopped her.

She raised her ears. It was a tiny squeaking cry and it stirred her. She was confused. Her own cubs should have been far behind her, at the tree. She veered off and came to another fence, then paced around the small enclosure.

Three little faces appeared through the gloom, calling to her. She regarded them through the flimsy barrier. Had she been a male she would have killed another lion's cubs on sight. She sniffed at the babies, who were the same size as her own. They came to her and tried to nuzzle her through the fence.

She looked towards the anthill where the warthogs would still be sleeping. She had until dawn. She started to claw the earth and when the scrape was deep enough, first one then the other two cubs crawled through to her. They saw her as an aunt, perhaps, but certainly not a predator.

The lioness opened her mouth and closed her fangs around the first cub, gently picking it up and carrying it safely back to the tree, where she deposited it with the rest of her brood. She returned for the second and then, finally, the third which had been trotting along behind her on its tiny legs, and took it to the others, carrying it just as tenderly.

When she was sure her cubs were safe, the lioness returned to the hunt.

Historical Note and
Acknowledgements

This is, of course, a work of fiction, but some events in the story are true, or based on fact.

There was a battle at Fort Namutoni in January 1904 between the German *Schutztruppe* and the Ndonga people. While an invasion of the north of Namibia after the battle was considered, it never happened as the Germans were preoccupied fighting the Herero and the Nama in the south of the country. However, I have altered history a little to work this into the story and set my fictitious archaeological dig in the vicinity of the fort and Etosha National Park.

The town of Wilfriedstein and its *Schloss* Hähner bed and breakfast are fictitious, but other towns and locations in the book are real.

I found the following books very useful in researching the history of Namibia and other issues covered in this novel: *A History of Namibia* by Marion Wallace; *Killing for Profit – Exposing the Illegal Rhino Horn Trade* by Julian Rademeyer; *The SADF in the Border War – 1966-1989* by Leopold Scholtz; and *The Kaiser's Holocaust – Germany's Forgotten Genocide* by David Olusoga and Casper W. Erichsen.

Items in the news media in Africa are often a source of inspiration for events in my books. A number of rhino horns, origin unknown, were seized at Windhoek's Hosea Kutako International Airport when I was setting out to write this story and that provided the germ of the idea for the book.

I have long wanted to set a novel mostly in Namibia, a country I love visiting, but I couldn't have done so without the help of many people who generously gave their time to help me with my research, and to check the manuscript for this book.

Desiewaar Natangwe Heita, Deputy Editor of the *New Era Newspaper*, and Wilfried Hähner, Chief Executive Officer of Hitradio Namibia both answered many questions I had about Namibia's politics, culture and history, and read through a draft of the book. I am indebted to both, almost as much as I am impressed by their love for their beautiful country and optimism for its future.

Thanks also go to Matthew Kelly, Senior Archaeologist at Archaeological and Heritage Management Systems (AHMS) in Sydney, who gave me a basic grounding in his field and provided input into the story, and to Charlotte Stapf, a Sydney-based psychotherapist, who gave me an insight into my characters' minds and corrected my German language references.

I'd also like to thank Svetlana Aksenova, from Moree Community Library who helped me with Russian names and language, and, once again, my friend Annelien Oberholzer whh o continues to correct my Afrikaans and find holes in my manuscripts.

Dr Andrew Barrett, who at the time of writing was working in Afghanistan, gave me extensive advice on treating gunshot wounds in the field (including the nifty idea of using teabags in an emergency) and advised me *not* to have Sonja organise a direct transfusion between Alex and Natangwe in my story. I'm grateful for Andrew's assistance, however, I invoked literary licence to have this risky procedure take place – whatever you do, don't try this at home! Fritz Rabe and Dave Morley pointed out some firearms errors in the first edition of this book and with their help these have been corrected in this version (I hope).

Thanks to Wayne Hamilton from Swagman Tours Australia, who helps me with accommodation and new experiences in Africa, and to two excellent guides on my last trip to Namibia, Jimmy Limbo and Festus Mbinga of Wilderness Safaris, for sharing their knowledge with me. I'm also in the debt of Aggie Aikanga from Wilderness Safaris who helped my wife and me when our Land Rover's steering box decided to give out near Etosha National Park.

As with many of my earlier novels, I have handed over the task of thinking up character names to a number of worthy charities. The following people paid good money to various deserving causes to have their names assigned to characters in this story: Alex Bahler, Matthew Allchurch and Dorset Sutton all contributed to Worldshare to further its support of the Heal Africa Hospital in the Democratic Republic of Congo; Sueanne Gregg contributed to Leukaemia research at a fundraiser in her home town of Taroom and chose for inclusion in this book the name of her late father, Ross Coonan; and Ann-Maree Grant chose to use her husband Sebastian Lord's name after contributing to the Australian-based African wildlife charity Painted Dog Conservation Inc.

On the home front my ever-willing and tireless team of unpaid editors and proofreaders have once again helped turn this story from rough first draft to a finished work. Thanks to my wife, Nicola; mum, Kathy; and mother-in-law, Sheila.

I am and always will be grateful to my friends at Pan Macmillan Australia for publishing me, and special thanks go to Publishing Director Cate Paterson, Editorial Manager Emma Rafferty and copy editor Brianne Collins.

Lastly, if you've made it this far, thank you. You're the one who counts most.

www.tonypark.net

extracts reading groups
competitions books new
discounts extracts extracts
reading groups
competitions discounts
books new extracts events
events extracts discounts
books reading groups
new books
events extracts
new books reading groups
title
interviews events
events extracts extracts
books
discounts
new books events events interviews new books extracts
events new
discounts extracts discounts
www.panmacmillan.com
extracts events reading groups
competitions books extracts new books